4/21

BLACKLIGHT

BLACK LIGHT

a novel by

PATRICK MELTON
MARCUS DUNSTAN
and STEPHEN ROMANO

MULHOLLAND BOOKS

Little, Brown and Company
New York Boston London

Mulholland Books/Little, Brown and Company
Hachette Book Group
237 Park Avenue, New York, NY 10017
www.hachettebookgroup.com

First Edition: October 2011

Mulholland Books is an imprint of Little, Brown and Company, a division of Hachette Book Group, Inc. The Mulholland Books name and logo are trademarks of Hachette Book Group, Inc.

The characters and events in this book are fictitious. Any similarity to real persons, living or dead, is coincidental and not intended by the authors.

The publisher is not responsible for websites (or their content) that are not owned by the publisher.

Library of Congress Cataloging-in-Publication Data
Melton, Patrick.
Black light : a novel / by Patrick Melton, Marcus Dunstan, and Stephen Romano.—1st ed.
    p. cm.
ISBN 978-0-316-19671-0
1. Private investigators — Fiction. 2. Psychic ability — Fiction. 3. Supernatural — Fiction. I. Dunstan, Marcus. II. Romano, Stephen. III. Title.
PS3613.E4655B58 2011
813'.6 — dc23   2011022312

10 9 8 7 6 5 4 3 2 1

RRD-C

Printed in the United States of America

JULY 2012

Imagine this:

A coil of steel more than two city blocks long, moving faster than anything else on earth.

Even ghosts are afraid of it.

But you probably don't know what that means.

You have no idea that this roiling column of metal could rip you apart, soul and all—and that you might never come back. At least not as skin and bones. You don't know because most people don't believe in ghosts. They think this kind of stuff is just make-believe. Stories you tell kids around a campfire.

I guess I don't have to tell you, they're wrong.

Very wrong.

But I'm getting ahead of myself.

Let's talk about me first...

ONE

THE MARK INSIDE

It always goes down hard when a dead guy takes his first swing at me. Like an invisible club coming out of the dark behind my eyes, landing in a million different places—places of the mind, places of the soul. I've been told I have a pretty mean soul, but I always flinch a little. You'd think I'd be used to it by now.

He's tough, this son of a bitch.

He was a child killer when he was still alive. I can tell that right off. It's the Terrible Thing that fuels his madness, makes him strong. It comes at me like a ripe smell of sulfur and smoldering ash, his last moments flashing in the thundering sonic boom of a bad heartbeat—and then I see his *whole life,* man. I take it on fast-forward, a quicktime superhighway of images, scenes, tiny little details flashing across the electrified chambers of my mind. I get it in just two seconds. It's a lot to swallow. The moment is always terrifying.

Freefloaters, they're always damn hard to pull.

You never know how tough they are until they're right on top of you.

Usually, you have to go looking for them in places like this. These old Victorian houses are death traps. The nasty ones get in deep in all the nooks and crannies—there's a million places to hide. But sometimes you get lucky. Sometimes they're just cruising for a straight fight. Didn't even need to call this one out, he's just that crazy. Jumped me right in the middle of the room, saw me coming a mile away. Thinks he's a real Billy Badass. Tough shit, Billy—I saw you coming too.

He was an altar boy in school, a four-letter football athlete in college. He could have gone pro but he became a cop instead. All the while living with his dark secret: the desire to smash something smaller than himself. So many years of madness and self-punishment and playing chess with his best friends and his family, who never knew the monster he really was. His final mistake. His own little boy. Psycho killers with families always screw up like that in the end. They get convinced they can be normal on the surface, but remain tortured by their desires until they finally give in, and it's never pretty. I've seen the writhing lifescapes of at least a dozen like him. The trick is not to go too far when you pull a mark in. The trick is to use their own insanity against them.

See, it's the *crime,* their most agonized moment—that's what always brings these guys down. The moment when they finally fell, the moment when they lost everything, screaming that it just wasn't fair, every regret and every lie and every damn one of those tormented secrets rising to the surface like sewage, hitting hard and blasting them off the earth—but not into death, not all the way. Every bad mark holds that Terrible Thing right out in front of them. If you're like me, you see it superimposed on the world like a shimmering red serpentine coil, oozing and twisting and sluicing across everything else they possess, like a cancer. If you're like me, you can reach out and grab it.

And if you're like me...it *burns.*

Burns so deep you feel your whole body swell at the seams and threaten to blow right there.

But I hold him.

What's *inside me* holds him.

The Pull.

I keep my feet planted on the floor now, allowing the energy of his own attack to ground me there. It's an old-school martial arts technique—but it works, even when you're fighting something that isn't alive. I concentrate on the hard surfaces and familiar smells around my body, using them as an anchor to the world. The dusty living room, the antique furniture and ornate French doors. The sharp scent of old souls trapped in the carpet and the peeling wallpaper. The candles filling the air with ordinary magic—the false magic of men and faith, not ghosts and whispers. It armors me. Allows me to turn his own attack against him. Works every time.

I hear the desperate screech of his fractured mind do a midair whipcrack in the opposite direction, trying to resist the Pull.

But none of them can resist it.

I am a black hole and he is the light that cannot escape it.

I turn it on harder, feeling the burn as I get a grip on the twisting red ooze that flows through him. This always hurts the mark worse than it hurts me, even though it hurts me a whole goddamn lot, like ice daggers spiked with fire jamming into my eyes and my heart. The mark spits at me and curses, fighting dirty, kicking up a shockwave that shatters all the glass in the room, but I have him now, and he's coming in hard, the way most spirits do when they try to possess you, connecting to your nervous system, taking control of your bones and mind, like a spider spinning up a fly.

But my Gift is to withstand that, to brush it aside.

Drink them down.

Kick their asses.

He screams all the way, the formless mist of madness and unsettled rage blasting apart and sleeting through the surface of my skin. In this one kinetic flashburn moment, everything he ever was—his life, his memories, his death in madness—it all goes into *me*.

My body shakes and rumbles as the mark plunges down deep.

Deeper.

And then...

Touchdown.

My whole body lights up from the lowest depth, coils of living energy dragracing my bloodstream. His rage scorches my mind, the desperate whine of a dying animal run through a feedback loop. I get it under control, bearing down hard, my teeth clenching.

He's in *my* house now.

The scream fades to a rumble, then a low simmer, as the substance of his insanity fizzes and dissipates like acid seltzer. I feel it burst and become sour muck, oozing along the walls of my stomach and lungs, a living disease given terrible formless autonomy, still trying to scream its way out. It's ingested now. Way down inside me.

This part is bad.

It's the worst part of the job.

Then again, who said life—or *death*—was fair.

I glance at my watch and notice that I walked in here exactly three minutes ago. Just in time to crash the party. The woman is cringing in a far corner, near the fireplace, crying as she watches my body quake and rumble, my eyes jacked open, infused with the dull red glow of a madman's cancer. All his hatred of her and his secrets and his terrible acts of violence—the things he did right here in this room and out there in the city, for years and years, and she never knew—it's bouncing around in my guts like a pinball on fire, tearing me to pieces. It rips a month from my life in three seconds. Then another month. Then a year. Always a lot of damage when they're so far down in the sickness.

But I still hold him.

He still oozes inside me.

I take a few deep breaths.

You'd think I'd be used to it by now.

The woman is still crying in the corner, but her eyes are full like saucers, the startled whites beaming at me, even through the flickering half-darkness. I see her face shimmer in the light from the candles, and she lets out a long sigh.

And that's when the mark hits me again.

A sucker punch, right out of nowhere, deep in my guts.

I lose control for just a split second as the awful oozing cancer gets a grip on my mind. The world fritzes out…

And…

It spirals across my vision like an X-ray bathing the room in neon darkness.

A dark so bright it blinds you. A glowing blade of white-hot laser light, peeling back the skin of reality to expose new layers. My scleral contact lenses keep the sudden shock from scorching me sightless, but the water in my eyes sizzles away fast. Didn't see this coming. Have to pull back. Have to get him under control. Have to do it now . . . have to . . .

. . . but . . .

I see everything.

Everything the dead people see.

This is where they live.

It's beautiful and terrifying, and all the answers I ever looked for are hovering right here in front of me in a sea of shadows.

It feels good.

It's been so long.

It knew I would come back.

I smile in the Blacklight, feeling it rush into me.

I'm standing right where I was, in the same room, but the room is now revealed for what it really is. A flashing flipbook of half-images, all rushing in at once in a machinegun stutter. A million shapes swimming in translucent curtains, shadows of old lives, echoes of lost love and bad family business played out long ago. I see every story this old house ever witnessed. I see children giggling on the carpet in front of me. Toys spread out on the floor, which then turn into vases of flowers, and then I see the house built in reverse, the farmland it once stood on, and the years before that, all bathed in bright polarized shadows as the Blacklight shifts and pulses, taking me back in time, then forward again, ricocheting all over history, flickering images like changing channels on an old black-and-white television set. I stand here in this spot and see it all go down, and I can tell that it's the mark's madness forcing me to look at this — because he wants out. This is what dead people see on their side of the world, and he wants me to see it so I lose control of him.

But I've played this game before.

I know how to win it.

I ground myself again and bring myself back to the moment set before me. I concentrate on the room and it solidifies in ice-black glimmers, coming into sharp focus, so bright and so hot. I see the mark's terrible crimes in the room.

I see the candles transform into the knives he used to slit his own son's throat. I see the razor wire and the rubber gloves and the bottles of ammonia appear on the coffee table, where he prepared his tools in the terrible hours before his final crime. I could reach out and bring that razor wire back with me if I wanted to, the same way I can pull marks. I've done it before. No one has ever been able to tell me why I can do it.

I even see the faint trace of the mark's madness, floating in the air where it was just before I grabbed him, still hanging there, like the slime trail of a phantom slug.

The slime trail that allowed me to grab him in the first place.

I see it all.

It feels good.

Feels like I belong here.

It's amazing and overwhelming and brighter than a million suns, hitting me hard... and I know I can use this... it will lead me to the truth... I want to stay here... it's where I belong... it's so beautiful...

No.

Get down, you bastard.

I will not have this fucking shit from you.

I go for the tiny pocketknife in my satchel, snick it open, and slide the sharp end along my little finger—just a tiny scrape. Enough to ping my system, to remind myself that I'm still human in this strange twilight of dead things. The pain shocks up my arm, overriding everything. The mark thrashes and screams and kicks me, but I have him cold now, and he has no choice but to retreat. And as be backs off...

The vision recedes and fades away.

The room is normal again.

My eyes still burn.

I reach up fast, and pull the lenses, toss them on the floor, where they melt like translucent slag. Damn. Those things are expensive.

That'll teach me to forget my goggles.

I calm myself, measuring reality by the beating of my heart, making sure I'm still all here. Yeah. I'm still here.

And I win, you son of a bitch.

"Ma'am, your husband is gone. He won't be giving you any more trouble."

The woman shivers, and I think she says thank you, but it's hard to tell. She didn't see what I just saw. Nobody ever sees it but me. It's enough to make a man feel really damn alone in a mighty cruel world.

She rises to her feet, throws herself into my arms, crying. I never have any idea what to do at times like this. Pulling marks ain't easy, but it's easier than a woman's tears. So I tell her it's okay, tell her she's safe now. She smells like sweet things. I'm reminded of a hundred others like her. I'm reminded of things I can never have. I tell her it's okay now. That's all I can do.

The big man next to me puts his hand on my shoulder.

"Come on, Buck," he says. "Why don't you step outside? I'll take it from here."

TWO

CHANGE OF PLANS

That damn commercial plays again.

I try to ignore it again.

The urn sits on the bar in front of Tom, and I can almost see my face reflected in the silver surface. Almost, but not quite. Some kind of poetry in that, I guess.

The place is dank and greasy, the smell of stale beer and cigarettes wafting around like a roomful of drunk ghosts. Sometimes I can pick up on stuff that happened in rooms like this. Sometimes there's marks here, just visiting. They never stay long in grungy nightspots. Bigger fish to fry in a town like New Orleans.

Tom pulls a sweaty envelope from his jacket pocket. Hands it to me and slides over the silver. "Here's your cut. She was generous. Twelve large, plus the urn. Did you see her *eyes* back there? You prolly could've gotten lucky with that broad."

"I don't get lucky with clients."

"She was a looker. I woulda done it."

"You would have done a lot of things."

"Yeah, I'm no Boy Scout. Not like you." He rolls a grin at me when he says it, as if he's telling me something I don't already know. Loves to bust my balls when it comes to women, like I give a shit. His weird Italian voice sounds high and hardened, like Joe Pesci or some other tough guy in a gangster flick.

"Yeah, but you're still one of the good guys," I tell him, careful not to imitate his sleazy drawl. I do that sometimes, I think a lot of people do. You get around strange customers and you pick up on their inflections. Whenever I go out of town on jobs like this, people are amazed I don't sound like some grim midnight cowboy from a trashy Western. That's because I mostly do business out of Texas.

"I try not to think about good guys and bad guys," he says, sipping his whiskey, watching me pocket the cash. "And you should count that, Buck."

"I trust you."

"You shouldn't trust anyone, even your best friend."

"I don't have any friends."

"Ain't that sad? Years I've known you, Buck, and you don't think *I'm* your friend?"

"You never call on my birthday."

"I never call on anyone's birthday."

"Neither do I."

"Then I guess we're both scumbags after all."

He finishes off his drink, orders another. Jim Beam Black on ice. Doesn't ask if I want anything. He knows I don't drink, and if you order club soda in a place like this, they look at you funny. The bartender goes through the motions, a silent black sentinel without pity in a houseful of dirty jazz.

I inspect the urn. Solid silver, not plated. Expensive. Haven't seen one of these in a while. It reminds me of crazier times. I shut off the memories fast, looking at myself in the mirror across the bar.

A man turning old in a big hurry stares back at me.

My hair was black before I got in this business. Jet-black, the color of being young and reckless. It's half-white now, in weird little streaks across the sides of my head. I noticed it the first time I ever got rid of a mark. One hair, shocked straight to hell by what I do. Gray is the color of something old and worn—not really alive, not quite dead enough. White is something else.

I figure one day soon, when I've asked all the questions I can ask, when I've looked through the Blacklight enough times, when I've found my mother and father and figured out why I can do this thing I do...well, maybe I'll look like Edgar Winter or Andy Warhol or someone like that. It won't matter. I'll be in my grave by then.

Tom sees me staring at myself in the mirror, and he laughs. "Don't kid yourself, kid. You look great."

"I look like somebody dying."

"You *are* somebody dying. But you still look good. Not a wrinkle on your face. Not an ugly old fuck like me."

"You're not ugly."

"Says you." He cracks a smile, makes a quick circle with his drink, searching for something. "You look like that guy...you know, *that guy* who played the cop in that fuckin' movie. The one about the dirty Feds and the counterfeiters."

"*To Live and Die in LA?*"

"Yeah, yeah that's the one."

"William Peterson. He was a good looking guy when he was young."

"What's he look like now?"

"Kind of like I feel."

He shrugs, then belts the drink and stirs ice with his finger. "Well, you look like the young version, kid, even if you feel like shit. All cagy eyes and square jaw—and no wrinkles. I don't get that. Guys in our line of work are supposed to get old and craggy fast. I'da thought you'd be thirty-eight going on sixty-nine by now."

"Looks ain't everything."

"Must've made a deal with the devil, huh?"

"I don't believe in the devil."

"Maybe you should start."

"Funny."

He smiles, then almost laughs. Gives me a serious nod. "It's all worth it, Buck. You did a good thing back there. That little lady, she went through hell this past year. Her man had some screws loose, but she never figured his goddamn *ghost* was gonna be around later to make it worse."

"Nobody ever does." I close my eyes and listen for the voice of the child killer—it's still keeping its distance inside me, softer now since I kicked his ass.

He sighs, long and hard. "Man, I was on that case for *three months,* Buck. Tried everything to flush the bastard out. I was down to bone throwing—fucking *bayou magic,* man. It's all for shit when you're dealing with a real hard one. They live in the walls like cockroaches and laugh while you bust the place apart. There was a time I could've brought him down myself."

That surprises me some.

Tom Romilda is still a respected name. Fifteen years on the streets of the Big Easy. He knows the lingo and all the parlor tricks, which is usually enough. He doesn't have the Gift the way guys like me do, though. Tom's good with the research end, computers and cop records and stuff like that—he's a licensed private investigator with all the heat—but you have to bring in the heavy guns sometimes. The local dicks who work the Blacklight beat here are mostly crooks who talk a lot of voodoo bullshit. Tom ain't like that. He makes sure the client is always happy, even if he has to lie about how he gets there. That's why he used to be so successful. Knows it's all about referrals in this business. He's older now, but still respected. Probably just getting lazy.

"You really saved my ass this time," he says, turning to me with one elbow on the bar. "Let me return the favor. Got something serious to talk about."

I see where this is going already, and I don't like it.

"Can't pull two in a row, Tom. I'm out of practice."

"So give it a rest. There's no rush. You can crash at our place. Victoria would love to spoil you."

Victoria's his fifth wife. He goes through them like bad romance novels. The last one was an ex–Suicide Girl, arms covered in tattoos, heart made of stone. The one living in his house now is a twenty-seven-year-old Betty Homemaker with a nasty streak—she broke a lamp over his head last week while he was sleeping, then made him pancakes in the morning.

"Tom, I can't."

"C'mon, man, I know I threw you in blind this time but—"

"It's not that. It's not you. It's this *place*."

"At least hear me out."

"No."

I pull away from the mirror, settle back on the barstool, feeling the sticky fingers of the French Quarter pulling at my mind. This town has a vibe unlike anyplace else. I've been a lot of places, too. It tastes like swamplands and weird mojo tickling you somewhere deep and private, the gypsy scent of strange perfumes and incense teasing with the wistful afterburn of secrets you'd really rather not know about. And the food. That's the thing about the Quarter anyone can pick up on, not just guys like me. The smell of backwoods banquets wafting through the street, hickory smoked and Cajun fried. It's almost enough to distract you from the limitless evil that lives here.

I run my finger along the silver surface of the urn. It has holy crosses carved into the side, etchings of Jesus and Mary. A joke, really.

The remains of the child killer grumble in my stomach.

"I just wanna get back to my hotel room, Tom. Get this Billy Badass out of my guts. One goddamn problem at a time, man."

"You should make it easier on yourself. Sit here and get drunk like the rest of us. You'll be yodeling down the big porcelain megaphone in no time."

"If I got sauced every time I needed to get rid of a mark, I would have gone belly-up a long time ago."

"Fine, have it your way. But you really oughta listen to an old man when he's handing out free advice—even if he *is* an ugly drunk."

"I handle my own problems my own way."

Above the mirror, the battered flat-screen plays that same damn commercial that's run four times since I stepped into this place.

And I can't look away from it, just like before.

"Welcome to the future," says the TV, showing off a world of dreamlight. The spot is state-of-the-art filmmaking and digital-video trickery, and the voice is excited and young, announcing the opening of a new

multimillion-dollar playground in Vegas. Everyone knows about it. Been on every channel for the last six weeks.

I've known about it for a lot longer than that.

"The Dreamworld Casino and Theme Park! A whole new planet of entertainment and adventure! A galaxy of wonderment in the center of the universe!"

If you've ever been to places like Universal City or even Disney World, you sort of start to get the idea—shopping malls mated with movie theaters dotted among terrifying mile-in-the-sky amusement rides, all rushing to be consumed by causeway levels, all brimming with studded marquees and twists of sculpted light more dazzling than the gilded gates of Neverland.

But it's always the second part of this commercial that gets me.

Like the sharp stab of a dull memory in the pit of your stomach, reminding you to turn away, but you can't.

"And there's just one way to reach the center of the universe! On the Laser!"

A series of fast cuts and super-hip screen-wipe effects show me the bullet: a sleek steel serpent slashing through the desert. The fastest high-speed luxury rail train ever built.

I want to forget that it exists.

"From downtown Los Angeles to the heart of Las Vegas, with speed and style to spare! The ultimate VIP travel-entertainment experience! The Jaeger Laser! Punch it into hyperspace for the thrill ride of a lifetime—all the way to the Dreamworld!"

I look away from the television, as the hard-sell powers down and it goes back to some sit-com. The bartender reaches up with the remote, thumbing the canned laughter into oblivion, replacing it with a news channel.

"The Jaeger Laser," I say to no one in particular. "Fucking ridiculous name."

The big man next to me lets out a sharp huff, his eyes still on the screen above us. "I guess it's true what they say—the past always bites you in the ass just when you think you're done with it."

Asshole.

He should know better, tossing it in my face like that.

I shake my head. "I *am* done with it."

"Bullshit. You've had your eyes glued to that TV since we came in here."

"Ain't got nothing to do with me anymore."

"I know you don't really believe that, Buck. You've got serious history with that train."

He's going somewhere with this too.

And I still don't like it.

"Tom... whatever you have in mind, just forget it. The last time I went out there, I got somebody killed. Somebody innocent."

"I know all about shit like that. Before you were even born, I was knee-deep in a place where killing children was government sponsored."

"I'm not like you, Tom. I don't kill people. I don't kill *kids*. I don't care who's sponsoring me."

His jagged smile splits his face like a jack-o'-lantern with a dirty secret. "What if I told you I could get you sponsored by the guys who are *running* that train? Right now. Tonight."

Something turns cold in the air, and I smell the hard grime of dead things in my past, the Walkers in the slipstream whispering something just on the edge of hearing. They just did a little dance on my grave.

I look at him hard. "What the hell are you talking about?"

"I'm talking about the *big one,* Buck."

He points at the TV screen, as the commercial starts up again.

The fastest train in the world, running to the center of the universe.

Running straight through my past.

"They're looking for you," he says. "There's something going on and they want you on the team."

"That's... impossible."

"Believe it, kid. They called me. I got you up here so we could have a man-to-man about it."

"I only came here because I needed the money."

"Don't kid yourself, kid. You came because you're still hungry to *look across*. You're still looking for your folks. This deal I'm handing you now could put you right at ground zero. It's just like you always said: there are no coincidences."

His words sting me.

It always stings when it's true.

I shake my head on auto-pilot, starting to feel the seriousness of his words sink in, the dull panic of everything that made me desperate so long ago washing up in bitter waves. "I don't want it anymore. I can't go back there."

"You could at least hear what they have to say."

"I said *no*, Tom. It's over for me. They can ride their fancy rail line straight to hell for all I care. Whatever happens, it ain't gonna have anything to do with me. And I've got things to do."

I grab the silver urn and get up from the bar stool.

He puts up his hand, palm out. "Okay, okay, I'm sorry. We're still cool, right? I mean, the money's fine and everything?"

I roll my eyes. "Money's great. Go fuck yourself."

He laughs. "Look, do yourself a favor, man. Just *think* about this one." He slides a small slab of embossed-foil paper across the bar to me with one finger. A business card. "Think about it *real hard,* Buck."

The card reads in big letters:

JAEGER INDUSTRIES

And there's a phone number.

I take the card and pocket it, give him a shrug. He knows I'll be back. Even says so, with that big filthy grin of his.

You'll be back, Buck.

Story of my life.

Loose ends and bad ghosts, all hanging at the edge of oblivion.

All waiting for me.

I shake his hand and he leans in and grabs my shoulder. He squeezes tight, winks at me through a leathery road map of wrinkles and says I just need a good woman, like that's his solution for everything. Like it ever really works for him.

A woman.

They say women are life's great mystery, but I know better.

There's lots of other mysteries out there.

Like the one that's hovered over me in dark neon riddles since the day I found out what I am. The one that's coming back on me now, while the mark sizzles and burns from the inside, boiling against my organs and blood and who knows what else.

I stuff the urn in my satchel and leave the bar, drifting out into the steaming summer night, the cobblestones of ancient French streets under my feet like grave markers, vibrating with the frequencies of the dead.

I walk right past my cheap room on Royal Street.

Head straight for my truck.

Change of plans.

I have to get home, and I have to keep Billy Badass inside me while I do it. Have to drive all night with the remains of a child killer cursing me, just like in the old days. All the way back to Austin from the worst city on earth.

I have to.

Tom was right—I came here to help because I wanted to look across again. But I didn't know what I was really looking for until just now.

What he told me back there changes the game.

And there's only one place on earth I can go to know for sure.

And one place beyond earth.

Have to get back there, fast.

The mark rumbles, sensing my panic, wanting out. The buzz always turns into sickness when you keep it in too long. I force it down with sheer will, taking an anxious shortcut through a back alley.

They followed me three blocks before they made their move.

I was hoping they'd see my truck and give up—it's ten years old and beat to shit, makes me look like poor white trash. But no such luck. The smaller one steps forward with his arms crossed and his chest puffed out like some skinny lizard. The fat one points at the big leather satchel strapped across my chest and lays down the law:

"We'll take your bag, man."

The child killer senses the threat and smells their blood, its wordless voice rumbling like sour backwash up into my throat. I tell it to stay down.

They're a couple of dim ratfaces in greasy wifebeaters and shredded cargo pants, half defined in streetlamp shadows, like ghosts wearing flesh. But they aren't ghosts—they're not even armed, not with anything but raw knuckles and deep scars across their lips, telling tales of juvenile prison and bad fathers. They're still in their late teens, probably won't live to be thirty. Don't even need to read their minds for any of that.

Dammit.

I don't have time for this.

The child killer rumbles, bringing the Blacklight closer, just out of sight.

I tell it to stay down.

It doesn't want to hear that.

It smells blood.

No shadows moving over the ratfaces. No traces in the dark. I would see traces if there was something inside them. The smaller one takes another step forward, pinning me with yellow eyes:

"You *deaf,* man? My partner told ya to hand over yer *bag,* man."

Their voices are dumb and street southern—when this one tacks the word "man" at the end of every sentence, it sounds like *main.* I start smiling, then I laugh. Backwater stereotypes. Gotta love 'em.

The Blacklight screams for me. If this turns bad, it could be a problem. I should hand over the cash. I should play this safe. But I just chuckle at them while the child killer lusts for blood in my throat.

"Whut the fuck you *laughin' at,* man?"

He takes one last step forward. He has a tattoo on his exposed right shoulder that says in silly spiked heavy-metal lettering: HI, MY NAME'S MERCILESS CLYDE.

That *really* makes me laugh.

"Shut the fuck *UP,* man!"

He shoves me with both hands. I don't stumble back. I am armored by what rumbles in my body, the stench of blood and the voices of dead things making me clench my teeth, amplifying my senses. The ratty kid smells like whiskey straight from the bottle and sour sweat. I would smell dull steel if he were packing. I smell his soul, tainted and broken. The child killer screams for it. The anger and the lust wash over me again, stronger now, the threat upping my adrenaline, fueling my rage.

I stop smiling and force myself to warn them:

"You kids don't want any trouble. Go home."

The fat one sees my expressionless face when I say that, and his eyes get real pissed, like *Some jerks just never have any idea when they're knee-deep, do they?*

Like I'm nothing but an inconvenience to these fuckos.

Stupid, ignorant backwoods punks.

I hate them.

Kill them.

Kill them NOW.

The voice cuts through me like a blade, and my hands act all on their own. The one in front of me never sees it coming: an open chop across his windpipe that crushes his Adam's apple and almost cuts off his air. You don't need to be showy with guys like this, but I want to hurt them, hurt them bad, teach them a lesson—*teach you to fuck with ME, you fucking little shit...*

He makes a wet sound, those yellow eyes bugging all the way out, and as he reaches up to claw at his neck I grab his little finger and twist it back, a mean shockwave of raw inertia rearranging his entire arm at a crazy angle that drops him to his knees. The threefold multicrack of the bone rips out in a nasty compound fracture through his skin, popping the air like a string of Black Cats. Every punk on earth becomes a little bitch when you show him what the food chain looks like from the bottom. This one screams, of course, but there's still nothing inside him—I had to be sure. Never take any chances in a city that crawls.

And I want to hurt him.

I want to snuff him out.

You're going to die, you weak little shit.

I am going to kill you.

My other hand goes around his throat, crushing off the rest of his air. Merciless Clyde is a child again, helpless and crying wordlessly for me to stop, and I want to smother that helpless, crying child—*smash him, destroy him.*

Because you are smaller than me, and I am stronger than you.

Because I am filled with rage.

My eyes flood with blinding darkness as I squeeze him.

The Blacklight, jumping me without warning again.

Like you ever get a warning in my line of work.

It feels good.

It makes me powerful.

And I see his whole life, this stupid little punk, as he shimmers in layers of phosphorescent fog beneath my iron grip, and I see the secrets of every crime that ever happened on this street corner strobing all around us like blasted bits of nightmares, coming in fast and terrible, all of them rushing through me as the heat of rage and violence burns and boils in my heart, pushing me forward, making me KILL THIS LITTLE BOY BECAUSE I AM A CHILD KILLER—

No.

Pull back.

Don't.

Stop.

I let go of him, and the blinding blackness goes away in one blink as I force the awful alien madness down, pushing it back into my stomach.

It had me, the fucker.

That hasn't happened in years.

Merciless Clyde hits the sidewalk, still crying. I stand over him and my hands shake. Almost killed the kid. Damn.

The fat one ain't so merciless—he loses his balls and breaks for the street.

I knew he would run.

I knew everything about these two guys the first second I saw them.

It's a problem I have.

"Get a job," I tell Clyde, who's still crying on the pavement.

I pull out the sweaty envelope and peel off a couple of twenties. They fall from my hand like dead leaves, drifting past the punk's face and blowing down the street after his buddy, floating on the sour wind. I pick up the urn, then jump in the truck, toss it on the seat next to me. The keys jingle in my hand and the engine comes to life like a grumpy monster.

As I'm driving away, I see a trace of something—the shadow of a broken-down old man in rags chasing after the money, his fingerless gloves clutching at false prizes, cut loose among all the other bad ghosts in a city without shame. I always see traces brighter just after I come up from the Blacklight, and it always chills my blood. The money drifts away. The false prize. The promise.

The mark grumbles inside me, frustrated and defeated.

It wanted that little bastard bad.

Can't let it happen again.

I have things to do.

THREE

ARMED

When I was seven years old, my life began.

Everything before that is gone, not even fragments left.

The Blacklight keeps the secret.

It's a window to where my parents went.

The teachers and administrators at the institution told me I'd been found on a backstreet in New Mexico, in a little postage-stamp town called Carlsbad. Said they'd found me near suffocated in the front cab of a rusty old truck with the windows rolled up, my brain half baked by the sun, breathing my own waste, about to die.

That's what they told me.

I couldn't remember any of it, still can't.

They said it was the heat inside the cab that fried my memory. Said I was lucky they found me when they did. Maybe I was lucky, maybe I wasn't.

The only thing I could remember was my birthday: November 12, 1973.

They told me latent-detail recall like that wasn't uncommon among amnesiacs who've suffered a major break, but it's always seemed really strange to me.

The institution was where I spent a lot of my childhood, the part I can remember. A chalky gray building, full of voices. A lot of crying, a lot of screaming. That place taught me to be tough, how to take it on the chin. I started my martial arts training there, under a kid who was ten years older than me, a fifth-degree black belt obsessed with Bruce Lee movies. I always thought those movies were real silly, but Bruce was a scary customer. He could kick everyone's ass, one ass at a time. I learned how to do that slowly. You learn how to be tough slowly. The scar tissue builds on your mind and body.

They gave me a last name on the inside, but they weren't all that creative about it. I never asked any questions. I was too young to ask questions. Now, I'm just used to the way things are. I picked my first name on my own. Grabbed it out of thin air when they were doing the paperwork. The social worker smiled across the desk and filled in the blank. Someone asked me once if I was named after one of the kids in the *Little Rascals*. A guy picked a fight with me a few years ago because he thought my handle was some kind of weird cowboy joke. Most people in Texas don't like weird cowboy jokes. Welcome to the big, bad confusing world, Mr. Carlsbad. We'll just call you Buck.

I pulled my first mark at the institution.

In the town I was named after.

I was twelve when it happened.

She was attached to one of the orderlies, a big tough guy named Granger who used to give me a lot of grief. He shook the kids down, even beat up one of them. The ghost of his grandmother tortured him for almost a year before I figured out what it was. Figured out how to deal with it. Mediums usually find their abilities at the peak of their awakenings, during puberty, and I was no exception. A pretty early bloomer, actually. The girls liked me a lot at the institution, and I had just experienced my first real tryst in a broom closet with an overdeveloped redhead who smelled like acne cream and Cheery-Cherry bubble gum—and that was when it happened.

The very same night.

I remember lying there in my bunk, thinking about the tingling in my gut, the new sensations of manhood, the odd afterglow of weird pride, silent guilt, and sadness. I could hear old Granger walking the hall between rooms as he went on bed check, his keys jingling along the corridor like strange sleigh bells, almost there and not quite there at all. I remember the jingling seemed to become a laughter. And then the laughter was a roaring in my head. I stepped into the hallway and saw the old woman hovering over him, plain as day, her crackling aura lit up in the dark, though he couldn't see her at all. A stinging thunderclap hit me, and I knew I had been given something. The first seven years of my life erased forever and handed back to me as—*whatever this was.*

I reached out and touched the old woman's madness.

That final, tortured moment that kept her trapped.

The Terrible Thing, swimming in the air like a red serpentine coil.

And as I touched it, I could feel the power coming awake inside me.

The Pull, summoning her dead spirit deep into me.

The Pull...

And as the old woman's vaporous remains crashed over me in a wave and seeped through my skin like burning, drowning seawater, everything she'd ever been as a human being moved through every chamber of my mind in one flash...and I knew what she had done to her grandson. The awful things that kept her around.

I swallowed it easy that first time.

She went without a fight.

And then I could see as she saw.

I could see the Blacklight for the first time.

That X-ray vision splitting the world into superheated prisms of burning shadow and darkness. It hit me hard and made me blind. I squeezed my eyes shut but it was even brighter there. I felt the familiarity of it all. I knew what it was. This was the vision of the dead. The place where all the souls that ever lived and loved and fought and died had gone to rest, but they weren't really at rest. A place filled with echoes of terrible things. Remains and artifacts. Had I been there before? Was this where I'd find the thing that had been taken from me? Were those the voices of my mother and father calling to me?

I could feel the mark of the old woman inside my guts, and I knew I was seeing all this through her eyes, and that feeling was nothing that a young

mind could comprehend—even stronger than the great awakenings in my
manhood. I knew that it felt good. I knew that I wanted to feel more.

In the air in front of me in the hall, a pearl necklace appeared.

The beads strewn in a crooked circle, like someone had dropped them there.

I was blind, but I could see it.

I reached out and touched it.

It was real, not some phantom vision.

A solid object, trapped there between worlds.

My fingers touched the smooth surface of the pearls, and I held them, ab-
sorbing crackles of living energy that might have been memory traces.

And in that moment, the Blacklight was gone.

Just a glimpse that time.

I was blinded, but I could feel that the necklace was still in my hands.

And the mark sizzled and dissipated, deep down in my guts.

Ingested.

Old Granger stood like a stunned troll in the hall in front of me, knowing that he was free and that I had saved him. But even then I knew it
wasn't enough just to swallow her. She had to be put to rest.

I didn't know how I knew that, but I did.

That night he took me to the cemetery where she was buried. By then I
could hardly hold her in. The blindness had receded, my eyes full of tears.
The sickness, on me like nothing I'd ever felt before. My guts boiling with
the remains of something that was once a living human soul. My stomach
contracting and releasing in a terrible spasm. I opened my mouth and the
blackness came up, like something tearing away from me and taking half
my insides with it. It spewed and oozed along the soft loam and grass of
her grave, disappearing beneath the earth...because *that's where I told it*
to go.

The pain faded.

I could see again.

Granger gave me a lift to the bus station that night, put a few hundred
bucks in my pocket, told me he would make sure they never found out
where I went. Said we were even. He took the necklace from me. Said it
had belonged to his grandmother. Said he had no idea how in the goddamn

hell I got it, but he was grateful, and I gave it up without thinking twice. I would have agreed to anything, just to get out of there. In the bathroom at the bus station, I looked in a mirror and saw my first white hair.

And I felt old, beat to hell.

I knew I shouldn't feel that way, but I did.

I went a lot of places after that. Nineteen years, and marks everywhere. You wouldn't believe how many there are. I learned more about fighting, about ways to hurt people, about the dicks on the Blacklight beat. You don't do what I do for free, and you have to be ready to kick a lot of ass—one ass at a time. There's always someone looking to explain the unexplainable, and a few others looking to make a fast buck off the dead. I ran with a couple of groups, scored some cash, kept moving. Every time I did it, I got another white hair. By the time I was thirty-one, it was like living in a world of shrieking animals. I saw shadows hiding in corners and heard the voices everywhere I went. It took a long time before I could walk through your average city street and not go crazy. I learned about the bad cities, the ones you don't wanna go anywhere near if you're like me. The Southwest is particularly noisy. You stay right the fuck out of Louisiana, especially after Katrina.

There's levels, you see.

Level one is the world most of us live in. The dead people mostly can't see you there, and they stay out of your way. A lot of folks are Gifted enough to do silly tricks at level one, like read people's minds. It ain't easy to get to level two—where the Blacklight shines—and you need special glasses or contact lenses. I've had a lot of practice making the trip. I learned on the job, the hard way. Learned how you use a mark to see across into the world of the dead, when it's swimming inside you. Learned that physical pain is usually the only way to pull back from it, especially when you go real low. That's why I carry a knife all the time. That's why the scars on my right arm. That's why I wear a long-sleeve formal jacket everywhere I go. Most people who get a good look at me without the jacket think I'm just one of those lost-in-space thirtysomething cutter types, but I'm a creature of habit. Always do myself in the same spot. To remind me.

Of everything.

You have to cut yourself because the Blacklight is like a drug.

You have to be reminded that you are human.

That you are not dead.

Dead feels good—it's a rush like nothing I can describe in easy words.

And I've been feeling it dance in my heart and mind for so long, surrendering to the glow of darkness and the flow of voices and shadows, all tangled up in blue and then back to earth. And every single time you want it more. You want to know everything about that place. You want to stay there forever.

My right arm is a callused road map of winding reminders.

I stumbled into Austin almost by accident. I was traveling up the Gulf Coast and into Texas, on a job for a rich lady who said her little girl was crying in the halls after a car wreck took her. She thought it was happening because she never bought the little girl a pony for her ninth birthday. Those guilty-parent jobs are always bunk. You don't even lie to people like that. Some mediums do, just to cover their expenses, but that's bad business. Creates shitty word of mouth. I told the rich lady she was just imagining things, that there were no ghosts hanging around, and she gave me three grand anyway, just for being straight with her.

Austin became my home after that.

The voices there weren't so bad, but that's not the reason I stayed.

I pull my truck into the driveway at dawn.

The old bucket refuses to die, no matter how much abuse she takes.

Seven hours on the road back from New Orleans. I took one hell of a risk staying behind the wheel this long, and the mark is already squirming and biting at me, forcing its way up in nasty acidic bursts, climbing to get free. I'm tired and I want it out. But I have to keep it in. Just a little while longer. Questions first.

I click off the Walkman at my waist.

The music dies, like so many other things that come and then leave.

It's a run-down house dug into the east side of Austin, an old wood-frame two-story hanging at a weird angle on the far edge of the world. You almost can't see the place because it's surrounded by so many trees, overgrown and dark, like a bloated storm shroud hovering above something long dead. A pathway through the briar tangle is visible only if you know where to look. The rusty gate gives me some trouble today. I have to push through some low-hanging vines, and dead leaves fall on me as I make my way to the front porch. The wood creaks under my boots like the bones of an old woman.

My key doesn't work.

Damn.

Raina comes to the door on the third knock.

She's beautiful and sad this morning, black hair in an uptight bundle on her head, run through with a knitting needle, eyes green and lost. Her tank top is full of flowers, stained with chili from the night before. She stands there and doesn't say a word. Like she's accusing me.

"You changed the locks again," I say to her.

"Yeah."

"Wanna talk about it?"

"No."

She backs away and leaves the door open.

I step in carefully.

There's no foyer. You walk right into the living room, which is huge and annexed to a small dining nook and kitchen area. High-arching beams and low-hanging fixtures. A ceiling fan that was installed last year. Everything swimming in mists of dust and grime. Papers, clothes, old Jenny Craig boxes. A rock fireplace with a wooden mantel filled with framed photos. A Zenith cabinet TV set from 1975, which is officially an antique this year. Reminds me of how old I feel. I'm more than halfway through my thirties now.

She sits down on the couch and picks up her coffee from the end table.

"It's been a long time, Buck. I was thinking you'd never be back."

"I've been busy."

"You could have called."

"I guess I could have. Have you been okay?"

"I got fired last week."

"From the Magnolia Café?"

"That was two gigs ago, Buck."

"Were you dancing again?"

"Do you really care?"

She looks me in the eye when she says it, and I see the shame hanging from her face. Raina was always a hateful bitch when she had to ride the poles at the Yellow Rose. She's still young, two years younger than I am. I try not to think about the sweaty, glazed-over stares of men who pay, the smell of watered-down booze and disinfected leather seats, all that terrible jive. I shrug and let it roll off me like it doesn't matter.

"This place is turning into a real dump, Raina."

"Thank you."

She takes a sip from the coffee while I try to figure out where the hell my good manners went off to. I struggle for something better:

"It's good to see you."

"Do you really mean that?"

"Sure."

She looks at me seriously. "You've got one inside you now, don't you? That's the only reason why you came here."

I look at my feet and try to be tactful, but all I come up with is:

"I . . . wanted to see the old place again."

"At least you're not lying anymore, Buck."

"I never lied to you."

"You left out the truth."

"Maybe that's right. I guess I'm sorry."

"That makes me feel real special, Buck. Thanks."

"What do you want from me? You're not my wife."

"I'm your friend. Or at least I *thought* we were friends. You're just so damn good at compartmentalizing, aren't you?"

"Sometimes I didn't know what to say to you back then. So I left things out. I thought I was keeping you safe."

"From what?"

"A lot of bad fucking shit, Raina."

She shakes her head and laughs. "Listen to yourself. You didn't know what to say so you *left things out?* That's the way cowards think, Buck."

"Lots of people are cowards."

"You're always gonna go it alone, aren't you? You'll never let a woman get close to you."

"That's not for me."

"Why? Because you're different? That's bullshit too."

"I don't expect you to understand, Raina. It's just the way things are."

"I came around your place a lot of times. You never came to the door. I saw your truck outside. You never answered your phone when I called. I thought you hated me."

"I don't hate you. Why would I hate you?"

"What then? What did I do?"

"You didn't do anything. It's what I did. I guess I thought I had to close the door on all this. But...I'm not sure I can anymore."

"You should have told me what was wrong. I would have been there for you. I used to think you were different. You never hit on me like the others. I thought you and I were close. I think I even loved you. Is that why you went away?"

"Something happened. I gave up for a while. On everything, I guess."

She shakes her head and stares at her coffee.

I can see a tear forming in her eye, but she reaches up and wipes it out fast, before it can fall on her face. On any other day, I might be sad for that. Today, I just don't know.

She's right.

What the hell is wrong with me?

I let her in a long time ago, then I forced her out, haunted to the end of the earth by dead people and bad magic. I told myself that I was keeping her safe. What was I really doing? What was I really feeling?

"Well, don't let me keep you from your business, Buck. Go on. Do what you have to do. I'll be right here when you're done."

I don't know what to tell her.

So I don't say anything.

How do you explain that things like family are abstract concepts to a guy like me? I'd tell her I don't believe in love, but I'm not sure I even know what love really is. I've had a lot of women, but those comforts turn into sad feelings of emptiness so fast. You get really jaded when you know so many secrets about how temporary everything is. When you have things inside you that never let go. Urgent things that come back again and again. Like the desperate need to be here now.

"Raina...I'm sorry."

"Don't say you're sorry anymore. Don't mind me at all. Just go about your business."

"There's something happening. It could be...very important. I have to look across, and I need to be here when I do it."

"You don't need to ask permission. You don't need to say anything."

She looks away from me, and I feel like I should be ashamed.

But I only tell her I'm sorry again.

I met Raina Winston three days after I came to this city.

Her family had all moved on—her two brothers off to see the world as Marines, her father lost in the breeze with another woman. The house, left to her by a dead mother. She told me all about it when I came to her door for the first time, when I knocked and told her there was something about this place that wanted me to be here. That maybe I had seen the house in a dream, or maybe it was a memory I couldn't finger. I told her a story about it that was almost the truth, then I came clean not long after that and told her a little more. Not everything, of course. I never wanted her to get hurt. Maybe that made me a coward, maybe it didn't.

She loved me from the first time she saw me. I felt it strong, coming off her in hopeful waves. I thought she might be Gifted at first, but then I realized she was just a lonely little girl trapped in the body of a centerfold, filled with sadness for those who hunger with their eyes and lust for the obvious. Beautiful women who don't lose their souls in this terrible world sometimes end up like that—hopeful romantics skirting the outer edges of something they'll probably never find.

I was attracted to her, like any man would be.

I slept with her, like I would have been a fool not to.

But the *love she felt for me*...it was overwhelming and desperate. Something alien, even beyond my inability to understand the basics of human nature. She gave it to me without thought of reward, and I never gave it back. Because we were not the same, she and I. As much as she wanted to believe that it was fate that brought us together, endless oceans of time bridged by some amazing series of cosmic consciences...I always left her bed before morning.

See, Tom was right: I've always believed in fate.

But I don't know if I believe in love.

So I always walked away and left her wondering why. And still, her eyes were big and hopeful, every time I came back.

Back to this house.

This house is the reason I stayed in Austin.

I lived here when I was a child.

Nobody ever told me that, nobody ever gave me papers that proved it—but I know this is where I was born.

I know, because the first time I saw the place, I had a mark inside me, and when I saw the house through the Blacklight...the overgrowth was gone, the paint was shiny new, and the faint traces of things long departed danced in the front yard, like shadows undefined, cruel teasers of a life that seemed like it belonged to someone else...but it was *mine*.

Through the Blacklight, I could see myself in that yard.

Myself as a two-year-old boy.

And then it was gone.

I came back here again and again, searching. I never found my mother and father, never saw them. But there were traces. Artifacts. Things left behind. I brought those things back to the world, one at a time, the same way I brought that pearl necklace back at the institution.

Raina stood there and watched me do it—the ghosts rumbling inside my body, showing me where to look, the Blacklight changing channels on me, making me feel as if I were home again, then jarring me into some other moment from some other family's private soap opera. I couldn't control it so well back then. I had to cut myself bad to pull back, and that terrified her. By then, my scars were pretty scary, but they were all I had to keep myself from looking too deep. Still, I found the evidence. Over seven years, I found it. Job after job, I would hunt the dead, and when I brought them back with me, I would go to the house, where Raina would be waiting for me, her eyes full of love I could never pay back, full of horror for the terrible burden I kept inside me and on the surface of my skin...and I would call on those marks inside to look across and feel the trace embers of my past. And the artifacts.

I found a pair of goggles—the ones I use now to keep the Blacklight from blinding me—and knew they had been used by my father.

I brought back a shattered shaving mirror and felt the moment when my mother had heaved it to the floor in mad frustration.

An old shoe with the laces missing.

A camera without any film in it.

After years, I hit pay dirt in the basement, prodded along by dead voices that wanted me to see a strongbox buried in the earth beneath the living room. Inside the strongbox, just past a rusted lock that gave easy with two whacks from a ball-peen hammer, was the game changer. The thing I'd searched for all my life.

A ripped and worn old road map of the southwestern United States.

It was dotted in red along the trail that led from Austin, up through El Paso, and into New Mexico and through the town where I was found.

All those little towns along the road marked.

The journey my parents took into the desert.

The trail continued through Arizona and ended near California, where a giant hunk of the map had been torn away, but I could guess what lay ahead. I hit the road, trying to trace each mark that had been left behind. I brought in another Blacklight dick to help me, called in some favors. That was how I met Tom Romilda.

Two years on the road, following my instincts.

So much sweat and blood and the screaming of dead things.

So many scars.

Tom set me up with clients on the road who needed help with bad marks, and I would step in and kick their asses. I'd keep what was left inside me for days on end, using the Blacklight to see what others couldn't.

There were a few clues along the way, things I brought back, but nothing that felt right. It was madness for a while. I'd wake up in a sleazy motel off some dusty back road in Arizona or New Mexico and wonder how I'd gotten there. I would scream at the universe to make some kind of sense, Tom would calm me down a few hours, and then I would rage again. Finally, he gave up on me and went back to New Orleans, but I kept going.

For two more years, I kept going.

There was no paper trail to mark the passing of my mother and father, no witness to their murder—if they even *were* murdered.

It was as if they'd never existed.

I followed my instincts, and at every turn my instincts betrayed me.

I even had a fucking map and that was no good.

It was starting to feel like one big cosmic joke.

I moved back through the Southwest and I never got near anything that felt like the familiar glow of the house—and the trace of it grew dimmer and dimmer as the marks mocked me. Until, finally, in a southern-fried podunk shithole halfway between the California border and the edge of nowhere, a place where the voices were louder than they'd ever been and marks filled the crumbling streets like shadows upon shadows set loose across the earth, all filled with bad memories and bitter curses...

I met a man who was like me, but a lot older.

He was seventy-three.

He had one tooth in his mouth.

He was the local sheriff.

His badge looked like something that had been unearthed from a tomb, and his eyes were dead and wise, cursed by all the things he'd seen and heard and dreamed. I knew he must know something. I could feel the truth inside him, the way I can read most people, but his pain was deep. And so I asked him where my mother and father were, what had happened to them...and he laughed.

The son of a bitch *laughed at me.*

You goddamned old man.

How can you laugh at my suffering?

How can you stand there and laugh at me?

His answer was something I'll never forget. I don't want to forget. I want it to haunt me until the end of time, because it was the truth I had been seeking all along, and that truth was this:

Nobody cares, son.

And he kept laughing when he said it.

As if it didn't matter at all.

He had the Gift, which allowed him to see that his tiny little town crawled with lost marks, and he *didn't care at all* how they'd gotten there.

Nobody cares.

That's how the bad people get away with it.

That's what the good people don't understand about America.

He told me there were hundreds of bodies found in the desert every year, sometimes thousands. All unsolved murders. The numbers get to you in the end, he said. It happens everywhere, all over the country, on back roads and desert terrains and stretches of endless wilderness, where a million secrets can be buried forever. *Truckloads* of bodies discovered, washed up without identities, without fingerprints, without faces, without flesh. The police never go near cases like that, not unless a Blacklight dick gets involved—and even then, it's always off the books.

The man with one tooth had been a cop in Texas and Arkansas, a sheriff in Colorado. He used to care when he was younger.

But the sheer weight of the numbers broke him in half.

That and the ability to see the spirits of those bodies walking the earth. To know there was nothing he could do to help them find peace. It's why he moved around so much in the beginning, and why he eventually stopped.

He asked me to kill him, so that he would finally be free.

Free from this world that just didn't care at all.

About anything.

I left him there.

Left him laughing.

Then I went back to the house.

Went back to Raina.

She was a little older then, like she's a little older now.

I never told her anything about any of it.

I left things out, to keep her safe.

I saw her a lot after that, kept hiring out on jobs, still obsessed, still addicted, still hoping for a trace that felt like home. Anything that could prove who I was.

Raina's love for me, still an alien thing I was never able to pay back.

Her smiles and her tears, silent and tragic in the dark, and I wasn't even sure I cared. I began to hate myself for that. Hate myself for allowing her the illusion, and always leaving before morning.

Until they announced they were building the fastest train in history.

Until I discovered the train was going to run right through the spot in California where the map had been torn away.

And that was when the fall happened.

"What are you waiting for?"

Her sharp voice brings me back from the memories, and I find that the mark inside me is desperate now, feeling my anxious heart inside this place that used to be my home. The mark feels me as I call on its power, controlling it.

I reach into my satchel and pull out the goggles.

Slip them over my eyes and pull the rubber strap back hard.

Here we go.

As I concentrate on the mark in my guts, I can sense what he's feeling, and it ain't pretty. The nasty bastard doesn't like being manhandled like this. But a nasty bastard gets only one sucker punch with me. Now you pay cash, Billy Badass.

It surrenders to my control, and the power fills me, flowing at my command, making my whole body tingle and my eyes fill with bright darkness...

The room around me polarizes, swirling in shadows, the walls bouncing dark neon blue against the triple-UV lenses, clawing at the glass, trying to make me blind. The contact lenses are good in a pinch, but nothing gets through the goggles. I move across the room, trying to ignore the pulsing X-ray life essence of Raina Winston slouched on the sofa, almost dead in her heart but never giving up on the flesh, twinkling there like the glowing coals of a long-gone fire that once reached for the sky. I looked deep into her one time when I did this. I saw her love for me, and her love for so many others, all swimming just above the surface of her skin, patterns of hope and loneliness and despair and self-hatred.

It was too much then, and it's too much now.

I move away from her and concentrate on the floor beneath my feet, keeping myself grounded. So many familiar things flashing across my vision, things only half formed, things I've felt before. Riddles in the blinding darkness. Nothing here I haven't seen already. Why am I here? I learned all I could learn from this place years ago.

I'm here because I want to be here.

Because it feels good.

I want to stay.

It flows into me like an old dream, directing my movements, telling me where to put my feet…and I follow it across the floor. Something familiar pings back to me like radar. Something I shouldn't know, but I do…something just out of my reach…

Something…

My foot catches on a loose board.

I haven't felt that before.

A sound like a wordless voice sings to me in that moment, tells me to stop.

I bend down and test the floor.

The board comes up easy.

Wasn't even nailed down.

In the space just under there, something sparkles.

It's a gun.

A .357 revolver, snub-nosed, brand-new.

It's loaded with one bullet.

My fingers close around it and I feel the rush again—purer this time, like a wave of euphoria washing over my entire body. Happiness is a warm gun. I laugh at the thought, hearing the voice of John Lennon, the voice of reason, pulling me back…and I bring the knife out, cutting myself just a little, along my wrist. The pain shocks me. The bright blackness fades…

The room looks normal.

The mark grumbles in my guts.

The gun is still in my hand.

It's rusted beyond use now, the bullet fused into the chamber, the trigger and firing pin frozen in layers of caked dirt and corrosion built up by years and years of waiting—waiting for me to find it. The floorboard is not loose anymore. It's not even the same floorboard. This place has been remodeled twice since the gun was hidden there, left behind by someone who wanted me to find it.

But why now?

It's been years since I found the map, and that was hidden deep in the basement. It was the last clue made known to me. And now *this*...

There's a nexus forming, and I can feel it all around me.

The shame of my past rushing to meet the fate of my future. All the things that seem like coincidences to everyone but me. The search I've nearly killed myself so many times for. And the train, out there in the west, running straight through it.

I was looking for a sign to point me back there.

And I just found it.

I've been armed.

"I never get used to that, Buck."

Her voice comes with a reverent sigh, and she stands up from the sofa, coming over to me. The first time I pulled an object in this room, she described what it looked like on her end. She said my hand just *disappeared* for a moment, like it had vanished beyond some weird invisible dividing line, and then I pulled it back, holding the goggles I'm wearing now. Said it scared the hell out of her, made her feel like she was living in a house of ghosts. But nobody can see what I see in places like this.

She touches the rusty gun in my hand.

"It belonged to my mother," I tell her. "I don't know how I know that, but I do."

"Just like old times."

"Yes. Exactly like old times."

"What will you do now, Buck?"

"I don't know. Something's going down...I can *feel it*...but I don't know."

"Will I see you again?"

"I hope so."

"Please don't lie to me."

"I never lie to you."

She smiles weakly, then opens her right hand, showing me the key she's been palming since I walked in. Gives it to me, her smile growing weaker.

"Please come back to me. I don't want you to die."

FOUR

THE FALL

My place is on the edge of town, out on the north side where there's lots of trees and the greenbelt river snakes in endless circles, making it smell like a swamp with the soul of a big city. There ain't any bodies buried out here. Believe me, I know.

FERNANDEZ CEMETERY AND FUNERAL SERVICE.

You can hardly read the sign out front, it's so weathered. They've been out of business for ten years, officially. It's quiet at the end of my street, not like on Congress Avenue, which is a lot noisier than it used to be. See, the bodies are all buried downtown.

I click off the Walkman and grab the silver urn from the seat.

My backyard is a country acre of headstones, all of them blank, most of them waiting.

Over two hundred headstones.

I helped out the family that owns this place. A nasty situation with an ex-son-in-law. They had no cash to pay me, so they let me live in the abandoned house rent-free for a few years. It was a unique fixer-upper opportunity, but I gave up on that. Now it's just a flytrap. I pay rent these days, but it's dirt cheap, even for a guy like me. A few bills a month, and the landlord is almost dead. The eldest child of the Fernandez clan tells me I'll inherit this shithole, lock stock and barrel, when her grandmother finally passes on. That's the way the old lady wants it in her will. Because of what I did for her grandkids.

Because I saved their lives.

I set the urn near the porch and dig the grave as the morning sun beats down, tired as hell, but it never takes long. The remains of the child killer swimming inside me makes terrible noises now—the soul of a maniac crying that it's scared.

Scared of what happens next.

Wherever it decides to go.

The marks make the choice themselves, that's what Tom always says. Nobody knows what really happens to a ghost when it's brought across and buried. Some people are just better than others at attaching names and labels and religions to things they can't understand. The Blacklight is the only thing I know for sure, burning me on the next level of sight, and the levels after that, down and down until you get into the worst places, where the really bad ones end up, swimming in nothingness, lost forever. I've only been to the bottom once, and it nearly made me blind. We call it the Big Black. It might be where they all go in the end. Might be heaven and hell, all rolled up into one endless stretch of nowhere. Not that heaven and hell were ever real to begin with.

That's something else most people don't understand.

Everything you think you know about life and death and some sort of God that loves you or a devil that hates us—well, guess what?

You're wrong about all that.

And what I do ain't about blessings or rituals or holy symbols, man.

It's about what's inside us.

That thing that never dies.

To send bad ones home—the trapped ones—you have to become *responsible* for what's left of them.

All that takes is a silver urn and a shovel.

And a special talent like mine.

The gravestones came with the place when I moved in. They're a nice touch, but you don't really need them. You just need to be able to reach out and grab the mark's madness. Then you put what's left six feet under.

Sometimes I think I know these things because my parents knew them. I'd *like* to think that, anyway. It's easier than believing in God.

I have the remains of seventy-six marks buried back here.

They've all gone home.

To the Big Black.

The place no one can see—not even me.

I can tell they've all gone because if they were still around, this place would sound like a stadium full of really unhappy football fans.

The summer sun pins me to the earth, and I shiver in the heat for a moment, lost in the earthen smell beneath my feet.

Summers are really hot in Texas.

And when it gets really hot in Texas, really bad shit goes down.

I pick up the urn and go inside, through the squealing screen door and across the rotten back porch, five locks and a deadbolt on a thick steel slab that keeps the bad guys out. You make sure your shit is sealed up tight in my line of work. Inside, the place is wasted. The work of a bachelor who ain't looking back. The kitchen needs a facelift, the dining nook filled with stacks of unpaid bills, a laptop on the table that barely works. One urn left in the cabinet above the fridge. It's made out of brass, plated on the outside with a thin sheen of flecked silver. I have the real thing today, etched with Jesus and Mary and holy crosses, so I leave my last one up there. Anything to save a buck. I'm behind on my rent by four months, and the city is going to shut my water off tomorrow. The cash in my pocket should cover me for a while, at least another few weeks.

The child killer rumbles in my guts.

Dammit.

Let's get this nasty shit over with.

The metal feels cool. My hands are hot.

Silver urns only.

I usually get the cheap ones these days, but you have to play by the rules, even if you cheat. I broke a lot of the rules when I was a kid. Most of that came back to haunt me later. Literally. That's when I dealt with it.

One problem at a time.

On the cabinet shelf where I keep the urns are rows of bottles with no labels—my own special mixture. Sea salt and Kaopectate in a castor oil base.

Really gross stuff.

This part also took me years to figure out. When I was younger, I'd sit around all day watching TV, swallowing all kinds of junk to force the marks up. The first one came out easy—the remains of the old lady when I was just twelve years old. But it got a lot harder every time after that. The other dicks told me to get drunk, like Tom always does, but I saw what that kind of thinking did to those guys. I really *would* be dead if I used booze to make myself puke. Most mediums self-medicate just to silence the voices—I tried it once and ended up constipated and fucked up, muttering curses at the mirror. I have enough problems without all that shit. Not that the alternative is much better when the chips are down, but I like being in control of myself. So fuck it.

I grab some old newspapers and spread them on the kitchen floor.

I uncap the urn and set it in the center of the newspapers.

I kneel down and pick a spot on the wall, holding my breath.

I raise the castor oil to my lips.

Don't ever do this.

The bile hits the back of my throat with a sting as it comes up in a black spasm—right into the urn, because that's where I *tell it to go*.

Then I swallow the castor oil and do it again.

And again.

And one more time after that.

It takes nearly an hour to get what's left of the child killer out of me.

Every single goddamn drop of it.

My guts are sore, the gag muscles clenched and hard as I choke one last time on a dry heave. So bad. The worst one in years. Fucking goddamn *child killer...*

I lie on the floor of the kitchen, staring straight up, the crying voice of the mark bubbling low inside the magnetized silver plating of the urn. It's trapped there now, and my own soul swims in hammered shit.

They tell me this is what a hangover feels like.

I can't imagine anything feeling worse.

The sickness that shreds my soul and my body. The cure that makes my hair white. I gauge reality by the beating of my heart, making sure I'm still all there, wishing I were dead and taking back the wish in the same second. I lie there a very long time. My body finally finds peace for a moment, but I never really relax, even after I win these little battles. Cry me a river, right?

I take the urn out to the graveyard and bury it in the fresh hole.

I'm thinking about nothing while I do that.

I want to sleep for a million years.

The shovel is rough and splintered in my hands, and when I am done with the task, I leave it leaning there against the grave marker, like some kind of reminder.

A reminder of everything.

The fall.

I don't think about it much when I'm awake, but it creeps up on me in my dreams. That's why I never sleep much these days, even when I'm dog tired, like I am now.

My second pilgrimage into the desert to find my parents.

I quit the first time and came back to the real world because the old man with one tooth had convinced me I was wrong for looking, that it was like searching for a dead man in a sea of dead men. I heard his voice every time I thought about going back on the road, and that voice told me:

Nobody cares, son.

Nobody at all.

But then the train came.

The Jaeger Laser.

There's a place in my house, just above the fireplace mantel, where I keep all the souvenirs I've pulled back from the Blacklight. I've lost track of how many mediums and hunters I've shown these things to, but not one person has been able to give me a decent explanation for why I can pull a solid object like that—not even the guys who can trance themselves deep enough to actually see what I see for a few seconds. And not all of those artifacts have given me familiar vibrations. The camera, for example. I think it probably belonged to another family that lived in that house, maybe one of Raina's distant relatives. But the more I looked at the broken shaving mirror, the more I could feel the scent of my mother's anger. The more I held that old toddler shoe in my hands, the more I regressed to the frustrated level of a two-year-old whining in the dark.

And the map.

Always something new there when I looked at it in the Blacklight.

In the world everyone else can see, it was just a moldy, torn-to-hell scrap of paper. But when I looked through the eyes of the dead—flickering backward through time in random bursts, like channels flipping on and off in shadows of phosphorescent darkness—new details of the map would become visible, sections long rotted or torn away reappearing for just a moment. I got crazy about putting together the pieces. I would pull a mark and keep it inside me long enough to look. I'd scrawl it out from memory on new scraps of paper. One entire wall in my bedroom became a hand-drawn map of southeastern California, where I knew the end of the line was located. I would volunteer for jobs with no pay just to get more than one in me, so I could go deeper and deeper, looking for more details. The more you have in you, the blacker and brighter it gets.

I remember the day they announced they were building the Jaeger Laser.

A prototype bullet train connecting Los Angeles to Las Vegas, running directly through a bad spot near the Nevada border, a place most guys like me never go near.

Some of us call it the Blacklight Triangle.

A lot of fucked-up business out there.

A lot of dead mediums left in the dark corners.

I didn't give a shit.

I followed the trail scrawled on my wall.

I followed the trail to the letter.

I shadowed the surveyors and construction teams they had out there working on the rail project, always staying out of sight, always looking just ahead of them.

Until I found what I was looking for.

It was in a spot just off the area of the map that had been torn, where the vibrations were so powerful that even a dumbshit palm reader without much juice could have picked up on it. The call was like a homing beacon and I zeroed right in. The Jaeger people hadn't gotten that deep yet—a stretch of burned earth just off the freeway in Teighlor where something was buried. Something screaming for help in wordless terror and straight-cold hatred. I dug it up. A mark, put six feet under—just the way I do it now, except that the urn was made of copper, not silver. That was why I could hear it and feel it. The job hadn't been done right. I didn't even think to wonder why at the time.

All I knew was that this had been left for me.

It was on the trail of my mother and father, and the spot had been marked on the map, right there where I found the shallow grave.

I had passed over hundreds of spots just like that on my first trip, but I hadn't heard the marks because they'd been put to rest the right way, encased in the magnetic void of a silver tomb.

This one was pissed off and unsettled.

The sloppy burial had left it hungry.

I kept the copper urn with me as I continued into California, and the vibe got worse. There were bad things all over the place. None of them were coming near me, though. I even tried to pull a few of them, but it didn't work. I was so close, but I needed to see as they saw. Needed to see through the eyes of the dead.

Finally, I got desperate.

I was holed up in an abandoned motel, and the mark in the urn was speaking to me. It had been pulled by my mother and father. It knew the secrets of where they had gone—I convinced myself of that, wrapped myself up in my own shameless mantra, rationalizing what I was about to do in so many hateful, obvious ways. I still can't believe I did what I did. It disgusts me to think about it, so I try not to.

And then it all comes back.

Unscrewing the cap of the urn.

Smelling the putrid, unbound remains boiling in there, swimming in traces of castor oil and blood from when it was regurgitated, years ago.

Sewage muck from a dead man's soul.

Rotten.

I picked a spot on the wall.

I held my breath.

It all went down in a few mighty gulps.

And the mark was inside me, doing its dance, oozing along my guts, filling me with sonic flashes and kilowatt bursts of terrible torture and murder and self-mutilation—not fully formed images, but diluted, half-digested slurs of insanity, a grotesque swarm of sick twitches and spasms. I couldn't feel anything but animal lust, primordial passion, the desire to kill and eat and be full of blood. It was an alien feeling, but it was also a terrifyingly *human feeling*—the basest feeling of all, the feeling that hurts most when we dream about bad things that touch us and turn us on with jaded cruelty and hopelessness. It wasn't the soul of a man, at least not anymore. It was the mulched remains of brute instinct and animal lust, mainlining directly into my brain. And I was a dog lapping up shit on the sidewalk and rushing from it like some delirious junkie wallowing at the wrong end of a suicide tear. At first I wanted it out of me. Then I rationalized some more. Then I called myself names. I put my fist through the mirror, repulsed at the sight of my own face.

Then I put on the goggles and let the Blacklight flow over me.

This time, I didn't hurt myself to come back.

This time, I stayed there.

I allowed the world of shadows to consume me, falling down and down. I knew it didn't matter, and I knew it would kill me. I wanted death to come so I would see the truth. I just walked into nothingness. The way doomed people do it.

I came to maybe a few days later, maybe a week, I've never been sure.

I was walking through the desert with the sun scorching my skin.

Two more marks inside me.

I can't remember how I pulled them, I was that far gone.

I kept thinking I could see something just over the horizon—images of people, blood, something like the sound of a gunshot ringing in my head, over and over.

The voices of my parents, screaming and screaming.

Finally—*their voices.*

The marks manhandling my soul and my mind, ripping at the walls, taking me down a little at a time.

I phased roughly in and out of consciousness.

The world flicked on and off in static bursts.

It was the end, I thought.

The end of my life and the end of my search.

They were right there.

Right in front of me.

If I just went a little farther.

Just a little more.

Just...

When I went under for the last time, I could hear the marks screaming in victory, and I knew that I was dead, that it was all over.

And I didn't care.

When I came up from the blackness, I wasn't dead at all.

I'd been found in the desert by a man with skin like red leather and feathers in his hair. His eyes were wise and calm, full of secrets. I was naked in a tent, surrounded by the smell of strange medicines and burning candles. I'd heard about the Kumeyaay tribes and the settlements in Southern California, how they were into all sort of mystical shit, but I'd never bothered to look into it. Always in my own world. Nobody really looks outside his own world unless his back is against the wall. Kind of pathetic, really.

I felt like a defeated child under the old Indian's wise eyes.

He said I'd outpaced the rail-line surveyors by more than a hundred miles, that it was a miracle anyone had found me, and I believed him. He said he'd taken the bad spirits out of my body, forced me to regurgitate them in my sleep. But it hadn't been easy.

Then he told me about his son.

One of the marks had gotten into him during the ritual.

Killed him.

I didn't want to believe it was true, but then I saw the body. The child had been torn to pieces from the inside out—a pile of human wreckage in the rough shape of a little boy, steaming in his own blood, watched over by eyes filled with tears. His mother, wracked with the worst loss a woman can know. Her silent, weeping form, hunched over what was left, praying in words I would never understand.

I felt the bottom of the world drop out.

Down and down, I fell.

The old man never cursed me, never told me I was a bad man, never even punished me, and that probably made it worse. He said I was one of many men he'd found in the Blacklight Triangle, and that it was his son's duty to stand by his side. He told me the bad spirits would never have the boy the way they'd had me or the others. That the boy had gone to a different place—a better place. He said it all with those wise eyes and never spoke of it again, never wept for the child.

Something glowed in his eyes.

Something familiar there, but I was too far in the zero to wonder what it was. Too ashamed of everything I had allowed myself to become.

Everyone feels that way eventually.

Everyone falls.

We only need to wait for it.

The old man never said a word to me again. Just gave me some new clothes and drove me to a bus. And I felt like a lost kid, just the way I'd felt when I was twelve, standing at the station with old Granger, not knowing what I had been trusted with and having no idea what the future would bring.

The old man waved good-bye.

I had no idea what to tell him, what to tell myself.

I didn't cry for the boy either.

I still haven't.

So I quit instead. Turned my back on the house and Raina and the horrible half-lives of evil men and women inside me. Turned on some loud music and tried to forget.

It was easy to become nothing.

Easy to pretend the world had no use for me.

I had done so much wrong by Raina, allowed her in and pushed her out so many times, that it almost felt right. Staying away from her, I mean. Ignoring her calls. Not coming to the door when she knocked. I knew it must hurt, but it was probably better than the alternative, which would have been holding her close to me in the dark, then running away again before morning. Every time I thought about picking up the phone to apologize, or returning to the house to see her, the more useless it seemed. I felt the terrible sadness Raina would leave with me on my front porch every time she came and went, like a wave that broke and rolled back, but her sadness left me cold, unmoved. I just sat there.

They built the train.

More time rolled by.

I told myself I didn't care.

Over and over, I told myself.

But the Blacklight always knew I would be back.

There's always a second chance to fall.

I look back at the grave again, and the shovel.

I roll up my sleeve and look at the scars covering my arm.

Reminders.

I don't want to be reminded. I spent almost two years running away from reminders. But things are changing now.

The nexus, slowly forming again.

It's always been there, hasn't it?

I can sense that coming thing in the hot Texas wind, the sun higher now and stretching my shadow long across the graveyard. There's a sort of comfort in that. I don't allow myself to feel it for long. I go back in the house and into the living room, which is filled with dusty light coming through windows that haven't been washed in years, and there's a dead man sitting on my couch.

FIVE

WHERE THE DOWN BOYS GO

You look like shit, Buck."

I move through the living room in a daze, almost not there. If I look half as bad as I feel, Darby's got me dead to rights. But he's a fine one to talk.

Heh.

Dead to rights.

Sometimes I just slay me.

"Had to drive all night," I tell him, almost laughing. "Need some sleep."

"Yeah, right. Like you ever really go all the way under when you hit a mattress. You're lucky if you can get, what? A half hour, fifteen minutes?"

"What are you, my shrink?"

"I'm the ghost of Christmas Past, come to tell you the future, Buck."

He makes a dumb little scary noise when he says that. Really annoying. Like someone calling you *sleepyhead* in a singsong just after you wake up from a terrible dream. His voice sounds just like it did when he was still alive: deep and with a neutral accent, like most street hustlers from Austin. That's a dumb little secret about this town. The indigenous criminals all sound like they're from Anywhere Else, U.S.A.

"The future's not what it used to be," I say to him, still almost laughing.

"Profound wisdom. Gonna tell me again how Facebook is killing my generation?"

"How about I send you a text?"

"You don't know *how* to text."

"And video killed the radio star."

"You're a *relic*, Buck. Nobody else would get that joke. Ain't you damn lucky to have a pal like me hangin' around?"

"Roosevelt would get it."

"The kid's got some culture issues, just like you."

"Thanks."

"I do my best."

He makes a sudden karate move—swings one arm around, like I showed him. Just playing, but he's really speedy this morning. Darby Jones is the only man I know about, alive or dead, who can do that to me. I still block him, like Bruce Lee to his Brandon.

"You're the fastest old fuck in Texas," he says. "I'll kick your ass one of these days."

"Dream on, ghost dog."

"My god, the *scimitar wit*. We're just a bed of fuckin' roses, ain't we?"

"To what do I owe today's pleasure, Darby?"

He narrows his beady little eyes at me, lowers his fist. Hates it when I call him by his real name. See, he was a gangbanger back in the world. They called him Crazy-D. That was years ago, just after my rep on the street in Austin turned mean and the gangs started wanting a piece of my action. I made them change their minds.

That's why this guy is still hanging around.

There's this funny thing that happens once in a blue moon. When a guy gets killed and he's got one foot in his own grave already, when he's full of conflict and he's not ready to let go. He gets cut loose and walks the earth at level one, sometimes attached to the man or woman who killed him. Walkers are not common. Darby's one of a small handful left, and you never see any new recruits these days.

Lucky fucking me.

"Your name's been coming up a lot," he says. "And it's not the usual gossip. Some of the mean ones have been seeing the future, for real. They see something big about to go down. Thought I'd pop in to let you know."

"Figures. I was offered a pretty heavy case last night. I don't know if I should run or sit this one out."

"I thought you'd say that."

"Everything's pulling me toward the same place again."

"The train, huh?"

"Yep."

I sit down in the Barcalounger, one of those old-style recliner chairs that nobody buys anymore, almost as ancient as this house. It sends up a poof of dust when my ass hits it, and the dust swirls in the gloom filtering through my dirty windows. It's the only light in the place, like a beacon from some dull yellow morning on another planet. The image reminds me of unsettled business. Reminds me of Darby.

I've seen into his past more than once.

We actually have a lot in common.

He was kicked around a lot between foster homes before he hit the street, at nine years old. That was in Houston, where he first got popped for armed robbery. The murder beef came later, but it was a trumped-up charge. He fought the prison rapists hard for three years before they showed him the door. By then he was real bitter and ready for more shit. How do you like that? Outside, he'd been more or less innocent.

Darby had to go to prison to become a killer.

He was doing hits by the time he was twenty-one, traveled all over the country with some mean kids. Came back to Austin after that, working for the cowboys and the gangbangers. An equal opportunity white-trash muscle thug.

This guy could have been anything he wanted to be.

He was smart and resourceful.

Everybody falls, and that's it.

But I guess it's probably easier when you're Generation Zero to begin with—one of those cell-phone-wagging Internet ghosts cut loose on the face of a recycled culture that doesn't even know what it's trying to mimic.

The funny thing is, Darby still has a Facebook page.

And he Tweets.

"I wish I knew how to take care of you," I tell him. "I'd send you packing if I could."

"You'd have to die."

"Stranger things have happened."

"It's damn dead in this town, Buck. There aren't as many of us as there used to be. They've been disappearing fast. And the *voices*..."

"Maybe I should do us both a favor. Might kill two birds with one stone."

"You don't have the balls."

"It ain't about balls. It's about some light at the end. I'm starting to think that the only way to find what I'm looking for is to go the whole distance."

He shakes his head at me. "Usually when you talk about killing yourself, you're not so serious about it."

"I'm tired, just like you are."

"Don't make me laugh. You've still got *skin*, man—what I do is hard work. You think I just drift around wherever I please?"

He starts bitching again about the life.

The world of slow molasses all Walkers deal with every day.

You can't pass by an old house without getting sucked into it. You can't truck near a troubled child and not hear every one of the worst secrets his parents make him keep. You struggle with your own substance and fall through the cracks every other second. It's like sinking in quicksand that burns your feet. And if you can't hang on, you descend into nothingness. The bottom level, where the Blacklight is blackest. A tar pit swimming with chummed remains, where you forfeit all identity, all purpose, every reason you ever had to go on existing. The Big Black.

I know all that because I went with him the first time he slipped.

I pulled him out, and lived inside the skin of his soul for just a quarter-second before I realized it was a life I couldn't consume like the others. He wasn't something I could pull and send to rest.

Because Walkers ain't really ghosts and they ain't really people.

They're bad dreams trucking the earth, wearing phantom flesh made from ten-ton resentment.

The smart ones are like Darby.

They look for ways to resolve.

They know it's probably the only way to avoid the pit.

Meanwhile, just about every story you've ever heard about a haunted house—pesky poltergeist action and all that creaky-floor business in the dead of night—that's mostly guys like Darby doing what they do, trying to find a way back into the world. Sometimes they just do it to amuse themselves. He's got six thousand virtual friends on the Internet, and not one of them believes he's really a Walker.

It's lonely out there, just like he said.

I remember the gun and take it out of my satchel.

It seems to vibrate under Darby's stare, sending familiar rhythms coursing through my blood.

"What do you make of this?" I say, holding it out to him.

"It's a revolver, a three-fifty-seven Magnum. Smith and Wesson. So what?"

"I found it in the house. When I saw it in the Blacklight, it was brand-new. Brought the thing out, and it was rusted and worthless. What do you see?"

He reaches over and takes the gun, holds it up in a practiced grip.

"Looks brand-new to me too." He looks at the chamber. "And one bullet, ready to shoot."

I can't see that—all I see is the rusty antique.

I need a ghost inside me to fire that last shot.

I need to be in the Blacklight.

Darby feels the weight. "This is probably a late-sixties model. It has no trigger lock, and the spin chamber is smaller. They developed the three-fifty-seven in the mid-thirties. It was based on the design of the thirty-eight special, but they were always fucking around with it, coming up with new wrinkles."

I wonder how many gangbangers know that much history about the guns they murder little old ladies with. Wikipedia—it's a lovely time killer for the living dead.

"I think it belonged to my mother."

He hands it back. "Kinda funny, don't you think? The voices lead you to a gun that can only be fired in the Blacklight?"

"I thought it was pretty weird myself."

"It could be something important."

"Or someone might be setting me up."

"Someone on the other side? Someone with a grudge?"

"Wouldn't be the first time."

I take the gun from him, set it on the wasted coffee table. Lean back in the Barcalounger, staring at the ceiling. My next words come after a dull sigh. "Did you ever regret killing someone? When you were still alive, I mean."

He thinks about it for a second. Then shakes his head. "No. I mean, you always think about it...but *regret?* It was all business. A way to make a score."

"You don't regret me?"

"I never killed you. Can't regret something you never did, can ya?"

"They say that's the worst kind of regret."

I stare at his face.

The scar from four years ago splits his lip at a bizarre angle, giving him a permanent grin like a crooked, upside-down triangle with teeth. His skin is chalky and almost translucent. You can't see through Walkers, they appear to you like normal people. Your average ghost is really strange-looking. Darby was twenty-four years old when my knife took him in the face. He's still wearing the same clothes he had on that night, and the scar never went away, either. He would have blown my head off because his employers gave him two grand to do it. You couldn't even buy a car with what my life was worth to those east-side shitkickers. They had no idea Darby would be so angry about the arrangement later. When Walkers are angry about something, they can do a lot more than make things float around or type angry blogs on a keyboard—they can kill the living and make it messy.

The gangs never fucked with me again after Darby was done with them.

And he doesn't even regret it.

"What if it's not really a sin after all," he says, his voice high and thoughtful. "What if we're just like all the other animals, cut loose and prowling for food in the world? What if God doesn't care? What if it was just three wise men and the ghost of Elvis calling the shots all along? *Man,* I'd like that."

I throw him a sideways glance. "God? You really believe in *God* after all this?"

"A man would be a fool not to. Someone's gotta be responsible."

"*We're* responsible. Blame it on Elvis if you need to."

Darby smiles in a weak sentimental way, shaking his head. "You were *always* the cynic, even back in the old days. You and me, we had a good run there for a while. I thought helping all those kids and families get their lives back would get me through the pearly gates for sure. I even read the manual."

He means the Bible.

Whatever.

I listen to him ramble on for a few more minutes. It's mostly stuff I've already heard. Old history, bad luck, downtown is for suckers. Like I need him to tell me all that.

I put a tape in the player, one of Raina's old mixes.

She loves the eighties.

"Down Boys" comes through the shredded speakers of a plastic compartment stereo I bought for eighty dollars at Walmart back in 1993. Cheap music for a cheap moment in history. Overwrought pop-metal riffs swimming in reverb, fighting for attention behind a wind-tunnel backbeat smothered in glamour-boy lead vocals. This band was called Warrant. "Down Boys" has a happy chorus that sounds like hot chicks with big, embarrassing eighties dos playing volleyball on a beach in California circa 1986.

Down Boys.

Raina used to call the ghosts that.

She said my graveyard was where the Down Boys go, just like in the song. That makes me smile sometimes, just a little. But not today.

"I can always tell when you want me to leave," Darby says. "You put on this turn-of-the-century fag rock."

"Metallica depresses me."

"Those guys saved American radio for the nineties, man."

"Get thee behind me, Satan."

He snorts, as if he can still breathe. Reflex actions of the living dead. "It wouldn't hurt you to get your head into the future one of these days, Buck. At least get yourself a better computer."

"It's on my to-do list. Right behind a shiny new iPod."

"Yeah, then you can retire your Walkman."

He points at the slab of metal and plastic I have hooked to my belt. I turn one corner of my mouth up. Walkmans are what they used to call iPods back in the eighties, before they turned into MP3 players. I really do need an MP3 player. I could get the whole Mötley Crüe back catalog on my little fingernail. There's nothing like loud music on a set of headphones to keep your senses distracted from all the bad noise nobody else can hear. New metal and emo punk and guys like the White Stripes make me very unhappy, but maybe that's the point.

They can have it. I want my MTV.

I sit back down in the chair and Darby continues to lecture me about owning a better computer, but I barely hear his voice anymore. The ghosts of young musicians pretending to be joyful float through the room like the faux-happy remnants of former lives. The voices comfort me, crazy and stoned and jaded behind the scenes. The voices make me think my mother and father are still here. Here and smiling at me. Family photos that never fade. Pictures I could never see to begin with.

"The ghost of Elvis, man," he says, getting thoughtful again. "That fat fuck. I'll kick his ass real good when I meet him."

I close my eyes and drift away while Darby is still talking. I know the rest won't last long, it never does.

Peace is something you only find when you're not looking for it.

I move in slow motion across a sun-ripped landscape, sinking in the sand just a little more with each step. I'm blinded by the light of the dead. My gog-

gles are burned through, my eyes bleeding like tears down my face. The voices of an angry mob hiss and scream at me, just out of sight. The waves of sickness crash and roll in, leaving the remains of rotten things washed up in my throat. I fall farther into the dark, way down and then farther still, with the salty wind blowing through my hair like millions of tiny tentacles, stinging my face with acid . . . and I start screaming because it's all so confusing and unfair and awful . . . and this is it . . . this is where it all ends . . . way down in the dark . . . where the Down Boys go . . .

They say Albert Einstein lived on two hours of sleep a day. I read somewhere that he took catnaps in his lab. He'd spend all day and all night finding solutions, jotting down numbers, all those things that geniuses do, and he hardly ever nodded off because he calculated that sleep was a waste of energy. He wore the same clothes every day, too. Had a closet full of dull gray sweaters and baggy pants, all of them identical. No time for fashion choices when you have atoms to split. Later, after the first atomic bomb went off in Hiroshima, old Albert said he wished he'd been a watchmaker all that time.

Funny, huh?

Most of the human race is asleep half their lives.

The rest of us split atoms.

Darby is gone when I wake up, and I'm thinking about Albert Einstein because it's just twenty minutes later. Catnaps in the lab.

There was a dream, but it's gone now.

Just the afterburn left, sizzling in my stomach.

Something about the fall. The desert out there. My shame and my fate, all wrapped up in the nexus.

I shake it off.

The room is silent, Raina's mix tape jammed at the end of the first side. The silence is almost deafening.

I get up from the Barcalounger and wander down the hall, into the master bedroom. I grab a shower. Throw on a change of clothes. It's almost noon. Day's half over for everyone but me.

The map of my journey through the desert is still scrawled on the wall, elaborate and detailed, like some demented trail to nowhere etched on the concrete slab of a prison cell. This room was my prison cell for years. I guess it still is.

The map points west, to the Blacklight Triangle.

Where the Down Boys go.

Everything's pulling me back.

I don't know what to do.

I see myself in the mirror on the closet door and I think of old Albert again. Black jeans and lace-up Dockers, Walkman at my waist, headphones around my neck, dark blue button-down shirt and black formal jacket with padded shoulders and dark gray pin stripes, the same one I always wear because I have ten on the rack just like it.

Atoms splitters are like superheroes, man. You can always see us coming because we always wear the same clothes.

I get the kid on the phone and tell him I need some information.

Some details on the Jaeger Laser.

Stuff only he would be able to dig up.

The kid appreciates a challenge.

Says to give him two hours.

So I pay my water bill at the grocery store, then stop in on Father Joe.

He's happy to see me, standing at the edge of an empty stage, doing something to his pulpit with a hammer and nails. He's young for a man of the cloth, his little hole-in-the-wall church located just inside town, in a cozy semi-rich neighborhood near a Baptist school full of cheering kids and anxious spirits. His full God-given is Father Joseph Angus Fay, but everyone calls him Father Joe, and he's cool with it. His dad left him the house when he was thirty, he took his vows of poverty and chastity two years later, renovated the place six months after that. In the beginning, I never had the heart to call him on the carpet about all this Jesus stuff. These days I kind of enjoy the sparring matches.

I pay him for the last case of urns and he counts the money twice.

I don't make a lot of small talk this time, and he can sense that I'm anxious.

We're going to spar again today, I can feel it.

He says something about faith, about rest.

I tell him I need another case of urns by Saturday.

I'd buy them somewhere else, but Father Joe owes me, and he still gets a good deal from the outfit that supplies his God-scent candles and holy wafers. Silver-plated urns are damn pricey, even when you get them wholesale from a funeral-supply company. I always put it down under "expenses."

Father Joe is thirty-three and looks like a teenager.

Maybe *he's* the one who made a deal with the devil.

Never can tell about these things.

"I prayed for you last night," he says, counting the cash a third time. "I see that it has brought fruit."

"Fruit for whom?"

"I was expressing concern for your immortal soul, Buck."

"Nice of you."

He sighs like he gives up. But Father Joe never gives up. He's right back at me. "I really wish you would reconsider your faith. You might find some peace. The Lord God is always ready to receive those who did not believe on the day before."

"Day before what?"

"You know what I mean."

"Maybe I do, maybe I don't. What I know for sure is that I've got a head filled with other people's bad business, and a lot of my own. I get to see little kids strung up by their own fathers. Nasty stuff. And I'm not talking about some bad daddy breaking down in the confessional. I'm talking about *full-color pictures* burned in my mind forever. What the hell did God ever do for *those* people?"

"He loves them. All His children are at rest when they leave this earth."

"Says who? I pulled a mark once, right here in this room, and he didn't go to heaven. He went into *me*. Does that make me God's son? Or does that mean it's all a little different than what the manual says?"

"If you don't believe, why do you still come here, Buck? You must be searching for *something*."

"I'm searching for a good deal on silverware."

"The urns are blessed when I give them to you. You don't think that helps?"

"No. They're just cheap."

He smiles. "You're incorrigible, Buck. But God loves you. He has given you this gift so that you may walk the earth and cleanse it of evil."

"I'm glad you believe that, Father."

"Are you really?"

"Everyone has to believe in *something*, even if it doesn't make a lot of sense."

"I believe in *you*, Buck. I know your burden is great, but your reward will be greater. You are touched by His hand."

"I'm glad you believe that, Father. No bullshit."

He smiles and tilts his head thoughtfully. "Where are you off to now?"

"Gotta see a man about a horse."

"Try to stay out of trouble. I'll have the new shipment in by Friday."

He starts to walk back to his stage, the hammer resting on his shoulder. Gets another thought and turns on one heel. "Incidentally, Buck...why silver? I've always wondered."

"Something do with the element. It reacts with the bile in a specific way that keeps it contained, kind of like a magnetic field. I'm not sure about the exact science, but it sure as hell works."

"How did you *learn* about that?"

He's trying to corner me. Wants to make it about God. The truth is, I don't *know* how I know. It just came to me one night after a few months of doing it wrong. It's the same way I know how to put them to rest in the graves. Maybe that was the good Lord shining a light on me, maybe it was my parents. Nobody's talking.

"Trade secrets," I tell him. "Call the head office, Father."

"I will."

I wink at him and he turns back to his pulpit again.

"My man Bucko—*Buck Oblivion!* Get the hell in here and have a toke of the smoke!"

Buck Oblivion.

A nickname a kid would come up with.

Or a guy like Franklin Delano Roosevelt.

His one-room apartment smells like marijuana and cheap sex, the kind you pay for by the hour. I can feel the remains of dead women in this room. They've been here for years. He can't feel them because he's always stoned.

"No, thanks," I tell him, holding up a hand when he offers me the blunt. Normally I might partake, but I hate the way he rolls his, half the joint laced with mint tobacco, like those guys in France do it. He pays three hundred a quarter for that stuff, then cuts it with over-the-counter menthol sawdust that costs a buck and a half.

Guess we all have our illusions.

I step into his command center, where he has his monster computers wired up to a series of giant-screen plasma televisions, laptops and keyboards and sensor rigs, a bulletin board tacked all to hell with memos, notes, printouts, digital scans that look like ultrasounds from the bellies of pregnant women, but they're really photos of infested houses.

"You've been busy," I say. "I hear there's been a run near campus, where they had that traffic accident at the Dobie Mall."

"Turned out to be bogus. Nobody got killed, and there weren't any latent projections, not on camera anyway. The big money's been in the *suburbs,* man. Those guys are fucked up and they've got deep pockets."

"Most of the time they just need a shrink."

"You don't have to *tell 'em* that, though."

"You never learn, do you, kid?"

"I learn a little. I learned from the best."

"Thanks."

"Sure you don't want a toke?"

He wags the reefer my way. I hold up my palm again. He shrugs.

"Suit yourself."

The smell of tainted hydroponic skullfuckery floats across the room like a ruined dream. His skin is deep black, his voice ultramodern, like his well-honed body, which is draped in typical Austin stoner garb. Everyone on the south side of town dresses like Kurt Cobain. Don't ask me why.

"Lots of new equipment," I say, checking out the infrared camera squatting innocently on a low tripod in one corner.

"Yeah, I've been playing around with a real state-of-the-art system. What I'd give for a full-bore infestation—I mean, a *real* infestation. I've got a multicam surveillance rig that would kill it, man."

He makes it sound like a termite problem, but that's the point.

Marks can be *worse* than termites when they go deep into a house or a school or an office building. The kid pulls down more bread than I do hunting termites because he hustles harder, and he's in the future, the way Darby says I should be, but Roosevelt can't do what I do. He's one of those mediums who'll lie to the client when the rent is due. Once nearly got himself shot for doing that. I told him it was a bad idea to hire out to NRA guys.

And yeah, that's his real name.

The hackers all call him the President.

I met this guy three years ago when I ran an ad in the *Chronicle* looking for an assistant on a job. Needed the session recorded on video—rich folks with a dead relative giving them shit. Roosevelt was the guy who showed me how to get a mark on tape and what to look for when you play it back. Later, tape became digital storage, which was more pure, he said. It's all the same to me.

Roosevelt may be the smartest person I've ever met.

He was my main man when I first got obsessed with the Jaeger Laser.

He can dig up dirt on anyone, anywhere.

And he's a walking textbook, plugged into everything.

"Have a seat, my man. Tell the President your life story." He kicks a stack of nudie mags off the couch and leans back in his command chair, spinning from side to side.

I give him a look. "No, thanks. I might stick to something."

"Pot kettle black, my man. I've seen *your* living room."

"Funny."

He takes another toke of the smoke and I see a million faces staring back at me through his eyes. The faces of his parents, overdosed and long gone. The many women he's conquested, because it's really easy when you know how to use your Gift. I see a lost child swimming in self-medication, hovering on the edge of jaded teenage manhood, brilliant beyond most people's comprehension and screaming for a miracle to make him happy. But who am I to judge anyone's manhood? I don't even remember being a kid. I don't think anyone can be a man unless they remember being a kid. A man like me, a man who can't remember...well, most of us are just looking at ghosts on film.

He sees me reading him, smiles and turns back to his console, scrolls of blackware data rolling across his face.

"Okay, so let's get down to business."

Click. Click. Click.

The center screen flashes up someone familiar.

An old man with thick eyebrows and a face full of power.

Sidney Jaeger.

"Your old buddy's been busy," Roosevelt says, speed-reading from five online blogs, three secure hacker chats, and two fresh news items straight from the CNN feed. "He's about to launch his train, and it looks like he's got some major players in his pocket."

"What players?"

"According to my sources, it's gonna be a big event. They haven't announced it officially yet, but we're talking about ten or fifteen of the highest-profile celebs in the business. You know the routine: multibillionaire industrialist invites a bunch of famous people to ride his train on the inaugural run. They've even got Bethany Sin showing up to sing the national anthem."

"Who's Bethany Sin?"

"Big pop star. You really need to get out more, my man."

"What's so weird about all that? Sounds like your typical red carpet to me."

"It's way bigger, Buck. He's got Bob Maxton."

"The hell you say."

"Straight up."

He snatches the remote to one of his flat-screens—the forty-one-inch hanging above his bed. A news channel blips on, and he uses his DVR to displace time, rewinding it to the top of the hour, which was just a few minutes ago.

It's the Carolyn Lewis show.

She's a celebrity political pundit who looks like a supermodel, showing off short bleached-blond hair and a voice like a high school teacher with a wry sense of humor. She likes taking potshots at conservatives, and Sidney Jaeger's been on her hit list for years, ever since he announced his bullet-train project.

But this morning's press conference has everybody buzzing.

This shit is big.

Roosevelt thumbs the volume up, rattling in an excited falsetto. "Bob just went public with an on-the-record endorsement. A lot of people are screaming that he's using it as leverage to back up his bill to legalize gambling in California. Check it out."

The video window over Carolyn Lewis's shoulder leaps out to fill the screen, showing footage from the press conference.

Maxton is young for such a popular guy in politics.

They say he's the youngest guy ever to run for president.

He stands next to Sidney Jaeger with a face carved in granite sex appeal, the two of them mobbed by reporters on the front steps of the Lost Angels Plaza, a ritzy high-rise. The strobe of cameras flicker around both of them like paparazzi at a big premiere. Bob's voice is filled with practiced vibrancy, more like a movie star than a senator:

"The Jaeger Laser is something never before seen in America. These are forward thinkers who have taken their cue from the Japanese in the efficiency and elegance of this project, which will help to create jobs, bolster the economy, and provide upscale travelers and tourists with something special for their vacations and family outings — but California and Nevada are just the beginning. I tell you one thing, people: this is the future calling, and we cannot turn away from it."

Sidney smiles:

"I think the senator took the words right out of my mouth."

More flashbulb frenzy.

A hailstorm of questions hurled at the two men.

It's back to Carolyn, who is smiling and shaking her head:

"My goodness. You start to wonder who's really wearing the pants at Jaeger Industries, don't you?"

The kid thumbs off the television and gets back to clicking his data scrolls.

A series of articles about Bob Maxton glow across his face.

"The way I've got it figured, man, Bob's gonna be one of the guests at the red-carpet premiere. The early buzz is huge. Those ads are running in prime time on every channel, and when they go public with everything, it's gonna be like the voice of God coming down."

"That's one hell of a ballsy move for a politician."

"He's a fuckin' *rock star,* man. Gonna be our next president. Won the nomination in a landslide."

"He was running against Sarah Palin. It wasn't a contest."

"Maybe. But this is gonna put him right over. He'll be Supreme Dictator for Life once he's in, just like George W."

"I heard he got caught in a hotel with some hot actress not long ago."

"Natalya Ustinov. And he didn't get *caught* with her. The guy *announced* it. Turned the whole thing into a photo op. He makes moves nobody else even thought of. Remember JFK? This guy's the real deal."

"How do you get away with that stuff in this day and age?"

"You're out of touch. The youth vote is *on,* my man. Welcome to the future, where we all dance naked in the street."

"The guy's crazy."

"Damn right. See the thing is, Maxton is *single,* and a Republican—a *conservative.* That's the secret to being a rock star in politics and making it stick. You gotta have the best of both worlds. The girls faint over you and all the guys wanna *be* you, and meanwhile you've got the rich bitches in Washington eating out of your hand. The talk shows love this guy. They call him Maximum Bob."

"Isn't that the name of a TV series?"

"An old one, from the nineties. It's a book by Elmore Leonard too. About a hardass Republican judge who deep-sixes convicts."

"Does the nickname have anything to do with his platform?"

"No. I think it just stuck because someone thought it sounded cool."

"So he's riding the bullet. Interesting."

"Word on the street is that Jaeger Industries has been greasing Bob's campaign to get the public blow job, and they're looking into expanding the railroad too. The guys at Amtrak have been screaming takeover for a year or so. I think the idea is to have a full continental bullet-train system within about ten years. The Jaeger guys are jumping through hoops right now just to make it all legal."

"What street did you hear that on?"

"Fire Dog Lake."

"What?"

"A political blog, man."

"When do you figure they're going public with the red-carpet launch?"

"Any minute now. The buzz about Bob is nuts. A couple of my guys are talking all kinds of conspiracy theories."

"There's always a conspiracy theory."

"I dug up something else too. Check it out."

He turns and clicks his keyboard, summoning up a clutch of icons that he separates and sorts through fast, finding an image that zooms out to fill an entire screen.

"Ever hear of this guy?"

It's a blurry photo of a tall man dressed all in white and surrounded by bodyguards and paparazzi heading into the Royal Albert Hall in Houston. Some kind of cream-colored theatrical mask over the guy's face, smooth and featureless—makes him look like a mutation of Michael Jackson and the Phantom of the Opera.

Weird.

"Who's that?"

The kid gives me a fifty-watt grin, biting his lower lip. "David Brannigan. He's Sidney Jaeger's competition. He owns a couple of Fortune Five Hundred companies, makes a lot of Ted Turner moves. It's come out recently that the rail system might have been his idea."

"Jaeger stole his thunder?"

"Something like that. Sidney moved faster than this guy did. Got the contracts locked before Brannigan could. They were bitter rivals for years before that, then Brannigan went all Howard Hughes and pulled a disappearing act."

"Looks like a freak to me."

"Haven't you heard? That kind of money makes people crazy. He went into seclusion. Rumor had it that he was into stuff like pulling marks, tripping the Blacklight—the things we do. His people were going head to head with Jaeger Industries for years...and then it just *stopped*."

"And he turned into the Phantom of the Opera?"

"He's always been like that. Nobody's ever gotten a picture of the guy's face. Walked around wearing costumes when he had to make public appearances. This was one of the last photos anyone got, and it was at a Jaeger function three years ago. Sidney went public with his rail announcement two weeks after that."

"So his old shadow popped up and scared him into making his move."

"There's all kinds of speculation. A lot of people think Brannigan might actually be a silent partner in the Jaeger Laser. Maybe they did a deal."

"One hell of a deal, if it's true."

"Everything's true on the Internet, man."

"Yeah, right."

"Whatever went down, it lit a fire under Sidney's ass, man. The Laser wasn't scheduled to be finished until nine months from now. They stepped up everything to get this show on the road. I've got that right from the labor delegates who nearly killed Jaeger Industries on a nice class-action lawsuit."

"Welcome to the union. We're all expendable."

He turns in his chair.

Looks me right in the eye.

"And speaking of expendable...I haven't asked you yet because I figure you've got a damn good reason for looking into all this shit again. But the inevitable question *remains,* my man."

"Yep."

"We were right about where that train is running. I guess you know that."

"Yep."

"And you nearly got yourself killed the last time you went out there. It weighed pretty heavy on me back in the day."

"It wasn't your fault."

"Says who? I was the one who told you about the Laser when they first started building it. Drew you a map and everything."

"I had my own maps."

"You know what I mean, Bucko. You're not thinking of going back, are you?"

"I was invited."

He scrawls on a strange sideways look. "Get the fuck outta here."

"No bullshit."

"Christ, man . . . what are the odds, after all this time?"

"No coincidences."

And I think about it hard.

When Jaeger first told the world he was building a high-speed rail system, he said it was a prototype. Now he's got plans to take it nationwide. And he's got one of the most powerful men in America backing his plays. Plus, the Phantom of the Opera shadowing him—maybe the man behind the man.

I sense plans within plans.

Something bigger than I could have imagined.

The nexus, tightening around me.

And a gun in my satchel, humming with messages from the Blacklight.

"What are you gonna do, Bucko?"

"People keep asking me that. And I still don't know."

"Keep me in the loop. If it comes down, I want in. For old times' sake, you know. I think I owe you that."

"You don't owe me anything."

"If these guys really invited you, Bucko, then they're having problems. Just like we always knew they would. Ghost problems."

"It could get sticky."

"It could get worse than sticky. Pressurized cabins at high speed. Moving right through the Triangle."

I remember the desert.

Dying out there, dying slow.

Turning my back in the terrible aftermath.

Years, trying to forget.

I would walk away again.

I would let it all go down without me.

But.

This is bigger than me.

They invited me.

I reach into my jacket pocket and pull out the business card from last night, the one Tom slid over with such confidence.

JAEGER INDUSTRIES printed in red letters against silver.

Tom, you son of a bitch.

In the truck, I pull out my cell. It's a Motorola, thick and dated, no frills. Looks like a garage-door opener. Smartphones happened when I wasn't paying attention. Congress Avenue speeds by me through a cracked windshield. Everyone's hitting the Continental Club downtown tonight, and the ghosts on the street are lonely. Neon shadows crying in dim corners, chased into nowhere by the scorching twilight. The bats are flying already, thousands of them—a black storm of screeching leather wings and sightless red eyes emerging from under the bridge just ahead of me and spiraling up into the dark blue like plumes of smoke from a burning skyline, shitting on everything and searching for food. Following radar instincts. Blind and starving.

I think I know how those goddamn bats feel.

The gun in my satchel hums.

And I finally say fuck it.

I dial the number, cruising across the bridge.

The bats scream.

I get a cool and measured voice on the third ring, an older man. He doesn't even say hello. What he says is this:

"Hello, Mr. Carlsbad. I've been expecting your call. You've come highly recommended."

SIX

SPOOKS

Three days later, I pick up the urns from Father Joe.

Then, the Driskill Hotel.

The place overlooks a well-traveled corner on Sixth Street, the nerve center of downtown Austin. Every capital city has its mainline party drag, and this is it: eight blocks of bars and restaurants and touristy spots lit up like a string of sleazy Christmas lights, slicing through the high-rises and posh spots to I-35, which runs through the east side like a main circuit cable. The Driskill is one of the oldest buildings in the heart of Texas, five stories of old-school elegance, retrofitted and modernized on the inside. The lobby smells like something brand-new, polished-rock floors and chrome surfaces merging with columns and stone trim from a hundred years ago.

I pull the satchel tighter against my jacket, feeling the heavy comfort of my gear. I don't go anywhere without it, even if it's just an interview.

Never can tell.

I can't get much of a vibe from this place. Too many people coming and going, too many changes over the years. It smells more like cold cash than humanity.

Elvis definitely left the building a long time ago.

I stand in the lobby for five minutes before I check the time on my cell and wonder where the bar is. Ten minutes to six. It'll start to get dark soon. Hate daylight saving time. I look up and there's a big man in a black suit standing in front of me.

"Mr. Carlsbad?"

"Yeah."

"Mr. Tate is waiting in the smoking room. Will you please step this way?"

"Sure."

I want to ask him how he just appeared like that, but it seems kind of pointless the more I turn the idea over in my mind. He's a spook, not a ghost.

We walk across the lobby and into a fancy lounge area that has a small bar and lots of couches. A few tables sprinkled here and there. Jazz-piano Muzak floating lazily. Everything seems really red in this room, low-level lighting and mirrors on every wall.

Eric Tate stands up from one of the couches to offer his hand.

"Welcome, Mr. Carlsbad."

He's slightly older than he sounded on the phone, looks about fifty.

I feel deception and ambition in his grip.

His suit is tailored, his tie made of silk. He doesn't tell me his name because we did that already, and this guy obviously doesn't stand on ceremony. His skin is white and pockmarked, like a sheet of crumpled typewriter paper, eyes wise and blue and searing, handsome in a wrong sort of way. Old and dangerous.

Guarded.

Usually I can read a man pretty well when I shake hands with him—at least enough to stack the conversation in my favor.

But this fella...

The man in the black suit stands near us as Tate motions me to the couch across from him. I notice as I sit that there are two other blacksuits hovering along the mirrored walls on either side of us, and I say the first thing that pops into my mind.

"Are those guys government-issue?"

He makes an amused noise, glancing at the worn leather satchel hanging from the strap across my chest. I could be packing anything, and he knows it.

"Private security," he says. "Mr. Jaeger likes to make sure his people are taken care of."

"I'm sure he does."

"I can dismiss them if they make you uncomfortable."

"It's okay. Just wasn't expecting such a reception."

Tate waves his hand, and the spook who brought me in here vanishes. His buddies stay on the mirrors. He sits, picking up a box of expensive-looking cigarettes from the table next to him. "Do you smoke, Mr. Carlsbad?"

"No."

"Good for you." He sets them back on the table, not lighting one. "It's a rather unbecoming habit, I admit. The pleasures of youth die hard."

"I wouldn't know."

"About smoking or being young?"

"Both."

"An intriguing answer. You're not a drinker either, are you?"

"No."

"That also intrigues me. Most of the men we've interviewed for this job are heavy into the booze—it seems to come with the territory."

"I never needed it."

"Mr. Carlsbad, how much do you currently know about Sidney Jaeger and his company?"

I have to be cool about this. It always makes me nervous when I play poker with a guy whose mind I can't read.

"As much as anyone else," I tell him, hoping he's unable to sense the lie. "He's heavy into a lot of political lobbying. Made his fortune in stock trading and real estate, am I right?"

"That was how Sidney *started,* yes. The company has experienced a massive growth since 2001, with the addition of our film division and the mass-transit investments. I am the company's head of development and promotion."

"Big job for one guy."

"I have a large staff."

"I noticed."

"For the past several years, we've concentrated a great deal of our corporate resources into the transit project. It's the way of the future."

"I hear Amtrak is worried about a takeover."

"Don't believe everything you read on the Internet, Mr. Carlsbad."

"Okay."

He pauses, narrows his eyes at me. I see him almost reach for his cigarettes as he checks with his gods for a moment.

"Yes, it's true," he finally says, slowly. "More than a rumor, really. We're closing on a merger with several companies. The goal has been to convert existing systems to high-speed rail within fifteen years. The Jaeger Laser is our prototype, and it's been designed with an eye toward public support. That's the reason why we chose California and Nevada for our initial run. Los Angeles to Las Vegas. There's a certain sort of theme-park aesthetic that sells the idea to the common man, and to certain government types as well. There's never been a high-speed rail in this country before, and a lot of that has to do with the political climate of the United States."

"I thought it was just the hills and valleys."

"Mountains we can handle, Mr. Carlsbad. *Lobbying* is what gets things on track in America."

"On track. Funny."

I know all this.

I need more.

Need to know why I'm here.

He sees my eyes narrow and nods a little, sensing my question linger in the air before I ask it. The guy's good.

"You'll have to sign a nondisclosure agreement, Mr. Carlsbad, and then I can fill you in on more of the specific details . . . but what I can tell you now is that Sidney is planning an *event* to coincide with the inaugural run of the Jaeger Laser. It will be televised."

The kid's good too.

Had these guys pegged.

I chuckle inwardly and tell him I don't do TV.

He chuckles back. "That's not exactly true, is it? Your appearance on *When Ghosts Attack* was…rather amusing."

"I had no idea there were cameras in the room. The client did a deal behind my back."

"Why didn't you sue them?"

"Suing people costs money, and I work for a living. Anyway, it was all schlock. Nobody believes anything they see on those reality shows, even the ones that ain't about ghosts. It's like professional wrestling."

"Sidney is the executive producer of seven reality shows."

"Good for him."

"We don't want you to appear on camera, Mr. Carlsbad. It's true that there will be a great deal of media attention focused on the Jaeger Laser, but we would like to hire your services for our behind-the-scenes team. Sidney thinks we may have a few bugs to iron out."

"You mean spirit bugs?"

"We're not sure. It may be nothing. But if it *isn't*, Sidney would like the best to be aboard the train to handle things."

"He heard I was the best?"

"From very reliable sources."

"Sources like Tom Romilda?"

"We can discuss that later. Are you interested in the job?"

Careful, man. Play it cool.

"Your train may be running through a…very dangerous area."

"It may?"

"I got in a pretty nasty scrape there once."

"Would you care to fill me in?"

"It's a long story."

"I'm all ears."

Bullshit. He doesn't believe, never did.

As if I care.

I fold my arms and thicken up. "None of this is an exact science, sir. Sometimes we have to play some jazz as we go."

"Jazz?"

"We improvise. Shit happens."

"To be sure." He chuckles again, and I see that he hardly stops his eyes from rolling. "Do you bill your clients extra for such complications?"

"Not that time. It was a personal matter."

"I've heard about your method of reclaiming souls. Fascinating."

"It's tough work. Especially in that area. And we're not even talking about the dangers of pulling marks on a bullet train."

"What dangers?"

"Well... you're traveling at a high rate of speed in a pressurized cabin for one thing. Spirits are bound to certain locations or individuals at a kind of *frequency* which most people ain't tuned to. Moving fast like that, they're harder to see, and it's tough to get a hold on them and keep them under. Plus, there's nowhere to go once you've pulled the mark. That can be a death trap for mediums, especially if there's more than one spirit. Your back is against the wall and you take major damage, with no place to run."

"How do you know that?"

"I pulled one on board an airplane. It was a nightmare."

"You look like you came out fine to me."

"Looks can be deceiving."

I run one finger through the shock of white hair along the side of my head.

He shrugs, tilting his head back. "So this wouldn't be something you'd be interested in?"

"I didn't say that. Let me think it over."

"I need an answer *today*, Mr. Carlsbad. I was sent to Austin to extend an invitation. Sidney would like to meet with you to discuss the matter."

He's playing it close to the vest also.

"Your boss is in Hollywood?"

"Yes. Sidney's overseeing final preparations for the inaugural run."

Damn.

I hate that fucking town.

He leans forward on his knees, clasping his hands together with a tight-lipped little grin. The grin of a man who knows when he's already won.

"Mr. Carlsbad, I propose we continue this rather fascinating discussion at the Lost Angels Plaza. Sidney's private jet is fueled and ready. It's a short flight. And I promise, no spirits will ambush you." He starts to chuckle, then sees I'm not laughing. "Sorry, bad joke."

"No harm done."

"Anyway, if you aren't interested in what Sidney has to say, we can have you back to Austin in time for lunch tomorrow afternoon. Or breakfast, if you're in a hurry to get home. We'll take you directly to the airport from here. There's a car waiting outside."

"What about my toothbrush?"

"The clock is ticking, Mr. Carlsbad. This whole business has come at a very late hour. You can send for your equipment and personal effects in the event you decide to join our team. I'll have my people fix up everything."

He motions to the big guy in the black suit, who nods without smiling. Gotta hand it to these people. They know how to sell something in a hurry.

I size up Eric Tate one last time before I make my call.

He's more than some condescending business executive calling the shots from the back of a limo. He came here personally. He's ambitious even beyond his very high position in the company, and he's not telling me everything.

"Mr. Carlsbad, may I ask you a question?"

"Okay."

"You haven't mentioned your standard fee once in this entire conversation, not even when I asked you about charging extra. Why is that?"

"It kind of sounded like you were needling me."

"I was. And I apologize. Still, I wonder why you haven't talked at all about money. That's usually subject number one with the other men I've interviewed."

"I'm not those other men."

He nods. "I suppose that means you're still undecided about getting on a plane with us?"

"I'm still thinking."

"Five minutes, Mr. Carlsbad. We're busy people."

He sees me reading him now, and he has his guard up.

I can smell the faint traces of destroyed men wafting in the air between us, the screams of old friends and partners betrayed, all for the better good of some higher mission that seemed like a terrific idea at the time. Money and schemes. He wears that part of him on his face with no shame, doesn't have to hide it. The kind of monster that walks right up and shakes your hand. His secrets worry me.

But the offer is real.

The nexus is real too.

I was a fool to deny it.

SEVEN

AT THE MERCY OF OZ

We touch down at LAX three hours later, and it's on to Hollywood. An incredibly ugly little town.

A lot of people who don't live here have a really idealized version of all this in their heads, mostly from watching movies, but even the tinsel and glamour stuff is pretty tarnished, pocketed away among skyscrapers and scummy neighborhoods, all compacted together with about a hundred thousand million billion people coming and going. That's what makes this one of the biggest cities on the map—the sheer number of people in it. Hollywood Boulevard is full of homeless types in Halloween costumes, off-duty dishwashers spare-changing the tourists, trannies and hookers and pimps who don't look like pimps. There's a skinny guy in flannels and a red top hat camped in front of the Grauman's Chinese Theatre where they have a lot of big premieres—and he's sitting in a lawn chair, offering a set of headphones to anyone who will listen, waving a cardboard sign on a big stick that says: JESUS IS BACK AND HE NEEDS A RECORD DEAL.

There's a lot of guys like that on this street.

You have more flashing lights and glittering signs on this one stretch of real estate than most any other city in America—besides Vegas, of course.

It doesn't look nearly as interesting during the day.

Los Angeles is basically a series of smaller towns all grouped together. Drive far enough, and Hollywood turns into Culver City, which turns into Beverly Hills, which turns into Long Beach. All of it swims in a bleak undertow of greed and deception and dead people screaming their heads off about how life is really unfair.

The good thing is that the whole bloody mess is perched on the edge of an ocean, and the climate is cooler than Texas because the breeze of the sea washes through at night. It blows a lot of the bad stuff away, but not all of it. New Orleans is a backwater knife fight built on a swamp—Hollywood is a lot of lying and ruined dreams wrapped up in a dazzle of lights, hidden in canyons of unforgiving concrete and steel, like stars twinkling deep in piles of shit.

I keep my headphones on the whole way in, reading the five-page nondisclosure agreement they handed me when we left the airport. All pretty standard stuff. Eric Tate sits across from me in the limo, cursing at someone on a cell phone.

I sign my name on the dotted line.

The Lost Angels Plaza is a shining steel mirage against the backdrop of a painted city buried in its own sin. It looks a lot like a Vegas casino.

It takes up twelve city blocks.

The main building is ten stories built at a futuristic slope, towering above the street at the far edge of Hollywood Boulevard.

Roosevelt told me they had to create new zoning laws to get the thing built. Took them a year just to grease the LA politicians, two more years to do the real estate deal. Schwarzenegger was a big advocate back in the day, of course. Another three years and the hotel plaza was open for business, and since the gala opening in 2007, they've been constructing the raised platform system for the Jaeger Laser. An ambitious project requiring two billion in labor alone. The rail runs from the heart of the Lost Angels Plaza and snakes through the city on an elevated track. Looks like something out of an old sci-fi magazine.

Yeah, this Sidney Jaeger, he thinks big, all right.

The limo comes to a stop in a huge semicircle full of other limousines right on the massive front steps of the plaza. The mouth of the great city of Oz, welcoming us.

I get out, and a very large man is right there at the bottom of the stone steps. Should have known it would be him. He tells me I look like hell, waddling toward me with a gigantic shiteater set deep into his wrinkled face. I tell him that's the second time this week I've been fashion-policed by a fair-weather friend.

Tom Romilda holds out his hand and I shake it with a silly little grin.

"I said you'd be back," he tells me.

I reach down and click the tape player off.

Mötley Crüe dies, leaving me at the mercy of Oz.

The lobby could be half the size of a football field at first glance, like a train station gene-spliced with a theme park mutating into a shopping mall, with a thick sheen of chromed metal and plastic over the whole thing, keeping the sci-fi magazine illusion going in a pretty major way. Giant columns reach up ten stories to a domed ceiling filled with old movie-poster reproductions, like some overblown temple of postmodern gods bound to earth. The levels of the hotel are visible through walls of glass, encircling the giant chamber, ringed with catwalks and VIP boxes. It's all designed to look inwards at the bullet train platform, which is just above us at the fifth floor, like a raised subway car landing that runs through the room overhead, encased within an elaborate construction that you can see through like the skeleton of a crystal robot, held aloft by two of the columns, and great steel supports glittering with chrome and lights, like nothing else in this city or on this earth. Luxurious lifts rising and falling into the lobby on all sides of us. Golden carriages filled with precious humanity.

The place is giant, the way you think of alien worlds as giant.

I feel like I'm on Mars.

Eric Tate walks in front of Tom and me, his bodyguards flanking us at a respectable distance, his expensive Italian shoes clocking on thick marble, motioning in wide circles like a tour guide. "How do you like it, Mr. Carlsbad?"

"It smells like money in here," I tell him.

"There's four hundred million dollars in this room alone. The platform is a marvel of modern engineering and rail technology. The track extends through the nerve center of old Hollywood and provides a dazzling view of the entire city during departure from Los Angeles."

Sounds like a press release, this guy.

He doesn't miss a beat, aiming at the walls of glass all around us with his sunglasses. "The hotel was built with the lobby and the platform in its center so that guests in their rooms and on the walkways surrounding us can view the train as it enters and leaves the station. It's quite the spectacle. People will come from far and wide just to watch the train pull out."

"I don't doubt it."

"There's already a six-month waiting list, Mr. Carlsbad. Pre-sales of our VIP packages have paid nearly a third of our construction costs."

Jesus.

What the hell does a room go for in this place?

I rub my chin, thinking about that kid on the street with the record-deal sign, and I choose my next words very carefully. "What about the average Joe? Don't those guys wanna see the paradise too?"

"Of course. Sidney wants *everyone* to share in his dream. There are several five-star restaurants located in this lobby and on level three. A shopping center with a fast-food court, movie theater with stadium seating. Vendors, video games, you name it. We even have a tattoo and body-piercing shop."

"How hip of you."

"This place is a *happening,* Mr. Carlsbad. We expect people from all walks of life to participate."

"But they mostly just get to *watch* the train, right?"

"Money does have its privileges."

"Guess you can say that again."

"As the years go on, we hope to make some of the accommodations more affordable to the working class."

"Hooray for us."

"Do I sense sarcasm, Mr. Carlsbad?"

"No. I just don't have any money."

He laughs. "Our sales department projects that within the first year of the train's operation, more than half a billion dollars in revenue will be generated from the hotel alone. This brings something far more valuable to the working class than E tickets on the Jaeger Laser or seats in one of those fancy opera boxes up there—it brings wealth to the community. *Jobs.* A change for the future."

"All paid for by the rich."

"Exactly, Mr. Carlsbad. Exactly."

Tom pats me on the shoulder. "These guys got their act *together,* Buck. Believe you me."

Yeah.

Kinda makes you wonder what they want with scumbags like us.

I feel the bottom fall away from my stomach as the golden lift floats us in space above the gigantic lobby. He was right, the view from up here is spectacular. It looks like a small, compact city built on multiple levels, teeming with ants, all centered around the train in its elaborate dock. The floors that streak by on all sides of us are like crystal walkways leading to luxury suites and shopping levels. Eric Tate tells us it's all open to the public and I have a hard time believing him. You could get away with charging twenty bucks just for the elevator ride.

We step out on a glass walkway near the giant temple ceiling with all the movie posters. Tate leads us down a hallway with high column arches and fancy carpeting. I can't get any kind of reading here.

It's dead, no life at all.

Executive penthouse level.

The hall terminates in a wide marble staircase, and there's a really big door at the top of the stairs, set into a small section of marble with more columns.

A guy in a suit on the door, who nods at our bodyguards.

He says something into a handheld device, and it glimmers, talking back.

One of them gives my satchel a weird glance, but nobody searches me.

Good thing.

I have a gun in there.

Never mind that it's thirty years old and rusted beyond use—I'm sure the threat is just the same to grunts like this. I'm not even sure why I brought the damn thing. Just feeling the nexus, man.

Going with it.

The guy at the door steps away, and it opens wide, like the arms of a rich Greek god welcoming us.

Eric Tate's expensive shoes clock through the door, the sound leading point into the chamber beyond, which flows in a circle all around us, layers of black glass shafting in prisms, creating frames for artwork and movie posters—probably the originals, if anything about this place is as real as it seems to be. The windows of the suite are slotted in twenty-foot slices, surrounding the whole room in a 360-degree panorama of the whole city, which winks at us with a billion all-knowing eyes. From up here, you'd almost think it was something beautiful, civilized. A great glimmering mural immortalizing some epic dream you once had.

There's a man in the room.

He's wearing a dull gray suit.

His stark form stands out in sharp relief against a center window he's looking through, an ivory cane held at his side, no bodyguards next to him.

He's much taller than I expected.

Looks about six and a half foot.

A giant, really.

Figures.

"Hello, Mr. Carlsbad," he says, not turning around, though I can see his face reflected in the glass in front of him. "I'm Sidney."

His voice is not what I expected either.

It was different on television.

The tone is smooth and practiced, even theatrical. All these rich fellas tend to be like that. It comes from a lifetime of pretending to be humble in rooms made of gold. But there's something human about the way he speaks too. Something that betrays secret parts of him. I'm reminded of a doctor I once knew—whose daughter fell from the earth and came back to him as a monster in the dark.

And I'm reminded of something else too.

His face and his eyes, younger than they should be, a deep passion running beneath the surgically reworked contours of his decades-old skin.

Something cold in his eyes.

Something I can't figure right off.

It'll come to me.

He starts off by welcoming me to the hotel, and we go through the introductions. He tells me I have a suite just below the penthouse. Anything I want, it's mine. He says he likes my jacket, and I tell him I have ten just like it. He finds my Walkman quaint and turns his mouth into an odd shape that almost looks like a smile, motioning to several glasses of champagne bubbling on a table made of polished volcanic rock. Everything in this room is black. The couches, the chairs, the giant flat-screen television. There's a glossy-gothy elegance to it.

"Shall we have a drink, Mr. Carlsbad? To celebrate our new alliance."

"We haven't talked about an alliance yet."

"You spoke with Eric?"

"He saved the big pitch for you."

"Of course he did." His smile widens and he forgets about the bubbly, standing there with both hands in front of him, resting on his cane. I'm reminded of a Marvel Comics supervillain. "Mr. Carlsbad, let's discuss the future. After all, that's where we're going to spend the rest of our lives, isn't it?"

Sheesh.

Fortune-cookie philosophy from the Fortune 500.

"Yeah, I guess you're right," I tell him, trying not to laugh.

"Of course I am. We are privileged to inhabit a very exciting period of history. The discoveries of fractal equations in relation to microtechnology and computer components, for example—these are miracles that our forefathers could never have imagined in their wildest dreams. But it all comes at a heavy price, and one must *pay* that price to those who are still wary of things to come. You've no doubt been made aware of the controversy surrounding my rail project?"

"A little bit."

This time the lie is easy.

He's performing, not reading me the way Tate was.

"That's where it all falls down a lot of the time," Sidney says. "Controversy can work both ways. With patience, however, everything moves ahead. At a slow pace, perhaps, but *ahead,* Mr. Carlsbad. Part of the process involves the participation of certain...shall we say, necessary persons?"

The way he says that, it kind of sounds like he means necessary *evils.*

"You're talking about Senator Bob?"

"Him and men like him, yes. This entire country is built on a delicate latticework of political systemetry, and it's all fueled by cold cash."

"Surprise, surprise."

"But we've been given a hostage to fortune in the senator. He's corrupt, like most politicians, but he possesses a sort of public charisma not seen in politics before. It's unprecedented, really. Money makes that happen too. When you have a big enough machine working for you, the opinion makers can be easily manipulated. My analysts project that by the year 2030, youth will control society as we know it."

"Good for them."

"They will also be directed in their opinions and philosophies by men such as Bob Maxton, and his campaign platforms are radical, particularly for a so-called conservative. His bill to legalize gambling in this city, for example. It will be passed next year, without a doubt."

"That's the plan, I hear."

"It's a plan backed by a lot more than public opinion, I assure you."

Welcome to the next generation, where everything's for sale.

I almost say that out loud but decide it's not a good idea.

The gravity in this room is almost crushing me now.

The nexus, tighter than ever.

"So," I say, then take a few steps toward him. "You're launching your bullet into the future in a few weeks and you think you've got a...problem?"

"It is a distinct possibility, Mr. Carlsbad. And the launch is not in a few weeks. It's happening in just four days."

What?

They haven't even made a public announcement about it yet.

He sees my face screw up in confusion and laughs.

"Tomorrow, you'll hear about it on every channel. Another seemingly impromptu press conference with Senator Maxton. It's all been carefully orchestrated. Our moles inside the Internet blogosphere and certain controlled leaks have already set the media on fire. This will guarantee a turnout of epic proportions. It's the kind of press you can't buy."

Brilliant, Sidney.

I'm almost amazed the kid didn't predict this.

So I take a deep breath, sit down next to Tom, and jump right in.

"Tell me about your problem."

EIGHT

BLACKJACK NINE

The image on the screen comes from a surveillance camera in a white room, somewhere deep in the bowels of a hospital for crazy people. The man sits at a table, bound in a straitjacket, his face a grim pock-marked zigzag of scars and burns, his eyes almost sparkling somewhere in the landscape like bloodshot crystal. His voice is brittle, his words forced out in confident spasms through a wrecked smile.

He's talking about men and women and children being killed.

Giving every detail.

He talks about it with an insider's ear, like he was there.

Creepy as hell.

He talks about slitting a four-year-old girl's throat, the way her voice sounded just before he did it to her, innocent like a child in a fairy tale.

He describes the eyes of a man with dark hair in the moment the knife went in, the way his startled brown eyes bugged out and then went dead, like destroyed planets.

He spreads both forefingers apart to indicate the amount of blood that came out of an elderly woman's chest cavity, a flowing river of deep, deep red.

He says it was all done so that the way could be cleared.

So that the Blacklight could shine on them.

A video time stamp at the bottom of the screen says the man's name is Adam Protextor and that he's twenty-nine years old.

The video is dated four months ago.

Jaeger stands next to the screen as we watch the man in the white room speak, allowing us to absorb a full ten minutes of it before he freezes the image.

"Terrifying, isn't it, Mr. Carlsbad?"

"I've seen worse."

"But it's still terrifying. For one reason, more than any other."

"What's that?"

"The man in this video was not a participant or eyewitness in the murders he describes. He's relating stories from *someone else*. It's a phenomenon that might possibly be more in your line of experience than mine."

"Tell me what happened to him. I need details."

"There was an accident on the rail line about four months ago. You've heard the stories in the media about the Jaeger Laser being nine months ahead of schedule?"

"Yeah, I heard that."

"Spin control. It's actually a year *behind* schedule. We've had labor difficulties, of course—all the usual setbacks that occur with a project so ambitious. But what happened earlier this year was almost completely inexplicable."

Eric Tate steps up, his face illuminated in the glow of the big screen, and the picture changes to a digitized topographical map of the rail line. "The Jaeger Laser is powered by a nitrogen-cooled electrodynamic suspension system," he says. "It's state-of-the-art magnetic-propulsion technology. They call it maglev in Europe."

"Magnetic? You mean the train never touches the track?"

"Yes, but only at top speed. A wheel array is used for takeoff and docking due to limitations on guideway inductivity. That's because of the massive magnetic field generated by the engines and the track system."

"Like landing gear on a plane," I say.

"Exactly."

"Isn't a field that intense dangerous in other ways?"

He titters some. "To people carrying laptops and credit cards, yes. Lead shielding is the key. We worked all that out years ago."

"Good for you. Wouldn't be much of a railroad without credit cards."

He waves his hand, brushing it off. "Our main goal is innovation and efficiency. The Laser is capable of doing well over five hundred miles an hour. That's faster than the most sophisticated Japanese bullet train ever designed. Our team is way ahead of the curve. Naturally, our engine has required years of development and research. A lot of trial-and-error comes into play. During field-testing, there were a few accidents. This one was the worst, and the most recent."

A video window zooms in on a section of the topographical map and expands it, showing a spot where the rail runs through the desert.

"Here's where it happened," Tate says, pointing at the area highlighted in red. "We were running a speed test on a section of the completed track in the desert just inside the California border. There was an accident at three hundred miles per hour."

"Your train crashed?"

"Just the engine," Jaeger says. "The problem may have been a construction flaw in the track. Our inspectors went over every square inch before the run—there was nothing left to chance. And yet nearly all seven employees aboard that train were killed in an instant when it flew off the rails. My people still can't give me a straight answer on what exactly happened."

Eric Tate looks at his feet when the old man says that.

I point a grin at him. "Sounds like a lot of people afraid for their jobs."

"Maybe, maybe not." Jaeger turns to the screen as it flicks back to the image of Adam Protextor in the white room. "The man you just saw in this video was the only survivor of that derailment. He emerged from the wreck a broken mess, babbling about men and women he'd seen murdered. He claimed the murders were visions given to him by God in the moment of his death, and that he'd been returned to earth to warn us all. He tried to kill his doctor with a hypodermic needle and was sent to a state hospital for three months."

"But you kept him on a short leash, I bet."

"Naturally. I own the building."

"Figures."

"I can't take any risks in cases like these, Mr. Carlsbad. On the day before the accident, Adam Protextor was a valued member of my team—a respected man in the engineering community who held advanced degrees and pulled down a six-figure salary working for government contractors. A young professional with a very bright future. On the day after the accident, he was a mental patient."

He points at the screen, and the video window switches to the topographical map again, expanding to show an area ten miles beyond the track in every direction. Three glowing points at the edge of the window.

The points of the Triangle.

He raises an eyebrow. "Do you know what you are looking at?"

"Prisons," I say. "Where they send the worst criminals in the world. Three maximum-security pens housing death-row inmates, all within about three hundred kilometers of each other. At the Johnstown facility they were putting people to death by *hanging* as recently as 1987."

Jaeger raises an eyebrow. "You know your history."

I shrug, wondering what he expected. "I call it the Blacklight Triangle. It's one of the worst spots ever recorded for paranormal activity. A lot of bad marks out there. Hanging is a nasty way to die, and bad death is what keeps most people hanging around later."

"You have a way with turning a phrase, Mr. Carlsbad."

"I wasn't trying to be funny."

"Eric tells me you have some experience with this area."

"It's not uncommon, really. You have drifters and seekers in and out of the Triangle. Serial killers. Cults. Mediums die there all the time. I was almost one of them."

"Tell me more."

"I'd rather not."

He shakes his head slightly, rolling with it. Then gives me a sideways look, his eyes slitted slyly. "In any event, I imagine you'd like to know why we're running our train through such a bad area."

"The thought did cross my mind."

A chuckle rolls toward me, as he places his tongue deep in his cheek. "To a man of your experience, I expect it must be the equivalent of building a shiny new mansion over an ancient Indian burial ground. Isn't that the old cliché?"

"Something started the rumor."

He laughs thinly. "The answer is *efficiency,* Mr. Carlsbad. Our train is the fastest ever designed, but it's also the most expensive. Before I can get my rail system on track, I have to prove that it works. The shortest distance between two points is a straight line, and that line runs straight through Johnstown and your Triangle."

"The Johnstown prison was a hellhole. They closed it down in '99."

Jaeger takes a few steps toward me. "You probably also know that one of the most notorious inmates of that facility was a very charismatic individual who called himself Blackjack Williams. He was arrested in 1973 and confessed to his crimes. The descriptions were entered into the court records and then sealed by the judge in order to protect the families of the victims."

"Those are the crimes *Adam Protextor* is describing?"

"Down to the last drop of blood, Mr. Carlsbad."

"I guess it would be silly of me to ask how you got your hands on those sealed files, wouldn't it?"

"Yes. Very silly." He doesn't smile at all when he says that. "As you probably know, Blackjack Williams committed suicide in the Johnstown lockup following his trial. That was in early 1974. No one ever interviewed him after he spoke in the court, and Williams never wrote a tell-all book either. There's no way any employee of mine could have known about those murders in such detail without being *told* about them."

"So you think Mr. Protextor is possessed?"

"What would you think?"

"I'd need to speak to the guy to know for sure."

"Not possible."

"Why?"

"Adam Protextor is dead. Suicide. He was released from the care of the

State and threw himself in front of a subway train in downtown Los Angeles just two hours later."

"Ironic."

"Obviously."

Adam had had a head full of bad shit.

And whatever it was, it didn't want him talking to a professional about it.

"That's not all," Jaeger says. "Protextor also dropped some names. Eight, to be exact. They all turned out to be notorious criminals executed in the same prison. Some of the worst killers on record. We did a little research."

Eric Tate picks up a dossier from the black table and hands it to me.

It's a thick file, full of photos and papers.

I thumb through some of it, just glancing.

Crime scenes and mug shots.

Bad shit.

"There it is, Mr. Carlsbad," Jaeger says. "An interesting equation, wouldn't you agree?"

He centers his gaze on me, and I see wary fascination and vague concern on his face, like he's asking me a question about all this. Asking if I buy it.

"One hell of a rap sheet," I say, closing the file. "So let me see if I got this straight. You think these nine bad guys might still be out there giving you trouble?"

"I'm not saying it's a possibility, and I'm not saying it isn't. These are simply the facts as we know them."

I look Jaeger right in the eye. "What other incidents have there been?"

He smiles proudly. "None at all since the one with Protextor, actually. We managed to keep the derailment quiet, and all further construction and speed tests have gone along swimmingly. In fact, during the last trial run of the train, I personally rode in the main passenger car."

"Then why do you need me? Sounds like all your problems died with Mr. Protextor."

"I didn't get where I am by leaving things to chance."

"You said that before."

"I did."

"So you want me along for the ride, just in case?"

"Important deadlines are imminent, Mr. Carlsbad. The election is in just three months. When Senator Maxton becomes president, he will push phase two of the Jaeger Laser rail system through Congress. The groundwork is already set. The launch of the project can no longer be postponed. When the Laser runs publicly for the first time, Bob will step off the train at the Dreamworld Casino and Theme Park in Las Vegas and announce his intentions to back the project at a VIP political rally, which will be held at the park's amphitheater. It will become the backbone of his entire campaign strategy."

"A political rally in a Vegas casino? I think now I've heard everything."

He leans in on his cane one more time, and levels a serious eyeline at me. "I'll be very honest with you, Mr. Carlsbad. I'm not a man who normally endorses the occult, or whatever you people like to call it."

"We don't call it that."

"Fair enough. These recent events have made it necessary to adjust the parameters of my beliefs, but I'm not sure what I expect you to actually *encounter*. This is all very new to me. I'm taking a great deal of it on faith. But I have the means to cover our bases, so to speak. What is most important is the success of my train project and the safety of my guests."

I take a deep breath. "If I do this job, it has to be done my way. And I'll need some backup. At least one or two good men I can rely on."

"That's a reasonable request."

"And I need to know every detail of that train. Need to be able to keep an eye on every compartment from a switchboard. That means electronic surveillance. I have a guy back in Austin, he can handle that."

"I can allow that also. Within *reason,* of course."

"There's one other thing. This whole magnetic-propulsion system gives me the creeps. If there *is* an infestation and something bad happens, I can't guarantee preventing another crash."

"You won't be held responsible."

"I want that in writing."

"Obviously."

He looks at me with a dead stare, and he can tell I'm scared.

I've never pulled more than five marks at a time. That was years ago. And I wasn't standing in a magnetically powered bullet going five hundred miles an hour straight through the heart of fucking darkness.

Blackjack Nine.

Eight bad ghosts led by a madman out of the Triangle, unbound and bad enough to knock the most powerful train in the world off its rails.

Is that what my parents found out there?

It could kill me, just like it might have killed them.

But this is the will of the nexus.

This is my last chance to go back.

There's no choice.

Damn.

"Do we have an alliance after all?" Jaeger's question floats across the dark room.

"I'll think about it."

"No time," says Eric Tate. "We need an answer now."

I think about it.

For about ten more seconds.

Then I tell them I'm in.

Jaeger's smile is quick and inhuman, then he nods his head. For a moment I think he's nodding at Eric Tate, giving the seal of approval to his hard sell. Then something moves in the room behind me, and I realize he was signaling to someone.

She was there all along.

Goddamn, why didn't I see her?

Nobody can sneak up on me like that.

"Mr. Carlsbad, allow me to introduce you to a very important member of our team."

Jaeger's voice is proud, like he knows he's surprising me.

Make a note of that.

Rows of dim lights come on, adding a rich yellow glow to the contours and shapes all around us, bringing the room into sharp amber focus as the ebony woman comes from behind me, her lithe form draped in formal yet formfitting black, mirrored sunglasses making mysteries of her eyes. Her skin the color of deep shadows, her long black hair immaculate in a tight professional braid. She moves with precision grace.

When she reaches up to remove her shades, the lights are all the way up.

Blue eyes in darkness.

"Hello. My name is Lauren Chance."

She extends her hand, slipping the sunglasses into a pocket of her black jacket. I can see the nasty hidden glimmer of a Colt Python semiauto handgun resting in a shoulder holster under there also. She's dressed a bit like the other bodyguards in the room except she's wearing tailored slacks and a blouse beneath the jacket that hugs her curves. I'm reminded of Angela Bassett as a young woman, or a blacker Pam Grier. As I touch her hand, I expect to feel icy professionalism, programmed false piety, maybe even a stone-cold killer, but none of that comes. I can't read her at all, the same way I couldn't read Jaeger or Eric Tate.

I finally decide it's the room.

It's like a tomb in here.

It doesn't distract me one bit from her eyes.

"Mr. Carlsbad, may I have my hand back?"

The spell is broken, and I let go, shaking my head like a schoolboy.

"Yeah, umm...sorry about that."

Jaeger chuckles. "Lauren makes quite an impression, doesn't she?"

I don't lie. What's the point? She can see my eyes moving all over her. "You're very pretty, Miss Chance."

"Please call me Lauren." Her voice is like frozen honey, confident and sleek. She almost smiles at my compliment but stops herself.

Jaeger leans forward on his cane. "Lauren is the head of my personal security force."

Figures.

She has the eyes of something deadly.

I search for the proper response but find myself saying:

"Cool."

She almost smiles again.

"I assure you, she is quite a bit more than a pretty face," says Jaeger. "She'll be with you on the Laser, along with Senator Maxton's own people. The Department of Homeland Security has assigned a small complement of men to safeguard Bob during his trip. I can tell you, it hasn't been easy coordinating our efforts. Secret Service men can be very... *impersonal*."

I shrug my shoulders. "They guard the president while he sleeps."

"And Lauren guards *me* while *I* sleep, Mr. Carlsbad. She's the best there is at what she does."

"Is that so?"

"That most certainly is so," she says.

"So," I say to Jaeger. "You'll be on board the train with your bodyguard?"

"No. Eric and I will be at the other end, in Vegas, awaiting your arrival in the Dreamworld amphitheater. I've assigned Lauren to protect you and our guests aboard the train."

"I'm not very good with an automatic weapon," says Tate, shrugging in a fake way.

"So you guys are going to miss your own train ride?"

Jaeger chuckles again. "I've already ridden the Laser many times, Mr. Carlsbad, and so has Eric. It's more a... shall we say, political move? The inaugural run must be focused entirely on Senator Maxton and the selected guests who will be riding. The Jaeger Laser needs a brand-name face—a champion. I am content to place the keys to my kingdom in Bob's capable hands."

I put my own hands in my pockets, keeping an eye on Lauren Chance. "They were calling you on that. On the news, I mean. I think it was the Carolyn Lewis show. Something about who wears the pants at Jaeger Industries."

Tate makes an amused noise, shaking his head. "Lewis has been one of our most acidic detractors. She's a liberal pundit inhabiting a notoriously left-wing cable-news network. Bob Maxton is often the brunt of jokes regarding conservative political candidates. But it won't be a problem."

I raise an eyebrow. "That's sounds a little sinister. You guys have plans for Carolyn Lewis?"

"We signed her just this evening," says Eric Tate. "She'll be riding the Laser next week as our guest. The first rule in politics and good business is to keep your friends close but your enemies closer."

I shake my head. "They say that in the Mafia too."

"We all play by similar rules," Tate says. "And anyway, there's nothing sinister about it. Carolyn's people actually approached *us* two months ago."

"She's been sniping at me on the air ever since," says Jaeger. "But I find it all very amusing. She's an *opinion maker,* after all—and as I said, opinion makers can easily be swayed."

I wonder how much they're paying her.

It can't be enough.

Welcome to the future again.

"Speaking of enemies...I heard you had some competition a few years back. The freaky Phantom of the Opera guy."

"You mean David Brannigan," Jaeger says. "He's very...*theatrical.* Hasn't spoken about anything publicly in well over seven years."

I smirk. "Have you ever met him in person?"

"Nobody even knows what the man looks like. But my people did have some rough dealings with his company in the early days of the Laser project."

"Some people think you bought him off—that he's a silent partner."

"Some people are misinformed."

I'm not convinced. He doesn't give anything away though.

I shrug it off, and Eric Tate gives me a strange little smile.

"You'll be briefed on the rest of our guest list and given a full rundown on the layout of the train and its speed capacities," Lauren says. "I'll walk it with you personally in the morning and answer any questions you may have. Along with the Secret Service people and myself, we will have a full complement of six agents holding down security. I am instructed to assist you in any way relevant to your assignment."

"I don't need a bodyguard. I don't even carry a gun."

"That seems odd."

"You can't pump a spirit full of lead, not the way I work. Some other guys like me come packing, but they're usually only gunning for the living—unhappy clients, bad neighborhoods, all that."

She gives me a suspicious look. "A black jacket and a Walkman isn't a bulletproof vest. I find it hard to believe you've never been *assaulted* by a client during one of your...I'm not even sure what to call it."

"We call it pulling marks. And yes, I've seen a lot of trouble with the living on jobs, but I don't kill people. You run the risk of becoming attached to the dead when you do murder. Plus, it's against the law."

She comes closer, begins to circle me. "That's very interesting, Mr. Carlsbad. Our files tell us that you *have* been known to hurt people."

"That does come with the job."

"Pray tell."

"There's different kinds of ghosts. The most common are the ones you hear about on TV. Walkers are different—they can become attached to their own murderers when they die. It doesn't happen that much. But they're mean bastards, and they can do major damage on our side of the world, even kill people."

"Poltergeists," Lauren says.

"That's the popular term. You have to be ready to go hand to hand with them. They can be really tough. As in *superhuman* tough. Other kinds of spirits possess human minds, and that gets tricky too. You have to use bioelectric shocks to shake the mark loose. The brain senses acute trauma, and the body goes into a sort of adrenaline arrest when you hit it in the right spot."

"And gives up the ghost?"

"Yep. A mark is always at its weakest when it first enters the host's mind. The longer it settles there, the more control it has over the body. Usually takes about ten or fifteen minutes for it to take over, sometimes less. If you get to the mark fast enough after it enters a body, you can pull it easy, without much of a fight. But that doesn't happen a lot. I pulled one a few years back that was hiding out inside an old man for months—had to get really nasty with him."

"I can only imagine," Lauren says.

"You don't want to."

She sucks in a quick shot of air to distract me from her coiled fist, which slashes the air to my left in a blurred sucker punch that would catch anyone else off-balance—I saw it coming three seconds ago. I put up one hand and block her delicately at the wrist.

She pulls her blow and smiles.

Just a love tap.

Testing.

"Quick, Mr. Carlsbad. You have training."

I nod as she takes her hand back.

"Started with *jeet kune do*," I tell her. "Old-school Bruce Lee all the way. Then I got into some Filipino boxing, street-fighting techniques. Less elegant. Dirtier."

She spins fast and puts one of her pretty legs in the air, sending the stiletto heel of her shiny black shoe like a guided missile just past my jaw, which I move quicker than she can see. But she's fast on the rebound—tries to fake me out on a right hook, and comes back in with another wheel kick. I sidestep it with my hands in my pockets.

Neither of us have broken a sweat.

This isn't even foreplay.

"My sensei told me it's all about staying three moves ahead of your opponent," I tell her.

"Which sensei?"

"All of them."

She puts both hands into it this time, more aggressive now. Wants to see what I'm made of. I keep one hand in my right pocket, bobbing and weaving in a casual step away from her classic *muaythai* combination attack. She pulls each punch back hard when it connects with nothing, recoiling and striking again and again, all her forward thrust redirected and channeled with amazing control. She plays speed chess like a pro.

But *classic* is another word for dumb.

Ask the man who can't stop listening to hair metal.

"It must be easy for a man like you to stay three moves ahead of your opponent," she says calmly.

"When you fight the possessed, you need every edge."

I almost don't see the next attack coming but I duck it anyway, riding an adrenaline rush as one of the big guys comes in from behind me. Dirty motherfucker made his move when I was looking at the cute chick. She smiles and steps out of the way as he plunges into the center of the room, hammering the air I just occupied with his meaty fists. Those fists are as big and obvious as canned hams once I readjust my focus and bounce back in his direction, my hands still in my pockets.

This one I can read easy.

His flight plan is scrawled on his face like a tattoo traced in neon lights.

"Ghosts are sneaky, Miss Chance," I say, circling him. "They often choose their hosts for the power of their bodies and the force of their minds."

He swipes with those canned hams and misses me by a mile.

"But bigger isn't always better," I say, not even looking at him.

He swipes again, misses again.

Classic.

"Some people actually *welcome* a mark," I say. "Those are harder to spot—the marks get together with the living, and the living take it like a drug. They cause all kinds of damage and you never even see them coming until it's too late."

Swipe.

Miss.

Hands in pockets.

No sweat.

"But in the end, those kind of marks all have the same weakness, Miss Chance—they're riding the electrochemical impulses of a *human body,* and a human body has six nerve centers that engage a psychoplasmic entity."

Swipe.

"The one that works best is coupled directly to the easiest bone in the human body to break—"

Miss.

"—and that's *this one*."

His fist is still missing me when I grab it and twist his meaty arm back hard, dropping him to his knees as the pain of his twisted-up muscles stabs a knife into his nervous system—and while he's down there, wondering what happens next...

I break his little finger.

Then drop him there, this little piggy screaming all the way home.

Look back at Sidney Jaeger.

I shrug and put my hands back in my pockets, as if to say *and now, for my next trick*... but instead I lay it down calmly:

"If this man had been possessed by a mark, that mark would be all mine now."

Sidney chuckles.

Claps politely.

"Son of a *bitch*," says the blacksuit, waffling on one knee, his finger twisted like a mauled pastry stick. Knows better than to get up.

Demonstration over.

Lauren glances at her boss. "I think we're done here for the moment, Sidney."

I still can't read her at all.

Couldn't even do it when she was trying to kick my ass.

Strange.

She leads me from the room, and I feel the uncertain stares of Sidney and Eric Tate on the back of my neck, while the nexus burns in my heart.

Right here at ground zero.

The hotel suite is obscene, like a space capsule for rich folks.

A normal person could drown in here.

I'm escorted by one of Jaeger's bodyguards though three rooms filled with thick white plush and expensive gold canyons, and he leaves me there to sink slowly. The bed lies in the rear section of the suite like a big pink monolith, or an expensive call girl waiting on her back for me, all done up in lace and ribbons.

It's one fifteen in the morning.

My soul feels scattered.

One entire wall in the living room area is dominated by a giant screen and it's already tuned to a news program. People in suits are arguing in a circle about the Jaeger Laser. Pat Buchanan thinks it's a great idea, all full of his usual harmless piss-and-vinegar pep, laughing like your daffy drunk uncle at a Christmas cocktail mixer. Bill O'Reilly agrees with him a lot and tells a skinny kid who's supposed to be some kind of political analyst to shut the hell up every other minute. I pick up the remote and click through the channels. It's everywhere, they're all talking. Big moves and future shock, coming at me in Technicolor and 3-D.

Tomorrow, Sidney drops the atom bomb on all of them.

Roosevelt is already on the way, and the urns are being delivered. Tom will be our backup on the train. And Lauren Chance. A wildcard that worries the hell out of me.

I pull my satchel off my shoulder and set it on the table.

Fall into the bed and stare up at the mirrored ceiling, seeing my reflection trapped between worlds.

I breathe in and out slowly, concentrating on Sidney's words.

The image of Adam Protextor.

The Blackjack Nine.

Did they kill my parents?

Are they the monsters I couldn't see when I was lost out there in the desert, hovering between death and the Blacklight?

The Pull glows inside my body, hungry for the truth.

I hover there on the edge of consciousness for a few hours.

Riding the Pull.

As the sun breaks over the plaza, I nod off for nearly an hour and dream about nothing. When I wake up, a suitcase sits on the floor in my room, filled with dirty clothes imported from Austin.

Next to the suitcase, a large crate from Father Joe.
I crack it open and inspect the urns.
Twelve of them.
More than I'll need.

NINE

PRE-FLIGHT

We stand at the entryway to the golden lift that opens five floors above us on the elevated train landing. It's eleven fifteen in the morning.

Workers are finishing a large stage near us in the lobby, where the press conference will take place just before we pull out. A giant video screen has already gone up, and it's looming over the stage. That's the satellite link from Vegas. A whirlwind of activity and excitement. I keep my headphones on for most of it. Too many voices.

Lauren Chance, Tom, and me face a phalanx of very serious men.

Five of them.

Homeland Security agents are always exactly what I expect—young men in suits and mirror shades with their ears wired. Bluetooths and shoulder holsters. Standard-issue sidearms. Thick revolvers made by Smith and Wesson. The man standing in front has white hair but a young face, slightly craggy and set in stone, built like a retired linebacker. His shirt is blue, his cufflinks made of gold.

His grip is laced with hidden agendas and tragic family issues.

A lot of it trickles through as he shakes my hand. It's the only read I've gotten from anyone so far in this place. He's a real case, this guy.

"Mr. Carlsbad, it's a pleasure to meet you."

I remove my headset and tell him the pleasure's all mine.

"My name is Richard Dryden, special agent. My men will be in charge of Homeland Security measures during the trip. I'm sure you've been briefed."

"Yes."

"Then we'll try to make this as painless as possible. I'll need to know exactly what's going on with your team at all times. Miss Chance and I have already coordinated our efforts. We'll have a base camp set up in three of the main VIP rooms, and these four men will be on constant rotation through the compartments."

"Wait'll you see this train, buddy," Tom says, rubbing a little bit of his hangover out of his eyes. "You won't believe it. They've got *everything* up there."

Dryden gives me an easy-to-read look and I decide to freak him out. "Your father was wounded in the Secret Service, wasn't he?"

His eyes squeeze into slits. I feel his heart move faster. "How did you know that, Mr. Carlsbad?"

"Call me Buck."

"Okay...how did you know about my father, *Buck?*"

"Old wounds never really heal, do they?"

It worked. He's completely freaked. But not in the right way. "I don't have time for phony Jedi mind tricks, mister. I'll be right up front with you about that. I don't buy the psychic bit, never did. That works on TV, not on real people."

"Then you were lying."

"Sorry? Lying about what?"

"About it being a pleasure to meet me."

"I'm here to do a *job,* Buck. What I believe about your profession is irrelevant. But I'm also the law, so let's not play games."

"Just like to know who I'm working with, that's all."

He keeps his lethal glare trained on me. "Miss Chance will show you the layout of the train and get you settled. My other men are establishing a perimeter inside the hotel for the red-carpet business. That's on Friday, day after tomorrow. It's gonna be a circus. We have thirty agents in the building."

"This room will be filled with press and spectators," says Lauren. "The front steps will look like the Kodak Theatre on Oscar night."

"Sounds crazy," I say.

"My own security force numbers more than a hundred inside this plaza on a typical day." She doesn't smile. I notice for the first time that her hair is in a different braid, though her clothes are exactly the same, holding coy shadows over her perfect body, like a vampire afraid to see the sun. Still, she's stunning in bright light, even more beautiful than before.

Tom leans forward and smiles. "It's a big deal, kid."

"And yes, you were right," says Dryden. "My father is retired from the Secret Service. It's not public knowledge. How did you *know* that?"

"You told me just a second ago."

"That's no answer. Let me rephrase: You will tell me how you knew my father was wounded in the line of duty or I will place you under arrest and you can sit out this whole fucking train ride in an interrogation cell. Do I make myself clear...*Buck?*"

"There's no need for that," Tom says. "The kid's tuned in, he's the real deal."

"Bullshit," Dryden says, and he takes one step forward, squinting his eyes down on me again, like he's about to make a grab for his handcuffs.

"It was 1981," I tell him quickly. "The Ronald Reagan assassination attempt. Your dad took a bullet in the motorcade when the shooting started. Tim McCarthy was his partner. He got the NCAA Award of Valor for protecting the president. Your father got nothing. You were probably a teenager then. There was a divorce after that."

His eyes go from slitted to bigger than life. "You got all that when I *shook hands* with you?"

"There's more. Want to hear?"

He drops his shoulders in a way that reminds me of an exasperated babysitter. "Save it. We'll talk later."

"Okay, suit yourself."

He draws a heroic breath and aims his finger at my heart. "Here's the deal, Buck. This event has been under preparation for *months*. My men are used to certain methods of operation. My superiors saddle me with a cheap TV psychic three days before the train pulls out, and if you wanna know my opinion, it all smells like some kind of fishy promotional gimmick. Sidney Jaeger's people are *not in charge* once we get on that train—as long as the senator is aboard, you all play by the rules of the United States fucking government. I've allowed Miss Chance to come along for the ride, but as far as I'm concerned, that's just a formality. If you have any tricks planned, I need to know about them in advance."

"No tricks," Tom says. "Buck's the real deal, not a TV phony. Those guys on the Syfy channel just made him look bad. If there are any problems you won't be able to wave a gun at, that's where we come in."

Dryden sighs again. "I'm gonna take this at *face value* for the *moment,* gentlemen. Strictly on the assumption that you people will stay out of our way. Are we clear?"

"In Technicolor," I say.

"And just for the record, Buck, my father *was* a decorated hero. He just never went on TV like you. He didn't like publicity. It's not like he got to save JFK, but back then it was a big enough deal."

"I remember."

"He's all yours," Dryden says to Lauren, then leads his men into the lobby, where they join another phalanx of blacksuits, getting on with the program.

Tom shakes his head at me. "What the hell was *that,* Buck? You trying to get shit-canned before this thing even gets on the road?"

"He's got a lot of pain in him," I say slowly. "I thought it was strange that I could read him so well."

The face of Dryden's decorated father still lingers—an old man dying in a hospital bed, too far gone from bone rot and dementia to tell his son he was sorry for the way he was raised. Hardass lessons scrawled in leather and blood. Family secrets riding shotgun all through little Richard's illustrious career.

I keep my mouth shut about all that.

Sometimes it just doesn't pay to be a smartass.

* * *

The lift is big enough for twenty people, made of thick glass and welded steel, so that you can see the lobby as we rise to the platform. The Jaeger Laser waits for us, like a sleek steel serpent encased in a tunnel of transparent aluminum, like something right out of *Star Trek*. The platform that borders the track is ten feet wide, overlooking the massive front entranceway of the plaza. Lauren Chance steps out and joins Eric Tate, who comes toward us with a thick smile. He doesn't have any bodyguards today, wonder of wonders.

"Good morning, Mr. Carlsbad," he says, looking right past Lauren. "Come with me and I'll show you the train."

The main forward door slides open with a thick slash of pressurized air.

We move through the first car, a massive observation/passenger deck which looks like a luxury airliner that wants to be a ritzy cocktail lounge tricked out in reds and greens, full of tables and chairs and rows of seats and glass partitions, booths facing the windows with plush first-class recliner chairs. Chromed steel latticework and handrails tracing along everything. It's wide and roomy, designed less for function and more for show, though I'm sure the show is functional as hell. Guess that's the trick with pleasure cruises: how to make it look good and get where you're going on time. They spent a bazillion dollars cracking that equation around here. Steel-reinforced outer hull and lead-lined inner walls and ceilings in every car. Pressure-sealed windows and hatchways, like an airplane's. Bulletproof, no doubt.

Tate stops in front of a large flat-screen in the center of the car. It shows the layout of the track, from LA to Las Vegas, in a heads-up interactive-video display. You can toggle the screen to see different areas of the journey and enlarge the satellite view.

"We start here," he says, pointing at the cluster of shapes that represent the Lost Angels Plaza, then he moves his finger along the track to the desert just outside LA.

"The ride through the city is just for show. You'll be doing less than seventy-five per hour. As the Laser gains momentum on the straightaway toward Nevada, you'll be going for a new land-speed record in two phases. We expect to reach over two hundred and fifty miles an hour. That's phase one."

"I heard the Guinness people are already trying to disqualify the record," Tom says. "That true?"

"Yes, there's been a little bit of controversy. Technically speaking, this train is not really a land vehicle during the main trip—we're actually *flying*. But I think they're probably going to allow it."

"Sidney Jaeger can be very convincing," I tell him.

"That's true. Now pay close attention, this next part's important."

He moves the video along many miles through the desert.

I recognize the shape of the Triangle as the target blip passes through it. Ground zero, where the derailment happened.

It matches my map almost exactly.

The track comes to a large mountain range just a few miles past the Nevada border, and a narrow tunnel cuts straight through it.

Just on the other side of the tunnel, the lights of Las Vegas glimmer.

"This is phase two. A tunnel pass through a mountain rich with mineral ores that will greatly amplify the magnetic field propelling our engine. During the second hour of the trip, the train will build steadily to a much higher speed, until we enter the tunnel, which will slingshot us toward Vegas at over *six hundred miles per hour*."

"Holy shit." That's me, with my mouth open.

"Your average jet plane doesn't go that fast," says Tom, his jaw also on the floor. "How come nobody's told us about this until now?"

"The speed slingshot is theoretical," says Tate. "It's one of those crazy things that gets discovered through testing. Sidney doesn't want to crow about it until we're sure it works—if it does, he'll have more to tell the media later. If it *doesn't* work, we've lost no face."

I give him a serious look. "Isn't that kind of speed a little much, even for a train like this?"

"I told you, Mr. Carlsbad, we're ahead of the curve."

Fuck.

God only knows how fast this goddamn bullet is capable of going.

"We'll be topping out at higher speeds only at specific times throughout the trip," Tate says. "The stages of the engine burn on a time-coded release sequence. The last forty minutes will be very fast, but it's not far to

Vegas, as you can see. Three hundred and seventy-six miles on the route we've carved through the desert."

"So it's all worked out by computer," Tom says.

"Yes. We pull out of the station at exactly seven p.m. You'll reach the tunnel at nine fifteen p.m. It's the final approach into the city. Just three minutes inside the mountain. When the Laser comes out of the tunnel, you'll be at maximum speed, and then the nitrogen engines automatically begin to cycle down and we coast into Las Vegas. Braking happens only when we reach the city limits."

Outer-space technology bound to earth, multiplied by six hundred and sixty-six. I'm reminded of an old Iron Maiden song.

That worries me.

A lot.

Tom smiles, looking nervous. "Gonna be a wild ride, huh?"

"Something like that."

"It's gonna be like an acid trip for you and the kid," he says. "Going that fast, even with the cabins pressurized and the lead shielding. At that speed, you'll be struggling just to keep a straight thought."

I narrow my eyes at him. "If we have to pull marks, it'll get worse. Did you look at the file on the Blackjack Nine?"

"Yeah. Nasty bastards, man."

Nasty bastards are a million times worse at six hundred miles per hour.

But that can work both ways.

Marks have limitations, just like the men who hunt them.

The next car is a casino lounge, glittering with all sorts of bells and whistles. Gaming tables for poker and craps, video screens, a full bar in the center, orbited by stools made of ivory and velvet, something that looks like a crystal chandelier hanging above, but it's all one solid piece—my guess is that dangling bits of glass are no good in a pressurized environment floating at four hundred miles per hour on a magnetic force field. A blue lighting scheme in here, running in dazzling low neon along the edges of the ceiling, neo-Victorian architecture hanging over us in arcs and steeples, marble columns and mirrored surfaces bringing a bit of design symmetry from the hotel. You'd never know you were standing on board a train in this room. There ain't even any windows.

The main restroom area takes up a small sliver of space in a tiny connecting corridor that leads to the next gigantic observation deck, which has more seats and a movie-lobby decor, with classic posters from *His Girl Friday* and *Pulp Fiction* hanging in frames and several screens flashing with trailers and film clips, all very professionally edited together.

"Jaeger likes his movies," I say.

"Sidney grew up on the Walk of Fame," Tate says. "Many Hollywood-royalty types are dear friends of ours. Francis Crowe and Jerry Donaldson will be joining us for the opening of the Laser."

Heavy guns.

Crowe and Donaldson, the legendary Tinsel Town tag team.

Producers who eat people like Harvey Weinstein for breakfast and spit in the collective face of the Coen brothers while they're doing it.

Donaldson's the bad cop, makes all the headlines when he checks in to the Château Marmont on Sunset Boulevard with Scarlett Johansson and a pound of blow. Crowe's the nice guy, but he's quirky. Known for his weird little side projects, like gallery showings of photos he takes on the sets of his films. I read about that in the *Austin Chronicle*.

I make a face like it doesn't matter. "Who else is riding with us?"

"Bethany Sin just reconfirmed this morning. There were some problems with her management people, but it all worked out. We have a couple of society types. Very high-profile. Ever heard of Derek Pappas?"

"Sure, I'm from Texas. He's an oil giant."

"He's coming with a guest. Rashid Hopi. A blue blood from the Middle East. It was just announced an hour ago. The media's already going crazy."

"Then everything's going according to plan."

"So far, Mr. Carlsbad."

Just outside the main doors of the observation deck runs a narrow corridor with a slotted glass wall on one side. Through it, you can see the platform, five stories above the lobby. During the trip, you'd see the desert flashing by out there. A series of ornate doorways in a row along the other wall of the corridor, each leading to a private VIP compartment, ten in all. Senator Maxton will be in number ten. We have our base camp behind door number five. Eric Tate gets to the door and opens it.

The room smells like marijuana laced with mint tobacco.

"*Oblivion!* My man *Bucko!* Get the hell in here and have a toke with the President!"

Roosevelt stands up from a bank of laptop monitors as we enter, wagging the reefer in my face. I put up my palm and shake my head with a smile.

"There's no smoking on this train," Tate snaps. "Please let me have that."

"Aww, man, the spooks didn't mind. Ain't ganja *legal* in California?"

Tate holds out his hand, looking very unmoved. "They should have told you about federal smoking regulations aboard rail cars. Please let me have that."

"Shit." He hands it over, looking depressed. Pulls out his pill bottle and pops it open, chewing a Xanax. His look tells me Dryden's people never set foot in here. They would have arrested him. Likes to live dangerous, the kid does.

"Standard medication," I tell him, then I shake his hand. "Should have known you'd beat me here, kid."

"Got the place wired. Come check it *out,* my man."

This room is even bigger than I expected, splashed in luxury, designed to look like the place I slept in this morning, with track lighting and contoured surfaces. A twin bed scattered with gear faces Roosevelt's rig on a plastic wood-paneled table—three laptops wired to a network of tiny hidden cameras. Seventeen video windows show us the whole layout of the train. He clicks a key, and another seventeen show us more of it.

"I've got infrared and ultrasound in the main casino lounge, the movie room, and the restaurant. Standard cameras everywhere else, but I can bump them all up to full spectral using the console. That's worst-case scenario, of course."

"Let me see full frame," I tell him, squinting at the monitor.

Click. A window leaps out to fill one entire laptop screen, showing

117

us the five-star restaurant car—it's as dazzling as the casino, full of an old-school dining decor, lace and leather seats, giant panoramic windows, frozen crystal chandeliers hanging above.

"That's the next compartment over from these VIP rooms," he says. "After that, you got a subcorridor that's like a lobby into the movie theater—they plan on using it as a meeting room for things like conventions. That's the last car."

Click. The screen fills with an image of leather seats in rows. No windows. It looks exactly like your local movie house, only a little smaller.

"Check this out," says Roosevelt, and clicks again. The room on the screen goes white and then red, with scan patters moving through the image, readouts counting off in alien languages. "It's clean as a whistle in there, Buck. Nothing on spectral at all. If anything spooky goes down, it'll have to come in over my tripwires. We'll be one step ahead of the bastards."

"Let's hope that our ride is not spooky at all," Tate says, dismissing us with a roll of his eyes. "Mr. Carlsbad, would you care to see the rest of the train firsthand?"

"Sure."

"Would you be so kind, my dear? I have to catch a plane in ten minutes."

Her eyes betray nothing as she nods.

"You'd better hurry," I tell him. "LAX is a long way from here."

"Not to worry, Mr. Carlsbad. We have a helipad on the roof for such rushes." He checks the time on his smartphone. "And I'm late already. Turns out I'll be in Singapore for the big rally on Friday, but I'll be watching the broadcast with our Japanese friends. They're major stockholders, you see."

"Of course they are."

"I bid you good luck...or is it break a leg, Mr. Carlsbad?"

"That's for actors."

"But aren't we *all* actors?"

He giggles at his own weird joke, holding out his hand. I shake with him, trying to turn myself off to the evil that rides on the surface of his skin. It doesn't work. He's a real scumbag, this guy.

Or maybe he's just acting.

"Very well," he says sharply, as if he knows what I can sense. "I'll leave you in Lauren's capable hands."

"Sounds fun," I tell him, eyes on her.

"I'll hang back with the kid," says Tom. "I wanna go over some of this business with the cameras."

Roosevelt gives him a look. "What business? The President is a *professional*."

"You're a professional who smokes too damn much weed."

"Aww, man..."

Tate turns on one heel and leaves us without another word.

His air of deception trails him like a bad stench.

I put it out of my mind.

Almost.

The VIP corridor has another restroom area at the far end.

And right through doors beyond that, the five-star restaurant.

It's even more dazzling when it's not on video. It's not like dining cars I've seen on other trains, a center row dividing a few booths scrunched up against windows. This place looks exactly like a trendy European bistro, arranged meticulously to the last detail, ornate tables and chairs, an exposed kitchen you can see through a partition at the far end. A giant gas grill, designed for show, like everything else. Lauren Chance leads me through the room, toward the compartment door at the far end. It leads to a long corridor, which dead-ends in the movie theater.

Inside the theater it's dark.

Lauren hits a switch, blue fluorescents washing over us.

She solidifies like a dark angel in neon ice, and I can sense the cold uncertainty of a woman holding secrets.

"I thought we'd take a moment to talk privately, Buck. I think we may have gotten off on the wrong foot."

"Are you better with your *left* foot?" I rub my wrists when I say that, still a little sore from the workout.

"I needed to see your skill set. It's part of my job."

I pass her a knowing look. "So what's on your mind?"

"You need to be made aware of a few things. Sidney was very guarded about what he told you last night. He didn't give you any details about the accidents that happened on the rail line."

"I did notice that. Figured the details weren't important."

"Many eyes are watching us. And there's a lot of secrecy. Things even *I* don't know about. My impression of you is positive, and I don't want to see any of our people get hurt."

"So what's Sidney Jaeger hiding?"

"I know that three men died just a few days before the derailment. Construction workers. One of them went crazy and cut another man's throat. He threw himself on an electrified rail and took another with him. I saw the whole thing on surveillance video. They didn't fight like men—they fought like animals."

"Sounds grim."

"I knew there were other incidents, but Eric put a muzzle on everybody. He's the kind of guy who makes things disappear. I'm...*concerned*."

"You think he's whispering in Jaeger's ear to push things ahead?"

"Something like that. I think they might already have proof that the rail line is haunted, or whatever you call it. There's too many things that don't add up."

"Whatever's out there, it's biding its time. Hasn't attacked anyone in months."

"Maybe it's just waiting for the right people to attack."

"Bob Maxton?"

"Maybe."

"Don't you think Jaeger has considered that possibility?"

"I'm not sure *what* he's considered."

"Have you told him about your fears?"

"It wouldn't do any good. When Sidney sets his mind on something, nothing else distracts him from it. And Eric is a snake. He almost had me fired twice. There's other considerations too. Richard Dryden, for example. He could be a big problem for us."

"He didn't seem very stable."

"You didn't do yourself any favors with him, Buck."

"I was testing the waters."

"Fact is, Dryden's the wrong man for this kind of job. He's in over his head and has something to prove. I got a look at his service record and it was full of bad stuff—mostly out-of-policy shootings."

"Homeland Security usually send specialists. Why would they trust this to someone who didn't even believe in mediums?"

"Things fall through the cracks all the time. It could be more political."

I breathe in quickly and decide I can trust her, for now. "I saw some of that when I shook hands with Dryden. He kicked in the door of some suspected protesters during the Republican National Convention a few years back—ended up shooting one of them. That never made the news."

"Doesn't surprise me."

"Wasn't even reprimanded. Homeland Security must've bought off the survivors."

"They're notorious about protecting their own."

"And they tend to shoot first."

"We'd better watch our step. If things get weird, stay close to me."

"That's not a good idea, Miss Chance."

"What?"

"When I told you I didn't need a bodyguard, I wasn't just talking to hear my own voice. You stay too close to me and you'll put yourself in a lot of danger."

"Buck..."

"I'm serious. People have died around me. Because of what I have inside me."

"What's inside you?"

"Something that ghosts can't fight. And the crossfire's a real bitch when they try. I don't want to see you get hurt either."

"I saw the scars under your sleeve when we were sparring. Is that part of the crossfire?"

"Everybody has scars."

She lets my words drift silently in the space between us.

As if she understands.

"I apologize, Buck. I didn't mean to insult you. But I have a job to do."

"Okay."

I look right into her deep blue eyes.

And I say this:

"You are goddamn fucking beautiful."

This time, she smiles.

Coldly.

"This is a professional relationship, Buck."

"Just an observation. I have a job to do also."

"Then I think maybe we understand each other."

Yeah.

Maybe.

I spend the rest of the day walking perimeter with the kid. We re-place five of his cameras for an optimal view of all six main compartments, plus we rig each VIP suite. Bethany Sin, Bob Maxton, and the terror-twin movie producers have their own rooms, the other guests don't. This is a short ride and not everyone wants to spend it in private quarters, but the biggest stars always need a quiet place to hide.

Then we go over security.

Just like I figured, the kid's got the train scoped. Started hacking the minute he got here. I lean over his shoulder in the base-camp VIP room, looking at his screen as he shows me how he got into the system through an easy back door.

"They've got a lot of really advanced protocols guarding the engine mainframe," he says. "But the stuff inside the compartments is a lot easier to break. It's all on a separate series of circuits. Check it out."

His screen splits into a cross section of the train, and he points out the exterior observation windows and the seals between compartments.

"They've got sectioned steel emergency shutters at both ends of each compartment that slam down in the event of decompression. They can be triggered manually too, from keypads at each lock point. I'm guessing your girl Chance has the key codes."

"How do you figure that?"

"She's one of Jaeger's. Gotta know her way around, right?"

"What about the windows? Looked bulletproof."

"Fat chance, amigo. You fire enough shots into standard-issue safety glass and eventually it's gonna go—that's why they have a backup. More shutters that seal the observation windows automatically. The sensors key on any kind of pressure drop in the cabins, or on a fire. They have a halon system for that. For the worst-case scenario."

"Jesus. So if the shit goes down, we all end up sealed in a sardine can going a million miles an hour surrounded by deadly gas."

"Something like that."

"Can you get us out of the can if we need to boogie in a hurry?"

He smiles wide. "Who are you talking to, my man?"

"What about stopping the train?"

"That's harder. And dangerous. This is one fast motherfucker. Emergency braking past a certain speed could throw us a mile into the sky. Plus they've made it damn near impossible to get into the computer that runs everything. Lots of mean firewalls. I haven't ever seen anything this advanced. They don't even have an engineer watching the dials, man. We're talking total HAL 9000."

Of course we are.

It's the train of the future.

I let his words linger for a moment.

Then I tell him there's one more thing, reaching for my satchel. I need him to stash something for me in here, where these spooks won't find it.

He arches his eyebrows when he sees the rusty souvenir I bring out.

When he touches it, he feels the vibrations.

"No problem," he says.

Back in the hotel room, I lay my satchel out on the bed and inspect my gear.

Two sets of tinted scleral contact lenses. Custom made, damn expensive.

Two sets of brass-framed UV sunglasses. Heat resistant, unbreakable. I almost never use them anymore.

The goggles are better—two pairs.

My father's and mine.

It's all about protecting your eyes on a job.

Your optic nerves are the key to seeing the next level, and the levels after that.

The Blacklight wants to blind you so that you can't connect.

There's other ways to fight too. That's the rest of my bag of tricks. Simple stuff, but crucial to your survival. I've been trucking with this little black bag for sixteen years, since the day I became a real professional. Hell of a day, that was. Low-level trial by fire, all the way to hell and back again. The dead man at the end smiled and said, Welcome to the monster club, kid. *We'll see you real soon.*

A box of baking soda—you use it to trace footprints. Burns marks when they try to walk next to you. They call it mojo dust in New Orleans.

One can of Lysol—this stuff is so powerful it kills herpes, says so right on the label. Works like tear gas on spectrals.

The pocketknife that makes the scars on my arms—plus a six-pack of brand-new razorblades, still in the cardboard. You keep those handy for quick escapes, taped under your sleeve. Can't always pull out a big knife and go to work on yourself in mixed company.

And the map.

I unfold it and spread the old moldy paper on the bed in front of me, checking the route against what I saw on the video screen. The empty space where the trail rips away in the California desert is right where I almost died.

Where the fall happened.

Fifty miles from the Nevada border, on the edge of the Triangle.

Directly in the path of Jaeger's train.

I sit on the edge of the bed and I practice my breathing.

I concentrate on what lies just beyond the waking world.

The vibrations of the dead barely reach me as they move along the chambers of my mind like faded memories, attracted to the Pull that lives in my body like buzzing insects unable to resist the ice-warm siren song of a bug zapper.

I concentrate harder and the voices come closer, louder.

Just on the other side.

I close my eyes and put my thoughts there, almost feeling the heat tickle my skin.

Homing from years lost.

I concentrate harder on it, using everything I have.

Using the Pull.

I hover there on the threshold, staying focused.

Preparing for the big show.

I keep myself there for a long time.

It seems like days, holding at the ready position, poised to spring.

"I won't be able to come with you, it's too hairy."

Darby sits at the table looking over the map, his teeth showing through the crooked anti-grin permanently pasted on his face. I'm pacing around, drinking a Diet Pepsi from the minibar, trying to work through it all. This stuff tastes like shit, but no sugar before a job—it jolts my nervous system too bad, even on a good day. The caffeine is enough to keep me focused.

"You can still contact us on the train," I tell him. "You can listen for voices and report back."

"I might be able to. It'll be a little tricky. The Triangle is full of bad noise, and that bullet you're going on is a magnetized roach motel. I'll be able to pull secondhand messages from the slipstream, but that might be it."

"Great. My faithful poltergeist sidekick sits out the case of our career."

There goes my usual ace in the hole.

I used to rely heavy on Darby back in the day—his ability to walk through walls and knock down doors. Should have known this one wouldn't be so easy.

His weird grin makes a disgusted noise. "Look, I don't make the rules, man. I could get fucking shredded out there in that black shithole. I was with you the last time, remember?"

"You never said a word to me then either."

"I nearly died, just like you."

That's the way it happens.

You burn out and the ghost shadow eats it right alongside you.

He sighs. "I'll do my best to help, Buck...but if you want my advice, this is something neither of us wanna fuck around with again."

"I can't think about that. I have to go back. You wouldn't understand."

"I understand you're getting crazy again."

"What if I don't care? What if I want an end to all this?"

"Goddammit, Buck, you're not just playing with your life—you're playing with *mine*."

"You don't get to make threats."

He shakes his head and almost laughs, giving me that muscle sneer, like he's gonna slug me. "Big tough motherfucker, huh?"

"Sometimes."

"So you take the money, stick your neck over the chopping block, and tack on an ending? That's dumb, Buck. You're not thinking right."

"Maybe. But I have to do this."

I run my finger along the map.

The little red marks seem to glow as I stare at them.

"My parents buried hundreds of urns out there...but at the end...it was something else. Something different. Something they wanted to hide from me. If it had to do with the Blackjack Nine..."

"It could be anything, man."

I put my finger in the center of the section of the map that was torn away years ago. "But it also might be where they went to die. And Blackjack Williams could have killed them."

"So this is about revenge now?"

I glance up from the map, give him a real serious look. "It's about knowing the truth. And you better get on the right side of it."

"Okay, Captain Badass, it's your show. Just remember who warned you."

"And you just remember whose back you're riding on."

"I'll try to help. Keep an eye on the Web."

"I'm not on Facebook."

"Get in the future, Buck. It could mean your ass if you don't."

I look down at the map and I can tell he's gone now.

His words still linger.

The Pull glows in my body, hungry.

TEN

MAGIC CARPET RIDE

Friday afternoon.

We watch the pregame show on a monitor from our base camp aboard the train.

It's on every news channel, just like they said it would be.

We flip through and get a lot of different takes on the launch.

The kid snacks on popcorn, and I suck down a can of soda—Diet Dr Pepper, which was invented in Texas and tastes a hell of a lot better than Pepsi. Tom paces the cabin, waiting for our cue to join the famous badasses who are about to make their grand entrance. His hands are shaking, and he's talking a lot—he's not usually so nervous about stuff like this. I keep telling him to calm down, because the three of us are connected with wireless earbuds, and when he gets loud, it crackles hard and hurts my head. I have enough voices to deal with without Tom going all goofy on opening night.

"Sorry," he tells me. "I'm just a daffy old man."

These wireless jobs are something Roosevelt geniused up a few years ago—they don't even relay through radio or cell boxes on your hip. Everything's contained in a tiny nugget that fits snug inside your ear canal, microcircuits the size of a sickle cell beaming back to Roosevelt's console. Or something like that.

The Homeland Security guys look in on us every ten minutes, on the nose.

There's a blond guy named Bryan Jacques who looks lean and corded, like a surfer. His laminate IDs him—but when he shakes my hand, he tells me the name is pronounced "all-American style." *Jacks*. He's not even a little French. Says he comes from a long line of working-class business owners who pulled a scam back at the beginning of the last century to strike it rich, and that involved a switcheroo on the family crest. A high-society thing, he says. Like it makes him proud that he hails from a clan of liars. The guy has a really gung ho attitude and a swagger. He's partnered up with Scott Kendall, a thin weasel with dark skin and bloodshot eyes who looks pretty tightly wound too. I ask him if he's got any funny stories about *his* name, and he says he saw a slasher flick once where the hero was named Kendall. I saw that movie. The guy he's talking about gets his privates squeezed into jelly by a zombie just before fade-out. But this guy doesn't look anything like him.

The other two agents working under Dryden are your standard clean-cut government guys. They look exactly alike. Blue eyes and black hair. No real expression on their faces. Their names are Ben and Jerry. No kidding.

I can't tell which one is which.

These guys are all really slick and well trained. Their minds are full of deception and steel-hard focus. They know how to hide their pasts. I figure at least one of them has a criminal background—probably Jacques, based on his family tree. He's got the eyes. But it's hard to read any of them. Now, anyway. I'm thinking about too many other things. That's probably bad, but it can't be helped. Sometimes you just have to trust your instincts and what you see on the surface. Can't be a mind reader full-time. It makes you insane.

Just ask Roosevelt.

I check the gear in my satchel for the tenth time, right after Jacques looks in on us. I tape three razorblades under my left coat sleeve. The crate from Father Joe is latched shut on the table in front of me, ready. Insisted on bringing the urns with us, just to be on the safe side. Like there's ever a safe side in my line of work.

Next, the lenses.

I drop them in, one followed by the other, like ordinary contacts.

Everything gets a little darker.

I ask the kid if he's got my souvenir. and he shoots me a big thumbs-up, cracking open a compartment on his main console tower. He used it to smuggle his weed onto the train when he first got here. He reaches in and pulls out the rusty old pistol and hands it to me. Tom's eyes get big when he sees that.

"What's with the antique, Buck?"

I turn the useless weapon over in my hand, running my fingers over the corroded metal. "Let's just say it heightens my sense of security."

"I guess you never cleared that piece with Dryden, huh?" Tom's nervous tic gets worse, his voice shaky. But he reels it in.

"No, I guess I didn't. It's a piece of junk anyway."

"Junk or not, you'll be in deep shit if they search you."

"Something tells me they won't."

"It's one of your trinkets, isn't it? Something you brought back?"

"Yeah. It was hidden from me—but sometimes it changes. The trace I see in the Blacklight homes back to a certain point when the gun was new, and it's got one bullet left in it. I'm starting to think that if I pull the trigger while I'm there, it'll actually fire."

"And you think that bullet was left for you?"

"Maybe. Nothing in my life has ever made much sense—but when I have a feeling like this, I'm usually right."

Tom takes it all in, his nervous tic going away for a minute. He seems really fascinated. Tilts his head in a quick ponder as I stash the gun in my satchel and then zip it up tight in one of the hidden compartments.

Roosevelt snorts. "Weirdest thing I ever heard of, man."

I wink at him. "Weirder things have happened."

"Guess you got that right, Bucko. Just make sure your life ain't on the line when you test out your single-bullet theory."

He sounds like Darby now.

I concentrate hard to find the ghost shadow, but he's not with me.

My wingman is staying as far from this flying magnet as he can.

Waiting in the slipstream.

I tell Roosevelt to check for him on Facebook and his fingers hit the keys fast, pulling up Darby's profile on the wireless connection. His status reads:

BON VOYAGE, SUCKERS.

Asshole.

But he's keeping it subtle, just like he's supposed to. Too many eyes watch the Internet. Ghosts watch the Internet. You exchange messages carefully when you do it this way. And forget Twitter.

"Try this, my man."

The kid digs a thick plastic slab out of his junk pile—a smartphone all full of bytes and fast technology. Keys it for me, pulling up a preloaded Facebook application. He uses one of his ghost accounts, the one he keeps under the name Shecky Dynamite.

"Welcome to the future," he says, handing me the phone. "You can hit a button to get Darby's updates. It's idiotproof."

"Thanks," I tell him, rolling my eyes.

Tom paces the cabin, going back to being nervous.

I haven't seen Lauren Chance since we walked the train two days ago, but now I see her on TV, standing at the end of the red carpet on the stage inside the lobby with a few of her security guys. She's right under the big screen, which is filled with an image of Sidney Jaeger, remote linked from another stage in Vegas. A lot of the commentators and pundits know her name and what she does. One guy on Comedy Central calls her a tall drink of ass-kicking.

"She's a hottie, but she's a career creature," Roosevelt says, watching her on television. "Mark my words, she sleeps with an ice-cold dildo."

I shake my head at him, smiling.

The CNN newspeople cut back and forth from the hotel to Sidney Jaeger, who's giving a long press conference from his podium at the Vegas Dreamworld amphitheater, and they cut around the big theme park a lot, showing how big and shiny and new it all is. They weren't kidding: The place is its own city, a main drag teeming with people, surrounded by shops and theaters and restaurants and roller-coaster rides stacked on multiple levels. The Dreamworld is supposed to be twice the size of the Lost Angels Plaza. Some of it is still under construction.

Jaeger's a natural on camera, fielding questions from the news anchors and pundits via satellite with an expert's ear for spin control and public relations. His jokes ain't funny, but they make him seem hip in an odd way. It's been carefully designed. He knows the lingo. His image towers over the stage just inside the entrance of the Lost Angels Plaza, filling the screen from hundreds of miles away. The whole Big Brother aspect of it all suddenly hits me, and I find myself laughing.

Lauren stands at his service, awaiting the arrival of our guests.

Francis Crowe and Jerry Donaldson are the first to hit the red carpet outside.

Five fifteen on the button.

Sidney Jaeger announces them from his screen.

Their limo is long and white, and they arrive with a full entourage in tow: six women and a giant black guy who looks like a bodyguard for gangsta rappers. Turns out he *is* a gangsta rapper, according to one of the news commentators. Somebody named Junk-E. Apparently he has the number one single in America right now, and three of the girls are on his arm for the evening. I really do need to get out more.

"I hate rap music," Tom says. "Every song sounds the same."

"It's all about the lyrics," the kid says, switching the channel to MSNBC. "Some great poets come out of the street, my man."

"Tell 'em they can suck my dick."

"Tell 'em yourself—I'm sure they'd love to hear from you."

When the kid ain't looking, Tom shoots him the finger.

Sound like a couple of high school media nerds, these guys.

Francis Crowe drifts absently, a six-foot scarecrow in expensive silk clothes. He plays up his camera-nebbish angle in a pretty major way—snapping photos of the paparazzi army encamped on both sides of the red-carpeted stairs that lead up to the giant entranceway of the plaza. In a strobing sea of flashing bulbs and pushy jerks screaming for interviews, he is almost unbelievably calm, while his buddy Donaldson works the line of news cameras one by one, talking about their upcoming movie a lot, something called *Black Bart*. He's a big, longhaired crazy man with a face full of scrag who was lucky to survive the eighties, and he doesn't have to dress nice for anyone: he's got on a black blazer that barely covers a loud Hawaiian shirt, not tucked in. He talks faster than Satan, hitting one news guy after another like a sportsman knocking off clay pigeons. I'm stunned to discover his new flick is actually a remake of *Blazing Saddles*—starring Junk-E, of course. The girl on Donaldson's arm could be anyone in Los Angeles. She's silly and blond and looks good half naked in diamonds. One of the commentators finally IDs her as Donaldson's wife then makes a crack about Francis Crowe's reported homosexual affair with some actor I've never heard of.

Junk-E is big in the political underground, it turns out. He's all about civil rights and does Million Man Marches, shit like that. Has guys like Jesse Jackson and Spike Lee on his speed-dial. *Black Bart* is supposed to be some important statement about racial inequity disguised as a bathroom comedy—that's how you nail the masses where they live and breathe. He actually says that for the cameras. His voice is deep and full of power. Terminator tough. I can just see this guy standing over an army of angry brothers screaming for truth, justice, and the American motherfuckin' way.

"I need a smoke, guys," Tom says, adjusting his earbud.

The kid gives him a serious look. "Don't go out there, man. They'll eat you alive."

"Who said anything about stepping outside?"

He locks the door and lights up in the room, his tarnished silver Zippo clicking musically, the sharp scent of bad tobacco hitting my nose like mud. The kid disabled the smoke sensors in here last night. I shake my head at Tom, and he shrugs.

"Yeah, yeah, Buck, I know."

I give him a look like *You know those things will kill you.*

He gives me a look back that says *When you hunt the living dead, cancer is the least of your problems.*

Whatever you say, smart guy.

* * *

Now, it's Bethany Sin.

She glides for the masses like a dirty muse, her posse of beautiful young things spilling from a pink limo and scattering behind her like hand-maidens. No boyfriends. They're wildcats, on the hunt. These estrogen-powered postmodern pop divas all look the same to me, and they're easy to miss if you have no interest in modern music, but she turns out to be wild and sexy in an almost underground kind of way: bright red and deep purple hair warring for attention with several pounds of metal piercings and a tattoo of a serpent crawling up her right thigh. You can see lots of skin through her stylishly torn black wifebeater, which stops just above a flowing orange skirt-thing that wraps her waist and drizzles at her ankles, encased in gold rock-star platform pumps with six inches of sole she can't control. I only notice that because the Fox News guy points it out. One of the cameras even goes in for a nice close-up on the shoes—it's a pair from her own line of clothing, apparently.

Carolyn Lewis cracks an unfunny joke about her at the top of the stairs. Roosevelt laughs at it.

"She's hot," he says.

"Not your typical diva," I muse. "What's her music like?"

"I wasn't talking about Bethany Sin, man. *Carolyn Lewis*—now, that's a piece of talent."

Figures.

I don't even laugh at that, it's so bloody obvious. "Ain't she gay?"

He licks his bottom lip. "Yeah, that's even hotter. Ever bag a lesbian, my man? It's ten tons of trouble in a one-ton sack."

"That's a *good* thing?"

"Hell, yeah."

"You're *sick,* kid," Tom says, sucking back smoke. "Get some help."

He's still shaking, sweat beading off his nose. He reaches up to wipe it away, and I feel something shudder inside him. Something like a bad memory. Something shameful. He's hitting his old demons again, and it's making him shake. I don't like the shakes when it comes to a job like this. The shakes get people killed.

"Tom, you sure you're okay?"

"I'm fine, kid. Just got the jitters, that's all."

"That's not like you. Sit it out if you have to, man. I want this thing to go smooth. We've got some real hardasses breathing down our necks on this one."

"Hardasses don't mean nothing to *me*, Buck."

Defensive. That's not like Tom either.

"Just take it easy," I tell him. "This ain't the jungle."

He dismisses me with a quick snort.

I put my eyes back on Bethany Sin.

Her manner is charming, laid back. She rolls her eyes a lot in self depre-cation, making big movements with her arms. If she went nuts and shaved her head tomorrow, I don't think anyone would mind. She glows, in a way none of these others do. She's young and unjaded, full of life. Seems almost impossible.

Make a note, she might be Gifted.

A lot of rock stars are.

She is stopped by a guy from Variety, and gives him a wry wink, never breaking stride, kissing the young man's cheek and telling him in a funny cartoon voice: *"I must go now and gnash my teeth in the name of Mickey Mouse!"*

The kid sees me wondering what she meant by that and leans in to whisper in my ear. "She signed a deal with Disney last week. She's voic-ing the lead in their new flick about a duck who becomes a pop singer. Creative, no?"

"No."

"Stop staring, my man. You'll go blind."

Carolyn Lewis makes another joke about the diva.

Lewis has been here since last night, did a fifteen-minute bumper piece on the train this morning, and now she's coming at the world live with her exclusive report. That was the deal she cut with Jaeger—she gets to say whatever she wants and put it all on TV. When her broadcast ends, she'll have a camera guy following her around on board the train, picking up juicy bits which they'll patch together for tomorrow and the next day's shows. She already had a rail with one of Lauren Chance's security people, but she knows better than to pick a fight with Homeland Security. She's witty and masculine and platinum beautiful, a superstar, and she knows it. She's more full of herself than the diva, really. Tough on the conservatives tonight. Keep your enemies closer, said the man.

"Stop staring," I say to the kid. "You'll go blind."

Derek Pappas is a fat old man with loud clothes and a loud voice. Rashid Hopi turns out to be little more than a shadow next to the bigger-than-life oil tycoon. He wears the shoulder sash of Arab royalty, but nobody makes jokes about it, not even Carolyn Lewis. Maybe they were all muzzled by Eric Tate and his spin squad.

"Interesting," I say out loud.

Carolyn *does* talk about Pappas's bold new merger with Hopi's Middle East energy firm, a small but respectable company with rigs in all the right places, a few even in America, and she does it very reverently, with no jokes. Lewis can be damn serious and mighty convincing when she wants to be.

"Major players on the magic carpet," says Roosevelt.

"Goddamn sons of bitches," says Tom. "They're the reason it costs sixty bucks to fill up my fucking car." He drops the half-burned cigarette in my empty soda can with a hollow sizzle, then sprays some of his Binaca around, looking silly.

It all makes sense to me. Nobody's making jokes about the oil guys because they own the world, and they bankrolled half this train project under the table, even if Sidney Jaeger doesn't know it yet. Power is fuel, and fuel is what trains run on—even a train that flies.

Brilliant, Sidney.

"Okay, that just leaves the big cheese," Tom says, shaking off his jitters for a moment. "He'll be up in ten minutes. Look sharp, guys."

"I don't look sharp to you?" The kid snickers and tosses a handful of popcorn in his mouth. Switches to CNN. I feel Tom's heart flutter again, doing double beats in his breast. I have to watch out for him when we're out there. If he does something dumb it's everyone's ass. Have to be ready.

I open Father Joe's crate and remove a silver urn from it.

Number one.

I slip it into the pouch in my satchel.

Just to be on the safe side.

Maximum Bob hits the carpet solo.

No entourage, no bodyguard.

He emerges from the back of his limousine as a common man of the people, never mind the immaculate suit and tie. The Homeland Security guys keep a respectable distance, making him look good, selling the illusion. There's ten blacksuits on either side of the red carpet also—they've been waiting all day for him. Plus the fifteen agents in the building and the five already on board with us.

Agent Dryden walks ten feet behind Maxton at all times.

The crowd goes crazy for him.

This close, I can feel the power he projects, the reason for his celebrity. His vitality charges the atmosphere, something bigger than all of us. I can tell in this moment that it's true—he *will* be president, and when that happens, he will change the world. I see no compromise in him, no looking back, no mercy for his enemies. A throng of teenagers near the velvet rope scream for him like he's John, Paul, George, and Ringo all rolled up into one. The redhead with braces even faints. I would wonder on any other day if that was staged.

It ain't staged.

It's real.

It's scary.

The news guys yell for his attention, but he only waves, making his slow ascent among the fans, right at home in the center of the storm.

"He's the man," Roosevelt says.

I don't doubt it.

There's never been anything like Bob Maxton.

Even Carolyn Lewis is somewhat humbled by his slick entrance, but she recovers enough to talk about some of his campaign platforms. No jokes now. This is serious business, apparently. The gambling bill goes before Congress in five days. The pundits all think it will crash and burn. I know better. I met the man who bankrolled that bill.

At the top of the stairs, Maxton takes his place at a podium. He smiles down on his admiring public and waves again. Looks like an English lord addressing the peasants.

His elegant voice glides the air from speakers the size of someone's car: *"My fellow Americans. Welcome to the future."*

And the roar of the crowd is like nothing I have ever felt at once.

The rest of his speech is short. He thanks Sidney Jaeger and the company, he gives props to the special guests. He is dry and charming and statesmanlike. He acts hip like a twentysomething, even though he's thirty-five. Three years younger than me. One year younger than the youngest man who ever ran for president. The commentators on TV find his performance flawless. They sling his rock-and-roll nickname around like he's already president. Maximum Bob rules us all.

He says thank you and joins his fellow famous people, striding into the lobby in flashes of light.

Sidney waits for them on the giant screen.

They move quickly to the stage through a roped-off pathway that snakes through a sea of humanity, all of whom are screaming for a photo or a comment. I'm really glad I'm not down there. I'd have to listen to Megadeth just to stay sane.

And speaking of music.

The commentators all tell us now that Bethany Sin is going to sing the national anthem.

How old-fashioned of her.

She steps to the front of the stage, where another podium waits, but she doesn't go there. She has a stylish headset on now, with a tiny mic shaped like a pink flower. Her trademark, the kid tells me. Sidney Jaeger introduces her to a thunder of applause, and she tells the big screen thanks, it's a pleasure to be here, and she asks the assembled crowd of reporters and news media and roped off fans how the heck they're all doing this evening. A lot of cheering comes back. A few people hold up signs that say things like WE LOVE YOU, BETHANY! I see another sign near the stage that says MAXIMUM BOB IS THE MAN! and I'm reminded in an oddly matter-of-fact way that she's not the only rock star up there. Doesn't seem to bother her.

Bethany carries the tune herself, with no musical backup.

Traditional pop diva approach.

But she kills it in a way I don't expect at all.

Her voice is simple and beautiful—no curly-whirly R & B parlor tricks or flashy embellishment. She's just damn good, and soulful too. Hits it in all the right spots, brings the song to a final, sustained high note that floats out over the room like some beautiful bird with black feathers. It's over before I even realize how moved I am, and the crowd is cheering for her again.

She throws them kisses with both hands.

Senator Maxton steps forward and takes her hand manfully, throwing it into the air above their heads.

It's a photo op, but not entirely rehearsed, and you can see her sincerity.

His smile is less genuine, but everyone eats it with extra sauce.

They move to the rear of the stage as Jaeger's face fills the screen again:

"Ladies and gentlemen... I've had a dream for many years. A dream I've invited all of America to share with me."

The dog and pony show is over quickly, and it's time for the big game.

CNN shows us highlights from Jaeger's press conference, all intercut with the live event, as the VIPs get in the elevator one group at a time and ascend to the platform.

Carolyn Lewis is in the first group, making a few cracks about joining the party. She says it's time to get the heck out of Los Angeles. It's a little too hot here for her.

"Okay, Buck," Tom says with a deep sigh, looking at his watch. "Let's hit it."

"The President abides," says the kid, settling into his station.

I make sure the earbud is secure.

A knock on the door.

Six thirty on the nose.

Tom unlocks the door and Agent Jacques escorts us forward through the VIP corridor and into the main casino lounge, making a couple of bad jokes about the fashion victims we're riding with. I was right about this guy the first time: He has issues so thick I can hardly read them through the fog. Rich parents, college rape, groomed for greatness but fallen from grace—all with a dumb smile on his gorgeous face. He leaves us in the casino and heads back into the VIP corridor, his slime trailing behind him.

The place is half full.

Stars and their hangers-on, and agents watching over them, two in this room, the Ben and Jerry twins. It's like a party with security guards.

The movie guys are already shooting craps.

Bethany Sin gives an interview to someone with glasses, who writes down everything she says on a little white notebook pad, then moves to the next celebrity. When he's finished circling the room, Ben or Jerry escorts him out.

I move past the diva, toward the entranceway to the forward passenger deck, and I try to read her but it doesn't work. Too many other voices. She looks me over and smiles, but I only catch a tiny shot of it.

Interesting.

Tom stays in the lounge as I move ahead, just like we planned. Covering perimeter. His hands are still shaking. He's armed, too. Had to clear his pistol with Dryden's men. They made some noise but he has a permit for it. Me, I've never fired a gun in my life. I keep thinking maybe I should learn.

I keep thinking about the rusted antique in my satchel.

I *know* it will only fire in the Blacklight, or in the hands of a Walker.

And Darby ain't coming anywhere near this place.

I can feel it vibrating inside the satchel.

Sending me signals.

Carolyn Lewis was first on the train and she talks to each guest as they enter through the viewing deck, or at least she tries to. A camera guy immortalizes the whole thing on video, short and invisible—not too good-looking, not too nerdy, neutral blue suit. His camera is one of those digital jobs, small and compact. Carolyn wears her typical on-air outfit: silver blazer with beige tank top, low-cut to show off what she has up front, matching skirt with long black stockings. The clothes are sexy without being threatening—she could be the hottest high school principal in human history, but everyone knows better than to undress her with their eyes.

The oil billionaire and his Middle Eastern guest are next on board. Carolyn stops them for a comment and they politely engage her, sidestepping all the important issues like professionals. I size them up as exactly what they are, staying invisible along the forward wall, near the walkway to the engineer's compartment. Pappas has a Deep South accent thicker than chicken-fried steak in cream gravy, and he drops names and hundred-dollar bills on the serving trays of attendants, who circle the room with snacks and drinks. There's three of them, all beautiful ladies. It makes Derek Pappas happy to stuff money into the cleavage of a beautiful lady, especially when she's bringing out straight whiskey shooters. They smile at him dutifully.

My earbud crackles. Tom. *"How's it going up there?"*

"It's going."

"Stay sharp. Maximum Bob just got in the lift, he's coming your way."

"I want to meet him."

"Good fucking luck."

I can feel Bob Maxton step onto the platform outside even though I can't see him. That's because every living soul out there feels the whole universe alter when he appears. It creates a shockwave that rolls back like thunder and almost knocks me down. I'm still reeling from it when he steps into the observation deck.

He's tall, the way Jaeger was tall.

More than six foot.

Handsome and dark, even more so than he was on the tube.

I recover from the shockwave and I'm checking him out carefully as he speaks. Carolyn Lewis introduces herself and he says he's delighted to meet her. I can tell she doesn't believe him. He can tell, too, but he's a politician and doesn't speak the truth in plain words. He says they'll do an in-depth interview once we get to Nevada—he can't wait to tell Carolyn all about his new election platform. It's going to be a real exclusive, he tells her. A wingdinger.

Actually uses that word.

Seems kind of dated for such a hip guy.

Maybe it's irony.

Agent Dryden is never less than ten feet behind the senator. The three blacksuits in the compartment tense with every step they take. I can feel it in the room like cords of steel snapping back, then springing forward again. Serpents tensing, then almost striking.

I walk toward the senator with my hand extended.

He sees me and smiles on auto-pilot.

Dryden stops him before he can touch me.

He does it really smooth, blocking the senator politely, but he keeps his gaze on me the whole time he talks. "Senator Maxton, I'd like you to meet our special consultant, Buck Carlsbad."

"Oh, yes. Sidney's told me some about you. I hear you're a ghost hunter *par excellence.*"

"I always try."

"There are those who don't believe in such phenomena, but I must say that I find it all very fascinating. We'll have to find time to chat about it."

"Fine by me."

"And please let me know if any *scary business* rears its ugly head, Mr. Carlsbad. I would hate to miss it."

He smiles and moves on, then takes a seat at the window.

Roosevelt's voice crackles in my ear. *"That was awesome."*

"Oh, shut up."

"No, I'm serious. I was shitting my pants. How do you read him, Buck?"

"I don't. He's got a steel wall around him. Everyone else is real excited, though."

"My fuckin' hero."

Lauren Chance boards the train. She is professional and sleek, watching everything silently from behind mirrored shades.

A soft female voice comes over the speakers, telling everyone to please have a seat in the main observation compartments as we prepare for departure. I'm reminded of the movie *Aliens*.

Tom's voice, right in my ear: *"Kid, I'm headed back to base camp. You gonna stay in the forward observation deck?"*

"For now."

Roosevelt's voice: *"Copy that. We're all good in the hood so far. Nothing on spectral but the standard operational bullshit."*

"Let's get a head count," I say, scanning the room.

"Check. Stand by."

I take my seat at the window as he counts off the passengers one last time.

Twenty-four guests—the celebs and their hangers-on.

Seven staff members.

Five cops.

One security guard.

And us.

Forty people in total on this train.

That's just less than half capacity.

More than enough to worry me.

The crowd of reporters and news guys hover on the platform outside, hundreds more below us in the giant Lost Angels Plaza.

A rumbling of low thunder beneath my feet.

The doorway slides shut, sealing with a hiss just feet away from me.

The cabin pressurizes in that instant, and I realize with a bottomless finality that there's no going back now.

No going back at all.

The sun is all the way down now.

The thunder consumes me, as the night train begins to move.

I close my eyes, and I can almost see Darby Jones waving good-bye.

Good luck, man, he seems to say in the gathering dark.

You're gonna need it.

ELEVEN

THIRD EYE SIN

7:00
Two hours and fifteen minutes on the clock.

Two hours and fifteen minutes to Vegas.

The city of Los Angeles is a multicolored neon hallucination on all sides of us, a dazzling tracery of all good things that must end, moving fast in streaks and bursts and flickers, like the many lives I've seen on fast forward. They all ended too, those lives.

We rumble over the damaged skin of the city, seeing only the lights.

Above us, the full moon.

"You should see the view from here," I say to the boys.

Roosevelt crackles back: *"That's what I get for riding in the rear with the gear."*

"Anything on your screens?"

"You'll be the first to know."

"Tom?"

"I'm in the bathroom, man. *Gimme a break.*"

Roosevelt has a look at one of his cameras and comes back: *"Has your dick always been that little, Tom, or is it just cold in there?"*

"Fuck off."

In the seat behind me, Carolyn Lewis leans in toward Maximum Bob and aims her mic. "Senator, this is a truly historic moment. Would you like to be immortalized?"

"By all means, Carolyn."

"What are your thoughts on departing the great city of Los Angeles?"

"It's thrilling, of course. I love everything that this city represents historically and culturally, mind you, but look at this *view*. It's spectacular. I'm looking forward to hearing what everyone in America has to say about it."

"I'm sure America would love to hear a bit more about how Jaeger Industries plans to coordinate this inaugural ride with your campaign platforms. I understand the rally is already under way in Vegas."

"You'll have to wait for my speech, Carolyn. I promise you will not be disappointed."

She narrows her eyes.

Then goes for it.

"You've always been one for firsts in politics—how about an exclusive on the proposed amendment to the health-care reform act? It was your strongest debate topic last year, but now there seems to be very little talk about it."

He smiles under the ambush, gives her one chance to back off:

"I wasn't prepared to answer that."

She doesn't flinch.

"Are you telling us you have no comment on the issue or that the issue is moot?"

Bob keeps smiling.

"May I ask *you* a question, Carolyn?"

"Umm...why not?"

"What is your fondest wish for America?"

She smiles with wide eyes, like *Are you fucking kidding me?* Then, slowly:

"I suppose I'd wish for...peace?"

"Exactly, Carolyn. We must all *understand* one another—and that requires connection. The train we're sitting on now is the first *and* second step. I have a message for your viewers, and that message is very simple: The political parties as we know them now must change so that this connection may happen. We must not allow ourselves to be afraid of difficult questions or fooled by antiquated concepts. We will move *forward,* not in *reverse,* and also at a great speed. I promise you, under my presidency, this will happen."

She's still looking like someone suckerpunched her when he smiles again and stands up, shaking her hand.

"I'm *so glad* we had this chance to dialogue, Carolyn. We'll continue our discussion in just a bit. Please enjoy the view."

Damn.

Not sure I've ever heard one man say so little with so many words.

He's a wicked creation, this guy. Not such a nice fella after all. That's the name of the game, but his angle is to make it seem like he's changing the rules. Moving forward in reverse. Other guys have tried it, but he's better and faster. State of the art.

Carolyn Lewis watches him enter the casino lounge, wondering what hit her.

Dryden is five feet behind the senator at all times.

Carolyn shrugs when she sees me looking at her, giving an odd little grin to no one in particular that says *What are ya gonna do?* Then she turns and gets in a huddle with her cameraman, pulling out her smart phone and dialing. Strategy time.

I turn my attention back to the streaking city as we slowly wind through and begin to leave it behind, making a break for the desert. The landing wheels rumble below us. We're still not flying yet. Any minute now.

Roosevelt, in my ear: *"Maxton just went straight to his private VIP room. Whatever Carolyn Lewis said to him, it must have been a real wingdinger."*

"He beat the shit out of her without breaking a sweat."

"That's why they call him Maximum, man."

"He doesn't scare me."

"Careful, Buck. You don't wanna mess with that guy."

A few feet away from me, Ben and Jerry are watching me talk to thin air, getting orders on their Bluetooths. Bad noise, I can tell.

I keep one ear on it for a moment.

Then they turn and leave us, moving into the casino.

The kid's voice comes back: *"They're making a sweep now. Jacques and Kendall headed back your way."*

"Check. I'll be a minute."

I watch the city rumble by, allowing myself a moment of peace.

Carolyn starts arguing with her producer, yelling into the phone.

Guess she's not such a nice fella, either.

I let it drift for a moment.

My reflection hovers in front of me like some odd work of art, a visual poem vanishing one streak at a time on the other side of the glass, lulling me into a place between the world of the living and the shadow speedways of the dead.

7:08

I close my eyes and feel them moving through me.

All of them now, moving faster.

Wanting desperately to be liberated from this place of lost marks.

Fallen angels watching and waiting, jealous because we are free and they are not.

I glide along with them on hundreds of separate trajectories, and I hover on the edge of consciousness, just for a moment.

I shouldn't stay here...but it's so peaceful.

I will open my eyes in just a moment.

Just one moment.

Back in the world, there are people bickering. I must protect them because they can't see as I do. I must return to them.

But it's so peaceful here.

Just one moment...

It hits me a thousand feet down.

Something that spook-dances over my entire being, like a shadow creeping across a dirty ceiling in a dark room, turning into a wall of concussive force, moving forward like the overpressure wave of a nuke blowing inside a city, flattening everything in its path. Something that transforms into a terrifying pulse-tone as it slams into my body, absorbing along every molecule in my mind, doing a mad dance deep in my breast, threatening to shake my atoms apart. Something inside the dream, calling me an idiot and telling me to wake the fuck up. All around me, the moans and cries of the Walkers in the Black-light, and the strong fingers of something that might be a taste of death jabbing me somewhere deep and private.

Darby slaps my face and tells me to wake up.

Something so close to me and yet a million miles away.

Screaming.

Laughing.

LAUGHING…

"Wake up, you dumb motherfucker! WAKE UP NOW!"

7:10

I glide back, not with a jolt, but with a cold sour burst, like rotten air swirling in my throat. The hum follows me across.

Something happened.

I can feel it from the dream.

I've never brought anything back from a dream before…but *now*…

"Kid, are you there?"

Roosevelt, loud and clear: *"Whatzzup, boss?"*

"Did you get anything just now? Something should have pegged your console."

"Nothing."

"Are you sure?"

"You're just feeling the burn, man. They engaged the maglev engines a couple miles back."

"Where are we?"

"We're on the straightaway, right on schedule. Doing about ninety, according to my screen. They just made an announcement they're gonna go for the phase one speed record in about forty-five minutes. We'll be hitting the Triangle in about twenty. You okay, boss?"

"I nodded off a few minutes. It hit me pretty hard, while I was under. Are you sure you don't see *anything*?"

"I'm telling you, my man, we're clean."

"Shit."

"You wanna come back and have a look for yourself?"

"I'll be a minute."

"Copy that."

I look up and an image of intense beauty shimmers before me, smiling with a mouth full of silver. Something sinful, reflected in the glass, superimposed over the speeding desert.

"You're Buck, right?"

I turn to face her, getting up from my seat.

Her eyes are like crystal spheres and they blow me away, this close.

"I'm Bethany."

"Yeah, I know."

"I know you know."

And the wicked smile she gives me is like a nasty cat cornering her favorite mouse in a dark alley.

"Buy a girl a drink?"

7:13

"Holy shit, Buck, did I hear what I thought I just heard?"

"Shut up, man."

She knits up her nose, shooting me sneaky eyes. "Excuse me?"

"Umm...sorry." I point at the earbud. "Comments from the peanut gallery."

"A *Howdy Doody* reference. Nice."

"You're a little young for *Howdy Doody,* aren't you?"

"I never trust anybody under thirty." She holds out her hand, offering herself modestly. "So...how about we drink to *Howdy Doody?*"

I almost don't want to touch her, but I do anyway.

And I was right.

She has the Gift.

It's at a low lull inside her, diluted by years of drinking and too many pills—I can tell Vicodin is her favorite, and Ecstasy, too—but it's there. Pacing like a doped-up tiger, caged down deep. She started medicating when she was seventeen to silence the voices, kept enough of herself to move people with her singing. She's been trading off her Gift for years now, it's made her a millionaire. She's twenty-seven and really doesn't trust anyone under thirty. That part was true. I get the history lesson of her life in three seconds and she gladly gives it up, even though she probably has no idea how honest she's being with me.

"That was *awesome,* Buck! It's been years since I got a real palm reading like that! It gets me all giddy!"

Or maybe she does.

I let go of her hand and she grabs it again, yanking me toward the door.

"What did you *see,* Buck?"

"I usually see everything."

"Then you know I'm an orphan, like you."

"How did you know I was an orphan?"

"I saw you on TV, silly."

"Oh. Yeah."

"I was on *Celebrity Ghost Stories* last year, but that was lame. They didn't have any real psychics on that show."

"I didn't see the episode. I'm...a little embarrassed to say but I never heard of you before the other day."

"*Awesome!* My music sucks anyway."

"Good for you."

She eyes my satchel with a rogue smile. "So what's in your bag of tricks?"

"Stick around, you might find out."

"A girl can only hope!"

We move into the casino lounge, and here's Roosevelt again: *"She's coming onto you like a megaforce, dude! Way to fuckin' ROCK!"*

Yeah, she is, ain't she?

Funny, that.

She follows me around for a while, and we talk a lot while I trade shifts with Tom, walking perimeter from one end of the train to the other. A faceless cook works his practiced culinary magic in the restaurant, rattling spatulas and slinging the hash.

Bethany rolls her eyes and makes jokes about the food.

Says she had McDonald's on the way over.

She is an animated pixie, full of life—I can see her in a Disney cartoon, easy. I keep expecting her to lose interest in me as I stay on the move, keeping watch on the observation windows, and the desert unfolding on all sides of us, checking for landmarks in the moonlight, comparing it all to the images burned forever into my memory—the map in my mind. She sees and feels my gears working, knows I'm not focused on her at all, and it's a challenge. She keeps insisting that I have a drink with her. The Homeland Security guys do their shifts, shadows passing us in the corridors and compartments. Bethany says they're like zombies. I smile and agree with her.

7: 20

The casino is in full swing now.

Dinner's been served and playtime's begun.

We're near the Triangle.

I can feel it coming closer.

Most of the celebs and their guests party all over the room, spilling from the restaurant like high school kids playing dress-up in rich people's clothes. Carolyn Lewis sits at the bar with Junk-E, and he talks to her seriously about his film career, letting her know all about the humor of *Black Bart* and how it will break through the stereotypes and tell the truth about the dividing lines between races. He lays it down with authority. She wrinkles her nose and blinks a lot, like she has no idea what he's talking about, but he's not really paying attention to her. He's playing for the camera. The oil millionaire and the sultan are still in the dining car, that's what the kid tells me.

The maximum senator works the slot machines, joking with Agent Jacques and Agent Dryden. Bethany Sin's three-girl posse eye him girlishly from across the room. Do I sense a scandal in the making? Probably just another photo op for him.

My mind swims against the increasing speed of the train and I have to concentrate hard to keep myself focused. Like standing against the roll of some miracle drug's first rush with your heart peeled wide open. Bethany leans over a Bloody Mary, aiming her words at me like lasers, her eyes full of stars. I can't look in her eyes for long. Too much information.

"You're very handsome, Buck."

"Thank you."

"You kind of look like William Peterson. Anyone ever tell you that?"

"Nope."

"Liar."

Lauren walks back through the casino and sees me sitting with Sin at the bar. I wave back at her with a thin smile.

Bethany doesn't let it go. Jacks up her eyes. "Friend of yours?"

"Just met her, really."

"But you get to know people fast, don't you, Buck?"

"That's true. Sometimes."

"When I was a little girl, I had the same problem. I'd tell people things they never even knew about themselves. Now, I do it with music. Something like that anyway."

"I thought your music sucked?"

"Well...*some* of it does." She giggles like a cartoon again. "The last album, it was super trendy, all trip-hoppy and shit. You gotta do that for the label. The last single was more rock and roll. I'd like to be like Gwen—she's one of my heroes."

"Gwen Stefani?"

"Yeah, her early stuff really rocks. I met her once and she was mean to me. I was just starting out then."

"You're very young to be so successful."

"That's how it works, right? Young and hot and full of marginal talent equals big paychecks for everyone around you?"

She tosses a sideways glance at her crew: girls gone wild on the blackjack table, doing a lot of yelling at the dealer, still eyeing Maximum Bob. There's three of them, color coded by flashy hair in red, yellow, and purple. The purple one has a face full of freckles and glitter, a neo-hippie thing going with a silver paisley dress. The blonde wears stylish spandex stripes over enormous talents, like a groupie at an eighties metal show. The redhead is sassy in black, her hair falling straight down her back like a sexy ribbon, almost touching her butt, which is exposed like a cherry apple through skintight leotard pants. They look like time-warped teenagers waving cash at everybody, shrill voices bubbling over like the pricey glasses of champagne in their hands.

"They're my best friends," she says, a little too seriously. "Who knew we would all end up here? Gotta take care of your friends, right?"

"You're a very kind woman."

"I got excited when they told me you were going to be on this trip. I actually wanted to meet you a long time ago when I saw your show on TV, but you know how things get."

"I'm sure I don't have your problems."

"I could tell you were the real thing."

"So are you."

"There's not a lot of people who know that, Buck. I had to hide it from almost everyone, even them." She jerks a thumb toward her multicolored best friends. "It's good to be in the company of people who truly understand you. Doing what I do can be really lonely if you don't have a sense of humor."

"Guess so."

"I sense a lot of loneliness in you, Buck."

"What's wrong with loneliness?"

"It can kill you."

"I'm not dead yet."

"Then you must have a good sense of humor."

She pulls both feet together, sitting in a lotus position on the bar stool, giggling like a dark fairy in golden shoes. Pins me with her stare, and I don't look away this time.

"You have to pay attention with your third eye," she says. "It can show you things, special things. I've let it guide my professional life on more than one occasion."

That explains a lot.

Her career directed by vibrations, the same way a lot of Gifted people use it to bring themselves to moments like this. Maybe she heard the whispers the same way I did. Maybe she can feel the Pull.

She senses what I'm thinking, though she can't read it all. "My manager didn't want me to do this gig. He said it was beneath me after the Grammy and all. But my third eye didn't blink, you know? So here we are."

She looks deep in me, and smiles.

"You're wearing contact lenses, Buck. They hide the color of your eyes."

"They hide more than that."

"I don't doubt it."

Something sad coming at me now. Something lost, boiling deep within her. This ain't what I expected from Bethany Sin at all. I'm pretty sure she hears me think that, because the next thing she says is this:

"I like your Walkman. It's cool."

"I'm a fossil."

"I like fossils."

She slides her hand across the bar, her finger pushing the sleeve of my coat back a little. Sees my scars and smiles sadly.

"We have a lot in common, Buck."

"Do we?"

"Yes."

Her third eye, full of hopeful sin.

"Could we go somewhere a little more private, Buck?"

The soft female voice on the loudspeaker comes again, telling everyone that the magnetic drive engines have been engaged since we left the city and we are now officially the first American bullet train in history to *fly* on a long-distance trip.

Bethany smiles and closes her eyes, allowing her body to feel it.

The voice tells us we're going to reach record speed in just over an hour.

Everyone in the casino cheers.

I feel their drunken happiness shock through me in a slurred instant, and then it's Bethany, filling my head.

"Can you *feel* that, honey? It's *exhilarating*. Like a million whispers moving through you on a lonely road. I used to feel like this in airplanes. Like my own soul was traveling behind me, desperate to catch up with my body. Wrote a song about it once."

"Some people think mediums lose their souls completely when they travel fast."

"This is *amazing,* Buck. I've never felt anything like this."

"You should be careful. You could overdose."

"Can't you feel it?"

"Yes. It's . . . interesting."

And there's something else, too.

Something that hums along the magnetized outer hull of the train and creeps like microscopic insects in my bones, synchronized with the fast moving earth on all sides of us. It's almost like *music* . . . getting louder . . . and I can tell she senses it also, just outside her immediate pleasure. Nobody else notices.

It's the Triangle.

Coming up on us fast.

A place full of bad things.

I have to be ready for it.

She smiles at me like a flower child in an acid trance.

"Come on, Buck. I want to be alone with you."

She moves her hand close to me again, stroking my little finger. I get up and smile at her, letting out a long sigh.

"I'm on the clock."

She gets up and licks the air, staring me right into my soul. "So am I. My VIP room's number seven. Ten minutes and I come looking for you."

She trots away with orange silk trailing in a shimmer at her feet. Looks back at me once and winks, then vanishes into the next car. Reminded me of a sorority sister just then. Someone used to getting what she wants. Still, I'm intrigued by her. Something floats in the air where she left me, the glowing remains of a million lives maybe, inspired souls, all inspired by her.

Christ, Buck.

A rock star.

"Dude, if you don't hit that shit, I'm gonna hit you in the face."

"Shut up, kid."

"I'm serious, Buck. What the fuck are you waiting for?"

"Keep your eyes on your goddamn screen. We're coming up on the Triangle."

"Whatever, man. There's nothing out here. We would have picked something up by now."

"Just keep your eyes open, dammit."

I move across the casino floor slowly, following in her footsteps. The smell of her hangs in space, fighting the insanity of a million other lives, the floor under my feet still humming with mysterious frequencies, the world outside moving faster now.

Faster still.

My legs slow down against the forward momentum of the train, the low hum encasing my heart, the rumble of alternate dimensions anxious at the back of my neck. I ask the kid if he's seeing anything, and he says there's still nothing. I ask him if he can feel what I feel—the intensity of the train itself—and he says hell yeah. But nothing on spectral. Just one hell of a fast machine we're riding on. I wonder for a moment if the quick ride and the magnetic fields could hide something from us or our machines, if we're not seeing as we should. What was I really feeling in the slipstream? What really hit me back there? The thought chills my blood, and I get out Roosevelt's smart phone, toggling the Facebook app to Darby's page:

STAY AWAKE. FAST MOVES HAPPENING.

Shit.

The faster we go, the louder the hum gets.

I move in a waking dream, sliding through the air of the pressurized compartment in slow motion. Traveling at this weird frequency, the thoughts of every person in the lounge now come crystal clear, like an untangled multi-symphonic code.

They're all drunk.

They're all possessed by their own demons and their own distractions.

They have no idea how close we all are to the edge of everything.

How honest they're being with all their deepest secrets.

Francis Crowe masks irrational contempt from everyone in this room, his thoughts drifting in semi-paranoia, wondering how much they all know and hating himself for being different. I notice for the first time that he has very long, very stylish fingernails—they're painted silver, one with a diamond stud run through it. Turns out he's not just gay, but *very gay,* and he's in love with three men at the moment, one of them his partner, who burns across the craps table next to him with all-male bravado on overdrive.

Jerry Donaldson knows all about his partner's crush on him, and he doesn't care. His boy has helped them both to become filthy rich, and Hollywood is full of perverts. In the heat of the moment before him, there is no past or future, just the gamble. That's what makes him a high-stakes shark in the cutthroat world of movie-making, which is mostly deal-making—a game he was born to play, with an ace in his shoe. He's fighting the urge to drink too much, his mind bouncing back against thoughts of the seven rehab clinics he's been tortured in, but he has to have at least *one more cocktail.* You know, to take the edge off.

Bethany's ladies all play roulette and jingle ice, laughing a lot.

Senator Maxton begins to drift toward them, slinking his way along the row of slot machines, looking very practiced in his big move.

No surprises there.

Carolyn Lewis listens to Junk-E's dumb-sounding voice, trying to fig-ure out how much education he has, wondering if street-smarts would have helped her any more than they've helped him to become powerful. She comes at the paradigm with humor and bemusement, allowing herself to have fun with it, rather than putting the experience down to numbers and graphs and charts, or even looking down on Junk-E because she's an academic and he sure as hell ain't. I wouldn't have thought that of her.

A lot of intriguing women on this ride.

Junk-E is *exactly* what you expect. He's very smart and tough on top. Thinks of money and managers and box office grosses. He freestyles new lyrics and tough witticisms inside his head, even as he jabbers on and on with his tongue about changing the world, most of it rehearsed earlier to-day in front of a mirror. He'll be doing a press junket for *Black Bart* in a few weeks and he wants to be on top of his game. Tells himself he could eat Carolyn Lewis in one bite and busts a rhyme in his head about it, way back there behind something he says out loud—something about working with Angelina Jolie, who was hired for twenty million to cameo in his film. She's playing the part originated by Madeline Kahn in *Blazing Saddles*. That should be darn interesting.

"Triangle coming up now, Buck."

"Check."

I walk out of there, leaving the pretzel highway of confused agendas behind me.

7:35

I walk into the next passenger deck, and stand in the center of the room, the giant observation windows on both sides of me, showing the endless roll of twilight desert. It comes ahead at incredible speed, like a sliding of molten metal through my mind. I see myself in this desert, long ago. I feel my death as it almost was, so close to me, the trace of it hovering out there somewhere, flowing... *coming faster and faster...*

And we hit the Triangle.

It blows over me and through me like thunder.

My ears pop under the hammer.

I hear someone laughing.

Flashes past my ears like phantoms.

I tense for a heartbeat, all the muscles in my neck popping and freezing.

I bring the Pull to the surface of my skin, scanning.

Nothing comes back to me at first... *but then...*

The world *shorts out* just a fraction of a second. And in the next second my feet are back on solid ground. It's like someone cut my personal film loop and let me drift in the splice for one long, elastic moment—a quick dip to black, quickly consumed by the slo-mo on all sides of me. I stand in the center of it, a few scattered people chattering left and right, the desert outside shooting past the windows like some weird half-remembered dream on fast-forward.

Son of a bitch.

I felt this way before.

Exactly this way.

In the moment I thought I could feel my parents, out there.

Before I can even say anything about it, the kid's voice crackles:

"Buck? You'd better get back here."

TWELVE

REAL ROCK AND ROLL

7:40
    He clicks the monitor to full screen and shuffles through the views quickly, showing five angles on the casino, stopping on camera sixteen. Hits a command and plays back something from a few minutes ago.

"Here, Buck. It pegged the spectral for just a second, and then it was gone."

"I think I felt it on the observation deck. What about you?"

"Didn't feel a thing. But you know better than me."

"What did you record?"

"I can't tell. It's at a really low frequency, whatever it is."

He freezes the wide image of the casino as something superimposes itself there. Something that looks like a dark red smudge on the lens, caught in layers of feedback static. It's just one or two frames, doesn't look like much of anything.

"Hold it there," I tell him, and I concentrate hard on the frozen image.

Part of a face there, hardly visible.

But I can see it.

A shadowy outline.

"Kid, you called it."

"Think it's still hanging around?"

"Whatever it was, I think I felt it move *through me* back there, like maybe it was sweeping the train. And there was something else earlier. Can't remember."

"Might be *anything*, Buck. We're inside the Triangle now. A latent projection, something floating around out there. Maybe a memory trace from one of the people on the train..."

"I don't think so."

"Look, man, all I'm saying is that two frames ain't much."

"Maybe the train is *cloaking* it."

"What?"

"The magnetic field. It could be hiding whatever we're looking for."

"Or maybe it's just making us jumpy for no reason. I've never felt anything like this. Bethany Sin was right—it's like a drug."

Yeah.

A really bad drug.

He throws a faux-macho eye at me. "I still say you should hit that shit, Buck. She's waiting for you in her stateroom. Number *seven,* man."

He clicks the monitor to the cam in her room.

She's sitting in her fairy lotus position on the bed, smiling with her eyes closed.

She's half naked.

I almost smile.

7:45

Tom meets me in the casino, looking bloodshot and tired, his voice still shaky. "Nothing's happening in here. I think you guys are just catching glitches."

"I needed to see with my own eyes."

And he's right.

There's nothing.

If something *was* in here, it would have attacked one of these people by now. I'd see shadows crawling on the ceiling, hear whispers, anything. The Pull would be burning inside me to get out, hungry for fresh meat.

Unless...

"Okay, you're the boss," says Tom. "I'm heading back to the front observation deck. Scream if you want ice cream."

"If you hear screaming, get back here in a big hurry."

His bloodshot eyes do a jitter, and he blinks sweat out of them.

He's tense and getting tenser.

I'm sensing real danger around him now.

I keep an eye on him as he moves through the door. When he's gone, I still feel the tension in the space he left behind. It's thick like syrup. Can't think about that. Gotta scan the casino, concentrate hard. Look for what might be hiding in here.

My eyes roll across the room...

Derek Pappas is being interviewed by Carolyn Lewis and her cameraman now, the royal sultan patiently waiting his turn at the bar. They just sat down together, but Pappas is already having the time of his life. He rolls and roars with laughter. I can sense that Carolyn is biding her time, circling Maximum Bob like a shark, who hovers at ten o'clock in the room, talking with the girls gone wild.

Asking them what their fondest wish for America is, no doubt.

Agent Dryden hovers near the door, giving Maxton his breathing room. Two of his boys along the walls—Ben and Jerry. Lauren Chance sitting quietly at a table near the senator, talking to someone on her Bluetooth. Probably Sidney Jaeger. I don't bother to find out. She gets up and heads out the door, toward the front compartments.

Derek Pappas lays down the truth, one eye on the senator: "I'll tell you one thing, by God—this whole damn country's going to the dogs. Used to be a time when you bought a politician, that son of a bitch stayed *boss!*"

Carolyn wrinkles her nose and smiles. "How many politicians have you bought this year?"

"You wouldn't believe me if I told you, honey."

"Try me."

"Well, now, ain't you the sweet-talker?"

Rashid Hopi rolls his eyes. I put a line out to him and find that his thoughts are very boring. He doesn't like the food here either.

The world shifts again and the slo-mo hits me harder than before, my legs wobbling like rubber.

And...

I see her face.

Bethany Sin.

Screaming right in front of me.

Screaming my name.

The world blurs back into focus, and I move back toward the door that leads to the VIP corridor, filled with an urgent coldness, my legs still moving in slow motion.

Senator Maxton sees me and narrows his eyes, seducing the young and beautiful with one arm behind his back. He can see that I feel something. A real multitasker, this guy. I'm impressed.

It's hitting the train again, whatever it is, more intense now.

Something penetrating the magnetic field and making weird stuff happen.

Stuff I can't see at all.

I feel a hundred voices at once now, as I step into the VIP corridor.

Bethany Sin, calling me from number seven.

Have to get to her.

Now.

7:47

The door is unlocked and I move through it quickly. She waits for me on the bed with a smile, licking her bottom lip impishly.

"Got my message, huh?"

"You were screaming."

"Only in your *head,* Buck. Had to get your attention."

That's an understatement.

She's dressed only in white athletic socks and a blue tank top. No panties, no G-string. The only thing separating me from her womanhood are crossed legs and false modesty. She aims her chest forward, showing me perfection that money can't buy. The smile that crawls across her face grabs me and doesn't let go.

Christ.

More rock-star games.

"Bethany, this isn't funny. I thought you were in trouble."

"I *am* trouble, Buck. Haven't you heard?"

She glides over to me before I can move away from her. Her hands are like quick wisps of silk against my jacket lapels, her face stunning in slow motion. My voice hardly finds its way out:

"There's something happening...on this *train*..."

"Sure is, honey."

I am breathless now, looking right in her eyes.

I hear the kid's voice somewhere way down low.

"Way to rock, Bucko! That's my man!"

She hears his voice and smiles.

"Your friend is funny. Shall we give him a show he won't forget?"

She nods at the camera hidden on the ceiling, licking her lips again. She knows it's there and it turns her on. Most divas like her would be pissed—they'd worry about ending up on YouTube. Not her. She's real rock and roll.

Licks her lips again.

Then her lips move fast for mine.

Her tongue slides in quickly, passionately. She really means it. The world tumbles around us, voices and memories and traces of old lives whirling in a waking dream, and the shockwave jets over my whole body, my soul sighing, and I hear her voice inside my head, telling me she wants me, telling me she's never kissed anyone with her Gift, that she's searched her whole life for a moment like this, firecrackers exploding inside my chest—sharp memories, passionate emotions, things that don't belong to me, *things she wants me to see.* And I see her as a child, lonely and screaming for attention. And I see her as an adult, getting away with tantrums and unhappy with it. And I feel her wriggling velvet fingers deep into my brain, and I am seduced, going down with her...

Deeper now.

Deeper than I've ever gone with a woman.

Buck, this is what it is to be with someone who understands you.

Love me.

I'm only vaguely aware of her lips against mine now, and I want nothing but this moment, way down in the most secret place, beyond everything made of skin and bone and sex. And we hold each other there, her eyes in the center of it all, glowing blue diamonds calling me to pleasure, and I can't look away from them... but I *have* to look away... this is too fucking intense...

Love me, Buck.

We hover here together for a very long time—it seems like hours.

Then the wave hits.

Explodes in my face, as I struggle back to my body for just a second.

All the hairs on my arms stand up.

Something tingles deep down, but not the way it was a second earlier.

A shriek of heat pounds my heart.

"Buck? Ummm... I think we've got a problem..."

The kid's voice crackles over my earbud, but I almost don't hear it. Her eyes are going black now, something cold coming straight at me, the thundering sonic boom of a bad heartbeat clobbering my skull from out of nowhere.

And a voice explodes in my head, not Bethany's at all.

Something real nasty.

Something real familiar.

The shriek of a dying animal run through a feedback loop.

She comes at me with an awful smile... and I see the monster underneath her skin, hissing like a snake.

"Buck! Get the hell away from her! She's..."

I brace myself and take the attack at point blank range. She slams into me, body and mind, knocking the wind out of my lungs. I stumble against the wall, my ears still ringing with the voice. I have a fast impression of something like slithering quicksilver rolling at me, and the ripple of it pins me there for just a second as she attacks again. My legs bounce me back on instinct. My shoulder angles into her face, her nose popping like a tomato. Blood bursts out, and she sucks it up between gritted teeth, the monster snarling just on the other side of her eyes in a bizarre amorphous outline, not allowing her to feel the pain. Her arms are blurred ivory clubs made of sexy muscle and flesh, swinging at me with metalstorm force, snarling curses sizzling over my head as I duck down and come up on the other side of her in a low crouch, taking her wrist and hitting the nerve cluster there, so that her fist pops open and I grab it, yanking hard. *Damn sorry about this, Beth...*

Her little finger breaks, sending the spike into her brain.

Whatever's in her screams and lets go.

And the monster spews into the air, torn loose and hovering.

Its madness materializes like a sizzling acid cloud forming and re-forming in bright red busts of free-floating mercury, coming in for a spitting serpent strike—a glowing, misshapen anti-creature, whipping and coiling in wild ribbons of teeth and tongue and spittle that slobber through space, slashing with near-invisible thorns, a crimson blur of unsettled madness shooting through its rolling, rippling, changing spectral form.

The red insanity.

The Terrible Thing that keeps its spirit trapped, pouring over everything else it possesses—the cancer that makes it a monster.

I make a grab for it and it *burns,* like it always does.

The Pull vibrates through my fingers, searing us both.

Its scream blows through the compartment and hits the panoramic window like an armload of bowling balls, but the safety glass holds. The mirrors blow. The light fixtures explode. Everything gets real dark, real fast, and I feel fragments of loose diamond dust tingle past my skin as the thing gets loose from my grip, thrashing. It bounces off the wall and comes back through the room in a strobeflash, making a savage move for my eyes—it's coming on like hell now, knows when to fight dirty. Its attack is so obvious, I see it in slow motion, traced in burning camera flickers through the dark.

My hand reaches for the satchel and I pull the Lysol canister.

Whip it right into the thing's murky substance and hit the spray.

Its scream shocks through my head like a pissed-off nightmare.

The chemical compound fans out and blisters into the mark's psychoplasmic flesh and it recoils, screaming a little more.

And I focus the Pull.

Weakened, it can't resist now.

The crushing gravity of my attack blooms from my body and sucks it toward me.

This time I get a good grip on the thing, grounding myself against its thrash. It forms part of itself into a double-pronged ice blade, makes another jab for my eyes and I spray it again with one hand. The Lysol cloud rips it a new asshole, disintegrating the improvised weapon.

And it screams again, fighting the Pull.

I bear down with both hands clenched into my sides, dropping the canister.

And as the force in my body finally begins to reel in the shrieking vapor on all sides of me... *I can feel its mind.* But it's coming in weird, garbled, like some strange radio signal beamed from an alien world. In this moment, I usually see everything—the entire life of the mark, when it was still alive. But I'm getting a real fight this time. I only get little pieces. Shards, and then less than shards. Like a glass goblin bursting in my face, each jagged bit slashing at me without mercy.

But I'm better than you, asshole.

I'm going to win because I'm better than you.

The Pull oscillates in the room now, the mark going down finally with a final spasm that smashes against my electrified flesh. And it explodes, absorbing, everything it ever was *whirlpooling deep into me...*

But I don't feel its life history.

I don't get all the details in three seconds.

It rushes in like a feral superflow—animal instinct, primal lust. I went through this once before, when I drank a mark that had been reduced to muck, and now I feel it again, filled with strange flashbacks of shame and guilt, heeled by distorted almost-emotions trainwrecking against my heart.

It's something pre-digested and hotter than the surface of the sun.

Hitting me like the clumsy tree trunk attack of a savage caveman.

Smashing my mind and pummeling my body.

I lose control *just a moment...*

Darkness burns on all sides of me as the storm of the Blacklight kicks in, and I feel it exploding and shifting at damn-near four hundred miles per—it's intense this time, even worse than on the airplane—and I know I can't stay long, my body fighting for its life, struggling to remain in place, the speed of the train and the magnetic field like a pain amplifier on all sides of me. I can still see the outline of her VIP room, vague and glowing like a video diagram drawn in Scotchlite—it pulses and burns. The lenses hold, my eyes squinting down hard . . .

A second later, the Blacklight is gone.

It was only there an instant—didn't have to hurt myself.

I open my eyes and I see Bethany Sin on the floor in front of me, smoke rising from her skin.

The kid's voice in my ear: *"I got all kinds of visuals on the spectral, Bucko. Ain't no doubt about it this time."*

No shit, kid.

It's inside me now.

It let go of her hard—the train helped to shake it loose, but it's kicking my ass now. I sink to my knees. An invisible fist piledrives into me. Stabs of razor pain slash my mind. The overdriven boom-sizzle of the mark's unsettled madness absorbs like electrified seawater, going down . . . down *deep* . . .

And it's not going easy.

Get down there, you son of a bitch.

Go into me.

No.

It's fighting me hard.

I feel its living essence expand like a fist and land in every living cell of my body, burning months and months off my life in a flashfried instant, smoldering like napalm, swelling and then bursting again, spidercrawling my skin, like hot black blood pooling in my stomach, leeching my bones. It wants to possess me. It wants to take over my muscle reflexes and command my mind. I can't let it do that.

I clench my teeth and fight it off.

My whole body lights up, my hair streaking white, two more years going away from me as the mark plays pinball with my guts.

I convulse on my knees, trying to scream, trying to bring it up now...to bring it up and puke it out...but that doesn't work either. My gag reflex is nullified. And the mark is going the other way, going deeper now into my private places. Grabbing onto the flesh of my soul. Laughing the way animals laugh. It's not even *digesting*—that's why I can't bring it up. I push a wave of raw anger at the thing and it almost backs off, then it springs again, frying my nerves. I squeeze my eyes shut and see the mucky cancer of the monster dancing in terrible formless desperation on the back of my eyelids as I beat it back...

It roars and swirls inside me, staying right where it is.

Ain't going anywhere.

And something comes into my head now...something that feels like it could be a memory...*or...a dream...*

The gun roars.

The woman's voice, screaming.

The sun beats down on all of us, the desert scorching our skin.

This is the moment that changes everything.

A voice I've heard before:

Very clever, bitch...

What?

What the hell was that?

Roosevelt, in my ear: *"You okay, my man? What's happening?"*

My voice is like a wheezing furnace. "I can't get this son of a bitch in me to calm the fuck down."

"What's the game plan now?"

I don't answer him, gritting my teeth down on the mark.

Forcing it down.

DOWN, you son of a bitch.

It backs off, reluctantly.

Growling, frustrated.

Like an animal.

But it doesn't explode into fragments.

It doesn't become muck in my stomach.

And it won't leave me, either.

It's holding, just beneath my control, circling my biorhythms.

The speed of the train blurs me again, making me dizzy and sick.

This is agony.

I force myself to rise above it, using my deepest meditation techniques, imagining myself at sea, adrift, with calm peace on all side of me. It floods in and smothers the bad shit, but just for a moment. Then I will my heart to slow down, riding along the magnetic hum of the engine pulling us. I take it down... and *down*...

I open my eyes.

Get my bearings.

I crawl toward Bethany, a cloud of some deep dark nothingness hauling me along as I look at her. Her face twitches in catatonia, and an odd sadness kicks over me. It's the empty feeling that comes with knowing you've been lied to—as if I really could have found a kindred spirit in this magical diva. As if it wasn't all some strange game I can't fully understand yet. And the mark, lurking in my living biorhythms, wanting to possess me, swimming and circling. I keep it down but it's hard work.

Those latent images in my head.

Are they memories?

Is that what happened to the mark when it died?

Gunfire in the desert.

The sun beating down.

A voice I've heard before...

I concentrate hard and keep it at bay.

More urgent problems right now.

Bethany Sin lies on the floor in a passed-out heap.

"Tom, did you hear all that? Get in here now."

7:57

A little over an hour on the clock.

The shit's getting thick.

I pull Bethany into the bed and have a look at her. She's breathing, but busted up pretty bad from the fight. Broken nose, broken finger. Still out like a light, her eyeballs bouncing all over in the dark, dreaming about nothing. I'm catching my breath. The mark is still deep in me and still screaming in frustration, confusion. All without words, without humanity.

No more images from the past.

Just the screaming tantrums, animal distortion.

Tom hits the door and I sense his dick nerve spike the red when he sees Bethany. His voice is full of panic. The danger pushing on all sides of him now, hot and awful. "What happened to her? She looks beat up."

I squint back, feeling the thing inside me dance on my grave again.

"We've got a situation," I say in the calmest voice I'm able to cough up. "She was under the influence of something and I had to act."

The kid's voice crackles: *"It was a major mark. He's still got it in him."*

"There may be more on the train," I say. "The kid caught a trace just five minutes before she attacked me. About twenty minutes before that, something else pegged us but we got nothing on spectral. That means some of them are making more noise than others. We could be traveling along some kind of gravesite inside the Triangle."

"The gravesite of the Nine," Tom whispers low, trying to keep his heart under control. "Why now? Why tonight?"

"It targeted *me,*" I tell him. "It was using Bethany to get in close. And now that I've got it, I can feel..."

The mark growls again.

Tom moves closer. I can smell his sweat. His heart races. He's gonna lose his shit any minute now, I can feel it. "Feel what, kid?"

"It's been consumed once already. I'm holding *mulched remains* from a sealed grave, just like before. They're getting loose somehow and coming on board. And if I got it figured right, the maglev field surrounding the train is keeping them here. This son of a bitch is a fighter—I can barely hang on to him. If the rest of them are this bad, it's gonna be a shitstorm."

"Fuck me," Tom says, choking back his beating heart.

"There's something else. Some kind of memories. It's really fuzzy and weird. But I think...I think these bastards really might have killed my parents."

Tom chokes again, this time on disbelief.

He wants to tell me it's impossible.

But I knew this was coming.

That's why I came.

He sucks in a quick gulp, then blows it out hard. "If they killed your folks, how the hell did they end up in sealed graves? Only your *parents* would have known how to do that."

"I don't have any idea, Tom. All I know is that every minute we waste talking about it is another minute their buddies could be sinking deeper into human hosts—we've gotta sweep the train again."

Roosevelt chimes in quick: *"Use the mark inside you. It'll let you see them."*

"We've gotta keep this quiet," Tom says, rattling now, his frayed edges coming undone. "If Dryden and his goon squad see the rock goddess here all beat to shit, they're gonna flip right the fuck out. Christ, they could shoot us all..."

"Just calm down, Tom. I don't need you losing it on me."

"Who's *losing it?* I'm just saying we *have to be careful,* man."

"I know what you're saying, but I can smell you about to blow."

He jabs a finger in my face, sweat dribbling. "I was hunting marks when you were a fucking punk *on the street!"*

"Just calm the fuck down, *I mean it!"*

He reels it in for a moment. "Okay...okay, goddammit. So what's the plan?"

I size him up carefully.

Gotta handle this right.

"You stay here with her," I tell him, pulling out Roosevelt's smart phone, thumbing the Facebook app. "Don't let anybody in. We'll figure something out when she wakes up."

"You *need me* out there, Buck."

"I need you in *here.* We can't let anyone see her until we know what the hell is happening. Are you *listening to me,* Tom?"

"Yeah, I'm listening."

But he doesn't like it.

I look at my phone screen and Darby's status line reads:

PLAY GAMES.

"Casino," Roosevelt says.

THIRTEEN

SHEER SECTION EIGHT

8:01
When a mark hides behind a face in a crowd, you have to be careful. They can jump you out of nowhere.

They can put up smokescreens and fuck you up real bad.

And if they go too deep inside a host, they're like hell to pull.

If you've been hunting marks for thirty years, you figure out how most of them think—but these are different. Insane and powerful, reduced to essence. Hard to see and tough as nails. And I've already got one bouncing inside me, hanging on way down in my dark places, cutting me up bad.

But I can use that.

As I walk through the crowded room, I slip on a pair of my shades from the satchel. I palm a razorblade, too—put it in one hand so its hidden, ready to bite me hard when I need the jolt. I do it casually. The shades aren't as good as my goggles, but they blend right into a party. Nobody sees me at all.

Good.

I slowly begin to release the power of the mark, carefully at first...then a little more...until...my vision begins to polarize...*and the room goes neon dark*...

Now, the Blacklight.

I see the people in here split into X-ray shapes, the form of their own emotions and obsessions and addictions playing in the air above them like crawling sea creatures that hover and skitter and wriggle. The world moves fast, vibrations shaking me bad as the train accelerates my senses. I slow myself down, trying to ride the storm... but it's terrifying, even as I focus on the members of the party:

Jerry Donaldson, still shooting craps, drunk as hell now.

Francis Crowe, chatting him up, talking about a movie deal.

Senator Maxton, surrounded by ladies half his age, who fawn over him like he's Frank Sinatra back in the day.

Carolyn Lewis, conspiring with her cameraman, plotting her next ambush.

Agents Dryden and Jacques hovering near Maximum Bob, looking serious, passing the odd remark.

The bartender, serving a drink to Junk-E, who quaffs it fast and shouts for another, his eyes scanning the room.

His eyes...

I put out a line to him and search for his thoughts. No freestyling now, no business numbers or thoughts of civil rights speeches. Nothing at all.

And he's a big guy, too.

Big and powerful.

I move toward him, and there's something...

Yes, something.

I lose it in the wild accelerated slithers of phantom darkness, layers on layers of memories, projections—bits of old lives flashing past me, shaking me hard. Just standing in a room is bad enough when you're on solid ground. This is a million times worse, entire worlds built and destroyed in split instants as I walk forward through it. My body begins to flicker in and out. I clench my fist and the razorblade cuts into my hand. The pain hits me sharp. Blood drizzles along my closed palm. I pull back...

And the world moves slower now.

I refocus on Junk-E, moving toward the bar, still a little dizzy.

Have to move fast.

He sees me and does something that looks like a weird smile, one gold tooth peeking out the corner of his mouth. "What's up, man?"

"Just a fan," I tell him. "Thought I'd say hello."

"Who you be with?"

"Hired help."

"Hired by who?"

"Doesn't matter. I just like your music."

He looks at me funny.

Nothing.

I feel nothing coming from him at all, not now. Solid steel wall up, on all sides of him. It could be my own mind playing tricks. Never been in a room like this. A room that moves this fast and this hard. Have to stay focused. Gotta try something bold.

"So tell me something," I say slowly. "How do you like being black?"

"What the *fuck* did you just say to me?"

"Think you heard me just fine."

He jabs a finger in my face and I sense something move inside him. "You get the *fuck outta here* before I snap you in half, *punk!*"

I reach up and grab his hand.

His little finger breaks easy.

He spits out a howl, but nothing comes loose. His eyes fill with water. He grits his teeth hard, takes a swing at me, snarling, and I feel his mind flare white-hot with rage. I sidestep him and grab his right arm, sending him into the bar, where shot glasses shatter.

I was wrong—*it's not in Junk-E.*

It might not even be in this room now.

Maybe saw me coming and hauled ass.

And meanwhile, I have a very pissed off black man coming back at me, blind with pain and rage and a broken finger. The room freaks out a little. One of the girls screams, then laughs. Carolyn Lewis nudges her cameraman, who starts filming the whole scene. Jacques and Dryden don't unholster their weapons, but they start to come near us, looking like this is all they need right now. But the room is packed, and the fight is on. Some people even start cheering. The two agents are almost swallowed up in it.

I aim my fingers for the nerve center in Junk-E's right shoulder, hoping to end this fast, but something punches me in the gut before my blow connects—something already inside me. The mark. I go down on the floor, doubled over, and the big rapper is on top of me fast, his whole weight pouring in like deadly lava, his hands around my throat.

While I'm down there, something comes straight out of Junk-E's eyes.

Like crawling red fingers—laughing, pulling his strings.

Played me like an amateur, dammit.

It was in his body, but deep down—took longer for the nerve spike to reach it. I curse myself as it spews over me, the mucky red ooze homing toward the Pull. But the son of a bitch is scrappy, just like the other one.

I get it all the way out, but it clobbers me hard.

Junk-E screams as the mark leaves him, blasting backward and into the bar, his head smashing against the polished wood, knocking himself cold. I dance to my feet, wrestling with the skittering mist. It claws at my face like a crazy dog, screaming wordless curses. I bear down hard, getting a good grip on the goddamn thing, the Pull coming down mercilessly...

The mark shatters against my skin and goes deep.

The desperate animal cries oozing directly into me.

It joins the other one, overloading my senses, scorching my lungs and my heart and my stomach and pulsing along my bones, swirling in the center of my body, in the roaring black hole of the Pull, which expands like a negative fist clenching my heart. My mind registers it as a complete fucking overload, all my bells and whistles lighting up in the red. I sense the same trace memories from before, smothered in sticky unformed animal mulch...and for one long second-and-a-half that crunches in my skull like dirty electric blowback, I hover there in slow motion, allowing myself to feel the primal truth of it—these spirits who've gone beyond rage, beyond revenge, beyond humanity. They are the worst parts of everyone. They are the worst parts of me. The screams and the blood and the eating of flesh...and...*and*...

Another one hits me from behind.

Right out of nowhere.

Its invisible attack lands like a bomb in the whirlpool center of the Pull, almost breaking my hold over the marks.

They don't come loose from my body, but they start pounding me hard.

177

Start grabbing for control.

Their combined assault smothers me in long terrible bulletflashes of absolute hopelessness, hitting me in all the worst places.

Places of the mind.

Places of the soul.

It's been years since I was ratpacked like this.

I reel in the undertow, pulled almost under as the gored remains of writhing animals twist my mind to hell and back. My world spins out and almost crackles away, and I expect the hot blast of the Blacklight to hit me in the face but it never comes. The magnetic force of the train speeds in on my senses, combined with the sneak attack of the mystery mark, plunging straight down on me, my mind exploding with fragged images, shuffled and blown apart and seared back together in tracerfire sequence, like some video-stitched montage, overdriven and loud...

Razorblades covered in blood.

The smiles of blinded men and women, possessed by marks.

The gun, exploding in my face...

A face like an angel, hair blowing in the white hot breeze.

The face of my mother.

MY MOTHER...

The shock blasts my heart as I come back from it, but I have no time to ponder.

The two marks inside me have the upper hand—and it's merciless.

People scream.

The world shifts and boils like smothering ooze.

I am dazed on my feet.

I hear the kid scream Francis Crowe's name in my earbud just before the guy sits up from his chair near the craps table, and something like a ten ton kinetic deadweight smashes into me. His hands never touch my body, but the air turns into a battering ram and does me hard. The floor under my feet vanishes and I fly back, clearing ten feet, slamming against the slot machine on the opposite wall. My ribs start screaming at me and I slump over, dazed.

Crowe.

The mystery mark is in Crowe.

And it wants in the game.

Wants the marks inside me.

The images from the desert pound at my mind one more time:

The gun.

The razorblades.

A face that could be ... could be my ...

Agent Dryden shouts my name and aims his gun at me. It's a monster, that thing—a Ruger P345 Centerfire pistol with a laser sight. Major stopping power, high velocity. This guy doesn't fuck around.

Tom appears at the far end of the room, his gun up. What the hell is he doing here? He was supposed to be ...

I throw out my hand. "Get back, all of you!"

Tom freezes, his hands shaking on the gun. "What is it?"

"It's *Hollywood,*" Crowe hisses with a wicked grin.

The mark inside him takes another swing with his invisible fist, and the world fritzes out again as the pain rips into me ...

Blacklight.

The room swims in neon shadows.

The rush is pure now—overwhelming.

None of the people in this place can see what I see hovering over the little guy now. Another one of the Nine, swarming its essence just inches above his flesh, making his eyes dark, manipulating his body like a herky-jerky meat puppet. He steps forward now with staccato grace.

I pull myself back, the Blacklight ripping away painfully ... the two marks colliding inside me, hitting hard ... *and* ...

Crowe attacks again.

He narrows his eyes at me. The invisible force slams into my stomach, and this time I manage to summon the Pull, which deflects some of it, spinning the shockwave across the room to knock down Dryden. He crashes into Jacques and his Ruger goes spinning across the floor like a toy. Dryden recovers fast and looks up, his eyes wild, as the panic in the room escalates into a full-scale terror scene.

The marks bounce back inside the walls of my soul—and it's complete fucking torture. Like rows of scalpels and ripping claws peeling back the skin of my youth, robbing me of everything. I barely manage to stand on two feet. I concentrate on grounding myself. Summoning the Pull. Trying to rip them out of my biorhythms and digest them. But they still hold out against me.

Crowe attacks again.

His hands never touch my body.

The invisible fist punches a double whammy, folds me in half, pinning me to the deck, and I crumple there, my soul buckling under the strain. *I lose control...*

And the Blacklight shatters the room again.

No coming out of it now.

I'm in for the long haul.

The air swims in surreal shadows, moving faster than the speed of sound, the screaming and crying people letting loose with terrible formless essence that swirls and crackles and blows like multicolored bombs. It's crazy. Total insanity. Crowe pushes past two of Bethany Sin's crew and lunges forward, focusing his attack again. This time I see what the fist looks like—a malformed shape like a steel battering ram with bad memories and movie scenes and spatters like blood and piss and semen flowing just under its liquid metal surface—and it forms into a knife and scrapes into me, tearing a deep gash in the worst spot—deep down, where the real Bethany was when she tried to seduce me. The private place where you give up everything. The marks inside me are street fighting now, kicking me while I'm down and pissing right in my face. I clench my teeth and take it on the chin. A vein pops somewhere in my head and a teardrop of blood streaks down from my right eye. I actually feel my hair go white in this moment, damn-near paralyzed.

I have to get up.

Have to get what's in Crowe.

My legs won't work.

Tom sees it hit me again, the steelbar force keeping me down. I smell his adrenaline blow bad in his heart, mixed up in the ripe blowback of several dozen panicking men and women. He runs forward, re-aiming his gun at Crowe, who is rapidly turning black, his eyes glowing with strange neon. The monster winks at Tom and licks his bottom lip, the mark crackling over his body like a storm of dead things that only I can see, a voice full of playful malice that everyone can hear:

"Let's wrap this one out, shall we?"

The force hits Tom and he stumbles back, the cloud over Crowe amping up, and it starts really screaming now, infusing him with twisting veins and blotches like living bruises, crawling all over every inch of his skin. Tom's eyes go white and wide like a shocked china doll, his whole body quaking and rumbling, terror striking through him like a sledgehammer.

Hell of a time to go crazy on me, Tom.

Dryden crawls along the floor, to where Senator Maxton is crouched in a corner, yelling at him to stay down, retrieving his gun. I see his panic materialize in the space above him like glowing blood diamonds, and his eyes are full and nuts—he's about to blow, too.

Crazy people everywhere.

Sheer Section Eight on both sides of me.

The thing-in-Crowe comes at me and I roll out of the way. It smashes against the bar and snarls there, hunched over like some bizarre nightmare about flesh and blood made dark and wrong. Crowe stands in the center of the hissing cloud of smoke and tendrils, enveloped in black stinking anti-flesh. He channels it with charcoal eyes, the will of the mark somewhere in there, pulling his strings. His movements are fast, the hatred under his skin commanding muscles at superhuman speed, coming right at us again.

Tom raises the gun and almost fires, his panic-on-overdrive killing all common sense in his strained mind... but I grab his hand.

"You'll kill him! Don't!"

The thing-in-Crowe pauses—snarling, laughing.

All the muscles in his body snap and pop, like the pistons of a machine.

His charcoal pupils dilate and recede into black infinity.

A billion thoughts crash through my mind in this moment, and not all of them belong to me. I focus up, bringing the Pull to the surface of my fingers *again, aiming myself at him. I can't lose this battle. I can't let Crowe die. The marks inside me scream and tear at me, slowing me down.*

The Pull comes painfully to the surface, knocking them back.

Calling for the thing inside Crowe's body.

It snarls and spits at me, digging in deeper to the little guy.

Telling me to come and get him.

Calling me a fucking asshole.

Agent Jacques closes from the other side, puts his sights right between Crowe's eyes, telling him to drop to his knees with his hands over his head, his voice calm and professional, like he's the only sane man in the room who has a gun. There's a bad joke for you. The black cloud is invisible to him—all the cop sees is a pissed-off movie producer with baby blues gone black.

Crowe snarls and screams at him to go fuck himself.

"Mr. Crowe, I need you to calm down," Jacques says, slow and easy, taking three slow steps toward him, riding the trigger heavy with each breath he takes.

The thing-in-Crowe turns and jumps at Jacques, its hand scraping across his face—an inhuman blur of stylish silver fingernails and thick spritzing blood. The cop staggers back like a drunk puppet and I leap up to take the thing while he's distracted.

And in that moment, time seems to slow in the Blacklight.

And I see a shape moving toward me in the corner of my eye.

Tom.

His gun raised.

His finger squeezing the trigger.

His panic blowing all the way now.

Right in time with the flashbomb of the high-caliber discharge.

It resounds like a god exploding in the casino and the bullet zangs just over my shoulder, going right into Crowe's forehead.

The back of the little guy's skull opens and the shot evacuates his brain in a chunky-pink goosh, like a scoop of mulched Silly Putty scattering in the air.

Hollow-point round.

Nasty.

The sound is still keening sharply in my head as the next shot comes, drilling out his heart and blowing apart one of the slot machines. A flower of blood detonates through his spine and the mark tears free, coming right at me, homing on the Pull. It looks like a blurred thrash of chitinous arms and legs, almost insect-like and changing shape from millisecond to millisecond, full of bad memories and animal instinct, a raging, roaring missile of pure supercolliding hatred...

The force of the blow knocks me off my feet.

I hear another shot as I go down.

Dryden's gun.

It hits Tom in the shoulder, scraping blood into the air and dropping him to one knee, his pistol falling from his hand. Jacques is still on the floor with blood in his eye as his boss pins Tom with his little red dot and tells him to get on the floor, right the fuck now. His voice is crazy, out of tune and warbling, like a heat-scorched record album.

Tom, you crazy fucked-up son of bitch...

The thought goes through my mind in bullet-time, before I realize there's still a mark on top of me, screaming, clawing at my face. But it's weak from throwing so much into the fight—weaker than the others. The Pull takes it into me, but it comes through my skin hard, crashing into the other two in my guts like merciless surf. I spiral faster on the dark downward as I feel the force of the train slushing and pounding and pulsing like wet electricity, just outside of sight. And I can feel the marks dive-bombing, writhing on multiple trajectories, the force of the train accelerating them into some weird black overdrive. Their screams buzz the magnetic field, pulling me under with phantom talons, kissing me with smells of dark oozing liquid, like oily lifeblood swirling and boiling and screaming, taking me back... making me see...

...and here come the memory flashes again, stronger now, like they're all of the same mind. Shattered glimpses, vague whispers, slashing across my mind like projected bits of an old life blown to hell and arranged in the wrong order...

The face of a madman smiles and makes promises.

Jack's face.

Blackjack Williams.

He opens his fist and the razors glare in the sun.

Someone tells me everything will be okay.

Someone tells me I will be safe.

The gun roars...

I can't stay in this maelstrom. It's burning me too bad and there's a war on. I have to break away. Break away NOW. I grit my teeth and find my center. I concentrate on nothing but grounding myself in my own humanity. I am not the marks—the marks are mine. I am not the memories—the memories are long gone.

The power of control slides in.

I grit my teeth and bear down.

The marks hurl slashing curses at me as I bring them under my leash. Bits of screams. Fragments of faces. All splattering against the chambers of my soul... but not digesting. Instead, something else happens. I feel them combine into a deep black burst of superheated energy—something that seems to feed directly from the Blacklight, focusing into power... and the power runs through my nerves, scores my brain and bounces back, making my body hum and rattle and speed faster than light, in synch with the massive drug-rush of the train beneath my feet...

And it's good.

Power.

Glowing, churning... coalescing.

Inside me.

Like nothing I've ever felt.

It pins me where I stand like jagged bolts of energy whipping through a lightning rod. My eyes glow with it. My lips are red from it. Tears streak down my face, dark with blood and strange humors, smoldering like the souls circling inside me. It's my birthright. It's where I belong.

Here in the Blacklight.

Yes.

YES...

Something hits me in the face as I begin my ascent to godhood—something hard and cruel, yanking me back to earth. A sharp pain opens a gash along my right cheek, and I see Dryden as he pistol-whips me again, and I go down on the floor like heap of dirty laundry. My shades fall off my face, and the Black-

light cuts across my eyes like a laser beam. The lenses hold, but the pain blasts through everything...

...brings me back...

And it's a total clusterfuck.

The room full of chaos.

One VIP dead, another out like a light.

Tom on the floor with Jacques digging a knee in his back, telling him not to move one fucking muscle.

And Dryden standing over me, his gun aimed right in my face.

8:05

There's a lot of screaming.

That's the first thing you usually notice in these situations.

The marks do another crash-and-burn in my mind, then I fight them back, as the unbound napalm blows fireworks again and again, just under my skin. They still won't go down. How much longer can I hold them? I struggle up on my elbows, but Dryden keeps the gun in my face and I don't get very far with that idea. He spits rage, but his voice is like a whoosh of angry air that makes no sense under the punishment tearing me from the inside. I try to keep focus on the room, which swims with sharp panic and frenzied voices—all kinds of voices. The kind you can hear out loud and the kind people come up with inside themselves when they're afraid to die.

The only one controlling himself is the senator, who stands near the center of the room like a Roman statue—he looks damn confused and even a little grossed-out, but he ain't showing a trace of fear. Jerry Donaldson is a different story: he's a racetrack full of drunken frenzy and shock, screaming his dead partner's name over and over while his arm candy clings to him in desperation, crying. Carolyn Lewis chokes back tears, the cold fingers of some inevitable bottomless despair clutching her heart. Bethany's posse all huddle together in a corner, hysterically shrieking, abandoned by Maxton—and not one of them wonders where their magical diva wandered off to. *And Tom...*

I feel him bottoming out again and again, consumed by his own panic and desperation, kept on the floor by Jacques, smothered in his own sweat. It mixes with the insanity rumbling in the room and pours in like a punishing wave, the speed of the train accelerating another notch on program, the world screaming by at *hundreds of miles an hour now*...

It's too much, but I steel myself against it.

Finally...somehow...the world starts to ooze back into some coherence, and Dryden is wild-eyed as he yells in my face again:

"I said what the fuck just *happened in here,* Carlsbad? I wants some answers out of you now!"

I fight the marks and try to make a normal voice happen:

"The train...we're under *attack*..."

"You'd better start making some sense, buddy—*I'm not kidding!*"

Agents Ben and Jerry come into the room from the forward observation deck, pulling Lauren Chance between them.

Agent Kendall brings up the rear, hefting his thick revolver.

Dryden sees them and hisses his next words in quick bursts, like machinegun fire. "Get that bitch over here! On your knees now! Hands on your head!"

They shove her next to me and we both put our hands on our heads.

"Cover the senator," he barks to Ben and Jerry. "I want all these people and the staff members rounded up now. Everyone is on lockdown until we get to Vegas. I'm getting to the bottom of this one way or another." He turns to me and spits in my face again, his gun held tightly. "You hear me *talking,* Buck? You and your pals have officially fucked yourselves."

Tom doesn't say a word, his mind slushed, Jacques still holding him down with his knee, gun aimed right in the back of his head—looks like he'd really relish an excuse to do some wasting right about now.

Ben and Jerry cover the senator.

Agent Kendall just looks confused.

"You can't put all these people in lockdown," I tell Dryden, starting to get a grip above the pounding in my head and guts. "There's something loose on the train. If you put them all in one place, they'll be sitting ducks."

"Shut the fuck up," he yells. "You are a *terrorist,* Carlsbad."

"I was hired to *protect* these people!"

"And you did a bang-up job, buddy—be sure to tell that to the judge."

"Didn't you see what just *happened,* man? That guy on the floor turned black and tried to kill me!"

"What I saw was you picking a fight, buddy-boy—and your friend here *blew his goddamn head off!* Is that the way you deal with ghosts down in Texas?"

"You have to listen to me..."

"Just shut up, boy—*shut the fuck UP!*"

The force of the train comes in harder when he screams at me.

The marks scramble to get a grip on me.

It's so hard, keeping them down...

Carolyn Lewis and her cameraman keep their heads, but just barely, on the floor with Senator Maxton. Derek Pappas is shouting that he wants to know what's going on, and the blue-blood from the Mideast looks real nervous. Donaldson and his arm candy are shaking in each other's arms—their crying boiling into a mumble paralysis, unable to speak. Bethany's posse hold on to each other for dear life.

The senator doesn't say a word. Kind of scowls in my direction.

Cool as ice under fire.

I sit there on my knees, feeling the burn inside, the speed of the train rushing toward hyperspace on all sides of me, blurring my senses.

Tom shivers and quakes under Jacques's knee, wounded and sideways.

Roosevelt, stuttering in my ear: *"Buck...holy shit, man..."*

Dryden hears his voice and snaps to Agent Kendall: "I want that kid with the cameras brought in here with the rest of these terrorists—all of them are under arrest."

Kendall does a quick *yessir* and bolts from the room.

"You hear that, kid?" I say into my earbud. "Looks like the big show's been cancelled."

His voice comes back: *"Fuck me."*

One of the girls gets hysterical, the one with purple hair. She's pretty far gone, her two friends crying at her to calm down.

I check for shadows, listen for voices.

Nothing else in the room, just panic.

Tom grunts as Jacques hauls him up on his knees, slapping iron around his wrists. I look Tom in the eye and he shivers, like he has no idea what to do. He's delirious now, in shock. Just doesn't make any sense. I'd think he was possessed, if I didn't already know better. I hear Roosevelt being arrested over my earbud—and then the signal shuts down, terminated at the source. There goes our eye in the sky.

Dryden fires his next words in a half-stutter, struggling to keep himself in charge of everything, his adrenaline pumping double-time: "Mr. Carlsbad, I'm supposed to inform you of your rights—but you don't *have* any rights as a terrorist. I'll give you one chance to confess."

"Confess *what?*"

His mind does a terrible snap, and I feel it like a bone breaking:

"Who are you working for? Who paid you to assassinate the senator?"

Lauren spits at him: "Have you *lost your mind?*"

He aims his gun right in her face.

"No, Miss Chance. Have you?"

The room freezes.

Agent Jerry gets wide-eyed. "What the hell are you doing, Richard?"

Dryden grinds his teeth hard. "Everyone just needs to relax . . . the situation is *under control.*"

He doesn't sound convinced.

At all.

I struggle to keep it together, squinting at his gun.

"You can't do this," Lauren says, very calmly.

"I can do anything I want. This is an emergency situation."

She almost laughs. "I'm a employee of Jaeger Industries—a goddamn *security guard.* I didn't have anything to do with this."

"You were *all* hired by Sidney Jaeger, which makes you all terrorists as far as the law is concerned, and terrorists are guilty until proven innocent—or don't you watch the news? How about it, Buck?"

He thumbs back the hammer, re-aiming at me, his eyes glimmering with something that looks like madness shot through with macho.

"You gonna shoot me right in front of all these people? I thought you spook-types were sneakier than that."

"I'll blow you away and they'll pin a medal on my chest for it."

"Just like your dad, huh?"

"Fuck you, terrorist."

He explodes inside himself, his mind doing backflips, his finger on the trigger.

Sheer Section Eight.

"One last chance, Buck. *Who are you working for?*"

Carolyn Lewis nods to her boy, who still has his camera rolling, getting everything on video. The senator finally notices that and takes a cautious step toward Dryden, his bodyguards moving with him, his voice strong and measured. "Richard, you need to lower your weapon. I am *ordering* you to lower your weapon."

"Sir, please remain calm," Dryden says, his voice still mad-on-macho. Terrifying. "The situation is *under control*...we need to have everyone move quietly to the rear of the train...need to ask each of you a few questions..."

The senator doesn't back down.

"Richard, I'm going to tell you one more time and I want you to listen carefully. Lower your weapon. Arrest these people by the letter of the law and the courts will decide if they are guilty. You and I both serve the public trust and this will not stand."

He's playing for the camera now.

Turning a bad situation into a chance to be a media hero.

I want to tell him to back off—that this guy is a hair-trigger lunatic with a death wish, but he keeps coming forward, even when Agent Ben slaps a hand on his shoulder and tries to pull him back.

Dryden's finger almost curls on the trigger.

"Senator...the situation is under control."

Maxton, cool as ice: "You're right. It is. *Now lower your weapon.*"

I feel Dryden's mind make a crazy dive for a black zone I can't read, and the marks twist and burn inside me, screaming for him, sensing fresh blood in the water. Everyone in the room holds on the next three seconds, as they stretch to the end of time, Maxton reaching out to Dryden, his hand unwavering.

"Richard, give me the gun."

Dryden blinks twice and says:

"No."

Then...

He lowers the gun. Slowly. Turns to Maxton with a stone expression, everyone in the room breathing again.

"Get these people to the rear of the train," he says to Ben and Jerry. "We'll hold them in the movie theater and sort this out when we get to Vegas."

"Thank you, Richard," Maxton says, and follows after Rashid Hopi, along with the others. They move toward the door, led by Agents Ben and Jerry.

Dryden looks back at me with disgust.

His eyes, stone cold and desperate at the same time.

He wants to shoot me so much it's like a bad taste in his mouth.

I stay focused on his madness, the Blacklight hissing just out of sight, the marks clamoring for my surrender. I begin to concentrate on their wordless voices, bringing the power forward just a bit...*so that I can see*...but I decide that's a bad idea and force it back down. I size him up on instinct.

Nothing in Dryden.

Nothing I can see.

He would have killed me, like the others tried to.

Jacques drags Tom over and tosses him alongside us. He's half conscious now, blood trickling down the scrape on his arm, his shirt sleeve dark with blood. Agent Kendall brings Roosevelt into the room, his hands locked behind his back in cuffs. Dryden orders the kid to his knees, and we're all in a row now—all us nasty terrorists.

"So where's the booze?" Roosevelt says.

Dryden turns on him, the gun still at his side, gripped in a nervous fist. "Shut your mouth." He redirects his eyes to Agent Kendall. "We'll hold these suspects in the forward passenger compartment. I want them cuffed and interrogated."

"Thought we were saving the party for Vegas," I tell him.

"Mr. Carlsbad, if I were you I'd get smart and crack a tab on a nice frosty can of *shut the fuck up*."

When he says that, something shifts in the room.

Something like the shockwave I felt before.

Something moving toward us.

I concentrate on it, *focusing all my energy...*

And the Blacklight spirals into view, washing the room in dark heatwaves, splitting apart everyone and showing me the shape of their fear. Dryden is a mess of writhing blue panic, but there's nothing riding inside him—he's just a crazy man. The agents are all clean, too. But I can hear the screaming now, like the sounds inside me, and it's terrible and piercing, feeding back in my head, filling my senses.

Crawling along the ceiling are two marks.

Their madness rolls the air into boiling red muck and the sound of their tantrums solidifies, blasting in circle after circle.

It's a thing of intense, terrifying beauty.

No one can see it but me.

I get a dirty lungful of what they are, reaching out to touch the smell... which burns like flesh set on fire, blood and sweat dripping from an open wound. I see smiles set into malformed faces, like cancers giggling, boiling skin and viperous plasmic substance doing whirlpools, upside down and right side up—the bitter shape and stench of unfocused insanity—coiling through the air like slime slithering through a drain... slithering down from the ceiling to strike home.

Right in Carolyn Lewis and Rashid Hopi.

No.

Goddammit, no.

I feel the wave hit me, as the marks inside my body shift again, kicking up a lot of shit as they see the touchdown. Lewis takes it with a rough jolt. Hopi has no idea it even happens. Nobody would know if they didn't see like I'm seeing now. And what I see is terrible, like a couple of spiders spinning up flies in a million tiny membranes that go deep into every pore, every orifice, then burst with a sick red glow, as the marks slide home, riding along the nerve impulses, dragracing through their bloodstream, hissing and laughing all the way. Carolyn Lewis really feels it now, and she goes down on one knee, as Rashid Hopi begins to convulse, still holding it together.

"It's in her! Carolyn Lewis! Don't let her go with the others!"

Dryden is shocked by my voice, then he hears someone scream and spins to see Lewis on the floor.

I scream again: "Get her away from the others!"

He hisses at me: "Shut your mouth, terrorist."

"I'm telling you—they're gonna lose it, just like Crowe did!"

The kid pipes up: "Listen to him, man. The shit's going down now."

Dryden punches him in the face and he shuts up.

The marks are going deep now inside Lewis and Hopi.

Taking control of them.

I have to do something.

Dryden takes three steps away from me, sizing up the situation, with Agent Kendall right behind him. Carolyn Lewis is on the floor now, moaning. Rashid Hopi shaking it off, feeling the burn, but he still has no idea what's happening to him.

In ten minutes, he will know.

They'll both be at the mercy of those sons of bitches.

And I'll be cuffed on the other side of the train...

I reach up and jam my finger along the wound Dryden cut into my face when he hit me with the gun, and the pain shocks me...

I bring myself back and focus up, the Blacklight spiraling away.

Have to make my move now.

I hear someone scream my name—I think it's the kid—as I jump up to my feet, coming right at Dryden and Kendall from behind, landing between them like a bomb. My left foot wheelkicks around and sweeps Kendall's leg at the back of his knees, putting him on his back. Dryden curses and tries to aim his weapon at me—but I intercept his move at the wrist, slicing two fingers along the nerves that govern his fingers and he drops the iron in a big hurry. My elbow comes into his face and he sees stars explode from the crack of his jaw, joining his buddy on the floor. I kick away Kendall's thick revolver and jump across the room in three fast pounces. Seconds later, I clear the space between the fallen agents and Carolyn Lewis and she's still shaking, the mark sliding along her bones now, having hell with taking control of her. Hopi is my first target.

But I never get to him . . .

Someone slams into me from behind in a full-body tackle.

The world tilts and then goes upside-down.

I look up to see Agents Ben and Jerry holding me on the floor.

Agent Dryden comes into my line of sight, rubbing his wrist, blazing down on me like a playground bully finally getting his way. Agent Jacques hovers there, too, pulling his revolver off his shoulder.

"That was real smart," Dryden says. "You just made my whole day, Buck."

He nods to Agent Jacques and says:

"Book him."

Smith and Wesson slams down into my face and all the lights go out.

FOURTEEN

DOWN TWISTED

I'm floating at the edge of everything.

I'm fighting them as hard as I can, putting up wall after wall to keep the bastards from breaking me. I can't tell them apart. They crash into me again and again and bounce back, gliding and twisting and screaming just at the edge of the Pull. The black hole in the center of my heart that wants to yank them all the way down, pulverize them, make them into muck. It's a Mexican standoff. They run at me and crash away screaming, riding the whirling black surf. Formless monsters running on brute force—animals let out of their cages, ready to rip me apart to get at the goods. An endless roll of slobbering thunder in my ears. Primal. Disgusting. But it feels good. The fight infuses me with desperate humming power, unchecked and flowing fast, flickering at my command and spinning out of control, feeding back against the Pull. I want to stay here and see everything. I want to lose myself in this endless void of the dead. I feel the slipstream of the Walkers roaring just beyond the magnetic pulse of the train, but it's far away now, and I'm standing in an infinite space of complete blackness, battered on all sides by three angry marks, who scream my name and curse me . . . because I am something they remember . . . and they hate what they remember. Their memories flow like syrup, distorted and slimy, freezing and breaking apart as they come in for their licks, hitting me in time with the punishment, and then receding away to surf the event horizon of the endless nothing that surrounds us:

The sun, beating down.

The blue sky above them all, as they kneel in a row.

The face of Blackjack Williams hovering above them, blotted and feature-less, an evil outline, backlit by the scorching day.

He stands on a high dune, looking down on them.

Raises his fist high in the air.

His fist glitters with thin silver...

...and now the dream shifts bizarrely, jarring my gut and making me scream as a knife twists hard, and the images pour in faster as they hit me with new resolve, all at once, throwing everything they've got like a clusterbomb that explodes in my face, and I know this is what happened to my parents, and I know this is how they died, and I have to stay here, have to fight them so that I know, but something is calling me back, something pounding me back in the real world of flesh and bone, something like a splash of blood in my face, tearing me away from this endless nothingness where I'm getting slaughtered by angry animals... but I want to stay and take it...I want to die in the cold embrace of the Pull so I can know the truth...let them kill me so I can feel what they feel...

...let me stay...

...LET ME STAY...

...let...

8:25

I buzz back to the world, as straight whiskey drizzles off my face, oozing down in hot rivulets, mingling with blood from the pulsing welt on my forehead and the cuts on my face, the sting of the alcohol tingling and burning. It's the pain that wakes me up. I feel my whole head doing four-alarms now.

Agent Jacques smiles when he sees me come to.

Splashes the rest of the burning liquid in my eye from a plastic cup.

"Rise and shine, asshole."

His tie is loose.

His smile is sadistic and disgusting.

Both of my hands are cuffed behind my back, through the chromed arm of a seat in the forward passenger deck, and the desert flashes by one of those huge panoramic windows. The train is going much faster now, accelerating toward its top speed on program. It blurs my senses on top of the pounding in my head and the pain stabbing me there. The marks roll and grumble in frustration. They almost had me while I was under. I'm barely keeping them down now. I have to get rid of them soon—but I don't know if I can. Tried that once and it didn't work. They're like heatwaves full of angry curses, undigested, swimming along my bones, still looking for a way to crack my soul. Trapped between the barriers of my flesh and the black hole of the Pull. And I can feel more of them on the train, close. Skittering like termites. Homing.

This is really bad news, man.

I look up and see that the sectioned steel emergency door has been slammed down at the end of the compartment.

Agent Kendall keeping us all covered with a nasty-looking compact machinegun.

Looks like an Uzi.

We're locked in here tight.

Lauren and Roosevelt are cuffed to the chairs next to me. Tom is passed out on the floor, one wrist cuffed to a steel bar—he looks almost dead, his breath coming short and wheezing. A pool of blood spreads slowly under his great weight. I see him and then look right at Jacques: "He needs a doctor."

Roosevelt lets a sneer roll off his chin. "Forget it, Buck. We did that song and dance. They don't give a shit."

I try to find my center, but it doesn't work that good. "You guys okay?"

"Never better," Roosevelt says. "What's it look like?"

I notice the entire right side of his face is bruised and swollen. It's fresh work. They did him bad when I was under.

Jacques says nothing.

His knuckles are red and scraped.

He pours another drink into the cup from a bottle of Jameson's and shoots it quick, his eyes wild, full of hot mean.

I feel the marks shift, and my control almost slips. It's harder than ever to face them down, to back them off. I feel the sick tingle and the raw smell of the Blacklight, just on the other side of the pain inside me, and the Pull. It keeps rising to the surface and I keep fighting it. I will lose soon. The darkest part of me—the part that almost died in the desert—it wants me to surrender. It wants to let these bastards consume me. This is something more than ghosts. It's a feeling I can't resist. The power, lurking just beyond my reach... waiting for me to let down my guard...

No.

Can't pussy out now.

There's other people in this equation.

I can't fail them.

I choose my next words carefully, looking right at the spook in my face:

"Listen to me. We're all in big trouble."

Lauren Chance rolls her eyes—guess they tried this already, too. But I have to keep trying. Have to make them understand.

"Two of the people you locked in the back are under the influence of something really nasty. Carolyn Lewis and the Mideast guy."

Jacques says nothing.

Just looks at me with that sadistic grin.

His breath full of booze.

I try again. "Are you listening? You have to get those two people isolated—or stop the train."

Nothing.

I might as well be talking to a wall splashed in whiskey.

Finally, after what seems like a scowling century, he says something. Says it with a steel tone and a disgusting I-don't-give-a-shit grin:

"So what you're saying is that those guys are possessed by demons?"

"You're close."

"Funny... your friends here have been trying to sell me the same bullshit for the last twenty minutes."

Twenty minutes?

I was under twenty minutes.

That means Carolyn Lewis and Rashid Hopi are already under.

The marks have complete control of them.

"Tell your boss to get in there—all those people are in deep shit."

He smirks again, speaking into his Bluetooth. "Jacques here. We got any demons in the movie theater yet?"

Dryden's voice laughs back—I can hear it loud and clear. He says all is quiet on the home front, and asks how the confession is coming. Jacques says he'll break one of us really goddamn soon, reaching for the bottle again and filling the plastic cup. Doesn't shoot it this time. I think about screaming something so Dryden can hear me...but the thought dies fast, as I realize how completely alone I am. The marks are hiding, just like they were hiding before. The spooks have got everyone rounded up in the last car of the train—the movie room. Either it's gonna turn into a bloodbath or the marks are going to walk when the ride ends. They'll walk in the bodies of two very powerful people. If I can't do something about it.

And the marks inside me know they've won.

They're the strongest I've ever been up against.

They're riding my biorhythms, withstanding the Pull.

They're laughing now—those sick bubbling animal sounds.

I'm fucked at both ends.

I look over at Lauren, who keeps her silence, her eyes sizing up the room. I can sense her mind pinwheeling fast, figuring our chances of escape, but she knows we're in a damn hopeless situation.

Roosevelt bites his tongue, his face busted up and bleeding.

Jacques looks at Tom, passed out on the floor. "You're right about one thing, Buck: Your trigger-happy friend don't look so hot. He could bleed out any minute. This is the part where you find out who your friends really are."

"What the hell are you talking about?"

"I mean we can do this hard or easy, Buck. If it's hard, nobody will ever know the difference. Be a good boy and tell us what we want to know, or your friend dies. Just that simple."

He tosses the booze in my face.

I shake my head and feel the burn as it bubbles in my wound—the pain fueling the rushing marks inside me, fighting back the rage. "You'll never get away with any of this. Your boss went nuts in front of a crowd of famous people and a video camera."

"You mean *this* camera?"

He picks it up from one of the seats and wags the thing in my face.

He's got my satchel on the seat, also.

Tom's revolver, Lauren's Colt Python, all arranged in a neat row.

Stripped us good—every one of us.

And the one witness who could have blown the whistle on national television—Carolyn Lewis—she's possessed now.

Fuck me again.

"Guys like us make things go away," Jacques says. "It's our job."

"Like shooting protesters in broad daylight?"

"Like I said, nobody will ever know the difference."

"Your mother must be real proud of you."

"My mother's dead."

"Good for you."

He sizzles when I lay that down—I knew it would spike him. He's got unresolved issues there. A shit-ton of unresolved issues. I'm starting to feel more and more of them edge in as he begins to let down his guard, working on a slow burn.

I look at Tom, passed out on the floor.

Have to do something.

I begin to twist my right thumb.

Might be my only shot.

Jacques clenches his teeth, setting down the empty cup and the video camera, opening my satchel. Rifles through it, making smug faces. He tosses the baking soda on the floor, and it spills a long spatter of snow. He does the same with my goggles and sunglasses. Ignores the urn and my two bottles of castor oil mixture. Gets to the can of Lysol and grins.

"You been fighting ghosts with *herpes* or what, Buck?"

"Ask your mother."

This time he only makes a dull dry chuckle, keeping his burn under control. "I know what you're trying to do and it's not going to work. I'm not gonna touch one hair on your head, Buck. But I am gonna let your friend die. Unless you give me something."

Roosevelt shifts with his arms screwed up in an awkward position in the chair. "We're *not terrorists*—your boss is crazier than Norman Bates on Mother's Day."

"You might be right," Jacques says. "But it doesn't matter."

He holds up my earbud and smiles at me.

"Fancy piece of work, this little gadget of yours. Real James Bond, man. We don't even have stuff this advanced."

He finds the rusty gun in the zippered compartment of my satchel and pulls it out. Holds it up, whistling loud.

"But this...now here's some *real* hardware. Damn high-tech. Who were you planning on shooting with this thing?"

"It's a long story."

"Tell it to me, Buck. It's the only way your friend is getting out of here alive."

Have to stall him.

I work my thumb against the metal of the handcuff, feeling the blood as it bites me hard. Have to keep him talking.

"Listen to me, Jacques. *Just listen to me.* This train is turning into a death trap. Have any of you been paying attention to what's been going on around here?"

"We've been paying attention. Good work on Bethany Sin, by the way. She's in a coma. So is the big black guy."

"They were under the influence—"

"Stop right there, buddy." He gets in my face again. "What you are telling me is bullshit. You could at least make up something that sounds sort of like the truth. And if I were you, I'd do it really god-damn fast."

He turns the rusty gun over in his hand. Tosses it over his shoulder. It clunks onto the floor near Tom, almost hitting him in the head. Gone now. No use to me. I have to get loose. No other chance...

Jacques laughs at me. "You're totally disarmed now, man. And you're all alone. I'm gonna give you thirty seconds to get wise. And then we're *gonna get twisted.*"

An important bone gives in my thumb.

Hurts like hell—but I was ready for that.

The pain shocks down the nerve center on my arm, and tingles the marks inside me...and for a long second, my eyesight blurs...*and the room polarizes...*

I see Jacques as a tesla cluster of tightly wound agendas hovering above his body.

I see the gun through the eyes of the three marks inside me, all at once, and it floods me with a burning lust for blood, the control of it all wrenching from my body in just one shatter-shard moment, the lenses over my eyes fogging under the intense bright light of the darkness...and then I reel it back in, screaming inside me for them to get the fuck DOWN...

My thumb breaks again, bringing me back.

The marks scream, but I hold them down.

They bounce back against the Pull and hit my nerves again.

The pain blows through me.

This Mexican standoff is running on borrowed time.

I move my hand behind me, feeling the blood slick against the rough furrow the handcuff is carving in my wrist, my thumb almost flat against the palm of my hand.

I look for the gun—my mother's gun—and I see it on the floor at Tom's head.

My hand is almost free.

And that's when I notice something moving above us.

Shadows, crawling along the ceiling.

8:30

Freefloaters.

Always damn hard to pull.

They move fast, and I sense the marks under my skin scream for them as the shadows descend from above with rough animal grace, pouring down like before.

The mojo dust on the floor burns, and a scream rips through my head.

Both of them solidify in that split second.

No one can see it but me.

I see it as a vague mist, not fully defined—and for a minute I'm not sure what's happening—but then they pour themselves back into the air, their psychoplasmic flesh scorched, hovering for one long slo-mo instant, writhing in agony... *and I see their eyes.* Beaming from the Blacklight, oozing through like a spill of strange glowing toxicity. Just like the trace that was burned on video by Roosevelt's console.

Two of them.

Mad bastards.

They hang there, picking their targets.

Roosevelt sees it and screams at Jacques: "They're right behind you!"

When the kid's voice cuts through the room, one of the marks spins in slow-mo, moving for him. The smell of its burned flesh bursts across the room like oozing scum in a basement full of bodies. Streamers of shadows shred the air, zeroing right in on Roosevelt's radar ping, and I smell its breath lingering there, the sour smell of dark desperate hunger...

I release the Pull.

It's hard.

Painful.

I almost can't do it with so much feedback.

The bolt tears from me, takes a year of my life with it—and it gets to the mark just a second before the mark gets to Roosevelt. I feel the white-hot frenzy of shredded insanity as my mind connects with its murky, burning substance for just one second, and it fights me hard, screams like razors inside my skull as I knock the shit out of it in mid-air.

Damn, that hurt.

And it's getting worse.

The razor screams blow apart and spray acid across my electrified mind, as the shadow of the mark cracks backward, skidding on the floor again, screaming as the mojo dust takes another bite, still clawing and ripping, screaming in pain, still trying to escape the Pull. It's strong and I can't hold it. Too much pain. Have to... *have to...*

Jacques is confused for about three seconds.

I think he even hears the screaming.

As the burning mark rises from the floor and looms inches above him.

He sees me turn white, my eyes re-focusing. And as he leans forward to get my attention again, the shadow over his shoulder lunges in.

I focus the Pull again, but the pain ruins my attack.

The shadow hits Jacques. His nervous system takes the charge like a champ. He hardly even notices, blinking twice and staring me down like a maniac.

Agent Kendall feels his knees go weak, the Uzi almost falling out of his hands.

As the other one slides easy into his body.

I feel the shockwave blow in the room, the two ghosts screaming together, voices-on-voices, modulated and run through with distortion like a choir of ill children as they strike pay dirt, the explosion of the new union blasting backward from their bodies to pin me to the chair.

And...*I see again...*

The twisted shapes spin each man up in their webs, oozing into them. It fills Jacques with an intense burn of power, and he thinks it's just the adrenaline of the moment—the thrill of the gig set before him. The thing settles inside his body, finding his wasted humanity and torn-to-hell family issues easy to get a grip on. A kindred spirit. It's like watching two amoebas make out in a hellish mutant dance...

I flicker back and forth.

Feeling the Blacklight, and then seeing the room...

Roosevelt doesn't see it, but he feels it.

Knows exactly what just happened.

My hand...almost loose...

Lauren's eyes are wider now, as she struggles with her cuffed wrists.

Jacques shakes his head and I see the monster inside him, spreading across his body, translucent just beneath the skin, though he has no idea what's happening to him.

I lurch forward in my chair. "You feel that, Jacques?"

"Shut up, asshole."

"You're gonna lose complete control of yourself in about five or six minutes. You've got one inside you now."

He almost snarls at me. "Shut your mouth, asshole."

"I'm telling you, man..."

"You're some kind of fucking hypnotist—*this is all bullshit.*"

Agent Kendall rubs his eyes, shakes his head. "He's right...I don't feel so good."

"You're both holding weapons," Roosevelt shouts, his voice run through with panic. "You'll kill each other when the marks get control of you—maybe worse!"

"Good one, kid," Jacques says, his sadistic grin coming back in a major way—only this time it's darker. He pulls a black handle from his back pocket and hits a red stud on it. A steel blade pops up and catches the dim light. He picks up the bottle of Jameson's and fills the plastic cup again.

Walks toward the kid with the knife and the booze.

His ice-killer intensity focuses into a sharp stream and cuts through the air, stinging me hard, and the marks inside me eat it up, coming to the surface like starving convicts sensing a free lunch. I force them down, managing a weak scream in the backburn: "Jacques, don't hurt him anymore—come *over here,* you jerk!"

"No dice, Buck. You're gonna watch something really nasty now. Unless you feel like telling me something."

"I'll confess! I'll confess to anything—*just don't hurt him!*"

"I don't think you're telling me the truth."

The blade moves closer to Roosevelt's face, and Jacques hisses at him: "Do *YOU,* kid?"

Roosevelt jerks away, but he ain't got nowhere to run, his hands looped through the arm of the chair. He's feeling the burn of the thing under Jacques's skin: his controlled madness, and the animal essence of the mark swimming levels below that, spewing out into the world in bursts of psychic blowback that throttle us both. It flashes in on me, strobing my senses, teasing the marks, bringing them up, and I smash them down. Barely. Just hanging in there now.

As the blade slides into Roosevelt's face.

Jacques cuts shallow at first.

Then works his way a little deeper along his chin.

The kid sucks in air, toughing it out—and Jacques stops the blade and twists it in the muscle, looking back at me:

"You were *saying*, Buck?"

I don't say anything, held fast by the smell of his cruelness and the dark stink of the monster roaring in his blood...and as it slowly oozes across his consciousness, eating all it can eat... *I see him, all of him, clear as day:*

Jacques was a bully in school, a killer by the time he was fifteen. Lit up bums for fun with his rich redneck friends back home, wherever the hell that was. It was easy for him to become a stone killer, he never had a moral compass to begin with. I feel all that in his past, and I see him standing in other rooms like this, twisting the knife, just like he's twisting it now, giving into the worst sort of inhumanity, the purest essence of savage animals disguised as human beings, all in the name of the God-Almighty American Dream. Guantanamo Bay. Iraq. Rooms made of unforgiving steel, his heart corroded and punished by bloodlust, his darkest self set free in ways he never would have imagined. Ways I never could have imagined, either. Because, like most professional killers who hold dark secrets, he's an expert at hiding it. Even from guys like me.

But now it's cut loose in the room.

Cut loose and bleeding.

And in just a few minutes...it will be controlled by something even worse.

His voice is already starting to change:

"I'm supposed to get a real confession out of you, terrorist. Not some made-up ghost story. It's going down, one way or another. We get what we want. Even when it means going down twisted."

He takes the knife out of Roosevelt's skin and holds it up for me to see.

Dumps the whisky right in the open wound.

This time Roosevelt screams, real loud.

Jacques's voice dips low again, oozing:

"What say we cut this short?"

He aims the blade for Roosevelt's neck.

And my thumb finally gives.

The crack of the bone snaps the air, my hand going free.

* * *

8:33

Agent Kendall sees me whip the handcuffs through the arm of the chair and slash them around in a deadly arc, right toward his face—it all goes down in a second-and-a-half, and he's dazed from taking the mark, his machinegun thumbed to semi-auto. That gives me half a chance. His finger hits the trigger in the same moment I get to his jaw with the cuffs. The bullet shrieks across the space above my head as the barrel jerks upward, and the modified high-velocity round strikes home in the big window behind me, making a dent in the safety glass. It holds, with a hairline crack that sizzles.

And I'm bringing my right elbow up into Kendall's nose as he stumbles back. I score his jaw again instead. He bites his tongue in half when that happens and spews blood all over me, dropping the Uzi. The gun does a heavy metal clatter in the room and I kick it toward Lauren, ten feet across the metal floor, just as Kendall comes back at me with a blurred fist and Jacques spins with the switchblade, reaching under his jacket for the revolver. My thoughts speed forward like turbine thrust—a silver flash of muscle memory and iron auto-pilot cutting through the pain writhing mercilessly in my body as I duck Kendall's blow and whip my leg around his ankle, dropping the bottom from his center of gravity. He falls on his ass. I hear the hammerclick of Jacques's gun—the thick steel ratcheting back so hard it sounds like an anvil crash.

Then the room fills with thunder as Smith and Wesson preach the word.

The sermon misses me by inches.

I duck and roll as the shot thunders past my ear, his aim spoiled by Roosevelt, who tangles up his feet with a sneaky move. The gun goes off three times more as Jacques struggles to stay upright, his bullets cracking the safety glass again. The agent stumbles, hatred spilling across his face, distorting in a bizarre series of other faces that ripple out from the surface of his skin, making his eyes turn red—and then he spins on Roosevelt with the gun, yelling:

"You son of a bitch!"

The kid jerks his head out of the way of the next shot, jamming his eyes shut, the ignited gunpowder scraping his skin, his hair sizzling back in frayed crispies. Jacques grabs him by the throat and starts to force the gun into his mouth, the hot metal burning the kid's lips.

"Hold still, you little fuck—*you FUCK!*"

I get to him a half-second too late.

His finger hits the trigger.

The gun clicks empty.

I hit Jacques with a slash-and-kick combination from behind. It seems almost impossible, but I hardly phase the son of a bitch, and he spins fast, slapping me hard across my face. The knockout reflex goes to work on me, screaming at my legs to call the game, but I stay on my feet, bringing my arms up as he tries to clock me with the empty gun. My block is a steel bar that sends shockwaves back through Jacques's whole body and makes him drop the weapon.

Now, I go for the nasty.

He sees my nerve pinch coming a mile away when I aim my good hand at his upper arm—I'm making a try for the heavy damage score, and he blocks it hard. That's good. It distracts him from what comes in on his left: my bad hand clutched into a solid fist, like a white-hot ball of complete fucking agony with knuckles riding point, crashing directly into his teeth in a straight-arm power piston right out of *Enter the Dragon.* The monster inside him screams as he loses ten of his pearly whites and chokes on blood, stumbling back. And I press the attack, hitting him again with both hands, feeling my thumb break in another spot as I connect with all his worst places—his soft places. You never aim for hard bone. You strike where it hurts and where it can't hurt you. But everything hurts when you have a broken thumb. He puts up his right fist to block my next three shots and then I go for his finger, but he fakes me out and grabs my wrist, tossing me head-over-asshole into the next window over. I bounce off the glass and slide down the wall, land flat on my back, the world jittering in and out of focus...

Blacklight in rough bursts.
Cutting me like flying glass.

Like a strobelight going off in my face.

The rushing, throbbing, rematerializing room vibrating in on all sides like a million phantom movie scenes at once, jumbling everything...

Agent Kendall stands to his feet, joining his buddy. The marks inside them glow brighter now, taking control, spreading through their veins and boiling to the surface of their skin like some shifting black-and-blue disease—the lifeblood of tortured animals rushing to meet the ferocity of human killing machines. Jacques is a bad kid torn to hell and reassembled as a monster wearing flesh—Kendall is a different sort of crazy, an ex-Marine with real passion for hurting people, but not as crazy as his partner. His eyes wink back his raw insanity, blood drizzling down his chin and neck from his bitten-in-half tongue. The two agents move toward me from both sides... the room blinding me with darkness that flashes... the thunder and speed of the train rocking me on my feet... shaking my senses loose in wave after wave. How fast are we going now? Has to be more than four hundred. The speed tunnel is coming up soon—we'll be faster then than any land vehicle has ever gone before. It's shaking me to pieces.

I have to get past these goons, to the locked door.

Lauren will have the code key.

Maybe.

I struggle to pull myself back...

It flickers in and out again.

The marks in my gut jab me and make me see...

I pull back, concentrating on the pain sleeting through my nervous system.

It strobes over me, blasting me backward...

I fight hard and put my feet on the floor, anchoring myself.

Yes.

Back now...

The two agents come in for the kill.

With their bare hands.

I've got one good hand, and it's weighed down with steel bracelets.

Can't use the Pull again until the marks cut and run, and I'm already weak.

The odds are ten to one against.

And they know it.

They smell what's inside me and home in on it like deadly robots.

I look for the Uzi—it's ten feet away on the floor at Lauren's feet, but she can't get to it with her hands cuffed.

I look too late.

They hit me once and it's the fight of my life.

8:35

I feel the hot force of the mark possessing Jacques—it cuts across my airspace with a hammercrack that turns the blur of his fist into a deadly missile as he stabs at me with a stunning right hook. I turn my head fast before it gets to me, and I duck under his next swing, right into Kendall's roundhouse kick, which takes my midsection, imploding me like a sub hit by a torpedo, blowing all my air. In that frozen moment I feel the gag reflex twang my gut and it comes whizzing up to score a direct hit in the back of my throat. I think I might actually puke—which would be really goddamn good right about now—but it only hurts. A thunder wave of nausea and black sickness ripples across me and I double over as Kendall slaps my face backhanded, spitting blood in my eye. Nothing breaks, but the blood stings and I fly back into Jacques's next right hook, which ricochets like a stone against my forehead, right where he clobbered me with his gun before, and the pain drills a hole in my brain.

The contact lenses keep the blood from blinding me.

But it burns like a son of a bitch.

I manage to kick Jacques away and pull one of the razors from my sleeve, swinging around as Kendall comes at me again, his fist just missing my midsection, and my elbow slams against the back of his head as the momentum of his charge carries him through empty space. Bone smashes against bone. It dazzles him, but he spins back fast, and I cut across Kendall's face with the razor, scoring deep gashes in his eyes, sending him to the floor just in time to avoid the next series of merciless mid-air slashes that come from Jacques—he's faster than hell now, controlled by newfound power, his reflexes superhuman, his skin crawling with blisters and cold black blood. I see an opening and kick him again, much harder. I feel his ribcage shatter and mushy things become paste inside him. The voices of the marks yell curses in my ear. My feet stab at him again and again, smashing...*smashing*...

He just smiles.

I just burst his liver to shit and *the son of a bitch is smiling*.

Kendall is slithering away from us, his face running between his fingers. Screams tear their way out of his lungs—modulated multi-tones composed in a nightmare and cut loose through a bad channel. I pull myself together through sheets of blurred vision, weird noises, the speed of the train slurring me worse than ever...and I face the thing-in-Jacques on my feet. He plunges in again and I sidestep his attack, try to grab for his hand, try to break his finger, but he blurs away like a mirage, consumed by the streaks of light and shrieking voices...*then he comes back hard,* materializing in the mist, screaming my name. As he burns forward, I do a spinning backward kick that lands in the center of his throat, breaking something. The force of it staggers him back, but he recovers instantly. I block three more quick punches. He catches my bad hand on the third and twists my thumb back, the sheer electric shockwave dropping me to my knees. Holds me there while he reaches for my throat. Gets both hands locked on me, cutting off my windpipe, bearing down without mercy. Can't breathe now. Can't pry his hands loose.

He's going to kill me.

He's hauling me off my feet, and my feet kick at him, but he's turned into steel—nothing hurts him, it just fuels him.

I'm going to die.

In the corner of one eye, I see Kendall clutching his own destroyed face, hobbling back in the direction of the fallen machinegun—and Lauren kicks it out of his way, sending it back down the aisle of seats. He roars and backhands her—and as he turns to follow the spinning Uzi, Roosevelt trips him. He falls on his face, screaming again.

I grab for Jacques's eyes now. He's got me three feet off the ground and I have nothing left to fight with. Except my thumbs. They plunge deep through the irises, the blood and humors pouring down across his face—and he doesn't even yell.

It doesn't slow him down at all.

I bury my thumbs to the last knuckle and it still does no good.

I'm starting to black out now . . .

Images reaching me now . . .

Voices that might be memories . . .

Signals . . .

From the Blacklight . . .

And Kendall is stumbling to the Uzi.

Picking it up.

Turning back toward us, almost blind.

His ripping, modulated snarl cutting through slashed and pulverized flesh, which now begins to bubble and shift, blotches breaking out, making him a monster with alien cancer. He raises the gun in our direction and fires. The blood in his destroyed eyes ruins the shot, and the bullet bounces off the lead-lined walls like a steel insect. I hear it buzzing around the compartment as Jacques tightens his grip on my throat and I know I have about one second to live and I have to try something else . . . *anything else . . .*

The voices, screaming now . . .

Screaming . . .

I lurch my entire body weight forward, my hands buried in Jacques's face, throwing his center of gravity off as the next shot blows through the room, missing us both again, hitting the safety glass instead. I hear something crack loudly and I realize it's not the window—but Jacques's spine, as he falls on one of the chair arms, the hard chromed plastic elbowing into his back. He hisses as the pain rips through. It's enough of a shock to make him let go of me. And when he does, I wrench my hands loose from his face and grab his little finger, bending it back like a Popsicle stick, the bone splitting with a deep red *KRAKKKK!*

The sharp jolt travels up his arm and throttles his brain.

Shaking what's inside him loose.

I dive for the floor again as Kendall opens fire again. The mark shrieks into the air above Jacques, who now lies across the seat, crippled and blinded—but it doesn't matter because his life is over. He takes Kendall's bullet, and the one after it. And then the one after that. The shots perforate him in a gory connect-the-dots pattern, like a swarm of angry wasps coming in for a divebomb, blasting his body all over the place, chewing what's left of his wicked smile into bloody chum and exploding his heart in black crimson through his black suit and tie. Kendall keeps on firing, still half blind, shredding his partner as I scramble toward him, my head low, the pain in my guts prodding me forward. He can't even see me when I come up on his right and chop the gun out of his hand, then slice an uppercut with the handcuffs, cutting his mouth in half. Teeth fly like bloody pearls. Blood flows down his face. I think he's crying now.

Have to wrap this up in a hurry.

I get to the bone in his little finger and it goes easy.

Kendall falls over, his human consciousness shocking back into his nervous system fast and putting him under as the mark abandons ship in double time, flying into the air to join the other one, the two entities spiderwalking in space again, but now I can see them clear as day: faces that becomes daggers that become teeth that become slobbering caverns full of primal ooze, all of it shot through with fire and ice and passion and deep black hatred. It swims there—one big nasty mess of the worst things on earth and in the Blacklight, coiling in space.

They're wide open.

Defenseless against me now.

I reach out with the Pull.

Calling the nightmare toward me.

Calling on the power of the marks already swimming in me.

This is suicide, just like Darby said.

Taking in this many.

But I have to see like they see.

I have to know what they know.

These creatures were once men, and those men killed my mother and father.

I will know why.

I will see the truth.

I'm almost there and the answers hover right in front of me—right inside of me.

I have to do this.

The marks rip at the air and scream, trying to pull away as I reel them in. They can't fight me. They're weakened now, and I'm better than they are.

Do you hear me, you sons of bitches?

Come here now.

Come into me and eat shit.

I ground myself into the floor as the Pull brings them home, down through my outstretched arms, pinning me there like lightning, and I ignore the pain as they go, tuning out the pulsing throb of the broken bones in my hand. I only hear the relentless screech of the marks sheer across my mind like blades. I only concentrate on their attack—and using that attack against them.

Using it to Pull them in.

I bring my fists to my side, *my whole body infusing with the glow . . .*

And I stand in the Blacklight, seeing what they see, the memories, surrounding me now, brighter and more vivid than ever, five bad marks accelerating my vision beyond all reason—five dead men who were there to see it all go down . . .

The eight followers of Blackjack Williams kneel in the scorching sun.

His face breaks the silhouette that shrouds him, as he steps forward, his hands full of razors.

And his face is my face.

I am Jack and Jack is me.

Jack is my father.

I pull back, the marks blowing my mind and tearing me down, riding the stabbing pain inside my body.

My father.

I hit the floor in agony, my hair frying white, the inside of my skin burning.

He is my father . . .

My teeth clench hard—so hard, one of them shatters in my mouth.

And my mother blows his head off . . .

I scream to get control, the sound of my own agony rippling through my body.

...blows his head off...

Five marks, down deep, exploding in my guts, wanting control of me.

...with the gun.

The gun.

Where is it?

Lost in the fight.

The Blacklight hits me one final time—and this time it stays with me. The bright laser glow flares up as I go deeper, pulsing against the contact lenses, almost melting them. I see what dead people see, and it takes over my entire body, burning and crackling and filling my eyes with blinding darkness. It feels like I am a god again. It's where I belong. I don't know if I can pull back this time, and I don't care...

I take the charge again and I'm deep now.

Deeper than I've ever gone.

The room sizzles and hisses on all sides of me. I stand there in the center of the storm. The train accelerates faster now. It's a long dark tunnel to infinity—I see the faces of a million lives shattered and blown back to me, floating in mid-air and then vanishing, clouds of nothingness, superheated and translucent, there and not there. The lenses hardly keep the light from burning a hole in my mind, but it doesn't matter. I'm almost blind, but I don't care. The marks scream inside me, and I can't pull back from what they see... but what they see is my birthright... what they see is where I belong... it moves through me like the sweet electric hum of memories brought back to me. Things I've been searching for all my life. So many souls inside my body now, powering the burn—but I control them now, standing on my feet in the storm. I only have to look deeper to see everything that was lost to me.

My mother.

My father.

The gun... the gun...

The hard metal click of the hammer brings be back to earth.

I look up and I see the gun.

Held in a clenched fist.

Aimed right at my heart.

By Tom.

FIFTEEN

THE GUN

8:46
 "Sorry, buddy. But you have to admit, I *did* warn you not to trust your friends."

The marks growl, and I slide back under again . . .

Blacklight.

The neon glow, outlining him in cruel shadows, making me see his treachery and deception—it floats over his skin in boils of red energy, dancing like jiggers of blood and flaming coal, everything revealed to me. His hand doesn't shake. He stands on his feet, one arm still cuffed to the steel pole, but he has me dead-bang. The wound in his shoulder ain't so bad after all. He was playing possum, and the whole nervous thing was an act. Pretending the whole time, so he'd have an excuse to unload on me when the shit got thick—and plausible deniability if his shot missed.

Goddamn you, Tom.

The power to see him as he really is electrifies every nerve ending in my body, the marks inside me powering it. I lunge forward with a snarl that comes from the unsettled rage of five dead men, but he re-aims the gun at my heart and spits:

"Stop right there. It's the end of the line, Buck. I have to take you out."

The gun, aimed right at my heart.

But he hesitates.

He doesn't want to do it.

Our friendship, all those years together, seeking bad marks and blowing them to shit—all of that was real.

This is just business.

"Who paid you to do me, Tom? Was it Jaeger?"

"No. It wasn't the old man. And that's all I'm gonna tell you, kid. Except that I'm sorry. I didn't want it to come down this way. But I've got problems you don't know about."

"And every man for himself, right?"

"You're a mercenary, too, Buck. We all are at the end of the day. Some of us just have a better excuse for it, that's all."

"So what are you waiting for?"

His hand shakes on the trigger.

On my side, it's the gun that killed my father.

On his side it's a rusted piece of shit.

But what happens on this side is all that matters.

And he knows it.

Still, his hand shakes.

I have to pull myself back again…I have to…

…but I don't want to.

I want to stay.

I belong here.

The power hits me again and again, like the purest drug, and I don't care that it means my death. This was always where I was meant to be. I knew it when I was a kid. I've denied it all my life. I never looked deep enough because the world of men seduced me. But this—this place of shadows and voices, rushing ahead and clobbering me at hundreds of miles an hour—this is the speedway and the slipstream that gives me the power I always deserved.

I belong here.

This is mine.

Kill me, Tom.

Make me stay here forever.

So that I can see everything.

He sees my eyes flash red with cancer—even from his side—and he smiles his dirty jack-o-lantern smile:

"I knew it would come down to this one day, Buck. We both knew you would fall again. All it took was a little push, huh?"

The marks speak to me in animal voices and they know they've won.

I am glad they have won.

I want them to win.

So many of them inside me now, showing me the way.

They scrape and bite and scream. They are bare essence and sheer brute force. Truth. Knowledge. They pull me down and down, where the Blacklight is blackest, where the Pull will consume us all in one big bite...

...and I see the gun going off in my father's face again... and again... and again...

I see my mother leaning over his dead body, crying...

And it fills me with hate...

...as Tom clenches his teeth and sees my death, his finger closing...

No.

You backstabbing piece of shit.

You are not going to kill me.

Not with that gun.

I push against the desire to stay. It fights me, but I do it anyway, struggling for the surface of the real world, everything flowing past me like sulfur and ash and seawater... but I can't... I want to stay...

His finger squeezes the trigger.

My death.

But it never comes.

The gun doesn't fire.

His eyes go wide as he realizes it isn't going to work. My mind explodes with hate again, the world pulsing and spinning. I jump up and tackle him from six feet away in a running leap, and he falls backward, his wrist twisting against the handcuffs that hold him to the pole, the gun clattering from his other hand and spinning out along the floor, swallowed in neon blackness. I punch him across the jaw with my bad hand, and another one of my fingers breaks, the pain shocking up my arm, blazing into my brain like a needle of pure adrenaline—and it sends me to the surface for just a moment. The marks scream and recoil, giving up control of me, and I go for it, punching through the maelstrom...struggling for air... Yes... YES...

8:50

I come back with a terrible kick.

The Blacklight hisses under my line of sight, hovering like a restless black surf just below my chin, like I'm breaking water just barely, pulling in desperate air. Tom lies on the floor and I hunch over him, my fist still pinned to his jaw. He's half awake, stunned. The gun lies next to him. I grab it and check my heartbeat, making sure I'm still there.

Yeah.

Still here.

Just barely.

"Buck...holy shit, man." That's Roosevelt, breathless, blood sleeting down the side of his face.

I struggle to find my voice. "Did you...see all that?"

"Yeah, we saw it. The son of a bitch was gonna whack you."

"Didn't work because he wasn't standing in the Blacklight. Gun's only good for killing ghosts." I stick the rusty antique in my jacket pocket.

"Or someone else who can see like you do," Roosevelt says.

"Maybe."

And who the fuck hired him to kill me?

It doesn't make any sense—maybe it's not supposed to.

Dammit.

I want to punch Tom again. I want to rip him apart with my bare hands. I settle for hitting him a few more times with the handcuffs, just to make sure he's out.

No time for righteous revenge.

The shit is thick and I have to move fast.

Have to get to the other marks on the train.

Have to get these mean bastards out of me.

If I go under again, I really will stay.

I'll never come back.

I stumble to my feet, rusted, shoving the gun in my jacket pocket, the fingers of the Blacklight tilting everything and nothing, hovering my whole body at the edge of oblivion, making me smell old lives I've forgotten, teasing me to come back and feel it again. I fight it and stumble forward. I feel like a lumbering shell—some kind of half-animated dead thing, running on empty, reaching for traces of myself on instinct. I hardly hear what Lauren says next:

"Unlock these cuffs. I can get the emergency doors open—I have the passkey."

Roosevelt lets out a huff. "What'd I tell ya, my man?"

Lauren nods in Kendall's direction. "I think he has the keys. Hurry up."

I move past the exploded and mutilated body of Agent Jacques. His buddy is still passed out on the floor next to the bloody remains, drawing short breath, abandoned by the thing that possessed him, bleeding and out for the count. I come up with the keys, pocket them fast. I move toward Lauren and the kid, looking around for the Uzi...

I hear something rise from the floor behind me.

Hissing.

8:52

I turn to face Tom, and I don't even need the Blacklight to see that a new mark lives just under his skin, laughing at me. Slobbering. Wrapping his whole body in shadows, making his eyes fizz with bloody stars and ice blackness. His face breaks out in blotches as it manipulates him. It's been hiding out for a while. Slipped inside him while the fighting was going on—I never would have noticed the change, I was so busy getting my ass kicked. He jerks it back for a few seconds, and it clamps down harder. I see the muscles shift and reorganize under his skin, his rolls of fat pulsing and the wrinkles on his face shifting in waves. He makes awful bone-shredding noises, his tendons snapping in his neck as he twists and bends, controlled like a puppet, the last trace of his last mission as a human being stumbling through his lips in broken syllables:

"I have...to kill you, Buck."

"Why? Who paid you to do it? Tell me, *you son of a bitch!*"

Usually you can get them to say anything when they're under the influence—but his iron will keeps it back. The same iron will that made him a stone machinegun killer back in the bush, made it so easy for him to sell me out:

"I can't tell you...I need the money...*I'm sorry...*"

His voice pitch-shifts again, into a dirty whine—a sad, pathetic sound, like children begging for their lives. He takes two lurching steps toward me, his right hand tearing through the handcuffs with a wet cracking spray of arterial red. The bones snap, spiking his nerve centers, but it's just like I thought—the mark has been in him a while, and it's not letting go that easy. I feel it shake and quiver under his skin, its grip loosening, as he slips forward in his own blood and keeps on coming:

"I HAVE TO KILL YOU!"

The Uzi is three feet away from me.

As he slamdances forward, screaming my name in a drunken slur, I grab the gun and hit the trigger. I've never fired a gun in my life and this one punches me on the recoil like a heavyweight fighter, right in my midsection, stinging my bruised ribs, as the bullet tears loose and misses Tom completely. My next shot hacks into his shoulder just before he gets to me, a rooster tail of blood *plooshing* into the air behind him as his hands reach out to claw at my eyes.

I use the gun like a club, straight up into his chin.

His head cracks back at a crazy angle, long enough for me to bear down on the mark with the Pull as it starts to come loose from his body.

I hear it scream inside Tom, knowing what I'm up to and not liking it one damn bit. He slashes at me with a mutilated fist, cutting the air over my head as I duck and roll, coming up behind him, the gun still in my hands.

I aim again and click empty.

Shit.

He turns into a blur, leaping away from me, the mark struggling with the shock to Tom's system—the bullet in his shoulder, the broken fingers chiseling at its will over flesh. It hangs inside him, just barely.

Tom opens his mouth and a stream of garbled alien noise comes rolling out—some bizarre feedback produced by an animal squeezed half to death, pulverized and back to earth as a creature of supernatural instinct and intense power barely held in check. The thing inside him sees the marks floating under my skin, screaming to be free...and it *wants them*. Wants to be *joined with them*.

And it senses that I will beat it, like the others.

I see Tom's eyes scan the room, the mark under him looking for a way out of here, and it sees the damaged window just feet away, pockmarked by bullets, and the desert moving fast *just on the other side...*

No, you bastard.

I take a step toward Tom, and it manages to scream words this time: *"NO...YOU'RE...NOT...GOING TO...WIN..."*

It grabs onto Tom's entire body with all its power. His feet leave the ground and he goes helter-skelter in midair, flying for the window.

His head smashes like a bloody fruit when it hits the glass.

The splattering sound of bone and brain and iron-hard spirit force hammers through the entire compartment as the mark tears loose, using Tom's abandoned flesh like a battering ram, heaving him into the glass twice more...

And the window finally gives all the way.

8:58

The cabin decompresses instantly as a thundering fist of heat and dust sucks all the air out of the room and replaces it with a rushing chaos. Roosevelt and Chance are nearly torn from their seats as the blast hits them, but the handcuffs keep them down.

The handcuffs...*yes*...

As I am knocked down by the blast, I grab for one of those chrome steel handrails and manage to slap the open bracelet still dangling from my good wrist around the metal. With about a half-second to spare, I use my bad hand to do it and it hurts like fucking hell, but then I'm anchored in the center of the compartment, as the storm levels off and the force of the sucking blowback calms down some—we're not in a plane or in outer space, so this isn't gonna kill me. Just have to stay on one piece for a few more seconds. Just have to keep control of the marks. Just have to... *have to*...

Emergency lights flare on and bathe the room in rolling loops of red-and-blue.

A siren shrieks.

I look up at the window.

And what I see happen next I will never forget.

The mark is a boiling, shifting spider-shape, full of red teeth and split-changing appendages, clawing at the jagged exit of shattered glass, still holding on to Tom's destroyed body, riding it for dear life, desperate and screaming—it wants to ride him right out and be free. But it's not going anywhere. The magnetic force of the train is holding it back. I was right about the maglev field keeping them on board, and this son of a bitch is finding out the hard way.

But Tom's body is another story.

It's only human.

The bloody mess shudders and cracks and smears, surrendering its substance a little at a time, an unrecognizable wad of decimated flesh and bone wearing cheap shoes. And it finally gives in to the laws of physics and tears away from the grip of the mark, exploding into a million glittering fragments, the pieces of Tom splashing from here to eternity, most of it sucking through the destroyed window. The mark screams again, bouncing back into the compartment. It sees me cuffed to the railbar, sees that I'm helpless on the floor—and I can almost sense it licking its lips as it homes in on the shuddering marks inside me. And the Pull. It's thinking fast, this son of a bitch. I don't even bother reaching for the keys to the handcuffs in my pocket—no time. It's coming in like a bat out of hell.

It hits me on the floor.

I take it head-on.

The sirens blare. The lights roll my senses. The mark slams my mind with everything it has—it knows damn-well how disoriented I am. It wants to take the marks inside me, wants to take everything I've got. This was its backup plan. It knew I would be helpless. It knew I'd be weak.

It's smarter than the others. I feel its cruelness slice in. I hear its voice mix with the high whine of the sirens. It's calling me names, spitting in my face, wrapping me in thorns, bringing me under fast.

Yeah, well fuck you, too.

It doesn't see my attack until the Blacklight hits us both. I channel everything into it, not going under like a drowning man, but calling the power to me like a pro. The rush of the Pull blows into my mind and blasts out in a stream of pure white energy that blinds the mark, then pulverizes its rolling plasmic form in mid air, as we tumble in alternate spaces, the shadows and ice-blue darkness bright and terrifying on all sides of us. It tries to back off, but I come at it hard and it screams again. I ground myself, getting to my feet with my hand still cuffed around the pole. The emergency shutters are sliding down over all the windows. I can feel the room re-pressurizing automatically. My lungs work overtime to find purchase in both worlds, and I am the master of it all—as I drag the son of a bitch down. It crackles like lightning channeling along my bones. Number six. Spiraling deep into me, and it's the rush of rushes as it collides with the others, scoring a bomb blast dead in the center of my soul.

And it's power.

PURE FUCKING POWER.

I can do anything here now.

I can see anything here now.

It all belongs to ME.

My mother looks at me and says that I will be safe.

We face each other and her face is beautiful, like the sun and the sky, just over her shoulder.

I see all this so clearly.

I smell her strange scent—like wildflowers shot through with gunmetal—and it reminds me of love that comes easy . . . reminds me of home.

My home is so far away now.

Our home was in Texas, and we are in the desert now.

She tells me this is the way it has to be.

She tells me I will have a life beyond all this madness.

I believe her.

I am seven years old.

She leaves me in the truck and tells me not to follow her.

I will be safe.

And now the vision changes... and I am seeing something I shouldn't see at all... something my mother protected me from...

The vision of my own father.

His wicked smile, like a monster outlined in the sun.

What he does is horrible.

I can't see it all... but I know it's there...

The vision tilts wildly as it shifts again, and it's fragments now, coming in like bits of falling lava rock, scorching my mind:

My mother and father face each other for the final time.

They both knew this moment would come.

They were both ready for it.

The eight followers of Blackjack Williams lie dead at his feet.

Blackjack is my father.

MY FATHER...

The gun kills him.

THE GUN KILLS MY FATHER...

But my mother lies bleeding also, crying over his body. I feel her bottomless sorrow as it takes her hard and deep. She knows she has failed to save him. Her plan was to save my father. Her plan has gone all wrong. I feel all this crash into me—a fusillade of dark emotions, all assigned to someone I can't even remember—someone I remember now, in a scene I was never supposed to see.

She places the gun in the hand of the old man.

She tells the old man to leave it for me.

The old man is a man I have seen before.

But I can't see his face, not here.

I strain to see his face...

I strain so hard it hurts me...

And she cries and cries, her failure consuming her heart and firing the most terrible shot into me... AND THE PAIN CUTS THROUGH ME...

* * *

9:01

The pain brings me back.

I hit the floor, sizzling in the afterburn.

Am I still alive?

The marks swirl and storm inside me, but I beat them back somehow. Something made them back off. The pain backed them off. The pain that runs through my bad hand, fresh and shocking, spiking my nervous system.

I look down and see that I've broken another one of my fingers.

I did it while I was trancing.

I hear Roosevelt's voice:

"Buck... *Buck, get us out of here, man...*"

The world slides apart, then reorganizes itself as I slip to my knees. I am on the brink of everything now. I see it all, but it floats in puzzle-pieces. And the real world has become a blood-and-guts freakshow. I almost can't tell what's real anymore. I'm going on reserves, feel more like a zombie than ever.

But somehow... I get it together.

Six bad souls inside me now—the bad souls who followed my father into the desert. But why did they go with him?

Can't think about it now.

Have to move fast.

Reach for my pocket and pull out the keys.

Uncuff Lauren and Roosevelt.

Reach into my pocket for the gun that killed my father.

When my fingers touch the rust, the marks jab me in my stomach, sensing the death of their master. It's contained here in this wasted artifact, *brought back from the desert after my parents died...*

By the old man.

The old man whose face I couldn't see in the memory.

Agent Dryden is screaming over Jacques's Bluetooth.

He wants to know what the hell is happening in here.

* * *

9:03

Lauren clips the cell onto her ear and starts talking to Dryden.

She tells him what's happened.

There's a lot of silence on the line before he starts making threats—tells her we're all coming up on criminal charges. His voice is rattled and uncompromising like before, sliding down the slope fast. I hear him coming apart.

She tells him she's seen the shit go down with her own eyes—there's no doubt about any of this weird ghost business at all now.

He doesn't buy it.

She tells him about Carolyn Lewis and Rashid Hopi again.

He doesn't buy it.

I scream at him to get those people away from the others and he laughs—there's nothing wrong with anyone back there. Says it like a man full of fear for his job and full-on panic—a man who never saw human flesh shredded by ghosts.

His voice breaks apart as he screams.

Crazy, getting worse.

Lauren keeps talking to him, keeps her voice calm and rational, tells him about his two best men who went berserk and wouldn't die, and Dryden gets angrier and angrier, making threat after threat. She finds her Python on the floor and checks the ammo—full clip, fifteen shots. Tom's gun is long-gone somewhere.

I waver on my feet, holding the marks down.

The kid sees it all swimming in my face. "Buck...you're looking bad, man. We have to get those goddamn marks out of you."

"It won't work. Tried it before. I think they *want* to be inside me. Something about my mother and father..."

"You're delirious, man. We have to—"

"I know what I'm talking about. *Believe me*. We gotta get to the rear of the train. There's at least two more back there, riding in bodies."

"You sure you can take them?"

"No. But I have to try."

"You're in deep, Buck. I know what that's like for a guy like you—you gotta ask yourself why you're *really* keeping those bastards inside you."

I trance again for a moment, feeling the truth of his words, *feeling the limitless power that hovers just out of my reach*...

"I can see it all, kid...*I can see everything*..."

"Buck, you're losing it. You've gotta take a breath, man."

Lauren clicks off the Bluetooth in the middle of Dryden's next rant and checks her watch. "There's no time. We hit the speed tunnel in fifteen minutes, then this train pulls into Vegas. With Dryden in charge of everything, those passengers in the back will walk."

Roosevelt makes a face. "Goddammit."

I turn to Lauren, righting myself. "Can we get back there?"

"I think so. Are you up to it, Buck?"

"I have no idea."

But some chance is better than no chance at all.

"I think it's a really bad idea," the kid says. "You're in strung-out shape. You should at least try to purge the ones you've got in you."

"I'm telling you it won't work. They haven't digested at all. They're trying to *possess me*."

"That's even worse, man."

Lauren is already moving to the steel emergency door. Her fingers fly over the keypad and it opens with a thick hiss. She looks back at us with a do-or-die coldness on her face. "Whatever happens, I'm doing my *job*. The people on this train are my responsibility and I can't let that maniac endanger their lives."

Roosevelt rolls his eyes. "So what's the plan? Shoot it out with them?"

"If we have to."

"Christ...I'm surrounded by heroes."

She gets back on the Bluetooth, and starts up with Dryden again.

Keeping him distracted.

We move forward through the casino and into the VIP corridor. Roosevelt breaks off into our base camp compartment and gets back on his console as me and Lauren make the next sealed emergency hatchway, the one that closes off the restaurant.

Beyond the restaurant, the movie theater.

And the last of the marks.

The last of Jack's eight followers.

My father's disciples.

I can feel them close, even this far away.

She keys the sequence, still jabbering to Dryden, who still hurls curses and tells us we're all under arrest.

Her code doesn't work this time.

SIXTEEN

HOSTAGE NEGOTIATIONS

9:05

I waver on my feet, surrounded on all sides by pain.

My ribs sting, my face burns with slashes, wet with blood.

The marks hover just below all that, the pain keeping them down, keeping me from going over into the Blacklight. It's almost all I have left to fight them. I concentrate on it, sensing the train's intense power, and the magnetic energy thundering forward, toward the tunnel, and the big jump to hyperspace.

The Pull, swirling within my heart.

The marks swimming at the edge of it...

The kid's fingers fly over the keys of his console and he spits curses, telling us half his programs have been wasted, mumbling a lot of technobabble I can't understand. I tell him to start speaking English and he makes it real simple for us:

"Dryden's guys back there must be wireheads—or maybe he's smarter than he looks. They crashed the security system with a series of really sophisticated viruses and just left the bones. Wiped out everything."

Lauren leans over his shoulder, looking at the computerized gobbledygook on his screen. "What about your cameras?"

"They're all out in the rear section of the train. They aren't taking any chances. Dryden's little wig-out in the casino must've put the fear of God into them."

"Can you get us past the door?"

"I can try—but I'm telling you, they fucked it up good. Scrambled the code combinations on the door to the restaurant from the other side. I've got some backup lockbreakers and I know my way into the system guarding the security protocols on the train, but it'll take a few minutes."

She looks at her watch again. "We don't have a few minutes."

"Tough shit, that's the way it is."

"Start working."

She clicks on the Bluetooth, as she walks through the open door to the VIP corridor. Stops at the locked restaurant entrance, still shuttered tight. I stand there in the threshold to the command center, keeping one eye on her, one eye on Roosevelt, my head reeling as the floor accelerates under my feet.

The kid's screen lights up as he gets to something important inside the computer brain running the show. "You feeling the burn, Buck? The tunnel's on the way, and it's gonna get lots worse. According to this, we've just reached four hundred and fifteen miles per hour."

"Get the door open," I say in a huff, hardly finding my voice over the magnetic hum in my head. "We have to take the marks while we're in the tunnel. They'll be disoriented from the speed jump."

"Yeah, and what about you, my man?"

"You asked me that already."

"You never gave me an answer."

"Just get the fucking door open, *Mr. President*."

His screen shows the speed counter, clicking higher and higher, as his fingers fly, trying to work the emergency doors. Trying and failing. The female voice of the computer brain suddenly comes over the speaker system, telling us all to take our seats, that the train is reaching maximum velocity, that new world records are being set with each passing minute...and then she starts counting it off:

Four hundred and twenty miles per hour...

Lauren tries her code again, and when it doesn't work again, she slams her fist into the shuttered steel. "Dryden? Dryden, *talk to me*—what's going on back there?"

His voice finally crackles back over the Bluetooth:

"You don't ask the questions, bitch. I'm the law on this train."

"You have to let us through to the passengers."

"We did this number once and I thought I made myself clear the first time. You and everyone else hired by Jaeger Industries are under arrest. I've already informed my people at the other end of this ride—they're waiting at the Dreamworld to take you into custody."

"So you've already won, Dryden. Just let us see the other passengers."

"Just how fucking stupid do you think we are, bitch?"

His voices rattles, all full of confusion and panic.

I tell the kid to check on Darby, and the kid says he ain't got time for that.

I tell him again, in a much louder voice.

Roosevelt's fingers fly. The update from Facebook reads:

SHEER SECTION EIGHT. DON'T TRUST THE SPOOK.

Great.

Four hundred and thirty miles per hour . . .

We're faster than anything on earth now.

Just a few minutes until we reach hyperspace.

Lauren screams at Dryden, hitting the steel again: "You fucking lunatic—you're gonna get those people back there killed! You don't know what's going on here!"

"I know you and your playmates are all terrorists. I'll see you all rotted in the worst hellhole the United States fucking government can stick you in. You hear me talking, lady? You're all going way the fuck down."

"Fine—arrest us! Just let us see the others NOW!"

Silence on the line.

Roosevelt hits a key and holds his breath.

Something beeps in his console and he looks hopeful for one second. Then it spits a mechanical curse at him and his screen goes dead.

"Goddamn black ice. Government-issue firewall. Ain't no way I'm getting through that."

"Keep trying," I say to him, holding it together.

"I'm telling you, Buck, I can't get it."

"Try again."

He clicks more keys. The screen comes back.

Four hundred and fifty miles per hour . . .

Lauren sputters into the Bluetooth. "Dryden? Dryden . . . *talk to me!*"

Nothing.

Super Spook ain't budging.

The kid makes another run at it, and his face lights up as he hits something that looks important. A series of algorithms scrambles across his face, insanely fast, like the train as it lasers forward.

Four hundred and fifty-five . . .

"Yes," he spits finally. "You little bastard . . . come here . . ."

His fingers click again and a thick metal beep sounds inside the walls of the VIP corridor. His screen goes dead again.

As the steel shutters on the door begin to rumble open.

"Ye of little faith," I say to him, smiling.

"Umm, Buck . . . I didn't do that."

The shutters open all the way.

9:11

Dryden stands in the center of the restaurant.

Rashid Hopi to his left.

Carolyn Lewis and Bethany Sin on his right.

His last two men flanking the party: Agents Ben and Jerry, their Uzis held right at our midsections.

"Hello, Buck," Dryden says calmly, his pistol aimed at Lauren in the open doorway, the laser dot shaking in the center of her forehead. "If you have a gun, Miss Chance, I'd let it hit the floor right now."

She takes the Python out of her shoulder holster with two fingers. She calmly sets it on the floor at her feet.

I see the shadow over Rashid Hopi—the mark possessing his body. It hovers and snarls there, and his eyes beam with blackness. Invisible to everyone but me.

I can't see the one in Carolyn Lewis.

Can't see it at all.

I look harder—strain myself to visualize that terrible shadow that should be moving over her, but it just isn't there anymore.

I take one step into the room.

Dryden makes a fast move and shoves the barrel of his big gun against Bethany's head, grabbing her throat, spitting at me:

"You stop right there."

I stop right there.

Bethany whines wordlessly, her mind radaring back to me in rough waves.

"You girlfriend is cute," Dryden hisses, forcing her to kneel in front of him, keeping the gun jammed in the back of her neck. "Let's not ruin her career any time soon. Just you stand there and don't move a *muscle.*"

The marks inside me scream for the prize just ahead.

They scream for what's inside Dryden.

Four hundred and fifty-six...

The world shifts and bends, the Blacklight spiraling at me and then bouncing back against the fast stream of the train, Dryden's voice coming again, distorted this time, black and malevolent. It's something I couldn't hear when he was just a voice on a Bluetooth.

Something really awful.

"I guess you can tell what side I'm on now, can't you, Buck? I was ready for that, too. *This* little lady here couldn't get you off her mind—even when she was out like a light. I think she might even be *in love.* That's always a pretty little wildcard, isn't it?"

It went into him.

It left Carolyn Lewis and went into him.

I should have seen this all along, dammit.

"Now what we have here, Buck, is a hostage situation. And in every hostage situation there are negotiations. I've done it a lot. I'm very good at this. You deal from strength or you don't deal at all."

Four hundred and sixty...

We stand in the eye of the storm, his voice spewing like insectoid tonalities filtering through a human voice box, as the thing inside him comes out a little at a time. He's controlling it and it's controlling him. They've welcomed each other. I can smell the fresh union of kindred psychos blowing across the fast-moving room, mingling together like slime on slime, disgusting and bitter. It jumped from Lewis and into him because they all knew he was in charge—and half-crazy in the bargain.

Dryden wallows in it, his grin slicing the air like a scythe.

Four hundred and seventy . . .

Bethany thinks to me again. She begs me not to let her die.

Says she loves me.

He spits in alien feedback: "Here's the deal. We hit the fast lane in about one minute. When that happens, you're gonna stand there and let nature take its course. Let what's inside you out for some fresh air. All we want is off this fucking train."

"Fuck you."

"Maybe I'm not making myself clear, Buck."

He pulls Carolyn Lewis to her knees and shoots her in the head.

The shot blasts through my mind, keening bio-feedback and terrible sounds of rending soul-matter flying apart as her brain scatters.

She falls forward, one eye drilled out, dead instantly.

Agents Ben and Jerry start to panic, heaving shockwaves I can feel hard, their mouths yapping open in complete shock. Lauren moves for her gun, but Dryden's next shot nicks her hand, bouncing off the floor and back into the room, where something shatters.

She freezes, the red dot hovering on her nose.

Dryden jams the gun back in Bethany's neck and snarls again: "It's like *this,* old buddy. You release the others. Let them *out of you.* We'll all go into fresh new bodies and walk off the train in Vegas."

Bethany, locked in terror, her eyes frozen and electrified.

Dryden, still hissing: "I'll let the other hostages live and walk off right alongside them. Starting with *this one.*"

He jams the gun deeper into her neck.

Four hundred and seventy-five . . .

"You've already got a bloodbath on your hands," Lauren says. "How the hell are you going to explain what just happened here?"

"I thought we were clear on all that, bitch? There was a *terrorist attack* and I just nailed the terrorists cold. They're standing right in front of me."

"You won't get away that clean," she says.

"I *always* get away clean, Miss Chance. I'm smart. Your cameras are wiped. The survivors can be bought off. We'll even use the senator, once he's ours. It all comes down to this, people: you're up the creek and there's nothing you can do about it. The only question is, how many more inno-cent people go with you?"

I look right in his eyes as the mark under there shifts.

It looks right back at me.

"Now give them up, Buck. Give them up *now*. I'm giving you five seconds before this little diva of yours takes one in her very *interesting* brain…"

He looks right at Lauren.

"…and then you're next, *bitch*."

Bethany closes her eyes and waits for it.

The mark inside Rashid Hopi slobbers for payback.

Ben and Jerry pass desperate looks between them. Have a feeling they're trying real hard to figure out which side to land on.

And I have no choice.

I step forward.

I concentrate on the marks inside me, pulling them to the surface.

Four hundred and eighty…

9:13

"That's it, Buck," the-thing-in-Dryden hisses. "Let it happen. Let them out."

One begins to undulate along my bones, crawling like a scared animal, tingling a tentative pulse over my arm as I reach out, aiming my fingers at Dryden. The mark slithers out in a dim fog that turns into a weird Tesla coil dance in mid-air. Dryden can see it and he licks his lips. Rashid Hopi takes two steps forward, ready to intercept the mark. It hovers there, still held by thin plasmic tethers at the end of my fingertips.

Dryden gets impatient.

"GIVE US THE OTHERS, GODDAMN YOU!"

Jams the gun into Bethany's neck again, *his finger curling...*

I force my words out against the force of the accelerating temporal spaces between us, the sound like beads of liquid metal squeezing through my lips, low and tortured, but I have to do it... *have to keep them talking...*

"It's coming... don't kill her..."

My voice slows and warps.

Five hundred...

Dryden grits his teeth and his mark shifts bizarrely, starting to ripple his flesh from the inside, his voice melting in reverse:

"She dies now."

Five hundred and sixty...

The mark inside Rashid Hopi tears loose from his body and shrieks at me, making a grab for the wasted, half-mulched vapor dangling at the end of my hand, and the invisible force slams into me like a jackhammer, coming down hard, just like it always does. Hopi's body jerks back and hits the floor as the thing that was in him attacks me, screaming, clutching at the mark.

Five hundred and seventy...

I put up a block and try to summon the Pull.

To reel them both in.

It crackles at the end of my hand.

The world oozes in slow motion.

I feel something cannonball back into me.

Five hundred and eighty...

Dryden clenches every muscle in his body, electrochemical energy on demon steroids forcing through every nerve ending as his finger squeezes down on the hair trigger, Bethany's eyes jerking open as the white strike of the bullet discharge lights up her head from behind in a flash outline—a terrible freeze-frame of light.

And we hit the tunnel.

Six hundred miles an hour.

Hyperspace.

* * *

9:15

The speedwave slams into the marks like the powerful cosmic doom-ripple of an exploding planet, as Dryden's bullet flashes past Bethany's face, scoring her perfect skin in a rough burn. My heart jumps into my throat, a jolt of panic freezing my senses into an elastic slo-mo as the mark at the end of my finger sucks back into me, the Blacklight kicking in hotter than hell and faster than light. But the one that was in Rashid Hopi still hangs there in space, fucked up and violated in the fast lane, dissolving into dust particles and coming back in rough blasts, the hanging vapor-glow shorting out in a Morse code rhythm, glittering on and off. The room spins with storm clouds of negative energy, as I see through the eyes of a crowd of dead people, all vibrating and sheeting in polarized layers and peels of sound and fury.

Bethany...

Her mind screams to me, the sound of the gun blast just micromillimeters from a killing trajectory—just missing, but blowing her right eardrum into permanent silence. The high whine of the tinnitus squeals through my head. She screams out loud. Panic still freezes me where I stand, as the Pull ratchets higher from my breast, seeking out the mark that was in Rashid Hopi, tasting its distorted vapor.

Lauren goes for her gun on the floor.

Dryden re-aims his laser dot at her.

Bethany goes down on her face, still screaming.

I feel the force of the speed slingshot at my back, accelerating the train beyond all reason—plunging down like hell on the marks inside me and inside Dryden—and they can't take it at all.

They SCREAM.

And their screams mainline directly into my mind, the slingshot hammering it home as we blast through the mountain, and it's an overload now, shattershocking me with the power, all of them exploding in a rain of heat and ice and shrieking agony, and I SCREAM it back at them, scream so loud that the sound becomes like steel clubs in my ears, and I almost lose the fight in this moment, almost stumble and fall all the way down, all the way to the bottom, but I hold it together somehow, my mind filled with the desperate burn of animal instinct.

And everyone else starts shooting.

Lauren's first bullet hits Dryden in his chest—he stumbles back, dark arterial crimson blasting out of the exit wound and hosing the wall behind him. It hardly slows him down as he fires again, putting the red dot where he wants his bullet to go, which is right over Lauren's heart. She gets to the floor first, diving into the restaurant, the lead burning air just above her. His next shot smashes through a framed portrait of Marilyn Monroe and bounces off the bulletproof wall, destroying part of the nearest crystal chandelier with a rough shatter. I throw myself on the floor, my hands over my head, riding the wave of thunder and speed toward Bethany, the marks clawing from inside my battered body, slobbering to get out. The room shifts and speeds at me, the bulletflashes and the sounds of slugs-on-flesh, shattering glass, blood going everywhere in sprays—all of it triple-amplified and streaking past my vision, leaving berserk tracer-blurs and hovering afterimages skidding in midair. The mark that was in Rashid Hopi still screams above my head, bullets whizzing through it, shorting on and off. The monster inside Dryden's body rips up the room with a fury Ben and Jerry have never seen or heard before, their boss going red and black in the face, screaming at them to kill the fucking bitches, all the goddamn fucking bitches—KILL THEM ALL!

They don't open fire on her.

They step away from him, turning their guns on the monster.

I can hear Bethany screaming my name.

The whine of her exploded senses crying at the highest frequency.

I look up just in time to see Ben and Jerry cap off several rounds each on Dryden, each one of them solid body hits, pirouetting their boss on his feet like a bloody weathervane shredded in a hurricane spiral. The shots do king-hell bomb bursts in the enclosed space and Lauren fires again, taking out the top of Dryden's skull—but he's still on his feet, snarling with blood oozing from more than a dozen high-caliber perforations, screaming "You fucking BITCH!" over and over in a voice that isn't really his voice at all. It's the mark's voice, run through a bank of special effects and ripping across the room like something out of a science fiction movie.

He takes a giant step forward and Jerry fires again, not believing his eyes.

Dryden readjusts his target priorities, spitting blood.

Bethany screams again.

The mark that was in Rashid Hopi still shrieks, caught in the air like a gaffed fish, pulverized by the speedwave.

Dryden's laser dot whips around and pins Agent Ben center-chest.

The shot comes an instant later, and Jerry fires again, as his buddy's mid-section takes a heavy dose of lead poisoning and evacuates in a splatter.

Jerry's bullet staggers Dryden back on his shredded feet as Bethany's next scream tears through the Blacklight, the shockwave hitting him hard.

Lauren gets up and fires—it's impossible but Dryden is still drawing breath—and one of his arms flies off in a fluid blur, coming away at the shoulder. He snarls at Lauren, stepping over the dead body of Carolyn Lewis, and he doesn't stumble at all or tremble even a little bit as he re-aims the gun, zeroing his target. Lauren dives for the floor again—two more shots miss her and eat the wall. Dryden's gun clicks empty. He ejects the spent clip with his thumb, then realizes he only has one arm, stumbling on blasted legs, the mark beginning to ooze out through the massive holes in his body, wincing still from Bethany's screams. He throws down the weapon and starts clawing for something under his jacket.

Jerry doesn't hesitate—he hits Dryden with everything left in his gun.

It's a roar like monsters that tears the room to pieces.

The hovering mark begins to lose form above me.

I grab for Bethany and start pulling her back toward the VIP corridor.

The bullets tear Dryden apart and zing all over the place, destroying everything, riddling the mark that was in Rashid Hopi, which looks like it's dying as it screeches in mid-air. I notice for the first time that the body of Hopi lies crumpled on the floor, out in a coma, like Bethany was before. The mark wants back in the body, but its substance remains webbed in space like a fly in a trap, damn-near shredded.

Dryden is an unwavering gory statue in the center of the storm, yellow eyes blazing back at his attackers, and at me—I can't believe he's still standing up.

He's pulling another gun from under his jacket.

A nine mil, standard-issue backup piece.

Jerry empties the pistol and tosses it—goes for his own backup, but Dryden is a lot faster and the bullets take his eyes out. It's like watching a couple of bloody fruits detonate in sequence. Jerry falls backward into the huge exposed grill, his finger clutching blind, his mind spasming in a final twitch of the death nerve, his bullets going crazy, ripping the propane jets to shrapnel—and I hear gas cut loose into the room like the terrifying poisonous hiss of a giant serpent, spitting deadly fumes.

Laughing, the thing-in-Dryden steps forward like some sort of bizarre jigsaw Terminator, spewing blood and hanging together by tendons, the vapor trail of the mark holding what's left together, screwing up its power to jump at me—to take what's inside me as they pry themselves loose from my soul in the speedwave.

Can't let him do it.

Can't let him take the marks.

Bethany's mind senses what's inside me, the power of it surging through my arms and into her body, and she responds with something I don't expect—a warm glow that rises above her panic and her fear of dying and the pain of her exploded eardrum.

A glow that lends me power.

She's helping me fight them down.

The-thing-in-Dryden is still coming at Lauren, hell-bent-for-whatever, as she aims at him one more time, squeezing down hard on the trigger . . .

The bullet jams in the breech.

The slide jerking back and freezing there, making her weapon useless.

The monster smiles through a face half blown away, covered in blood, his dead aim pinning her center-chest. She scrabbles backward on her hands. The gas spreads across the room in a shimmering wave. One muzzleflash and the room goes up in flames. I scream at him not to shoot. Dryden looks confused for a moment, firecracker remnants of thoughts and memories shorting and sparking in his half-destroyed mind.

The gas liquefies the air now, choking me—choking Bethany.

Something really bad about to go down.

A whole goddamn bunch of really fucking bad.

I can see Dryden trying to aim his weapon at Lauren through the spiraling gas fog in one long grainy second as she tries desperately to get out of his firing line, almost to the door that leads to the VIP corridor. He swipes at the air with his weapon, blood and gas in his eyes, like an annoyed beast clawing at insects. Jerry lies across the wasted grill, choking on the gas, covered in broken glass, nearly dead. The monster wails in the room. A fractured, kaleidoscoped vision, broken and strobeflash-kinetic and stabbing at my eyes, making me see double with dark red tears pouring down my face... and as I fight to see straight, one image crystallizes... and I can tell it's Dryden firing the gun through the haze...

I see the flash from the muzzle sparkjump through the shimmering air.

I pull Bethany back as the gunshot ignites the wall of gas.

The mark hovering above us screams one last time.

A vague glimpse of Lauren making a leap to safety, just at the corner of my eye.

The explosion comes, and it chases us all into the VIP corridor. I see the burst and feel the brutal heat over our heads like we're outracing the fist of god, the roaring column of fire spewing across the entire room behind us, engulfing Dryden as he screams. The thing inside him writhes and wails, feeling its host body blown to hell in the fractured half-second of the blast, the tattered coils of its powerful mind snapping the connection finally — the tenacious link with Dryden's kindred spirit and flesh going black and then vanishing, becoming nothing and then less than nothing. The ignited gas — blue and yellow and bright red — rolls in a long second of frame-jitter slo-mo behind us as I drag Bethany back into the corridor, and Lauren is right behind us. The big boom of the explosion consumes itself beyond the open doorway, shaking the floor of the train with a rumble like Kong.

Fire raging inside the restaurant now.

The train still going like a bat out of hell, sluicing my senses.

Dryden, finally dead in the explosion.

Lauren, just over my shoulder, asking if I'm okay.

No.

No, I'm not.

Something blows again in my guts and I sink to my knees, the marks cours-

ing through me. So many of them inside me now, rolling over each other as the vibrations in the train threaten to rip me apart. Sinking and then rising, struggling and losing, fighting and winning ... just making it up for air.

I roll over on my back and bear down hard on the marks, trying to keep it all from driving me insane.

I have to get them out.

Have to get them out or they're going to rip me apart.

The combined power triggers another load of TNT inside me again, and it's like napalm jungle warfare on both sides of my body, the fire raging just beyond the hatchway that leads to the burning restaurant, dead souls boiling, turning into liquid nukes in my guts ...

... and ...

... we come out of the tunnel.

Six hundred miles an hour.

I can feel it burning on all side of us.

Like the fire.

Like the marks.

It's too much.

The wave of thunder and speed blows again like another explosion some-where deep in me, as the ride slows down. I hear the engines shift below my feet, the nitrogen jets cooling the system, bringing us to earth. I concentrate on the pain in my body. The sharpness of it. The way home. But it leaves me badly ... leaves me like phantom sustenance washing down some invisible drain ... leaves me like terrible voices that know all my secrets, a tortured after-burn singeing my throat ... and I hover there again, wanting to see, wanting to know ... wanting to feel it ...

Images of my mother and father.

The combined power of a million voices and souls.

I could lose myself here and be sated forever.

No.

Something is pulling me back to earth.

Something warm.

Something that glows ...

* * *

And I'm out.

The marks inside weigh me down with power.

The train on all sides of me like the comedown of some nasty acid trip.

Lauren hunches over us, her face grunged-up with soot and sweat, her hair hanging in her face—she is so goddamn fucking beautiful.

My body is wracked with the worst kind of bad, and all I can see is her face.

All I can feel is Bethany's arms around me, the warm glow of her mind coursing through my flesh, pulling me back.

Is this what love feels like?

Am I feeling it now, warm inside me, the light at the end?

I want to kiss both of them in this moment, I want to thank them for standing by me—but then the moment is gone, consumed by the thunder of the magnetic engine as it calms, my head reeling away to be consumed by it, every thought I possess slowing down and then speed-ing up, flying away and coming back. The sound of rage held for years. The smell of insanity like smoldering sulfur—the same old smell from so many years of fighting monsters that never let go. The earth, speeding through a long dark expressway in a galaxy of unblinking stars, their light reaching us from millions of years ago, the dark formless taunt of dead men who came back to earth to live inside my body. A klaxon sounds. The shutters come down on the windows inside the VIP corridor, sealing off the galaxy.

I feel Roosevelt's hands on my shoulders. He's speaking to me, but I can't hear his voice. I feel the beautiful glow of Bethany's love, armoring me in the storm. The roar of the burning restaurant fills my ears—feet away from us, blazing out of control now.

Something moves in the fire.

SEVENTEEN

REVENGE ON EVERYONE

Lauren is halfway to her feet, her gun empty, her mouth hanging open. Impossible.

It's just impossible.

A charred, burning mass that might be a human shape solidifies in layers within the thundering restaurant, still held at its destroyed seams by the mark. It's a dancing stream of vapor ribbons organizing skeletal remains which lurch toward us painfully, taking slow steps through the blazing wall of superheated gas, kicking aside flaming tables and chairs.

It walks straight through the fire.

Coming right at us.

"Get behind me!"

I struggle to my feet as the thing pushes through searing curtains of yellow and blue and red, the flames tearing away what's left of its face, revealing raw skull, which blackens and oozes, brain matter boiling through the eye sockets. Bone claws reach out, stripped of flesh. Clawing at the prize just beyond the burning room.

And I can feel the last remains of Dryden's mind hovering there, willing the body and the mark forward—prodded hard to punish his enemies and get away with it, to re-make the entire world in his image. It's how he was able to control the mark when it came into him—the reason why the mark is desperate to stay with him now.

The charred corpse steps into the VIP corridor, screaming my name.

It's a sound that blows through my head, piercing the air above the fire sirens and the danger klaxons, summoning the marks in my body to the surface again. The creature reaches for me with bone-shard hands and calls them. The force slams into me and I stumble back for a moment. The concussive force expands from my body as I take the attack and it pegs Roosevelt and Bethany where they live and breathe, manhandling them into the nearest wall. The kid smacks his head and slumps, out cold. Bethany kisses the floor and almost goes under, but I feel her powerful mind force itself to stay afloat.

Lauren watches with her eyes wide as I stand on my feet and face the monster.

It screams my name again and I tell the motherfucker to bring it on.

I anchor all my power, summoning the Pull.

It spirals outward.

The sweet black swirl grounds me into the floor as the mark swimming in Dryden's burning bones stabs out and takes his next swing at me, the red contrails of psychoplasmic vapor-flesh bursting against my body. I reach up and the Pull focuses through me. I can take him, like the others.

You're no different, you son of a bitch.

Some of us just have a better excuse.

I grip the mark hard, and in this split-instant, the others try to get free. They hover in my body and jab at me. They piss in my face.

They want revenge on everybody, these animals.

The burning corpse unravels like an abandoned skin as I take the mark into me, and the pressurized deadweight of the descending spirit speed-balls into the spirits under my skin—rams them all down my throat, like an anvil crashing on cartoons.

Dryden's mark, it's the toughest one of them all.

It's Dryden and the mark joined together.

Dryden's blown-to-hell spirit wrapped up in the muck of unsettled madness—the two of them mated and coming in for a crash landing.

It can't resist the Pull.

None of them can.

And as it goes down into me, just like all the others, it's the monster's own animal toughness—its own cannonball insanity—that finally explodes all eight of them in my stomach.

It lights up my whole body.

Knocks them all on their asses.

My feet almost give, but I stay up.

I take them finally and they all explode inside me—like all the others. Deeper.

And then...

Touchdown.

The screams fade to a rumble, then a low boil. I feel it burst and become sour muck, oozing along the walls of my stomach and lungs, a living disease given terrible formless autonomy, still trying to scream its way out.

Ingested now.

This part is always really bad.

It's the worst part of the job.

Then again, who said life—or *death*—was fair.

The flames begin to fight it out with thick plumes of jet-blue liquid ice that pour from the walls of the restaurant. The burning room coils and writhes with tendrils and tongues, like weird sea creatures writhing in a deep-sea inferno, the klaxons screaming, emergency cherries rolling along the corridor. Lauren hardens up, making herself in charge again. "Fire's set off the halon system."

Another wave of thunder hammers me down low.

My guts boiling with molten steel, jumbled voices struggling to become one voice—I can't even tell who's who anymore, but they're finally muck—something living and oozing like acid in my stomach. Something that I can choke up and get rid of.

Need to purge them now.

Lauren sees me clutch over at the shock of pain, and I go under...

The marks.

My father's disciples.

The eight members of Blackjack Nine, imprisoned in the desert.

They're in me now, digested, and they're making me see all kinds of things:

Images I can't understand.

Tracerblurs of blood and flesh and the charred remains of half-burned memories and emotions, like the living-dead shambles of Agent Dryden, lurching ahead in my mind, coming on in jagged shatters...

I struggle to pull myself up from the muck.

I struggle really goddamn hard.

I come up for air, and fall again.

Come up and fall.

The world blacks out and I come back in shattered bursts.

I hold myself up the next time and I see Lauren wearing an oxygen mask just inside the restaurant, breathing hard from the tiny little mixture tank clipped to her waist. Swirling mist on all sides, faint traces of the gas fire that started all our problems, but it seems like the pressure is normalized in here. The bulletproof walls saved us, after all. Destroyed shapes and twisted bodies cascaded in velvet blue tentacles of smoky mist, smoldering flesh—the flesh of Carolyn Lewis and Rashid Hopi and Richard Dryden, blown to hell a dozen times over. Plus the agents who bought it in the shootout. Their souls are long evacuated, and I can't feel them in the room or even calling whispers just out of sight. If they're speaking to me, the roaring hiss of the halon drowns their voices, covering everything in a rolling, translucent cocoon of cheesy graveyard fog from an Ed Wood movie. Tom liked Ed Wood movies.

Tom.

Goddamn, man.

Who were you working for, Tom?

How much money did they give you?

My mind flashes with something long-gone, something he once said to me...something about the difference between the damned and the doomed...

I go under and fight the muck again.

I black out and then come back to earth seconds later, minutes later...

I feel the train coming in slow now.

The emergency shutters in the VIP corridor are sliding open, and a world made of candy mirages glitters ahead on all sides of us—final approach to Las Vegas. A dazzle of deep space nebulae and dreamtime starlight carved out of a desert wasteland. We punch through the heart of it, hovering above winking eyes and destiny-streams spelled out in neon. Just on the other side of the windows, Lauren aims the C-4 canister at stray flames, spitting at them in fast, efficient bursts. She doesn't wince at the smell of cooked skin below the chemical rush or the fog-shrouded shapes of dead men. She's an icy pro in a room filled with dying fire cooled below zero.

I feel Bethany Sin's mind reeling, as her hand caresses my bloody face.

I see my mother, blood falling from her mouth in thick ropes.

I see her eyes full of wasted love and loss.

I go under as the train stops flying, the clunk of the wheels kissing steel rails, coming into the Dreamworld casino.

Up from the dark again.

Fast impressions now.

Spews and streams, as I go to black and bounce back:

The footfalls of men wearing heavy riot gear.

Cops boarding the train.

Someone pulling me off the floor, getting my body onto a stretcher.

My mother lies still in her own blood.

Her mission has failed...

I'm surrounded by cops.

I smell their bad aftershave and cheap cologne.

I sense their confusion and feel the burn.

The platform in the giant theme park is full of cops and medics, all holding back throngs of reporters and spectators. Flashes sparkle in the crowd but there's only a few news cameras. This was supposed to be a gala opening and a photo op for everybody—it's sort of half that now, spilling over into a chaotic happening, all full of noise and light. I try hard to get a grip on all of it, but my mind is swimming nearer and nearer to the truth, the dense memories of the marks inside me triggering it finally...everything I ever wanted to know...it glows in my mind and seduces me...*all I ever wanted*...

The face of my father curses her.

Tells her she is a clever bitch.

Dares her...

Men in suits with their ears wired rush to meet us as the senator is hustled off the train. Chaos. Too many voices. The pit of my soul swims.

Blackjack Williams, dear old Daddy...

The other guests are herded into safe areas, people in uniforms barking questions and orders. Everyone shell-shocked. Derek Pappas and Junk-E and all the scared-shitless survivors get lost in the blizzard of faces, and I am pulled down deep, wallowing in my own despair, spiraling along the memories...

Where is Bethany?

Blackjack Williams, who murdered children and little old ladies, then confessed his crimes...

My father...

Men wearing government-issue black detain Lauren Chance and she doesn't look happy about it. Lots of questions. Looks like they might arrest her, too. I hardly sense it now—I am cuffed to a stretcher, hovered over by spooks with gruff voices. Jerry Donaldson is drunk and sheet white. Looks like he saw a ghost, someone says near me. I wonder for an insane moment if he's serious. I finally see Bethany vanishing on a stretcher among a galaxy of flittering lights, headed toward something that might be the multicolored outline of an EMS vehicle, somewhere in the melee. She'll be safe now. Not like me.

Did my mother know?

Did she know about his crimes all along?
Did she love him, even then?

I see Roosevelt in cuffs also.

Right near me.

He's surrounded by men with guns.

The train platform is big and crawling with humanity, the last stop on a track that circles the whole park like a rollercoaster ride, exposed to open sky on a giant slab of sculpted marble and steel at the far end of a valley of lights and towers and levels that seem to stretch to the horizon and beyond. It really is a *Dreamworld,* defined in pure gold and starlight blue, hitting me as a weird, epic backdrop to the scene on the platform, as everyone scrambles for the skinny.

Voices on voices, inside and out.

Echoes on marble, sirens and radio squawk.

Memories and marks, still lurking in my stomach, filling me with the desire to trip the Blacklight and stay there, to leave all this bullshit behind and be a god. Like my father wanted to be a god...

My father.

My mother.

Love and insanity, all rolled up into one terrible feeling.

Thirty years worth of searching, all boiling in my guts now.

The marks, screaming that I never should have looked for it...

A clutch of important-looking guys in suits take the senator aside— they've all been informed of the situation and there's a lot of talk now about shutting down the rally. More voices. People in suits talking to the news crews. Agendas and orders and damage control.

Mother... why did you love him?

Is that why you make me forget?

EMS guys hover like concerned worker bees around Maximum Bob, but he keeps shooing them away, as if they're annoying him.

They claw at me, hissing again in unison.

Their memories, still down there, stewing within rolls of fire and ice.

Blackjack's mission and my mother who loved him.

Why?

WHY?

Senator Maxton is coming over to me, saying something to his body-guards, motioning to the cops. They loosen around me, but only a little. One of them tells Maximum Bob to be careful and he says it's okay. What did he say to these people? Did he confirm Dryden's orders to have us all busted at the end of the line?

Why am . . .

The thought freezes in my head as Bob leans down to smile at me.

And I see a shadow moving over him.

"Tell me something, Buck," he says. *"What is your fondest wish for America?"*

I see the monster just under his skin, twitching and howling with victory—a sound only I can hear—and the laughter follows me under, way down under.

Into absolute blackness.

EIGHTEEN

EVERYTHING DEAD

Down here, I hear his voice.

Writhing among the faces and the broken maelstrom of tortured lives, screaming for my own resurrection in the flood rush of complete insanity, I hear his voice.

The voice of my father.

Coming closer.

I feel the breath of the others, hot on the back of my neck as I move toward the memory, but it's not any one person's memory—it's the memory of many.

The memory of all of them, cut apart and pasted back together.

A multi-camera passion play, flashing at the end of a long dark tunnel to nowhere.

The play of the Blackjack Nine.

Rushing toward me.

I run toward it.

My father's voice breaks the surface.

"I am the only god you will ever need."

He stands in the sun, his face baked in the heat that pours down from a bright blue sky, and his face is MY FACE, and I smile because it really is true—I'm one hell of a handsome bastard. My smile sparkles, all white teeth and square jaw, sleepy eyes that seem to withhold the secrets of the universe.

It all comes in sharp focus, and I see him from seven different angles—seven minds, taking him in all at once.

Seven, not eight.

There are eight followers, but I only see through the eyes of seven.

I didn't get all of them.

But in this dream...I still see all eight of his followers. Eight tortured minds who went free when they died in the Triangle and waited for years to find new bodies. Eight unbound spirits who found willing donors. The donors are drifters. Hippies. Failed seekers. The mid-seventies is full of them, and so is the Triangle.

They each kneel in a row.

And before each of them is a silver urn.

All in the name of handsome Jack, who stands on a grassy dune before them, his fist in the air. His voice again, my voice:

"You are all born again to the purest faith. I have given you the gift. If you turn away now, you turn away from immortality. If you believe in me, I will set you free. You have walked and cried and kneeled in the name of things that this world will punish you for. But flesh is only a means to an end. I am the only god you will ever need."

He's tricked these burnouts, every one of them—with his voice and his smile and the magic that burns within his body. Tricked them all into becoming possessed by the worst serial killers on earth. The spirits rumble inside their bellies—sour muck, like the muck inside me now. They want out and Jack will set them free. This is his promise to them. His plan. I sense it so clearly now—all their minds tuned to the same mission. Jack leads them, he is their master.

My father...

His fist opens and the razors glitter, rivulets of blood racing down his arm.

One razor for each of them.

Jack tells them the blood is good, that the blood will bring them life eternal—actually uses those cheesy words, like something out of an old Dracula movie.

But cheese works if you mean it.

If your voice is magical.

Jack is magic.

The blood is the life.

They take the razors from his hand. They do not hesitate. This is all part of the plan. They searched for years to find each other. This is the moment that changes everything. His voice makes them do it. The sound of his voice.

His power.

I see and feel and hear it all go down in adrenaline shocks that pound me on the outer edge. Bursts of red and blasts of venom. The razors in their hands, raised to their lips, swallowed whole like bitter pills. Ripping their insides apart. The marks inside the flesh tearing free in terrible spasms, coming up in rivers of bloody bile, splashing into the silver urns at their knees like wine, steaming and blackened. Reeking in the sun. Each soul swimming in its own filth, cut loose and screaming in the muck. I am each one of them, leaving those pathetic bodies that were so necessary just moments before, swirling down inside the urns, bouncing back against the silver walls, ready to give themselves again...

...and thirty years later, they are trapped in my guts...

...they are trapped within me now...

...making me have this terrible dream...

...just the way they were trapped then, by the power of his voice. The power that made them give up on flesh forever, so that they could be immortal.

That was the plan.

Jack's plan.

The host bodies lie in a row, abandoned, slashed to hell from the inside out. Their souls swirl in silver, ready to make the final leap.

Into Jack.

This is the moment that changes everything.

And I see my mother now, in that moment.

She walks over the dune, just behind him. She is beautiful in a pleated summer dress that ripples her body in the desert air. Her hair is long and blonde and tangled up in dreads-by-default. Her eyes are so blue they blow me away. Her mind is full of desperation and loss and disappointment—the kind you feel when you know everything you ever loved lies in ruins, and all that remains is the task. That thing you must do.

The Terrible Thing.

My mother's eyes tell all these tales and so many more, flowing across the dream in a crystal clear shot of pure insight—they all feel it hard.

Jack feels it, too.

As she walks over the dune rise, springing her trap.

The gun in her hands.

She has searched for so long to find my father. Her heart is full of burned-out love and screwed-up things that tortured her for years. The face of her one true love, needling her in nightmares, making her go on, knowing he was just out of her reach. She failed so many times, but then she knew . . . and she came here to this place to finish it.

But she doesn't come alone.

She hasn't been alone for a while now.

Someone helped her to find my father.

Someone saved her life, just like he saved mine—found her in this terrible desert that steals souls. He armored her. Took her to that place in the Black-light where only spirits tell. Allowed her to come to this very moment, where it all goes down, finally.

The old Indian man standing at her side.

The old man . . .

Jack raises the first urn to his lips, the empty host bodies of his eight followers limp and abandoned in a row before him, drained of the bile, all for him, all because it's part of the plan. My mother's hands grip the gun, aiming right at the monster that has my face.

My father.

He sees her and stops, his eyes wide, his smile jagged like lightning.

"I get it now."

His voice is displaced and strange—something out of harmony with the sneer on his face.

"Very clever, bitch. But you won't pull that trigger. I know you won't."

She knows it too.

If she pulls the trigger, she loses everything.

Everything.

"I DARE YOU TO PULL THAT TRIGGER!"

But the child is safe.

And she has no choice.

She looks right in my father's eyes and says:

"I love you, Buck."

And the gun explodes in a firebloom, sending me into a tailspin. And I struggle to make it up from the memory because it's too much now, the dream hot and slashing, like a mirror shattering in a superheated explosion . . . but I want to see . . . I WANT TO SEE . . .

And the bullet smashes into my father's heart.

He comes at her and she fires again and again.

His razorblade cuts her throat as her last shot takes him.

And he slumps over . . . crying . . . his terrible voice blasting into oblivion to join a million others in the Blacklight . . .

My mother bleeds.

The old Indian man holds her and she says to finish the task.

Bury them.

Bury them in the urns and never let them come back.

And she puts the gun in the old man's hand.

Tells him to leave it for her son.

Her voice croaks and fades away to nothing . . . and the dream fades away with her . . . the face of the old man . . . a face I will not see again for thirty years . . .

I come awake in a dark room.

My body aches. Broken bones, slashes and bruises. My left hand is set in a cast and bandaged.

The marks still grumble down low.

But they can't possess me now.

I've digested them.

I was tripping in their minds again—their collective mind, this time. The answers all there, but horrible and sour in my mouth. Rusty metal and blood. The pulsing heat lingering from the desert in my head, reminding me of so many years I spent on the road, looming like a shadow in the dust. Years and years, searching for an answer. Searching for them.

The old man, who saved me from it.

Who sacrificed his own son, so that I could live and come here.

Did he know all this would happen?

"You look like shit, Buck."

I look up and there's a dead man leaning against the bars of my cage.

We're in a police station of some kind. Empty holding cell. They brought me here fast. Took my Walkman and my gun, too, while I was dead to the world.

Dead like Darby, who I can hardly see, backlit by the dull fluorescents running along the corridor ceiling just on the other side of the bars.

I get up on the cot, squint my eyes to bring his image into focus.

It doesn't work all that good.

He's turned into a see-through anatomy model, half-there in little bursts through skin made of wavering liquid, like some matter teleportation experiment gone wrong. I can tell he's struggling to keep himself in this room, pulling at the air in desperate grabs with his fingers, which peel back and shred as he loses himself.

"Darby...what's happened to you?"

"I can't stay with you, Buck. Whatever happened on that train...it was *major*. You've got something real hot inside you now. Not just marks. Some kind of *force*. I can't get much closer. It burns."

His voice is crumbling, going all static on me.

"I'll pull you back, Darby."

"No, you can't. I made it back to *warn you...*"

The marks inside me hear his disintegrating voice and hiss in my blood.

"...you have to get that shit *out of you fast, Buck*...it's causing shock-waves all over hell and back on my side...do you understand what I'm saying to you?"

"I can feel it. A combined power."

"It'll consume you and eat up everything...Blackjack Williams knew it."

"Knew what?"

"Blackjack Williams...he was trying to tap into the Blacklight...trying to find a way to make himself immortal...but the power is *bigger than all that*... it's making everyone run for their lives in the slipstream... that's what they were all trying to warn us about."

"Blackjack was my father."

"I wouldn't... be... so *sure* about that..."

"What do you...?"

And it comes clear.

He couldn't have been my father.

Not exactly.

Jack was executed in prison—a notorious serial killer with years of cold-blooded murder to his name.

My mother didn't kill Jack.

She killed my father.

Jack's spirit had possessed his body.

"Stay with me, Darby. I need more answers. Why would Jack want to *destroy* the Blacklight?"

"Not destroy, Buck... it's all about controlling the *dead parts of the world*... don't you get it? Everything in the world is dead..."

"That doesn't make any sense."

"Look around you, Buck... the only thing living in this room is *you*."

My heart falls.

It has to be the truth.

All my life I've been surrounded by dead things, but I was distracted by the obvious—those moaning, screeching apparitions that whispered to me and hid in concrete corners, those phantoms and Walkers and ghosts that made me crazy and haunted. I was too blinded by the Blacklight to see one simple truth and that truth was this: Those concrete corners were dead, too.

The brick and mortar of every building I ever stood in.

The hard wood that made every door I ever walked through.

It was all alive once, part of an infinite cycle of birth and decay.

Everything made to serve man has to die before it means something.

And it all rots now under our feet.

Our own bodies are made of dead things—our hair, our fingernails, the cells of our skin shedding into the air to make dust particles.

The air itself—filled with poisons and gasses.

All of it dead.

All of it rotting.

I sense that rot, that final stage of the cycle...the terrible endless swan song of everything dead that surrounds me...as the Power courses inside my body.

And I realize that it's the power to control all dead things.

That's why Darby can't come near me.

That's why my mother killed my father.

He felt the Power and was seduced, just the way I was.

That desire has been in my blood since I was born.

The followers of Blackjack Williams were the pieces of a puzzle—and that puzzle was meant to create some sort of god on earth. They were stopped and buried. But how were they resurrected?

And why did his disciples hit us on the train—*why now?*

He hears me think that and his garbled voice electrifies the air again. "It was the *train itself*...something to do with the speed and the magnetic field...like a skeleton key...freeing them from their graves one by one..."

"And I came because the spirits told me to. Because *you* told me to."

"It was the ride to end all rides, Buck."

That's why my mother sacrificed so much.

That was why the old Indian came to my rescue.

He found her too.

And knew saving us both was the only way to prevent what might have been the end of everything—the Power to rule all dead things controlled and held in the body of one man. And that one man is me, now that Jack is long gone.

Jack went free when my father died.

His spirit was never buried like the others.

He couldn't have been one of the marks on the train.

It's a sick irony that swims in the pit of my stomach, like the fucked-up souls swirling there, screaming my name, ready to take on the world at my command.

But the circuit is still not complete.

Not without...

"There's one mark left," I say. "It's in the senator. I think it's the one I lost when the restaurant blew up—the one that was in Rashid Hopi."

"Good luck with that."

"I have to get out of here. Can you help me?"

"I told you, I can't stay with you...it's hard just staying in this room...*can you still hear me...*"

"Yeah, I can hear you. Like a bad channel on the radio. Just like you said before. Maybe you're finally going to see Elvis, man."

"He better hope not...*the fat...fuck...*"

Gone now, sucked back into the light beyond this room, his voice a dim memory.

Gone.

I get up and call his name, scream at him to come back.

My voice echoes down the corridor beyond the bars of my cell, and the tinny noise of a TV around the bend floats back. The sound of commentators and crowd noise—the rally, going on as planned. Someone casually yells at me from the front of the station to shut the hell up, then he calls me an asshole and says to sit tight. Shadows move at the end of the hall. Sounds of walnut heels on a smooth, polished floor. Cops pacing around, waiting for backup to arrive. I'm fucked.

But I haven't been here long.

If the rally is still happening, there's just minutes before Maximum Bob hits the stage. I concentrate hard and hear the voices on the TV. They're not talking about tragedy and death aboard the Laser. There was some kind of statement just made by Sidney Jaeger—something about how the show must go on. Technical problems. The speed test in the secret desert pass not going quite as planned. Not one word about the people who died, the fire on board. How are they keeping it quiet? Major people bought the farm—it was a bloodbath.

This is completely insane.

The commentators drone on and the moment of truth draws near. The senator's speech on the big stage. Nobody has any idea what kind of a monster lives behind his eyes now, what he could do if he becomes president with that *thing* still in him.

I have to get out of here.

Have to try something.

Anything.

I try screaming again. I yell that I need to use the bathroom. A bored voice floats back, telling me tough shit, kid, and sit tight again. It'll all be over soon, the guy says. I try to concentrate on his voice. Try to visualize what he looks like, what the room around the bend at the far end of the narrow corridor looks like, how many men they have. This place seems really small, really empty. Definitely a holding cell, somewhere in the Dreamworld. If this place is so big that it has its own zip code then it definitely has its own police division, the way most city hospitals do.

But...

The marks hit me again, real hard, in the stomach.

I stumble back as the Power rises to the surface and whites out my world, filling me with the anger and pain and undead ambition of seven bad motherfuckers. Snippets of crimes long buried in the desert come pouring in again, and it snakes through my veins, into my hands, crackling in my broken fingers under the cast. I ball my right fist and bear down hard, planting my feet, allowing the Power to ground me, controlling it.

I am the only god you will ever need.

Down.

It surges again, coming up like a spiraling tube wave. I engage it and ride the tube like a surfer from hell, sending my mind along the center of its gravity, getting a grip easy. I feel their voices and they tear at the walls. I feel the fragile strands of my soul going white—one hair at a time. This really hurts, but I'm keeping them down.

What happens when I can't?

What happens when they become too hot to handle?

What happens when it seduces me again, the same way it seduced my father—turned him into a willing vessel for Blackjack Williams?

The Power to destroy everything dead lives in me.

I have to get it out.

* * *

For the next few minutes, I try making myself puke.

I stick my fingers down my throat first—that's never worked on me before but I'm running pretty desperate right about now. It used to be real easy with a bellyful of bad gunk like this, but the gunk ain't moving. Sticking to my insides like napalm, hanging on for dear life, yahooing in my blood, joyriding my biorhythms. Laughing at me as I try to will myself to force it up, calling me a fucking moron as all my efforts fail.

Gonna take more than this, and I can't do it here.

It'll be really dangerous anyway without some way to contain the mess.

I once chucked up a soul in a parking lot and it was dirty, ugly business. I'm reminded of that night in living color, the memory full of deep black slime snaking across the pavement like devil seed. I couldn't keep that one in for long because she was a real fighter—the unbound soul of a teacher who loved her students the wrong way. She kicked and screamed, the same way these bad bastards inside me are kicking and screaming—but she *wanted* to come out of me. Wanted to get her hands around the nearest human throat and cause some major damage. Some marks have no idea when they're beaten. They stay unsettled in the muck until the moment you bury them.

The way my parents used to bury them.

I am the only god you will ever need.

No.

Don't think about it.

The moment—*concentrate on the moment.*

I sit on the floor, cross-legged.

I clear my head as best I can, the rumble boiling low. I take myself slowly to a place of calm. Guided meditation. I tell my body to keep this Power down. To bring it under control. I use the Pull.

It surges on me, filling my blood again, and I hold it down again.

An idea begins to form.

If the only thing living in this room is me . . .

If I can summon control over inanimate matter . . .

If what Darby said is really true . . .

I have to try.

I think about my mother, and her years of searching. My father, who allowed this same feeling that now lurks in my body to take him over and make him a killer. I have to honor them. I have to avenge them. I have to use this right. I feel like a junkie again—rationalizing, like I rationalized back in the desert. I got a kid killed that way. I could get everybody killed this way.

I have to try.

It surges one more time and I use the Pull to *engage it now,* feeling the flood shoot into me, taking it like an injection, seven souls combined into one soul, colliding with mine in a searing burst of lifelight. And I throw myself into them, the way I always do when I first pull a mark, pulling their madness close to me . . . *pulling it in . . .*

The heat washes over my body, weaker than ever before, but then I tighten my grip on the madness, giving myself to it . . . and the madness is good, the madness fuels my body in a dreamtime sizzle, bursting and flashing, energizing. The dark blue glow intensifies. The voices of a million billion angry bastards rip off in my ears, thundering in the infinite spaces set before me, the neon-striped outlines of the real world just outside the menagerie of slithering zero gravity shapes, like half-formed moray eels and faces filled with burning eyes and cursing tongues. The world changes and flickers, just like it always does. I see this same room, years before it was even built. I see the hundreds of people who have stood right here in this spot.

And it all comes clear, these things I see.

These things I've seen for years.

These are dead things.

And I see them here because this is the place where all dead things go.

They remain here forever, even after they are destroyed.

I've been able to reach out so many times and pull those things from this place—bring them back to the world through the lens of the Blacklight.

I've seen it hundreds and hundreds of times.

Everything that exists in the world—a map, a gun, a pair of shoes, an old camera—it all has to die before it becomes any of those things.

The world is made of dead things.

My father saw this, too.

I am my father's son.

And the seven mad bastards trying to focus themselves through my eyes now—these doomed, fucked-up killers who were promised immortality by a handsome liar—they want to use my eyes.

I am the crucial missing circuit.

I am the lens to the Blacklight they want to control.

I feel it powering through my bad hand, coming to my command—the Power to rule everything dead.

And in the moment it explodes from me, I scream.

I come out of the Blacklight with the sound of my own voice hammering the air, the force of my will sizzling through my broken fingers, instructing the bones to mend themselves as they fuse with white ice and burning lava, crackling and popping and pulsing.

A raw burst of energy so intense my fingers can't hold it for long.

It lights up my nerve centers.

It rattles my entire body.

The raw burst transforms into a thick shockwave which expands through my mended bones, seeps through the pores of my skin, blasts outward with a scream that shatters the cast on my wrist into dust...and I'm SCREAMING...

...SCREAMING...!

And the expanding shockwave becomes a wall of invisible fire, slamming the prison bars just ahead of me, materializing as a dark fist of neon, pulled from the burning essence of a million dead souls...*and it sets the iron on fire.*

The bars glow, and then crumble.

And then they are gone forever.

Gone because I banished them.

I pull the fist back into me and the Power thrashes like a drunk shitkicker, moshing me from left to right, manipulating my body in one wild stumble after another as I try to get a grip. It's still manhandling me when

the cops appear from around the corner ahead. I see them as black outlines in the hall.

One of them yells something intelligent: "Hey, you!"

The other one is going for the stick on his hip.

Something bolts through the muscles inside my arms, and the bolt explodes forward through the air to land an invisible clamp across the cop's
weapon. The polished wood was once alive, but now it's dead—and I
control it, the same way I controlled my own bones, which now sizzle
and hum, shot through and fortified with white-hot energy. The night-
stick spins in the air and bounces off the wall, clunking on the floor. My
whole body is flying as his face goes white with shock, and the second cop
can't even see me—I am a whisper and a blur, and my first blow hits him
hard in the chest. I hit him with my good left hand. His lungs give up the
goods as his rib cage implodes, and a cracking noise fills the corridor.

The Power, surging downward now.

As my human mind and my battered body remembers it's not a god or
a ghost.

Remembers my training, all in my hands and feet.

I focus up, the cop on the left wheezing and halfway out of the game,
watching his buddy take the full brunt of my attack as I spin with complete control, my foot in the sky, swiping across the guy's face, rearranging
his nose a little. He forgets how to stand up and decides to kiss the wall,
out like a light in two seconds, slumping like a sack of shit to the floor, out
cold. The one with the busted ribs goes down at the same time, begging
me not to hurt him anymore. They don't even have guns. Just wooden
sticks and pepper spray.

I just took out a couple of security guards.

The Power, ebbing low now, but making all kinds of threats. It got
a taste and it wants more—it senses everything around me, everything
dead, and it wants to smash every bit of it. I could control it all or destroy
it all.

I can't let that happen.

Down, all of you.

I am the only god you will ever need.

I flex the fingers of my left hand.

The power still sizzles in the freshly knit bones.

I can feel it healing the rest of my body.

Finding the dying tissues and restoring them.

This is a taste of what Jack wanted.

To be a god on earth.

And it feels good.

No.

Down.

I can't let it happen.

I get the stick off the guy who forgot how to stand and relieve him of his pepper spray, then put the business end of the weapon in his buddy's face, ordering him to grab his legs and open the next holding cell over. There's three along this little hallway, smaller than the one I was in.

He does it really fast for a man with busted ribs.

I keep the stick aimed at him the whole time like a gun. He unlocks the steel gate and pulls his partner in with him, slams it shut, wincing through half-assed curses that I'm never gonna get away with this. The FBI is on the way, I won't get out of here alive. Blah, blah, blah. The words don't even reach me in complete sentences. I'm thinking ahead, to what I have to do now. Bob Maxton. A hard target, if there ever was one.

I have no choice but to go after him.

The Power inside me likes this idea.

I feel it race with collective anticipation—jacked anxiety like a shot to the arm.

Down, you fuckers.

I tell the broken-rib guy to give me the keys and he hands them right over. I tell him to unbuckle his badass utility belt and he hands that over, too. Squeezes it through the bars with a jangle and a twist of leather. I see by the plate on his chest that his name is Ash Laurence, and I call him that when I tell him there's no hard feelings about any of this and that he'll be okay if he gets to a hospital eventually—there's not much a doctor can do with busted ribs, but if there's no internal bleeding, he should be just fine.

I tell him sorry again, rounding the corner into the main office, leaving his cries for reason behind.

The Power, letting me do this now, staying its hand, holding back.

Mexican standoff.

Today's just been full of those fucking things.

The front office is a tiny room, with a few desks. A pitiful sliver-view of the lights of the Dreamworld twinkling in the distance through a couple of glass doors. We're at the far end of the park, away from prying eyes. No cops out there. I wonder again what's up with all the lame security—seems like I oughta be on the Ten Most Wanted List by now, America's Most Armed and Dangerous, hogtied down in a hole somewhere, being drilled by hardass secret agents with their sleeves rolled up while they test out brass knuckles to make me confess my terrible crime and give up my conspirators.

But no.

They stuck me in a holding tank and waited for the cavalry.

Weird.

A wave of dirty nausea nearly flattens me, my guts rolling again, the voices jeering in the dark back there somewhere. I keep my feet on the ground. I think of an old movie I used to like and an imaginary cartoon voice starts squeaking in a chiding nursery-rhyme drawl: *feed me, Seymour, feeeeeed me...*

On the main desk is my Walkman.

And the gun.

My mother's gun.

The gun the old Indian left for me in the house.

The gun I was able to see and bring back because that's always been part of my gift. My way with dead things. The way that almost makes me a god now.

Almost, but not quite.

I reach out for the gun, and it moves all on its own, without my fingers even touching the rusted metal. The Power giggles again, coming loose in a thin stream which I cut off quick, balling my fist.

I said *fuck you*.

It slinks back up my arm.

I grab the gun and stick it back in my belt.

Then, the Walkman.

The flat-screen TV blares the big event, less than a few miles away, at the other end of the giant theme park plaza—the same amphitheater Sidney Jaeger was broadcasting from when we left Los Angeles. The commentators are going on and on about terrorist activity rumors, some kind of official statement to be made during Senator Maxton's speech. They keep cutting to a live newsfeed, with info bars rolling across the bottom: JAEGER LASER ARRIVAL SHROUDED IN UNKNOWN CONTROVERSY, HOMELAND SECURITY UNAVAILABLE FOR COMMENT...INSIDE MEN SUSPECTED IN RUMORED CORPORATE SABOTAGE...SEN. BOB MAXTON TO MAKE SPEECH WITHIN HOUR...

They buried it.

The whole thing, wrapped up in spin ribbons.

There's all sorts of new versions of the truth coming across the screen. I try different channels and it's the same there, too. Nobody knows what's really happening. Nobody's reporting the death of Agent Dryden or Rashid Hopi or the other cops who got wasted. No official statement has been made by any of the celebrities who were riding the train. Carolyn Lewis's death hasn't even been reported and she's one of *them*. That's why all the rumors are flying. Everyone is hanging on the edge of their seats, seeing bogeymen in every corner. It's all racing in on me at once, just as a gun comes out of nowhere and clicks itself against the back of my head.

Lauren Chance aims a resigned smile at me from behind the gun and tells me to drop my weapons.

I tell her to take it easy, dropping my weapons.

The rusted piece of shit that belonged to my mother clunks at my feet.

Lauren stands there like a statue sentinel, covered by two black-suits—Jaeger's men, not the cops. Her grim little grin softens as one of them retrieves the pistols from the floor. She lowers her Colt Python slightly, but I don't dare move.

"Are you okay, Buck?" she says.

"That depends."

"You went a little crazy on those two guys back in the cell. I have to be sure you're still one of the good guys."

"Do I *look* possessed to you?"

"I wouldn't know—you're supposed to be the expert."

I turn and look her in the eye.

She lowers the gun all the way.

"Come on, Buck."

She motions to the door. The two blacksuits fall in step behind me. We move quickly outside.

There's an unmarked car waiting for us.

I'm shoved in the backseat and Lauren slides in next to me. The blacksuits take the front. Doors slam. The engine guns. We take off on a road that snakes around the outer edge of the theme park. My guts do a crazy scramble in the sudden forward motion, but the Power stays in check.

I only notice that Roosevelt is sitting on the other side of me when I hear his voice rip off in my ear:

"My man, *Bucko*—back for the attack!"

The Dreamworld flashes by us. I look at Lauren, who slips the Python back under her black jacket. I tell her thanks for the save and she nods, still cool under fire. She tells me Jaeger's people acted fast when the cops arrested her on the train platform. Some quick negotiations and she was out of lockup and on her way to spring me. I don't wanna ask her what she means by "negotiations." Sounds grim.

"Welcome back on the crazy train," Roosevelt says.

She hands me her iPhone.

The video screen shows me a familiar face.

Should have known it would be him.

"*Hello, Mr. Carlsbad,*" says Sidney Jaeger, his tone measured and professional, not what I would have expected in this moment. "*How are we feeling?*"

"I feel like shit. Have no idea how *you're* feeling."

"I'm feeling a touch nervous, Mr. Carlsbad. I believe we have a situation on our hands, don't we?"

"You could say that."

"Care to fill me in?"

"You first. What the hell's going on? Why isn't there anything on the news yet? There were cameras all over that platform."

"They only saw what Homeland Security allowed them to see. In fact, I just came from an interesting meeting with some very upset government representatives. It seems they confiscated some video shot on the train by Carolyn Lewis's people."

Roosevelt holds up a flash drive and smirks. "Not to mention this bad boy."

I give him a quick shrug. "Your cameras?"

"Yeah, and I've got the data backed up in three remote locations too. You don't fuck with the President, man."

The Richard Dryden show—one night only, in living color.

"I bet it was fun viewing," I say to Sidney.

"To say the least. They're having a hard time explaining why their own men tortured unarmed civilians."

"Yeah," says Roosevelt. "And why when you shoot 'em, they don't die."

"To say that the powers that be are shocked and horrified would be a gross understatement, gentlemen."

"It gets worse," I say.

"What?"

"One of my own people tried to waste me. It was Tom. He said he was working for someone who wasn't you—and I don't think he was a spook, either. There's another player in the game."

"Tom Romilda was my employee. I paid him an obscene amount of money to guard your life on that train."

"And I'm telling you someone got to him. We can't trust anyone."

"Mr. Carlsbad, you're asking me to make some very extreme leaps of faith."

"Then how about this: There's a mark inside the senator and he steps on stage in just a few minutes. I'm going after the son of a bitch, and I think I have a few new tools to help bring the bastard down."

"New tools?"

"It's a long story."

The Power pulses inside me, sensing everything dead in the air, in the car—even Lauren's hair. Roosevelt looks at me funny, and I think he can almost sense it, too.

Jaeger knits his brow at me, considering all this.

"So you want to go in and get the mark out of the senator while he's making his speech?"

"If the thing settles in him for too long, it might never come out. I can take him from the audience, but I have to get in close."

"That's a bold action. It could cost you everything."

"I don't care."

He thinks about it for a moment.

Then, very calmly:

"A lone assassin is a doomed assassin, Mr. Carlsbad. History has proven that time and again. Allow me to assist you."

"What did you have in mind?"

"This is my house, Mr. Carlsbad. Make a wish."

Lauren Chance stays icy cool at my side as our car nears the amphitheater.

NINETEEN

LAST STAND IN FANTASYLAND

The Dreamworld is unlike like anything on earth.

Like a fantasy bursting from the depths.

Everything looks like candy laced with steel, wild explosions of color and glitter streaking and bursting over structures and substructures, noise from a million radios, laughter from a billion kids—and I can't tell how much of the laughter is real and how much of it is leftover from last week, all going off in my head like anti-symphonic atom bombs. I slip on my headset and kick it to the Crüe to get normalized. It's not working like it usually does. No small thing, that.

I see dancing bears in the sky and roller coasters made out of superheroes. I see swing sets circling on fifty-foot carousels, brimming with kids of all ages. In the center of the complex is the main casino and hotel, which is not as huge as the Lost Angels place but sparkles a lot more—ten levels of sparkle, all the way to the penthouse near the roof, where Jaeger has his offices. A helipad up there, too.

Just ahead is the Dreamworld amphitheater.

The place is so new that about a third of it is still under construction—sections are lain open to reveal skeletons of steel and scaffolds several stories high. The kid tells me that Sidney wanted to name the theater after an actress from the forties named Gaylen Ross, but her estate refused. You remember her, right? She was in *There's Always Vanilla*.

The place is nestled just between the train platform and the casino, peeled open like a giant seashell to reveal rows and rows of seats facing the giant stage I've seen so much on TV. Seeing it live, even from this distance—it really is kind of awe-inspiring. I feel a wave of bizarre idol-worship come on, and I manage to crush it quickly. That isn't hard. I've got a lot of other shit on my mind right now.

Lauren directs our driver into an alley alongside the area where the building is still unfinished. I turn up my headset because the voices in the stadium are just too much. Mötley Crüe dulls the background noise, but only a little bit. Goddamn, man.

Thousands of people, just feet away, all in that giant theater.

All cheering for Maximum Bob.

Fireworks bursting in rough intervals over the theater—the grand old red-white-and-blue showing off for God and country.

I peel one ear and we huddle up, talking about our approach:

Lauren knows every nook and cranny of this theme park, and the amphitheater is under serious lock and key now, the Secret Service agents double-fronted since the nasty business on the train. The senator's life has become top priority. I won't be able to get in through the main entrances—the spooks will be gunning for anyone who isn't with park security, and even those people are on the detention list. Lauren and Roosevelt's slip from the cops and my escape from lockup won't be noticed for at least several hours—they've made sure of that. Sidney's already working on buying the right people to make our pardons permanent, but right now we have to act fast.

Lauren knows just how they'll get me into the theater from here.

She's been putting it together for the last half hour, on the phone with each of the twenty-seven security peeps she still has in the building, all of whom have been triple-screened and fingerprinted by Homeland Security. These are the well-informed maniacs that hired a cold-blooded killer named Richard Dryden to guard our lives.

They're predictable, she says.

They follow patterns, even in a crisis situation.

That's what made it so easy to bomb the World Trade Center.

Secret Service agents are no better than airport security, once you strip away all the fancy hardware—they're just *human beings,* after all—and these human beings are behind the times, she says. At the very least, I figure they're behind the times of Sidney Jaeger's high-tech organization, the accelerated eggheads who built a flying train that could do six hundred inside a mountain—the people who built this five-mile nightmare-on-earth and called it a Dreamworld. Lauren says it will be fairly easy to slip me through the half-built section of the theater and into the main stadium deck. All government eyes are focused on the stage right now, plus ten backup agents in the building, walking perimeter like good little robots, checking broom closets, snack stands, talking to each other on commercial-frequency Bluetooth cells. Roosevelt has been able to crack their channels on a hand-held, and we're wired into every move they make.

Mission fucking Impossible, man.

She hands me and Roosevelt plastic laminates with our faces on them. Bar codes and big red letters that say VIP. We have orchestra pit press seats, fifth row center.

Roosevelt is my backup, wired to the network through his hand-held.

We're going in through a hole in the skeleton of steel that rises above us—it's where a service entrance will soon be built all the way, near the rear of a loading area that'll be clear for the next five minutes.

Have to nail Maximum Bob from the audience while he's on stage.

Once he steps away from the podium, he's under triple guard in every direction again and we won't be able to get near him—at least not any time soon.

He's going on right now.

I can feel it in my guts from here.

No volume of loud rock and roll can drown that noise out.

He might as well be the second coming of Axl Rose.

Lauren says there will be eyes on me at all times, once we split up on the inside. They'll have me covered. The men in there will know the faces of Lauren and her boys—we have to hope they won't know mine. Roosevelt gives me a new black jacket, just like the one I have on now, only not burned and soaked with sweat and blood. That's why you wear dark clothes in my line of work. Takes a licking and blends right in. Makes you look official too. Sort of square, with the padded shoulders and pinstripes.

Lauren hands me a new earpiece and I trade her the Walkman.

I ask for my rusty gun, and she tells me no way.

She reminds me that security will pat me down.

Her voice cuts through me like ice.

I tell her I'll go along with that if she kisses me for luck. She gives me a funny look. Says the pistol and my Walkman will be waiting for me when the job is done.

I don't get kissed.

The rumble in my guts intensifies, racing with jaded anticipation. I keep it down. It's all a blur now.

We hit the service entrance area just as the crowd goes crazy on the level above us—it almost knocks me down but I keep my feet. The voice in my ear, Lauren's voice, cool and measured, in control, telling me to stay focused. I hear the sound of our next president, rising like a great wave and breaking back.

"My fellow Americans, I have seen the future, and it must be protected."

Two blacksuits appear at the loading area. Friendlies, right on schedule. They join our grunts and escort us through a winding maze of steel substructures and concrete girder supports. Electrical cables blow backward and forward, clanking against the skeleton of the unfinished walls. The whistle and hiss of wind and blowback through the maze, as we get deeper into the place. I slide in behind Lauren and Roosevelt, the four spooks right behind me. The corridor ahead of us is narrow and empty, exposed without walls—like a giant beast cut open, ribs and guts rising from the carcass. Scares the shit out of me.

"When this country was first founded, our forefathers set forth a proposition that would carry us through marvels of science and revolutions of industry and

ideals. Today, we stand on a great frontier, and if we are to survive and flourish, we must not allow ourselves to bow down in the face of adversity..."

We move fast. This speech is the climax of the Dreamworld rally, and Maximum Bob is famous for keeping it short and sweet. They say he writes his own material. I'd believe it. He's really stirring them up out there.

"...we are not afraid because we are a country of free men and free women, and we embrace complex ideas and common sense solutions as no other nation on this earth. This is our pledge and our legacy to the human race. We are soldiers. We are scientists and statesmen. But moreover, we are warriors. We are the spirits of our forefathers, rushing to meet the future of the world..."

The noise of the crowd rises. Every shadow seems to jump, the unified boom of all good Americans crashing like deep bass percussion, just above us. Next level up, the big show. So much sound-on-sound now, I feel insane. Really need my Walkman right now. Lauren tells me to stay focused on her voice. We move toward a larger corridor, which also has no solid walls. An agent tells us to hold, his voice crackling over our earbuds. Secret Service patrol, moving through using a heat scanner. No sweat, Roosevelt tells us. Backwoods motion detection system. He has it jammed out already at the source. Like working beads on an abacus, he says.

The patrol moves through and leaves the exposed corridor empty.

Shadows dance through the beams of steel and rivets.

The wind, rattling the scaffolds.

We split up here and Lauren keeps her voice in my ear—me and Roosevelt and two of the suits head for the next junction without her. She becomes a ghost in the corridor, floating along the walls with the other two men, breaking off into another service tunnel, out of sight now.

"...we hunger for the next frontier, because we are Americans. We strive for speed and success, because we are Americans. We reach for the sky and the stars, pushing ourselves to new and greater heights of discovery and wonderment BECAUSE WE ARE AMERICANS!"

The crowd goes nuts.

Really cutting loose out there.

The Power ebbs inside me, riding the lightning wave of my adrenaline, keeping a scan hum buzzing in my chest, keying on the words of Max-imum Bob as I follow three feet behind Roosevelt. Lauren is still in our ear, telling us an elevator is just ahead, which will take us from the unfin-ished floor and open right into the central walkway on the level above us that borders the main seating areas of the entire theater. We wait there at the closed doors of the lift for Lauren's all-clear.

The crowd is still roaring, soaking up the great man.

"I welcome you all into a brave new future—a future in which all our great lands will be united as one under a system of transportation more ad-vanced than anything else conceived…"

Lauren tells us to key the elevator now. Roosevelt presses the button and the doors open quickly. The crowd cheers again. We move in and punch the number two button. All clear, she tells me. It's up to us now. She'll be closing with her men as we make our approach. We're going to walk right down into the crowd on the main auditorium seating deck. I have to be close to him for this to work.

It's going to be damn tricky.

The Power slurps hungrily inside my stomach.

"…and this technology that represents our future must be protected. We will not allow those with evil agendas to stand in the way."

We shift floors and the elevator dings.

We step out into the open cement walkway.

There are thousands of people down there in the stadium seats.

All of them held in near-rapture by the face of their next president.

He's pacing the stage with a mic in one hand, laying it down.

Looks like he really could be Axl Rose.

"What I am about to tell you will come as a shock to many, but I ask you to be strong and stand with all good Americans, for if we do not stand together, the forces of anarchy will surely consume us all."

Amphitheater security lined up in pairs along each entrance to the floor below. We show our IDs and get past them easy, without a second look. The two grunts on either side of us make our entrance really official. They look just like Homeland Security. The amphitheater guys don't even use a metal scanner on us. Could have kept my Walkman, dammit. Lauren's voice again, in my ear, telling me to stay focused on her voice, and on the senator. We walk down the concrete steps, right through the center aisle in the midst of the cheering crowd. The stage directly ahead. Bob's face's forty feet high on three screens, his voice booming out across the universe.

"Tonight, we must all be made aware of a terrible threat to our nation's shores."

The Power rumbles in me as we get closer.

Louder now.

Hungry for him.

Homeland Security agents camped on either side of the great man, five strong. Another row of men in a line just below the stage, arms crossed, like muscle backup at a heavy metal show, just beyond the steel cage bars.

The mark in the senator senses me.

I can feel it move inside him from a hundred yards away.

Maxton's voice rises, shifting tone slightly.

We move forward.

Roosevelt and me, and the two blacksuits.

"Tonight, aboard the Jaeger Laser, an attempt was made on my life. The perpetrators of this attack were citizens of our own country who have conspired against your government to destroy our future. They were foiled in their attempt to assassinate me, but many lives were lost. Among them was the great American Carolyn Lewis and several members of our own heroic Homeland Security force."

Shock breaks over the crowd.

A woman near me screams.

Lauren tells us to hold. Two men in the upper level have spotted us. They don't have a positive ID, but they see us in the aisle and they're alerting their buddies orbiting the stadium seating. We have to move fast. She says they'll do their best to cover us. The blacksuits on either side of me and Roosevelt tense, as the crowd shifts on all sides of us, restless and transfixed. I feel the fingers of a thousand angry badasses closing around my neck. Smothering me.

The crowd, like a rising storm.

"These deaths were senseless and criminal, but the gallant efforts of our own

law enforcement officials have foiled this insidious sabotage attempt, and pre-
vented the death of many others, including myself. But, my fellow Americans,
the nightmare is far from over..."

They rumble in their seats.

Maximum Bob rules them all.

Roosevelt looks at me, real worried.

We move in fast, almost to the orchestra pit.

"...because the terrorists responsible for this merciless and deadly attack on
our nation's soil are still at large. In fact, we have reason to believe that these
terrorists are now among us—in this very amphitheater."

Oh shit.

Oh fucking goddamn shit.

Another woman screams.

And another.

And another

And...

It breaks over the crowd like a disease.

The voice of Maximum Bob working on them like heavy drugs.

"These terrorists could be standing right next to any one of you, at this very
moment. They are prepared to kill your loved ones and your children—to de-
stroy our American way of life."

The giant video screen behind him flashes live with three still photos.

It's my face up there.

Me and Roosevelt and Lauren Chance.

Maximum Bob aims his finger at the screen:

"These are the faces of the murderers that are among you now—I say again
that WE CAN TRUST NO ONE!"

Lauren breaks over the earbud—tells us to get the hell out of there.

But it's too late.

Hundreds of people are screaming.

The first punch is thrown.

A bottle shatters.

And everyone within a hundred feet of me and Roosevelt get real crazy
in a big hurry, their eyes zeroing in on us, dead bang.

"My fellow Americans—YOU MUST FIGHT THESE TERRORISTS!"
Critical mass.
"They are AMONG YOU!"

A black woman with long hair screams in horror as a sweaty bearded man in an olive drab jacket jumps on her—she only bears a passing resemblance to Lauren Chance, but it's enough. Another man in a business suit jumps on the guy next to him, who could be me, tearing at his face.

"TRUST NO ONE!"

His words drop on them like a fever bomb as we make it to the orchestra pit, and the entire crowd explodes in a blind rage, held in the grip of their master, leaping out of their seats, ripping each other to shreds—men and women and children at the mercy of this insane cult of personality, rolling and boiling around us like lakes of superheated magma punching loose from the skin of the earth.

Roosevelt screams something like *"holy shit!"*

And I think I hear gunfire through my earbud, as the blacksuits on either side of us tense on the butts of their holstered weapons, panicking.

The crowd closes on us like dogs.

Senator Maxton snarls down, his hands held high in the sky, commanding them all, and I see the mark *appear over him* in this moment, a tracerblur of madness, laughing like a lunatic, working Maxton like a talking puppet—and I can tell the thing's *in deep,* that the senator has accepted it and he's riding the rush, which must seem like ultimate power to a man capable of inspiring such anger and awe and Nuremberg frenzy in the hearts of so many people—all of them young, all of them waiting for a chance to be special... *all of them out of their minds now.*

And his eyes fall on me.

His eyes see me.

And he smiles, his smug voice stinging in my mind:

Checkmate, buddy. Enjoy the ride.

And the riot he created engulfs me in its thunder.

* * *

A sea of flesh surges forward. Screams and cries and tears and blood. Arms like steel and tree trunk legs and gushing sweat from every borough of life. Voices ripping across voices. I almost go under it, as the orchestra pit swarms...but I can still *see* the senator through the blizzard...*I can still see Maxton...*

The Secret Service agents are closing to take him off the stage.

The rioters are closing on us.

No, goddammit!

NO!

The blacksuits on either side of me and Roosevelt draw their guns and tell these crazy people to back off, but that just makes everything worse. The ugly Americans get uglier, and I only hear one shot before the blacksuits are obliterated in the closing circle of mad humanity. Roosevelt screams something I don't understand.

I call on the Power.

A desperate wave of black determination does a red-hot flash through my body and I feel myself connected to all the dead things in the air, to the cement below my feet, to the clothes on the back of every crazy person coming right at me—and the flash of it *booms* like an invisible fist exploding in a circle, blasting out from my body.

The rioters surrounding us are blown backward like dolls.

Roosevelt is thrown to the cement, where a nasty-looking patriot in a business suit pounces on him, smashing the kid's head into a seat.

A woman in a red dress jumps on the business suit and starts clawing at his eyes.

A sixteen-year-old metalhead jumps on her.

Blood and hair fly all over the place.

Roosevelt is buried in the rubble of arms and legs.

I send out another wave but it does the kid no good.

Hundreds of crazy people on all sides of us, closing fast.

We're all fucked in about three seconds.

Maxton sees the wave emanating from my body and starts screaming into the mic, jabbing his finger at me:

"THERE HE IS! SHOOT THAT MAN! KILL HIM!"

The agents beyond the cage bars go for their guns. The agents on stage grab the senator. The screaming people on all sides of me are blown back one more time by the ripples of energy I'm putting out. Maxton lets out a big damn animal yell that charges through the giant auditorium speakers, his fingers reaching for the nearest shoulder holster, grabbing the Smith and Wesson revolver that lives there. The agent is too startled to figure out what's happening, even as Maximum Bob snatches the gun and aims it into the crowd. A new wave of horror breaks out over the screaming audience, the senator bearing down on me...and Roosevelt looks up from the concrete with blood in his eyes, shocked in awe as I aim everything I've got at the stage..._just like before..._

And the Power sharks out from my left hand in one mean bite, chomping through the air—fifty feet, a hundred feet, two hundred feet across the rows of panicking people...

And it hits right where I tell it to go.

I take control of the gun.

I stop him from firing.

The mark inside the senator curses at me, dazed by my attack—and the shock _almost gets the gun loose,_ but he's not letting go yet. One of the Secret Service men tries to grab the revolver from him, yelling something I can't hear, but Maximum Bob backhands him with the hard steel, exploding the poor bastard's nose. He swipes another set of arms away from him, knocking his protectors backward, aiming at me again, spitting more curses. As I redirect all my energy into what comes next, the rioters in broken circles around me get their shit together and close the gauntlet, screaming for my blood.

I hit the gun before he can fire..._and..._

Blacklight.

Blasting into view, just for one second.

Then I'm back in the world again, struggling to keep a hold on the gun.

Blacklight again.

Then back again.

He's fighting me hard.

The rioters who want to kill me freeze in place, feeling the burn of dark energy pouring out of me the same way Maxton does, the two of us struggling between worlds as we play tug-of-war with Smith and Wesson. It flickers on and off across our minds and inside our eyes like the stuttering shocks of an exploding neon sign.

He snarls and his finger hits the trigger.

More panic in the crowd.

The gun fires and there's a blur as Roosevelt springs to his feet, throwing himself in front of me.

The bullet punches him dead center, sprouting flowers of blood. I hear his lungs do a red-hot pop. His scream of pain is cut off as all the air inside him blows. The next shot tears into his head, sending plugs of hair and bone scattering. His brilliant, overloaded mind detonates like a supernova and scatters in a million directions.

Time slows to an infinite crawl as I feel the kid die.

Seconds become like lifetimes.

His body lies in a bloody heap, his spirit mark going free with a terrible, ragged wrench, hovering there in space, just feet away from where I stand. I'm the only other person in this room besides Maxton who can see it.

The mark hovers there, feeling the awful burn of the Power stabbing from my body.

It backs away from me, the same way Darby backed away from me, cracking like a shadow whip into the Blacklight, consumed by the endless nothingness on the other side of death. I almost hear Roosevelt's voice as he goes, and he's telling me *no hard feelings, man...just have to go...catch you later, my man...*

And I almost start to cry.

Because he's dead and it's my fault.

Because this is the way it always happens.

Because this world is cruel and nobody cares.

It fills me with rage, and the rage channels the Power, stabbing through space and toward the senator as he gets ready to fire at me again, everyone losing their minds.

I take control of the gun.

I take control of the dead air surrounding his hand that holds the gun.

He fights me again, but I clench my teeth and win.

The gun turns on him at my command.

The next shot fires into his right hand.

And as the white-hot flash of the muzzle detonates his flesh, the intense pain axes through his entire nervous system.

The mark lets out one last scream, knocked for a loop.

I let the gun fall as it tears loose, screaming in anger.

Bob Maxton crashes to the stage, abandoned, slumping to his knees, staring in horror at the massacre set before him, seeing his life and legacy and the lives of hundreds of innocent people sprawling in fragments and tatters, like the flaming slabs of Rome, crumbled and broken and splashed with blood. I feel the rage and the desperation and the panic wrecking inside him. His life in politics. His affairs and his rise to fame. His life that might have been, commanding people like this—people like us. The man who would be king.

Who now realizes *his life is over.*

His eyes fill with tears, as he picks up the gun from the stage.

"God forgive me," he says.

He turns the gun on himself and pulls the trigger.

And in that one fractured, punishing instant, as the bullet cannon-flashes through the senator's skull, blowing his last thoughts skyward in pulpy, syrupy slow motion . . .

. . . I release the Pull.

It expands in a wave from my body.

And the mark that was inside Maxton can't resist me.

It hovers over Maxton's dead body for just a moment, peeling in mid air, trying to escape the terrible black gravity of what I have inside me, but it knows it can't win.

So it *comes right for me.*

Does a screaming head-firster into my guts.

I feel the thing's subatomic particles shatter like ice against my skin and absorb into me to join the others, slamming my whole body backward as everything the mark ever was—the ruined, regurgitated animal essence of his life, his crimes, his death in madness—*goes into me . . .*

I stumble and fall, overloaded.

The concrete below my feet red with blood.

Roosevelt's blood.

Panic still skittering and screaming and flowing like rivers, everywhere, all around me. A lot of people running for the stage now, some of them making a break for the exits. Everybody crazy, frantic. The senator dead next to his podium, alongside the agents who were supposed to save his life, all of them shocked out of their skulls.

All on national television.

The Power breaks against the inside of my body, trying to find a way out, but I'm in control of it—at least for now. The chaos all around me threatens to overdrive my senses, but I am backing away slowly, at least for the moment.

Nobody wants to kill me anymore. Nobody even notices me now.

I'm one tiny ant in a smashed and ruined colony of the doomed.

Swarms of complete insanity, trundling away in a million directions.

I can hear Lauren squawking in my ear, and I realize that it's *not over the wire*—she's actually here, pulling me back through the crowd.

Came to my rescue, just like always.

Three of her men cover us. Pandemonium on a global scale. Like a war, rumbling inside me and outside of me.

The Power, surging in waves.

I'm controlling it, but just barely.

I'm feeling every dead thing in the world surging around me.

Pulsing.

Glowing.

Waiting for my command.

We head for the main walkway above, fighting through the dark circus.

I black out when we get to the corridor outside.

Sizzles of the marks burn themselves in the dark behind my eyes, over-driven traces of their memories and their insanity, all fused together as they coalesce in my stomach...then I'm back up, and someone is carrying me through a dark tunnel.

I short out again, and then there's a car waiting for us, in some dark place I'm not sure I've ever seen before.

Tracer streaks grabbing at everything I see.

Lauren's voice like some vague icy beacon from the real world.

I'm gonna pass out...*and if I pass out I could lose control...*

I won't let that happen.

It happens anyway.

TWENTY

PRIMARY OBJECTIVES

The surreal glow of the video washes over me. That's the first thing I notice as I come up from pitch-blackness. I was out cold, and I didn't dream. Something prevented that. Something cool and warm at the same time, racing just under my skin, holding the Power down. At first I think it's a miracle. Then I can tell it's some kind of drug, and I feel like a dumb kid fooled by a second-grade magic act.

I feel the ground rolling under my feet as they wheel me into the center of the room. Everything is black glass and chromium steel, the lights of the Dreamworld broken into a sectioned panorama, sprawled out ten floors below us.

Just like his place back in Los Angeles.

He stands in front of a bank of screens, all flashing up dozens of worldwide newsfeeds, all reporting the tragedy down below. Commentators and pundits shocked and dazed. Police and city officials corralled for questioning. Screaming families and crazed survivors. The official death toll from the riot something like eighty-five now, including the senator of course.

Sidney Jaeger stands outlined in the back glow of the monitors.

Leaning on his cane.

I'm reminded of a Marvel Comics supervillain.

Lauren Chance has her hand on my shoulder, and I finally notice that

I'm on a hospital gurney, an IV drip going into my arm, the rumble of the Power straining to make a frustrated growl in my guts as my body surfs along the happy potions guest-starring in my bloodstream. Sidney smiles at me, looking vaguely excited.

"You've done me a great service," he says. "And I thank you."

Then he looks back at the chaos unfolding worldwide on ten zillion stations. Even the regularly-scheduled sitcoms have turned into tiny windows at the bottom of emergency broadcasts, O.J. Simpson style.

He stares up at it, fascinated and sated.

Smiling.

He turns to me and walks over—an amber silhouette floating out of a sea of newsflashes, so I almost can't see his mouth move when he speaks again.

It's appropriate.

He was the faceless man behind everything.

"This is how the world ends, Mr. Carlsbad. With the screaming of the innocent and the destruction of false gods."

As I hear the dead calm in his voice begin to waver, something strange shifts through the room.

Something that isn't Sidney.

A whisper like a dark shadow.

My arms and legs are strapped to this gurney.

On a rollaway table, just out of reach, is an instrument tray full of needles and syringes. Scalpels and surgical gear.

My Walkman and my mother's rusted gun sit there too.

Just out of reach.

"It's so very beautiful," he says, looking at the screens again. Looking at the horror of lost lives, the chaos. "I'll remember this day forever. We *both* will."

Lauren keeps her hand on my shoulder, her eyes down on me.

Like she's saying she's sorry.

Jaeger smiles at me, and the smile chills my skin.

I struggle to make words happen:

"This whole thing... everything that's happened... it's all because of *you*."

"Most of it."

"You *wanted* the senator to be possessed."

"Not exactly. We had bigger plans for Bob. I was hoping you might take him alive. Suicide really is a coward's way out for a politician, isn't it?"

"You put him on the train...you put *all those people* on the train..."

"I put them there for a very good reason. To bring urgency to your mission—to distract you from the big picture, so to speak. Bethany Sin can be *quite* distracting, can't she? It all worked beautifully."

"Why? For God's sake..."

"Mr. Carlsbad, I've dealt with the rich and the powerful all my life. Rock stars and politicians are just blips on the radar screen of history. Easy sacrifices. I don't mind watching while they die. In fact, it rather amuses me."

He was full of shit from the beginning.

And I walked right into this with my eyes open.

Walked right into it.

I struggle up through the drug fog, focusing on his face, willing my voice to the surface. "You wanted the marks inside me all along, didn't you? All of them together, to create...this *control* over dead things."

"It was our primary objective. You thought I was just an eccentric billionaire with money on his mind, didn't you?"

"It did seem that way."

"Smoke and mirrors, Mr. Carlsbad."

"And all that bullshit with Adam Protextor in the video and the derailment—that was all a cover story, wasn't it?"

"Very good. The man who played the part of Protextor was an *actor*. There was *never* a derailment. We had to let you know what you were up against so you'd be ready for them and our explanation had to be plausible."

Yeah, and the slick way they grabbed me and threw me in a private jet, with hardly any time to think it over.

I wasn't thinking about that.

I was obsessed.

Just the way my father was.

"As I said, you've done me a great service, Mr. Carlsbad. My train was designed as a very high-tech resurrection device. The high speed and the magnetic field took years to work out...but we never could have pulled the ghosts aboard the Laser without the beacon of your unique mind to complete the circuit."

They homed in on me.

I was bringing them aboard his train and I never even realized it.

And he has more of those trains ready to run.

Ready to honeycomb the whole country.

"You set the whole thing up—all that media hype with the launch and everything—just to fool *me?*"

"Don't flatter yourself. Bob Maxton and the others were a necessary evil on many fronts...but you have to admit, it worked, didn't it? I knew we could kill two birds with one stone. Even with all your psychic intuition, you never once suspected what the real plan was."

"Bob Maxton could have destroyed the whole world."

"It *was* something of a temptation when I realized the senator was possessed. It might have been easy to control him, but I couldn't take any chances, not with my primary objective so close. We needed the eighth member of the Nine. And you're very right—he *was* dangerous."

"What if more of them had gotten loose in your guests? I almost didn't pull it off."

"Wouldn't have been a problem. We would have sent you after them the same way we sent you after Bob. I told you already, I have no qualms about collateral damage."

"You're a maniac."

"I'm much more than that. And people *need chaos,* Mr. Carlsbad. It prepares them for things to come. Softens them. Gives them a reason to exist. Just take a look at all of it—a *million channels* of chaos, for all the world to see. They'll be talking about what happened tonight for a long time, and why not? It's only a means to an end."

The son of a bitch.

He would have had me chase down every one of them, and he would have been happy as hell to see Bethany Sin lose her soul live on CNN. It was all a game to him. He built a house of glitter and fantasy—a Dreamworld on earth—and smashed it all down, just to watch people bleed.

And I walked right into it with my eyes open.

"How many people have you killed, Sidney? Your guests on that train were slaughtered. The people in that theater were *slaughtered*."

"Some of that was unnecessary. But it makes no difference to me. It makes no difference to either of us."

He laughs some—a dry, unamused sound.

And I realize that *either of us* doesn't mean him and me.

It means him and *someone else*.

He looks at the rusted gun sitting on the instrument tray next to the Walkman and smiles inwardly, picking it up.

"This is quite an antique, Mr. Carlsbad. Would you believe that I recognize it? From long ago? When it was used for the first time."

How could he know?

Unless...

The Blacklight rumbles, just out of view...and I sense what's inside him.

The thing that makes him recognize the gun.

He slips the antique in his pocket. "We'll just keep that safe for you, Mr. Carlsbad. Wouldn't want anyone to get shot, would we?"

He motions to one of his men, who rolls something over that looks like a large steel box on wheels. Sidney twitters a keypad with his fingers. Then he pulls a latch, opening the front of the box with a rush of rotten air.

Air that was sealed inside for a long time.

Something floats out.

Something real bad.

It's the strange presence I felt a few seconds ago, only now a million times more intense. Let loose and rumbling. A shadow given substance.

A living plague seeping in from all sides.

Sidney laughs as it fills the room.

* * *

It stuns me first with a series of images—things I heard described to me before on video, but I've never felt them first-hand.

A four-year-old girl's throat slashed, her pleading voice innocent like a child in a fairy tale.

A man with dark hair stabbed by a knife, his startled black eyes bugged out and going dead, like destroyed planets.

An elderly woman dying slow in a flowing river of deep, deep red.

And so many more.

So much death and torture, dirtied up in a lingering fog of pure fucking evil, swirling in the air.

It's coming from a small metal canister.

Sidney brings the canister out of the steel safe.

Brings it closer.

"Buck Carlsbad, I'd like you to meet someone."

When he says that, the images hovering in the fog become a quick needle spike that reaches out and pings my dull noodle for just a second.

Blackjack Williams just shook my hand.

Sidney sees that I understand and he smiles again. "We got to know each other *quite well* a long time ago."

He brings the canister closer and I can tell the sleek silver-plated surface is holding Jack's essence fast, but the black influence of his mind still fills the room like poison gas, *still fills me with images…*

I see it now, in the fog.

My father, driven by nightmares and visions.

Visions put in his head by Jack.

To find those eight souls who could give him control over the Blacklight—if they were tricked and combined in the right way.

He leaves everything to find Jack's unbound spirit in the desert.

He knows the only way to stop him is to join with him.

But going over is losing your mind and your body.

It's turning away from everything you ever loved or knew.

It's surrendering to the temptations of the Blacklight—the limitless power beyond human sight that only a man like him could see and feel and know.

Or a man like me, because I am my father's son.

I can see him out there—just like I was out there—going too far and taking too much, allowing himself to be consumed by it, all of his desire to serve humanity and protect the innocent falling in ruins beneath such obvious, ordinary temptations.

Because it's all so obvious.

This desire that powers the Nine.

This desire to eat everything and be full of it.

To kill us all and drink it down.

I've felt it so many times.

My mother knows, too.

She never gives up on looking for her one true love when he vanishes into the desert.

She kills my father to release him from the desire.

They kill each other.

And when his body dies, Jack goes free in the Triangle again.

Until Jaeger finds him there.

"Jack and I have planned this moment for a very long time," Sidney says, his voice slithering now in the powerful Cheshire fog of a killer's soul. "I built the train, with all the speed and technology to crack open those silver graves out there. He taught me the *truth* about the Power they all represented. And you stood in the middle and finished your father's work. You will become the *vessel of the Nine,* just as he was supposed to. There's a certain symmetry in this. I'm sure you can appreciate it."

Because I'm my father's son.

Because my father fell just like I fell and my mother pacted in blood to stop this terrible thing from happening, thirty years ago.

Father.

Mother.

How I've failed you both.

He smiles, the urn humming now in his grip.

"Fuck you," I tell him.

"Crude. And unnecessary. In just a few minutes, you will feel quite

293

differently. You will feel just as your father felt. Before your mother was forced to kill him."

He opens the urn.

The hiss and the smell of Jack fills my senses, much harder now.

"I expelled most of Jack's essence a long time ago. We've kept our pact ever since. You can *feel his mind,* can't you?"

Swirling there.

So much evil...so much *death*...

And Sidney, a sick old man poisoned and brainwashed by his power.

By everything.

Ready to kill anyone, ready to shake up the world—ready for anything at all.

I feel Jack pressing in on me, the fingers of his insanity tickling at my mind, and it's terrible—like demon seed drizzling in the air, something cold and wet and nasty in all the bad places. Disgusting.

"Back off, you crazy son of a bitch."

But my threats are empty.

My mind is dulled and helpless.

I can't fight him.

"He's *not* crazy," Sidney says softly, caressing the surface of the urn. "He's not even human—he was *never human,* Mr. Carlsbad."

Then, he looks right in my eyes, and I see how insane the old man really is, the sick trickles of Jack's madness breaking apart his eyes in thin red corpuscles, like blood-winding scars on the surface of his soul.

It's not all in the canister.

Part of Jack is still inside Sidney.

The old man sighs again, and says:

"He is a god."

I try to get free.

I struggle against the straps.

His voice, still calm and focused, full of Jack and full of madness:

"He was *sent to us,* you know. To bring the new age. All the wealth and politics and cruel machinations of the world we live in, every little thing that moves us closer to oblivion as creatures of flesh—this is all the way of *unenlightened beings*. And when Jack leaves this world and returns to it, every man, woman, and child who lives in their own human filth, all these ordinary beings who *believed in nothing* on the day before...they will see fire in the sky and *the face of God*. They will see every dead thing on earth rise up at his command. That's why Jack never died when your father did. That's how he survived for so long in the Blacklight and made me see the truth. He'll make *you* see, too, Buck. He'll make the world see. *I promise you that*."

"You're insane...you're all insane..."

Two men grab me and force my mouth open.

I can't fight them, I'm too weak now.

The marks inside are too strong.

The smell of Jack...*the destroyer of my mother and father*...

One of the men jams something plastic in my mouth that keeps it open.

I can see four more guys in a semicircle, all surrounding us.

Lauren Chance with her hands still on my shoulder, her face still apologizing.

Jaeger comes closer with the urn, opening his mouth, his body breaking into a violent shudder. Something cracks inside him. Something wet and ripping. Thin ropes of deep black muck push through his mouth, trickling along his lips and chin. The muck screams, and it's the voice of Jack, stretching like tortured music oozing within tangled membranes.

The tendrils drop from Sidney's chin and into the urn.

It goes home with a deep bass thunder.

And Sidney's body rumbles again, his hands clutching the urn, his eyes bursting with red stars and black ice. He laughs, and the sound fills my entire world. I can't fight it back. It smashes me. It twists knives in me. It brings me under.

He tips the urn just above my open mouth.

Jack's stench, pulsing inside there.

I see the old man's wasted, quaking smile just above the heatwave.

When the rancid liquid goes into me, the Nine will be joined.

The Power will be controlled by *Jack*.

Jaeger's voice, garbled and jagged, his humanity imploding:

"The world will change again soon...tonight, they've all seen how fragile the world really is...tomorrow they will be *ruled by the hand of God.*"

And I hear Jack laughing now.

Laughing because he wins.

Finally.

I feel Jack shriek loose from the urn as the muck slides down my throat. I try to fight it, but the ooze is quick and stinging, gushing down fast, like a snake sliding in caustic oil. The Pull explodes in my body like an animal reflex action, bringing the spirit in with a gutterspewing thunder that feels like a toilet flush tremor bolting to the core of the Earth. I sense lightning tearing across the sky of the Blacklight, the marks within me starting to boil again, just under the concrete drug block in my system. They see and feel their master, close now, all the masks off, the games played—and it's like fire inside me.

My eyes go red with a madman's cancer.

A terrible hatred boils beneath my skin.

Jack's voice, pouring on top of my mind:

"Are we having fun yet?"

The world of shadows on shadows forces itself into my sight, exploding the room in an X-ray-shimmer that ripples in layers—the Blacklight, blacker than ever.

And beyond that.

Deeper.

Down into the canyons of my own mind.

Surrounded by the Blackjack Nine.

They circle me like unformed animals—mutant plague streaming in desperate, psychotic layers, screaming at me.

Blackjack Williams, standing in the center of it now.

Coming toward me.

The Power inside my body surges.

I pull it to the surface.

It's like ripping at a wall of pain to make my own mind work right.

Jack laughs at me.

I see his true face now, outlined in swimming beads of electric neon black-
ness. A rough-hewn jaw cut into a stone slab of uncompromising cruelness and
jaded insanity. His terrible smile is checkerboarded with missing teeth, dissi-
pating in a blurred flicker into the outline of my own soul, infecting my living
essence and amplifying itself, feeding off a fresh new mind and sucking back
the juice greedily. We roll together, exploding and glimmering and oozing. All
I see now is the blur of the Nine as they surround us—and in the center,
Blackjack's smile.

That terrible, warped smile.

"You killed my mother and father, you fuck."

He laughs at me. "Your mother and father killed each other."

"It was your fault!"

I reach out to grab him, to tear him apart, my rage crashing out like molten
surf. His smile widens, then explodes, showing teeth like sharp stones and a
winding serpent's tongue, lashes of light setting the glowing black air on fire
between us, wrapping up my hand, burning my fingers, racing up my arm.
It pries the fight from my grip in a searing talon burst of clawing white-hot
agony, and the flames eat through my skin, there and not there, ripping and
cooling, and he shrugs as I grit my teeth through the pain.

This is not really happening.

My hand isn't really burning.

This is all in my mind.

This is how he possessed my father.

I'm not going to let him do this.

I won't let him win.

He feels my resistance come against him one more time, and counters again.
I feel his boiling substance inside me, settling through my body, his voice
pounding louder and harder, the Nine finally joined against me.

"We shouldn't be fighting," he says. "We aren't of this earth, you and I. Just
the way your mother and father weren't. Come and see for yourself."

The Blacklight shifts, and I feel the cold yawning bite of his power—the
power he used so many times as flesh and blood, and later as an unbound

spirit—as it plunges in on me...and everything changes, images shorting on and off in the blackness...

I see my mother and father, together.

I see them holding hands and making love.

I see them finding each other in a crowded bar in Austin—the Continental Club, where spirits linger and the lonely come to roost on dark Mondays, the skies of downtown filled with twilight bats screaming blindly for love and blood.

I see them discovering what they are together.

I see them hunting marks together.

I see them standing over the graves of a hundred men and women—unsettled spirits that were ripped from the Blacklight.

I see them in the house I grew up in, tortured by their own power to experience what others cannot, unable to escape for even a moment from the voices.

I see shards of their long voyage into the desert.

I see my father in the grip of madness, following Blackjack in nightmares that make him cruel and filled with hatred.

I see myself as a young boy, watching them fight each other.

I see the mirror shatter on the floor.

I see my father slap her hard across the face.

I smell the hot sizzle of her blood and her pain.

I feel the terrible burn of the love that binds them.

And Blackjack Williams, just over my shoulder, laughing.

The sun beats down on us.

The Blackjack Nine kneel in front of my father.

My father, possessed by Jack.

Jack, who stands next to me with his hand on my shoulder, making me watch the whole thing as it goes down again.

My mother firing the gun.

My father slashing her with the razor.

He plays it over and over, like digital video on a feedloop.

Making me watch.

"I would have joined with both of them, Buck. Your father was the vessel—he was my body, and your mother could have stood by our side. But she had to go and turn it into a train wreck. And all for what?"

I spit rage at him, trying to block out the images: "She released my father!"

"She ruined everything, Buck. Most people don't understand how temporary these things that hold us back really are—things like flesh and love and the promises we make to each other in the dark when we are weak."

"SHUT UP! GET OUT OF MY HEAD!"

"You know it's true, Buck. You've known it all your life. It's why you've been alone for thirty years. It's why you've tortured yourself in endless spirals. You know the truth your parents denied. That love makes us weak. That the only thing that holds us back from being gods is . . . this."

And I watch them kill each other again.

And again.

And again.

"I've searched for years to find you, Buck. I've guided your life, even though you never knew I was there. I felt you close, so many times. It took a lot to finally come to this moment. And there are no delusions of love to come in the way now. No delusions of anything. You and I are the last of our kind, like your parents. Let it happen now, Buck. Stop fighting me. Come into my mind, the way your father did. Give me my followers. Complete the cycle. This is your legacy."

"No . . . no . . . this is all a lie . . ."

"We are the last, Buck. Stop fighting me."

"FUCK YOU!"

I concentrate on shattering the image of the desert around me, and it almost works, the Power ebbing painfully from my drugged body, blasts of other memories bottlerocketing across my mind in jagged twizzles. I see Bethany Sin, crying and smiling. I see Lauren Chance, beautiful and deadly. Sidney Jaeger and Bob Maxton, mad with power. Roosevelt and Darby, dead and gone. The blown-to-hell shatters of my past—glimmers and tinkles like falling debris, faces rushing on faces, a broken mosaic of emotions, all piledriving me backward as the gun goes off in my father's face and the razor cuts my mother's flesh . . . and I scream . . .

...as my hands close around the throat of Blackjack Williams.
His face and the faces of the Nine snarl at me in unison.
The Power and the Pull electrifies through every nerve ending in my body.
He takes the charge and stumbles back.
I hit him again and it hurts Jack this time—hurts him bad.
He stumbles back.
I press it hard, coming at him in a full blast now.
I push him down.
I gain control.
He screams all the way as I struggle for the surface...
...and just as I make it back from the Blacklight...

Click.

...the gun comes out of nowhere. Lauren swings it up, and the sound of the hammer falling back in the second before the first shot is like the cold snap of an electric icicle. It's ringing so sharp in my left ear as I come up from my battle with Jack that I almost don't hear it when she blows the two guys away on either side of Sidney. It's a dull metal *poof!* of superheat, calmed down by a silencer. They take the shots right in their foreheads, spouting thick gushers and falling back like broken puppets. She works the rest of the room in a clean, professional sweep—*poof! poof! poof! poof!*—and the line of men all go on their backs in a row. The last one almost gets his gun out before she *poofs* him, but he's a hair-fraction too slow. The gun clatters on the floor next to him and he blinks blood from a crimson cyclops eye in the center of his forehead.

Sidney leaps back and brings his hand down on a console.

An alarm siren cuts through the room and the building.

"Lauren," he says in a long sigh, his voice still garbled. "You have sixty seconds to obey my next command. The police are on their way up. *Put your weapon down.*"

"I can't do that, Sidney."

Her eyes are calm blue, uncompromising.

She is so goddamn fucking beautiful.

"Very well," he says, reaching under his jacket.

She fires at him and the bullet chunks through his arm, but he still gets the tiny little Berretta out of the miniature shoulder holster near his heart.

She fires again.

The bullet hacks his left ear off.

He doesn't even flinch.

Straightens his wounded arm and fires across my chest, right at Lauren.

She ducks inhumanly fast, still cool as ice, and blurs away as he chews up the room with his next several shots. His hands are still shaking and the bullets get confused, zinging over her head as she pulls her duck-and-roll move, hot lead shattering the monitors against the windows. The faces of the brave new world blow to hell and rain on the black marble floor like burning diamonds. I think Sidney's screaming at her—or maybe it's Jack screaming inside me—when she locks him up from a crouch on the floor and blows out his heart with a single shot. This time he flinches.

This time, he dies.

He staggers forward and sinks on his knees, the gun clicking empty in his hand, looking at her with agony and wonderment.

I'm wondering too—wondering what he's thinking in this moment as whatever's inside him leaves his body.

It goes with a rough rustling sound, like palsied feathers straining against an invisible wind.

"Jack," he says.

That's all I get.

Then he just slumps his shoulders.

Sits on his knees, staring.

She comes over to me and pulls out the gag.

I tell her thanks.

Her icy face has gone red a little.

"We have to get you out of here," she says. "There's a squad of our own agents on their way up, and he wasn't kidding about the police. We can take the private elevator straight to the parking level."

I feel the Nine shudder inside me.

The voice of Jack, like bile rumbling up from the back of my throat.

You can't escape me, Buck. It's just a matter of time before you give in. Stop fighting it. Stop—

"I have to get this out of me."

She nods, stone cold. "I know."

She uncuffs me from the gurney and I rub my wrists, sitting up.

"Why did you do it, Lauren? You must have known Jaeger's plan all along. Why?"

She smiles, just a little.

Then she leans forward and pushes her lips gently into mine.

The kiss almost cuts through the drug fog in my head, full of things that might be courage under fire and sacrifice. I am lost for just this moment in the smell of her, so many confused moments dancing in my mind...

Pathetic, Buck. Love is a lie. You know it's true. Stop fighting me.

...and then I'm back on earth, and she's giving me that icy look.

"We have to get you out of here," she says again. "Come on."

Jack screams inside me as I get to my feet.

Jack throws tantrums in my guts.

Fuck you, Jack.

Sidney is still upright on his knees, dead and gone. I pluck my mother's rusty gun from his pocket. Stare into his eyes to see if anything's left.

Nothing.

The gun should be humming its messages, but it's silent now.

Silent, because we won.

The Blacklight thunders, just out of sight.

My stomach dips and glides.

Stop fighting me, Buck. You can't win. YOU CAN'T WIN—

Have to get Jack out of me.

I jam the gun in my jacket pocket and swipe my Walkman from the instrument table as she helps me across the floor, into the elevator. She punches a button on the panel. The door slides shut. I slump to the floor. The voice inside me is dulled for just a moment by the drugs. I swim in space as the car hovers us between floors.

She looks right in my eyes.

Almost smiles again.

I can hear something that sounds like a helicopter, coming closer.

And I realize we're going up, not down.

"I'm sorry, Buck."

Her cold voice stabs me.

I realize it's something bad.

Her eyes fuse with something merciless.

Something inside her?

I tense for her attack, waiting for the blowback to hit me in the face, just like it always does when a mark jumps me, but it never comes. It's just her eyes, cold and dead, removed from anything like remorse or conscience. Or delusions of morality.

Jack laughs inside me.

Jack screams inside me.

Jack knows how this all ends.

Fuck you, Jack.

The elevator door clunks open and two guys reach in to pull me onto the roof, their hands rough and huge. They were waiting here with three other men. Lauren's people. Waiting for this moment.

I hear Jack scream again.

Laughter in my head.

Terrible, smug, vindicated laughter.

The deep dinosaur roar of chopper blades explodes over us.

The roof is two city blocks of hard concrete, smoked glass, and chromium steel sprawled out in sections above the Dreamworld. We come through an archway like five others that lead to stairwells and elevator shafts. There's a luxurious glass escalator that reaches up from one of the upper floors and terminates into a patio restaurant with a big kidney-shaped swimming pool. Everything is dark and stormy. The helicopter hovers over a landing pad directly in front of us, which is outlined in glowing yellow beads, wind spewing across the tarmac. A big metal monster with plenty of room for company. I've never seen a chopper that big before. It has three tail rotors.

Godspeed within rolling thunder.

The cold stare of Lauren Chance never changes as she strides alongside me, her two giants manhandling the merchandise, pulling my half-wasted body across the smooth landing, toward the giant machine as it descends and kisses the pavement.

This was planned.

She's been working for someone else this whole time.

And that someone is stepping off the big insect now, his white pants and suit flapping in the prop wash, a featureless cream-colored harlequin mask hiding his face like he's the Phantom of the Opera.

I've seen this guy before…haven't I?

The Phantom pulling Lauren's strings since the start.

I look at her and I shake my head.

Somehow, I'm amazed.

Nobody can sneak up on me like that.

"I'm sorry Buck," she says again, as if she really means it. "This is a professional relationship."

The Phantom in white comes close.

A jagged man who looks like a doctor comes with him, two faceless cronies rolling a six foot steel anvil case along the tarmac at his heels.

He reaches up and pulls off his mask.

Holy shit, man.

He doesn't tell me his name because this guy doesn't stand on ceremony. His skin is white and pockmarked, eyes wise and blue and searing, handsome in a wrong sort of way. Old and dangerous.

"Actors," he says. "Aren't we *all?*"

I have to laugh.

He laughs also.

And for the first time since I met him in the Driskill Hotel, I can feel his mind exposed to me—his powerful mind. I can feel it in him, the way a twin can read her sibling from birth, the way animals running on jungle instinct know each other in the dark, just before the kill. He kept it from me before, but I feel it now. He has no reason to hide anymore.

He's like me.

He's always been like me.

"How long have you been a mole in Sidney's house, Eric? Or is your name David Brannigan?"

"You can call me Mr. Tate if you like. I've gotten quite used to it."

"You hired Tom to kill me."

"That was an unfortunate misunderstanding. Mr. Romilda was my operative, yes, but he was never instructed to *kill you.*"

"What the hell *was* he supposed to be doing?"

"He was in your confidence, and you were a wildcard. Or so it seemed at the time. I didn't know exactly what Sidney was up to until just a few hours ago. I knew he planned to use his billion-dollar skeleton key to bust the graves of the Nine, but I couldn't figure out why in the hell he would drop an *exorcist* into the mix at the last moment."

"It beat the shit out of me too."

He laughs. "Mr. Romilda acted on his own initiative, I suppose when he perceived your presence on board the train as a threat. You see, we originally thought Sidney was planning to infect his VIPs with the spirits...it seemed clear enough agenda. Control the president and you control the world. I didn't realize that it was much simpler—that *you* were the key to the whole thing."

"You were his number-two guy. What was so hard about figuring that out?"

"Sidney always kept his secrets close to the vest, even from his most trusted."

So Tom acted on his own.

Sheer Section Eight under fire.

Thanks a lot, asshole.

Brannigan tosses it away with a wave of his hand. "It no longer matters. Mr. Romilda got what he deserved, after all. And when we finally figured out that Sidney's plan was to reunite the Blackjack Nine inside your body . . . steps were taken. That's what I have *my* most trusted people for.

Lauren's cold stare never changes.

I remember that first face-to-face in the movie theater—all her talk about Sidney's maneuvers to keep the train running on time, her fake concern for my safety. It was all bullshit. She was feeling me out to see what I knew, just like Tom was. Neither of them had any idea Sidney was a crazy man brainwashed by Blackjack Williams.

She lied to me all along.

She's the best liar I've ever met.

Right down to the kiss that got me in the elevator.

"Sidney was right about one thing," Brannigan says proudly. "Lauren Chance is the best there is at what she does."

"You had a lot of lucky breaks," I tell him, wanting to spit in his face.

"We improvise. Shit happens."

I smirk at him, hearing my own words from what seems like a lifetime ago.

He smirks back, nodding to the guy who looks like a doctor.

The doctor nods to his cronies, who begin to unlatch the big steel case.

A machine lives in the case—something with pumps and tubes and clamps. A glass dome, like an aquarium, tops the whole elaborate contraption. They begin unraveling the components, using high-powered rivet guns to bolt steel legs into the concrete. It unfolds like some terrible medieval torture device, glimmering with weird lights.

The man in white smiles at his machine.

Then he smiles at me.

"Time to play some jazz, Buck."

The first sirens peal away in the street, thirty stories below us.

Lauren keeps her game face on. Cold eyes betraying nothing, as she glances at her watch. "This area is compromised, David. We don't have time for this."

"Time is of the *essence*," Brannigan says, looking at me. "Mr. Carlsbad is a professional, after all. He's holding something very special inside him and holding it well. But soon he will lose that control. It might be a matter of seconds."

"David, the police are on their way up here now."

"Let them come. In just a few moments, it won't matter." He gives me a crooked smile. Son of a bitch almost looks grateful for a second. "I should thank you, Mr. Carlsbad. Your actions have made this process much simpler. It would have been a terrible inconvenience to round up eight possessed celebrities with our little machine. Might have taken years, really."

But he would have done it.

He's been planning this for a long time.

We just handed him his kingdom.

He winks at me.

"So...*thank you,* Mr. Carlsbad."

He motions to the grunts, who haul me over to the machine. They go through my pockets and come up with the rusty gun. One of them hands it to Brannigan and he laughs at me, just the same way Jacques did. The same way all bad guys laugh when they think they've figured you out.

Jerks.

"You really are poor white trash, aren't you?" Brannigan says, turning the rusty old hunk of metal over in his hand. Then he lets it fall. Kicks it away.

The gun slides like a rough stone and plunks into the swimming pool.

A dull splash, and it's gone now.

Gone for good.

They strap me into a series of metal arms that hold me fast. I am held down by an Iron Maiden shot through with steel and leather. One of the flunkies rips my shirt open, exposing my chest for the Inquisition.

The doctor steps over to Brannigan, holding one of the machine's long tubes.

At the end of the tube is a six-inch catheter needle.

I struggle to get free. I call on the Power, but Jack blocks me, filling my head with smug laughter. He knows Brannigan's plan.

The machine is a transfusion device.

Brannigan opens his shirt and the doctor slides the needle into his stomach. He takes the pain with a long sigh and a dreary smile, like a lover humoring the inevitable, and he winks at me, the sirens getting louder now, more cops descending on the front steps of the plaza below us.

Lauren looks at her watch again, and her face begins to stitch with something that almost looks like panic. She just killed one of the richest men in the world—a man she's been planning to betray for years. The payback will be fast and major, and she knows it. She tells her six men to cover the stairwells and the escalator, reloading her pistol. They snap open metal stocks on compact machineguns. One of them pumps up a nasty pistol-grip assault rifle—a twelve-gauge monster. Away in the night, I can hear the rudder of more big metal insects.

Police helicopters, closing on us from miles away.

The doctor uncoils the other long tube from his machine and comes toward me with the needle. I struggle again, but the steel of the Iron Maiden has me hard. Jack still laughing at me, ready to bail from my body.

I ain't going nowhere.

But he sure as hell is.

"This may sting just a bit," the doctor says to me.

And the sting hits me in a lightning bolt as the steel rams home in my guts.

A crash of fire and ice in my heart.

Thunder in the sky.

The police helicopters closing—the cavalry, too late to save me.

Lauren's men open up on the riot cops as they stream through the escalator and the stairwells. The hard blast of shotgun shells and automatic machinegun fire cracks across the roof like dynamite. Glass shatters. Bullets skip through water. The first two cops are punched center-chest—Kevlar body armor saves them for about two seconds before head shots take them down. The troops sprawl in their own blood, faceless men in black, chopped and torn. Lauren orders her guys to keep firing as more cops run right into their guns. They get shredded just like the others, but there's more coming up the escalator, and they're opening up full auto with AK-47s. The bullets whiz and burn, blasting one of Lauren's men off his feet in a spew of thick crimson.

Brannigan hisses at the firefight as it kicks into a higher gear.

"Do it now," he says to the doctor. Then he lifts a cell to his lips and tells the man driving the chopper to start the engine.

The rotor blades begin to whirl, turbines wheezing back to life.

Lauren is a robot in the heat of battle.

She fires at the cops, as they come up in waves.

Three of them get through the line of skirmish and throw themselves on the cement landing, spitting rapid-fire, and I see her take a bullet in the shoulder. She doesn't flinch as a dark flower of blood sprouts across her black jacket and oozes slow tendrils. Doesn't flinch at all.

Brannigan smiles at her and she doesn't smile back. She blows another cop away, the one who shot her, and he flies backward, punched right between the eyes, smashing into the glass escalator, his gun sputtering curses into the sky, cracking and exploding.

She stumbles to one knee.

She doesn't retreat.

Brannigan orders the chopper to take off.

And the machine starts to kill me.

I feel a ripping kiss inside the needle as it hits me with something intense and cold—some sort of drug mixture blasting my blood and meat and muscle. It sizzles, then bursts, like the flameouts going on in my nervous system, a chain reaction doing guitar solos in my bowels, jumpstarting chemical reactions that trigger involuntary nerve reflexes. I writhe in the grip of convulsions so painful and intense I can't even feel them after a few seconds. I only feel what it's doing to my body.

It's hammering me.

Imploding me.

Forcing everything out in a flood.

My eyes filled with a blood-red sky—but the sky *isn't* red.

It's blood coming from my eyes.

My veins squeeze tight in my head, so tight that one of them bursts in my neck. Every cell in my body rebels and blasts inside out, all at the mercy of one overriding command: to force everything I have to the surface—every thought, every scream, every ounce of fluid.

Sweat and blood pour off my body in floods filled with poison.

And here it comes...

HERE IT COMES...

The firefight on the roof is crazy now. More cops go down, blown to shit. Lauren takes another shot and staggers back, returning fire. Wholesale slaughter in human waves, bullets stitching blast patterns in the concrete, men screaming as they die. The doctor and his cronies begin to retreat toward the escape chopper, but the big metal insect is already lifting away from the tarmac, hovering above us. Lauren falls to one knee and doesn't look back. She doesn't even look up at the chopper. She is ready to die. For Brannigan. For Jack. For the new world and the face of God—all promises made by a handsome liar.

She snarls through her teeth.

She spits blood.

She struggles to fire her weapon again.

Brannigan smiles at her.

The police helicopters circle in low.

The transfusion machine shifts gears on me, and begins to pull everything I have through the tube.

Everything, and Jack.

It all surges upward and outward, exploding like the sounds of gunfire erupting on all sides of me, like the shattered pieces of my life and my memories, ebbing away in wave after wave... *coming up from the lowest places... taking it all...*

So long, Buck. It's been real.

Fuck you, Jack.

He pulls out with a rebel yell and fires right into Brannigan's stomach.

And he takes the Blackjack Nine with him.

* * *

And Brannigan screams as he smiles, glowing black miasma tumbling under his skin like translucent beads of liquid metal. The black napalm burn fries his flesh from the inside as my body self-destructs, cracking and surrendering.

The black muck consumes him.

The combined Power of Jack's eight disciples.

A churning, transmogrifying soul-storm—a thing of terrible, horrifying beauty, forming inside him, leaving me more and more empty, staring straight into Brannigan's eyes, my mind pinging and jingling and popping and rattling and screaming. And I realize, as my life storms away from me, that David Brannigan trained his body and his mind painfully for this. He waited in the shadows for decades to make it happen. He was ready like none of us ever could have been. His disciples were ready to die at his command. They all knew this Power and were prepared to use it—every damn bit of it. Brannigan knows that if you control the dead parts of the world, you control the living. He wants to be God, not like me. Not like any sane man in a world of crazy fucking people, maniacs ruled by desires that make us into animals, make us into tyrants. Like the desire to smash something smaller than yourself. Like the desire to make the whole world bleed and burn and cry, just because you can.

Like the desire for revenge.

Just out of sight, Lauren Chance struggles to stay on her feet, her body splashed in blood, the cops storming the roof now, the police helicopters coming in for a landing.

She is the last man standing.

All the rest are dead.

She gets off one last shot before they blow her away.

I almost see her smile.

And then her head explodes.

The Blacklight hits me as I begin to go under.

I feel death dragging me down, just as death drags Lauren Chance down. I see her spirit shriek loose—something black and ugly, full of jagged neon rage born in the heart of a destroyed little girl who gave up everything to follow a madman to the end of the earth—and as it tears away across this flickering endless nowhere, I feel her kindred spirit pulling at my heart and my mind. Something almost irresistible now. The siren song of everything that must die, so that it can be controlled. The mistakes of every lost mark. The secrets and the sacrifices and the endless despair. The Terrible Thing that comes for us all eventually and kills us in the most hopeless moment. All of it calling me in ripples and waves and voices on voices. She vanishes into the slipstream and I am about to vanish with her.

I'm going to die.

The cops stream onto the roof in force, but it's too late.

Jack looks back at me through Brannigan's eyes now, his living essence enveloping the X-ray outline of a willing human soul like a spider spinning up a fly, micromembranes shooting and spiraling off on thousands of winding roads. Brannigan's body sucks it up with an overdriven sigh—something that sounds like a dragon having an orgasm, crashing and burning, then skidding in a bed of fire and ice, buried under the passion of a million dead men and women.

And in one amazing clench of his entire body, it's all over.

And he stands there, no longer a man or a ghost.

He's come down from the mountain with a message for all of us.

For the whole world.

The cops surround him.

They tell him to drop to his fucking knees.

They tell him he is under arrest.

He waves a finger at them and I feel his control over all dead things, Jack's terrible face strobeflashing through his skin, and the wave pulses out at the cops, taking command of the guns in their hands. It's all over in a few seconds. The muzzleflashes detonate across the Blacklight like tracer-streams skidding in a weird dream, and I hardly even hear them now. The screams of chopped and blasted men hardly reach me either, their garbled death rattles going away under my own heartbeat...

...my heartbeat...

I feel my blood seeping out in long dark tethers from the wound in my stom-

ach. The beats come slower now as Jack commands the Blacklight, forcing the cops to kill each other...and I try to hang on...try to pull myself up...I'm not done yet...

The gun...my mother's gun...

Just a few feet away from me on the tarmac...

I reach out painfully for it, feeling my bones grind against the metal restraints.

But it's over.

The machine has won.

My body is gone.

The Big Black calls me now.

All the life runs out of me, my next heartbeat coming in a painful thud.

The next one will be my last.

It's over...

Over...

The chopper hovers above us on the tarmac, the cops dead in a circle on all sides of us, their spirit marks dancing stupidly as they go loose. Brannigan hovers over me, his voice blasting above the whirlwinds, Jack glowing just under his skin as he laughs:

"Good-bye, Buck."

His feet leave the ground.

He begins to fly.

I feel his command of everything dead in the air, swirling the pollutants and the carcinogens and the remains of unsettled souls around him like lashes, and he uses those lashes to climb into the sky, screaming along with Jack. Laughing. Mad with hubris. They hover in space, just above me. Floating toward the getaway chopper.

The Blackjack Nine.

A god on earth.

It's the last thing I ever see.

Blackness seeps in from all sides as my final heartbeat crashes down hard.

TWENTY-ONE

THE BIG BLACK

There's this funny thing that happens once in a blue moon.

When you get killed and you've got one foot in your own grave already.

When you're full of conflict and not ready to let go.

Always wondered what it would be like.

I look back and see my flesh and bones, as they go stiff inside the metal arms of the machine, blood seeping slowly from the wound in my stomach, my eyes wide open and bleeding. I'm deader than fucking hell. But I'm still on my feet. I'm wearing the same clothes I had on when I died.

I'm looking back at my own abandoned body.

And my new legs feel like they're made of hot molasses, oozing along my very first step as a Walker.

Brannigan doesn't see me.

Jack doesn't see me.

They twist and writhe in the sky together, distracted by the act of becoming one a hundred feet above the roof, halfway to the hovering getaway chopper—a sizzling, electric ball of living energy wrecked in unison, pulsing and coalescing into some bizarre new form. I've never seen anything like it. I'm seeing it with new eyes—the eyes of a dead man.

I'm seeing Jack consume Brannigan's body in midair.

In a storm of light and noise.

I have to concentrate hard to keep myself above the cement ground. If I ooze lower, I'll slip beneath this level and into the Blacklight, way far down, and it won't be pretty. I've gotta concentrate. Stay focused. I have other things to think about.

Important things.

Unresolved things.

Above me, the Phantom in white hovers, and Jack hovers beneath his skin—a glowing, flying *thing* in the night.

The chopper rotors pulse the air just above him.

He levitates toward it.

I see the strange outline of Jack's organs solidifying in white-hot bursts.

His power and the sound of his voice shatters through my mind.

One of the police choppers finally lands on the roof.

Two others circle the building.

I can see men inside those choppers with their mouths hanging open in slack amazement, as they watch Jack ride the lightning.

None of them can see me.

My legs vanish and then reappear.

I stumble and ooze along, learning how to walk again.

I get the hang of it pretty fast.

Mother.

Father.

I am closer to you than I've ever been.

I am one of you now, cut loose on the earth in the face of my death.

Unbound.

Superhuman.

Speak to me.

By the time I get to my second step, I'm motervating pretty well, the tarmac gliding below me in a half-dream, Jack's crackling essence bouncing back from above like submarine radar. I stay focused on it.

And the voice comes:

This is the thing that was waiting for you, Buck.

Your birthright and your Gift make you different.

You can use this to be free in ways others cannot imagine.
You can still beat the bad guys.

Yes, Mother.

I hear you.

The gun...it was just out of my reach before...*but now...*

Moving up to my third step, I can feel Jack *from inside David Branni-gan's body:* the wind of the blowback in his face, the Dreamworld casino and the city of Las Vegas strewn below his writhing cosmic form like a glittermap of twinkling yellow starstuff, the amphitheater two blocks away, full of panic and terror. I feel the intense Power that now ebbs at his command. The terror of it all washes over me easily, but I find I am no longer afraid. This is where I have come to—where I was always supposed to be.

This is the moment that redeems the Fall.

My moment.

I move faster across the roof now. The gun lies at the bottom of the pool. Just feet away. Shiny and new, like it was that day...*so many years ago...*

...and the open air of earth smashes me in the face harder now. The song of our planet—a zillion voices, screaming and crying and laughing and sighing. I thought it was intense being a medium when I was still alive. But that was just a taste. A glimpse. This is really fucking intense. This is what Darby was always complaining about. Coming in rushes now, each more wild than the one before it. The roar of the chopper blades all around me is a dull *thump-thump-thump* behind the rolling voices, which I realize now are clusters of spirits cut loose and coming across the sky in pressurized blast waves. The waves ripple and boil, distorting the fabric of reality, creating a second atmosphere layer above the surface of the city, a living sea of human energy and unsettled remains interacting with the sprawl of man-made lights below us. All their voices are made known to me in this moment—*all of them, all at once*—and it's so overwhelming in one second that I almost collapse, but then I straighten myself and push through, riding my own abilities through it, using everything I have to focus.

On the gun.

And Jack.

He is almost to the chopper—hundreds of feet above me in the screaming sky. He looks down... *and he sees me.*

He finally sees me.

He feels me.

Just like I felt Darby.

I am attached to him because he killed me.

I feel the burn, running to the gun now.

The trace left for me by my mother.

The ghost of a weapon used to kill my father.

One last bullet.

I throw myself into the water and it explodes around my shadow substance. I fly in zero gravity, pushing aside the chlorinated shimmers, not breathing, no bubbles, sinking fast in the deep end. At the bottom, my hand closes around the handle of the gun and it charges through me. The Blacklight spews into my line of sight, *but it's different this time*—not something hot and awful, but an energizing *force* that knits with the slipstream of spirits, lighting my whole body up in darkness.

Darby calls my name.

All the dead people call my name.

I swim for the surface and break from the water with an explosion that hurls me into the distorted air above the roof—and I aim the gun into the sky.

I see my entire life as I put my finger on the trigger.

Jack laughs and hits me with the Power.

But I know this guy—know him well. He's been inside me, and I kicked his ass then, too. So I'm one step ahead. I grit my teeth and spit rage back at him. He shrugs it off and bears down hard again. He concentrates on breaking me in half, crushing everything that's left, ripping at the darkest, most shameful weakness he knows I still possess...

...my love for my mother and father... the love I always knew was there, even when I was a child... the love I searched for desperately and never found... the love I rejected from Raina and turned into bottomless despair, lost out there in a world that never cared, screaming for it all to make sense...

He burns me there in that awful place.

He concentrates on using his control over dead things to tear me apart.

But he's wrapped up tighter and tighter in Brannigan, still tied to something *alive,* and it's giving him shit. Shockwaves of frustration suddenly begin to pour off him, bouncing back on me like hard fists. He can't muster up all the Power yet, as he fights for control over Brannigan's nerve centers and muscle reflexes, struggling through the interference and screaming like an angry child to bring the thunder against me.

He finally gives up on it.

And makes a very bad call.

Jack tears from Brannigan's body, which falls to the roof like a spent shell, cracking and splattering against the smooth cement, just a few feet from where I died.

And now he hovers loose in the slipstream of the Blacklight, becoming something that flashes and ripples and glows with endless power, a roaring monster filled with everything dark and dead.

And I see his face.

I look into his eyes.

I fire the bullet right into his heart.

He doesn't even know what happens when the shot takes him.

It punches into his glowing body—that weird writhing mass of Black-light energy hovering in the strange sky, that *thing* that might have come down from the mountain as the ruler of us all—and it's the trace of something left for me long ago that explodes through its breast. A magic bullet that kills Jack dead.

Just like it was always supposed to.

There are no coincidences.

Asshole.

And the Power of the Nine blasts free in that one rip-roaring thunder-clap moment, sending a wave across the slipstream of the dead...but I don't let it knock me down. I don't fall all the way, not just yet. I have to see what happens next.

It's pretty amazing.

Maybe it was even worth dying for.

The twisted, transformed body of the ghost I just killed flies backward, sucked by the rotor pull of the escape helicopter, plowing upwards into the spinning blades. I can almost feel the whirlpool of slashing steel chop into Jack for just one second as he hits the fan hard, rending metal stalks blowing in shatters. I focus myself to stay in once piece—every memory, every mark, every last trace of desperation and courage I ever mustered up in the heat of a fight—all of it armoring me to keep my eyes skyward, as the armored blades bend against the remains of Jack's superhuman substance, peeling back, flying away into the swirling mist. The chopper tilts and shudders as it loses its ability to fly, the last blade cracking off and lurching the giant insect into an awkward lopsided roll, hovering there for just a few seconds in the rolling slipstream, hanging in a midair cocoon, in the center of a jagged fist of Blacklight energy. Tendrils shoot through the thick metal, writhing and spitting, skittering beads like white-hot raindrops racing moray patterns and talons, filling the sky with an angry new moon that screams and bursts.

And then it all blows up.

A giant flaming comet made out of burning slag and the scorched remains of a god streaks across the sky and crashes directly into the center of the amphitheater, two blocks away.

An explosion to shake the earth.

For real.

The flames kick up for one hot minute. Steel supports snap like Tinkertoys. Glass shatters and fuses and bursts like millions of crystal embers in a dynamited jewel mine. Rolls of fire blow through destroyed stadium seating and office spaces and half-finished hallways made of marble and plastic. It all crumbles and collapses. And I stand there on the roof, a strange ghost wearing phantom flesh, and I watch it burn...along with the rest of the world...until the vision fades...*and I am falling again...*

...falling through the Blacklight now...

...down...

...down...

* * *

The voices whisper at the edge of the universe, floating along the chambers of my mind, flowing like every dirty secret and empty promise and shattered life I ever had a look at back in the world, and I find that I want to stay here, I find that the voices give me rest, that they seem like peace and truth, everything that made no sense at all when I was alive, all transformed into real and lasting comfort and the promise of a new life, far away from everything that dies... in a world that doesn't care...

... and I realize I've felt this before...

... in my dreams...

... the years rolling back like fog curtains, rolling back... and back...

... back to my mother and father.

I see them now, and there's nothing bad about it at all. They're young, like they were when I first knew them. When I was first born. When I was first named.

Buck.

That was really my name.

That's what they call me as a baby, bouncing and pure and happy.

I am named after my father.

I see our lives together on fast-forward.

I'm a precocious kid. I soak up knowledge like a sponge. They make me feel special and loved on my birthdays, with gifts of song and sight beyond sight. Each year I learn more about what lies beyond the eyes of men in the real world. My father teaches me about marks and says never to forget the rules, because rules are important, and he says his father taught him, and when he is gone, I will have to carry on the family work—the work that has protected mankind for hundreds of years. And I love my father because he seems so strong and wise. And I love my mother because she smells like love that comes easy... and we travel the earth, helping people, making things right... until one day... I never see them again.

For thirty years, I never see them.

Until the moment when I feel their hands on me.

Feel them now.

The voice of my father, strong like I always knew he should be:
You have to go back.
The voice of my mother, like a memory of some perfect summer day:
Please forgive us, Buck. We failed you. People can be very selfish. They can forget what's most important. But we can make it up to you now. Go home.
My own voice, like a child again:
No, Mother. I'm dead. I'm here to be with you. Let me stay.
She laughs, and I feel her hand on my face, gentle and soothing:
It's not up to us. You don't belong here.
How can this be?
How can I not belong here?
I searched my whole life to belong here.
It feels good.
I want to stay.
My father's voice comes again, tough and wise:
Death is a funny thing, son. Most people have no idea when to let go. That's where you and me and your mother always came in. We helped those people along, just like you do it now. But sometimes we can help them go the other way, too.
And I feel his heart beating over mine.
Son... all you need is a little push.
The great courage he possessed when he was young, like me.
The truth of his words, as they pour over me like life-giving rain.
And now the rain becomes a thunder.
And the thunder becomes a flood of memories.
All my memories from the first seven years of my life.
All rushing back at once...
I take the gift as they move away from me, and I ride it all like a series of great waves, up from the blackness... up from nowhere...

And I open my eyes.
Alive.
Breath races through my lungs as I come to with a hot shock in my

breast, the wind whirling my hair. I'm still strapped into the machine that killed me.

The cop choppers have landed.

Men with guns are scrambling all around me.

I look down at the Dreamworld, and the million eyes of the city. The desert beyond, like the void that waits. Police cars and ambulances buzzing around the wreckage of the helicopter in the amphitheater. The lights trailing into the distance. Chaos and fire, fading into the canyons of forever.

I gauge reality by the beating of my heart, making sure I'm still here.

Yeah.

I'm still here.

I'm still alive.

And I win, you son of a bitch.

TWENTY-TWO

EVERY PROMISE WILL BE BROKEN

The world didn't really change much.

Not the way Sidney Jaeger or David Brannigan dreamed it would. The crazy, doomed bastards.

In the aftermath of Maximum Bob's meltdown at the Dreamworld, there was a lot of spin control and speculation, people racing double-time to cover their butts and professional debunkers talking in circles on every damn cable channel. It was nonstop for months. But then it kind of trickled off, like everything else that gets hyped and then loses luster, stripped down and burned up in the spotlight. It amazed me how much truth could be denied by people who saw it right there in front of them.

It was pretty easy slipping under the radar, in the middle of so much chaos. It was one hell of a mess. Lots of people dead, the great-and-mighty Maximum Bob included. They pulled me off the roof, asked me a few questions, then got on with more important business. My main accusers had been Maxton and Dryden, after all, and nobody was taking them seriously anymore. They shipped me to a hospital and I walked a few days later. Got out of the city. Got on a bus back to Austin. Slept for about three weeks. Thought about my dead friends. Got on with my life.

Raina was waiting for me at the house, and I told her everything.

Told her how I'd died and come back.

How I came back because of my parents.

She said she'd been so scared. She told me she loved me. I held her in my arms and she wept. And I understood what she had felt for me, all those years. Finally understood what love was. Or at least that's what it seemed like.

I said I would stay this time.

I would be her friend and not walk away.

I told her that I was sorry for the way things had been before, and that it was gonna take a long time to come back from it, for both of us. But there was no denying that I was a changed man — that I was starting over with a new look at the way things really are in the world, and a lot of regret for the way things had been in my life for so long. I told her I wasn't sure if I could love her the same way she loved me. Working through all that was gonna take time also. But I wouldn't leave again. I promised her that. Looked her right in the eye and said the words:

I'll never leave you again, Raina.

I am grateful to you.

I owe you.

You are my family.

She cried tears of joy.

A year went by and there were lots of unanswered questions, lots of people who wanted to know my story. Reporters. Cops. The grandfather of Richard Dryden came around once to ask me how his grandson had died, and I told him lies. I told a lot of lies back then.

The real truth is that people *want to be lied to.*

They want to be given puzzles without answers.

They want to know that the unknown will never be explained, even when it's trying damn hard to make them promises in plain English. It gives ordinary people a reason to believe they are special in a world full of ghosts. A reason to exist on a dying planet spinning in space. Plausible deniability on every channel, forever and ever.

Every promise will be broken.

My father said that once.

I can remember his words now, and that's the crazy part — the part I still have a hard time getting used to. The words he gave me when I was a child *all given back to me,* along with my mother's kindness and her scent that lends me comfort when I dream. Sometimes it isn't a comfort at all—sometimes it's damn scary. But I take the good with the bad. My memories made me live again, like broken promises given back at some crucial moment when you needed the voice of God to make you believe everything would be just great again. But it comes with a price.

Part of that is knowing that Blackjack Williams might still be out there. That he might not be dead.

That he might have made it back from the Big Black somehow, just like I did. That he might be wandering, like he did for so many years before he found Jaeger and they did their Crossroads deal and all the shit came down. I promised Raina that he was gone for good and that I would never look for him again. But I told a lot of lies back then. People want to be lied to. Every promise will be broken. Maybe.

Bethany Sin got out of the music biz for a year and made a movie with Jerry Donaldson about ghosts on a train. It came out six months ago and I never went, even though she invited me to the premiere. But I hear the reviews are pretty decent, and of course everybody's yakking about how real it all may or may not be. The poster and all the trailers say it's "inspired by a true story." Bethany talks a lot about her experiences at paranormal conventions these days, and tours around giving benefit shows for the victims of the Dreamworld Tragedy. That's what they call it nowadays—*the Dreamworld Tragedy.* Kind of tacky, if you ask me, but it's probably better than *9-11.*

I saw Bethany last week when she was in town on a tour date.

She looked amazing, and her mind was just as open as ever.

She said she liked my new hairdo—I wear it real short these days, now that it's completely white.

I was right about looking like Andy Warhol in my grave.

And I don't like hiding it.

I want to be reminded.

She ran her fingers through my hair and smiled, then she kissed me, and I felt that thing called love again. Stronger, coming from her.

Stronger, because she and I are the same. But sometimes I think it's not even that simple. Sometimes I think it was fate that put us together, the same way fate put me with Raina. And it still confuses me, those feelings. Makes me wonder about all the other simple lessons I missed out on when I was a kid. I'm working on it.

Bethany says she loves me too.

She says it's in the stars.

Whenever I'm ready, she will be.

That's what she told me.

I told her I would think about it.

She asked me to work with her paranormal research group—*the world has to know and you were right there in the middle of it, honey*—but I just smiled at her and said no thanks. The last time someone made me a similar offer, I ended up dead. She smiled in that amazing way she has, and she said I'd be back. It's in the stars, she said.

Story of my life.

Lose ends and weird ghosts, all hanging at the edge of oblivion.

Waiting for me.

You'll be back, Buck.

I never think about Lauren Chance. Not ever.

I think about Roosevelt a lot, but that's mostly because he's still around. He drifted for a while, the way most Walkers do, then found his sea legs. Darby showed him the ropes. Helped him stand up right. The kid's still a schemer and a hacker, just like he always was, and Darby's still a hustler with all the street moves—but now he's got serious backup on the World Wide Web. They make a pretty strange pair, those two.

Even with two smartass poltergeists riding my back, it's still pretty quiet at the ranch most of the time. I've kept busy, though. I have a lot of memories to work through and a roof to keep over my head. Been getting a bunch of calls from rich people these days. Most of the jobs are bunk, but I still take one now and then when the vibe is right and the rent is due.

Raina tells me I should retire, but that's not in the cards.

There's still good work to do.

Just like my father said.

* * *

I'm standing with my crew on the front lawn of a home for abused children—Austin's full of these places, and a lot of them are real hellholes.

It's summer.

Summers are really hot in Texas, and when it gets really hot in Texas, really bad shit goes down.

But you knew that.

Raina got me this case. She's been a pretty good partner in the last few months. Never really had a partner before, but it's cool. The kids here have been hearing voices in the halls at night. Voices just like I heard in the town of Carlsbad. Like we all hear when every promise is broken and the Terrible Thing comes back to hold us down in the dark. Maybe I can help these kids. We'll just see how it goes.

Raina smiles at me, her face filled with sweet concern.

"Are you sure you're up for this, Buck?"

"It'll be fine. I'm back in the game."

She leans over and kisses my cheek. So much love in her eyes, in her heart. I still ain't sure exactly what to do with that. She's happy just that I'm here with her. And that's cool too.

Darby and Roosevelt hang close, just out of sight—my aces in the hole, in case things get too rough in there. I can feel them smiling at me when I get kissed, the smart little punks. They like busting my balls on days like today.

I'm feeling pretty good for the first time in my life.

It's been a year since my life started.

So I guess I can't complain.

I guess this life is good.

I click on the Walkman at my waist and we walk in through the open front door of the institution, to where the down boys go.

TWENTY-THREE

BLESSED

Father Joe wakes from a dream he can't remember.

And he is filled with light.

The voice comes in his head again, just like it did the morning before, and the morning before that. He knows it is the Father. He knows he is blessed. Soon, there will be blessings for *all* who did not believe on the day before. And when that day comes—oh, praise God, *when that day comes*—there will be a sign from above and a glory beyond man and flesh as could never be imagined by all the ancient saints and sinners who went before him. All he must do is heed the voice. All he must do is wait.

The light fills him.

I am the only god you will ever need.

CREDIT ROLL

The magnetically powered bullet train described in this book is based on existing technology currently in use. However, because this is a *work of fiction*—in fact, one might even go so far as to call a good portion of it *science fiction*—the speed factor has been slightly pushed a few years into the future. We didn't do this to be cute or mock the laws of physics for no good darn reason. Our editor thought it might be a significant *story idea* to have the train go really, really fast and we agreed with him. We hope that the one or two learned scientists out there who've actually read our book—or perhaps those among you who obsess over little details like this and compulsively look them up on the Internet—will choose to be merciful and realize that this is an *entertainment,* designed to thrill and chill and all that. It's the same reason we also put ghosts in there. And lots of guys with guns. And a pop diva named Bethany Sin.

Obviously, the "2012" described in this book is not real, either.

Depending on when you read this, it will either be a few months in the future or many years in the past.

That's fine with us, and here is why:

Most works of genre fiction that deal with interesting political subplots like the one we have in here tend to take place within some fairly undefined *alternate reality* without a fixed date attached to it. This is an oh-so-very-darn-clever way of making your story "timeless," while automatically sidestepping the wrath of historical purists. That's how most movies are too. That's how you should read this one. It was necessary, however, because of the time-sensitive life history of Buck Carlsbad (in relation to the most appropriate election year on the Mayan calendar), to stick a "date" at the front of everything and hope for the best. We do not flatter ourselves that we've predicted the future of politics or public opinion in any shape, way, or form with the creation of Senator Bob Maxton and his whacky exploits—again, the idea of a rock star presidential candidate fast approaching his moment of glory was something that made the *story work better*. After all, it's *science fiction*, man.

Now, on to the credits.

A lot of novels come to the printed page or Kindle screen with the help of many people. But most of us aren't fortunate enough to have an editor as sharp as the one we worked with at Muholland Books.

That editor is John Schoenfelder.

John's is our esteemed collaborator and chief brain cell, who set this project on track in the beginning and rode the bullet right alongside us to its rather spectacular end. His boundless creative energy, wild enthusiasm, and sage advice kept everything humming along at six hundred miles per as we completed the book in record time—less than *six months* from conception to final proofs, in case you're wondering—and he kept us out of trouble when we were, many times, dangerously close to veering right off the deep end, bound for dark territory. John is the unsung "fourth Beatle" of our crazy little pop-lit power trio—or maybe he's our Kim Fowley, or Phil Spector, or George Martin, or...well, you get the idea. We are very, very, *very* grateful for his contributions to our "first album" at nearly every phase of its creation. Nobody does it like Schoenfelder. He's lightning and thunder wearing shoes. A total badass. Our sincere thanks to him.

Also, a big shout-out goes to Michael Pietsch, and the swell team at Little, Brown and Company who believed in a guy named Buck.

And a lot of sappy, sloppy special thanks to the following folks:

David Hale Smith, Trevor Engelson, David Boxerbaum, David Fischer, Sheryl Petersen, Dave Feldman, and Richard D. Thompson, all of whom are our agents and managers and lawyer, believe it or not. Miriam Parker, marketing director of Mulholland Books, who makes us look real good. (Darby Jones really *does* have a Facebook page, and it was all

Miriam's idea—go friend him!) Ruth Tross, our UK editor, for highly valuable observations and support. Lolita DePalma, our helpful intern at Little, Brown, for additional observations at the last minute. (For some reason, she called us on all the *Terminator* references too.) Peggy Freudenthal and Tracy Roe, our hard-working, long-suffering copyeditors, to whom we sincerely apologize. Ben Allen, associate copyeditor *extraordinaire* who stepped in at a crucial phase. Wes Miller, who calmly answered the phone all six hundred and seventy-nine times Stephen called the head office in a panic. Tom Piccirilli, who writes great books. Gaylen Ross, who wasn't really in *There's Always Vanilla*. Batman, just because we think he's cool. And a bunch of other guys and gals we're forgetting and who will be pissed off that we didn't mention them. (Insert your name here.)

On a personal note, special thanks to Patrick's wife, Eebin, and their three little hellions, Tai, Keke, and Easton.

In addition, thank you so very much to Marcus's parents, Maria and Tom, and his sister, Kristin, for supporting the strange, the dark, and the terrifying every step of the way.

Stephen would like to thank Patrick and Marcus and John for inviting him aboard, and also an amazing artist cat named Rock Romano, who is his father and best friend.

And Scott Hiles.

He came up with the speed tunnel, just when we needed another killer concept to make the train go really, really fast.

Thanks for reading.

Please let us know if you want another one.

We'll totally write it.

—*Patrick, Marcus, and Stephen*